The Seeker Academy

The Seeker Academy

A novel by L. D. Gussin

4361 Press

Published by 4361 Press
P.O Box 645
Housatonic, MA 01236
www.4361press.com

ISBN-10: 0-9789170-0-6
ISBN-13: 978-0-9789170-0-5

Library of Congress Control Number: 2006908015

1. Novel of ideas-Fiction 2. Mind-body-spirit movement-Fiction 3. New Age move-ment-Fiction 4. Romantic movement-Fiction 5. Counterculture-Fiction 6. Hudson Valley (New York)-Fiction

This is a work of fiction. Names, characters, places, and incidents are either products of the author's imagination or are used fictitiously. Any resemblance to actual events or locales or persons, living or dead, is entirely coincidental and beyond the intent of either the author or the publisher.

See www.4361press.com for purchasing information.

Book and cover design and cover photograph by David. R. Guenette.

Printed in the United States of America on acid-free paper.

Acknowledgements

I thank Kathryn Macdonald, David Guenette, Liza Nelson, Anne Williamson, and Jenn Pasternak, brave readers of my first draft; Christopher Noel and Madeleine Butler, who upon reading my third draft told me what it lacked; Leslie Cohen, who gave me a last critical read and a valuable copyedit; and David Guenette, again, who designed my book cover and interior. The circle grows as I thank some of these people, further, and thirty others for getting me through three long years. Ken Colgan helped keep me afloat, and bought me a great meal when I first felt I was done; Diane Rosenblum advised me that, no, I wouldn't be going 7,000 miles to have my teeth fixed; Howard Davis handed down pants, and Mark Mitshkun, shirts; and friends and family in six states got dogs and cats so I might take up pet-sitting. Finally, a pal graciously loaned me her shadow.

Parts of chapters 22, 23, and 24 draw on and interpret materials presented in a fine book of non-fiction, *The New American Spirituality: A Seeker's Guide*, by Elizabeth Lesser, Copyright © Elizabeth Lesser, Random House, 1999.

The cover photograph looks out from Poets' Walk, a public park dating to the 19th century where, as readers will discover, one long scene in *The Seeker Academy* is set. Poets' Walk is preserved by the environmental organization and land trust Scenic Hudson, which works "to protect, preserve, and restore the Hudson River and its riverfront as a public and natural resource." To volunteer with or make a donation to this worthy group, visit its website at www.scenichudson.org.

Acknowledgement is made to the following for permissions to reprint previously published material:

Shambhala Publications: Excerpts from "A New Rule" and "Be Lost in the Call," from *Love is a Stranger*, poems by Jalal al-Din Rumi with translations by Kabir Helminski, published by arrangement with *Threshold Books*, Copyright © Kabir Edmund Helminski, 1993.

Coleman Barks: Excerpts from "Say Yes Quickly" and "Quatrains," from *Open Secret*, poems by Jalal al-Din Rumi with translations by John Moyne and Coleman Barks, published by *Shambhala Publications* by arrangement with *Threshold Books*, Copyright © John Moyne and Coleman Barks, 1984. Excerpts from "Where Everything is Music," "The Many Wines," "A Great Wagon," and "The Guest House," poems by Jalal al-Din Rumi with translations by Coleman Barks, from *The Essential Rumi*, published by *HarperSanFrancisco*, Copyright © Coleman Barks, 1995.

For Maya and Zachary, from UL

Table of Contents

Prologue

The Seeker Academy's four-hundred-seat dining hall sat on a grassy hill, facing the algae-infested but pretty pond that lay, hidden by pine trees, a quarter mile east. Thus on early summer mornings the sun, above the far eastern hills, lit the porch directly. The land behind the hall was steeper, climbing through trees to the sanctuary and above it a spiritualist-in-residence tent and hiking trails atop an even higher rise. Planked steps and switchbacks helped with the rough way up. On a north-south axis, though, the land sloped more gently. At mealtimes, people strolled up on paths that crossed a kitchen garden or a lawn, hardly knowing—since nearly everyone who came here ate and exercised as if their body were a temple—that they were climbing a hill.

The hall and attached staff mess—both shaped for enjoyment— bustled at meals; anyway, buffet lines brought diners inside for a time. However, porch tables, seating a hundred, and below them ten picnic tables on a sloped lawn, were where many chose to eat. As Seeker policy was for its staff of two hundred to leave the porch to guests and teachers, staff eating outside usually found space on the lawn. Most were in their early twenties and from middle-class homes in North America or Europe: seated at picnic tables and on a low curb at the base of the building, they all were casually handsome. Nurture saw this as a birthright (to use a cliché many of them knew from school), while nature believed it to be unchanging. As they ate and talked—good talk was a Seeker goal and what Sophie particularly wanted—their limbs fell from tee shirts, shorts, bibbed overalls, and other loose, unmatched garments with thoughtless grace. Even the few who wore teasing sarongs or muscle shirts, to make the most of their handsomeness, were dusted by this grace.

Their conversation, or the half about holistic healing, showed them to differ from the main part of their generation. Seeker, many said, was their true start in life; it was where they could gain skills for the change to a new beginning—while for almost all the young staff it was at least an emblem of this change. Sitting down to organic grains, beans, produce, and, for the less restrictive, dairy products, they spoke of what in a working reduction they called "the opening of their hearts and souls and minds."

Above them on the porch, guests and teachers took their meals. In nice weather, porch tables filled long before those inside. So many people, on breaks from regular activities and schedules, treks to and from suburb and office, hungered for the rural air and view. Nor was the staff segregation strictly enforced: some older staff ate usually on the porch. Perhaps they were too used to comfort to want to balance, as did youths on the curb, trays of, say, tofu scramble, fruit, tea, and bread on their laps. Perhaps, too, they felt more at ease among people nearer their own age.

It was in many ways a different song, as of another tribe, that the older generations sang. Their laugh if as frequent was less staunchly brave; often, it wasn't brave at all. On the other hand, these guests and teachers, ages twenty to eighty, with most near fifty—life's midpoint as they saw it—sounded generally happier and more grateful than the staff. Soon—after Friday's lunch for weekday workshops, after Sunday's lunch for weekend ones—they would go home. So they had to show their high spirits now, while they still freely could.

As diners found seats at the round, eight-person tables, the talk changed speakers and topics easily. It was for many a welcome, unusual experience: finding a human chord with others they were just meeting. Or does this fully show the strangeness? For if some worked in business, where the tasks fed detachment and friendships were often too success-tied to root, others worked in nonprofit fields or the arts. Price-graded housing options and a scholarship fund kept Seeker affordable for these less-well-off professionals. So on the porch also were teachers, nurses, and others who tied their work to a human scale. They sought, beyond their own well-being, "against-the-grain" ideas and tools to use with the hodgepodge of individuals and groups they tried to help.

No, what truly marked midlife visitors, come from many kinds of work, were their layers of doubt and struggle beneath a savoring of summer. This likely was what had brought them, at least to a first workshop; the same money, after all, might buy them the exotic beach vacations their travel agents preferred. Seeker's directors, managers, and teachers, who saw it somewhat as a business, knew that the knowingly wounded made up the mass of paying customers. Seeker after all was a refuge from the madly devouring society. All who came joined a healing community.

Yet, so much against the grain, the refuge had to feel strange.

Helping to make it so were the juxtaposed generations, who could have been but weren't each other's parents and children. Warily, without family ties or habits, one generation saw who they might become, the other who they had been.

The hero Grace, Sophie, Trumpeter, Monk, Willa the Wiking, Deb and Anton Gold, Hans, sad Moira Kathleen, Franny, and even, yes, Pythagoras: all our players would be in the dining-hall at such a breakfast hour. To others (people behind Anton in a buffet line, or watching Grace refill a milk dispenser), they would not stand out. Like everyone, they would seem to be facing the day's opportunities, raised like another sun amid the shared enthusiasm. Willa, Hans, and Deb might look ahead to activities that would make them feel better: one whose body had begun to slow, another whose heart was torn, a third whose mind yearned for calm. Here again though, seeking wellness in the face of fear, the roads they set off on were strange. Some activities, like touching one's toes, were childishly sensible and helped right away; but others asked them to not be who they were at home. What an idea healing was! Could people find wellness and a spiritual anchor in what they knew? Or must they see themselves in a new context—and if so, what was it and how would they find it? Were there unseen forces that could help, or harmonies to slip into? Did their daily struggle even matter? Must people change how they thought, or lived, or both?

How could these questions, astir on porch and curb, seem so wild yet also pressing?

Monk, one of those who had long made a kind of home at the academy, had, while at the pond one night years before, watching the eastern hills in silhouette, thought how this earnestness was itself strange. People gave up so much so readily: it was like an emigration. To know them better, he had, in late October, with Seeker shut for the year, visited those eastern hills. He drove for half an hour and walked for an hour. The high ridge he reached faced west. He was south of the academy but had the northwest mountains to guide his eye. He couldn't pick Seeker out across twenty miles, but he saw about where it was. He also saw about where in the mountains a new similar retreat would be.

He liked this distance, as it let him imagine. He saw, or felt he might, the storied river that ran six miles west of the academy. The foliage was solidly orange, but there was that one dim arc that could be a bending river. Near where he looked, there was a castle, now a museum. Two centuries back, a rich dreamer had built it with old worlds still on his mind. The entire valley running two hundred miles and the mountains it snuck beneath were in fact splashed with castle-museums and, otherwise denoting old or anomalous worlds, monasteries and religious or cultural camps. If most such compounds were now relics, they showed that Seeker, writhing into life three decades before, had fit in. The strangeness, Monk saw, had been nothing new.

Part One

A Day Back in January

The Taste of Fig and Gorgonzola

A must-do that Saturday had been to get to the bank. She took Amos, who wore his nearly outgrown, green ski parka, patched at an elbow. But when she broached her larger plan, the boy, six weeks shy of twelve, was predictably reluctant.

"We'll eat lunch at that pizzeria we found last fall, which has a fig and Gorgonzola pie," she told him, bargaining. More than his friends, from what she had seen, Amos liked distinctly flavored foods.

"I can't go, Mom; you know I can't. I have geography homework."

But the real knowledge they shared was that Amos had a new alien-slaying computer game; and that, with Grace gone for half a day to see Alicia, he along with his father and maybe, later, a friend would have the time to get a sense of its controls.

An hour before, as she sat over coffee, watching from the kitchen as Henry filled the bird feeder, Grace had conceived the bribe. She still at that moment had hopes Henry would come along, as well.

"Gracie!" her husband had called through the windows as he brushed a window clean of frost with his bare hand. Next, he swung his body around and lifted to the windowsill, with his other hand, the fifteen-pound bag of bird feed. Grace saw from its anomalously pillowing bottom that it was nearly empty. Henry, who saw most domestic chores as her responsibility, smiled at her brightly.

Seconds later, he had begun to further disarrange the kitchen. This was something they both did well, but Henry's actions always bore a sense of mission. He made a sandwich from bread, jam, and cheese and poured a glass of orange juice. Knowing she wouldn't yet be hungry, he stood at the counter and, with a busied air, packed his breakfast down.

After some mouthfuls, he looked at her and smiled again. "It's winter, and our poor birdies will soon begin to starve."

"I'll get more feed tomorrow. But: what about today? We can go after lunch if you need the morning, and on the way back have supper at that pizzeria we all like so much. We can convince Nan and Steve to drive part-way back and join us there."

"I'd like to go, Gracie; but shouldn't I stay and work on our taxes? And there's that blowout sale at eleven. If we don't find an affordable kayak soon, it'll be a second summer of going without."

"They'd be happy if we all showed up." She said this without anger, because she thought he had a right to be afraid.

"We'll go next Sunday," he told her. "I swear I'll jump in ahead of you and shoot down all of Amos's excuses."

Amos, not very awake, had gotten in the car because at unimportant moments he still liked to be guided by his mother. They crisscrossed their hilly suburb, where it hadn't snowed in a week, leaving the snow in its own miniature set of damped-down valleys and hills. Finding the back way into the mega mall, they quickly bought the sneakers Amos already had shopped for, and then, on a bumpy old road that had once had more impact connecting local villages, they found the dowdy Italian bakery outside which, in their car, they would have their pastry breakfasts.

Mother and son had some similar rhythms; both were enlivened by the sweet odors and tastes. Bundled up, they chose to eat with the windows open to enjoy the crisp winter air. Amos had questions for Grace, who twice that week, on both short workdays, had gone to visit her niece.

Having finished his milk, he sipped twice from Grace's coffee.

"But does that mean she can't have more treatments?" he asked.

"No; they'll start up again when she is stronger."

"And that's why she's back in the hospital… to get stronger?"

"Yes," said Grace, finding it a relief to talk about this even if incompletely.

"But haven't the treatments been making her sick?"

"Yes to that question, too." She thought to find his gaze, but then allowed him his separateness. "It's a difficult time now," she added.

For three months, Amos had made it known that he wanted to be told; but he didn't want discussion or, truly, to see Alicia or his aunt and uncle. At infrequent intervals, he forced himself to be involved.

At the bank, she found a line longer than expected—well, she first thought so, but then saw that some in line were kids. One boy, whose name she had forgotten, was a classmate of Amos; her son took a temporary place a few slots in front of her. With the weather outdoors calm if cloudy and cold, few patrons wore hats or scarves. The bank's floor was also less dirtied and wet than it would likely be in the weeks ahead.

There was one seated teller; a second was often at a car-banking window. Amos returned when his friend's father began transacting.

"Just a few minutes more," said Grace. "Who is that, again?"

"Jeremy."

Grace chuckled. "How many does that make?"

"I guess, four. One Jeremy moved somewhere last summer."

"Has this Jeremy ever been at the house?"

"No, but he may come over this afternoon."

"I thought you might decide to come with me."

"But I thought we said I had to get my homework done." He looked up at her and presently clamped shut his teeth and spread his lips and stretched out his cheeks. She knew this grotesque grin was a reference back to his life as an indulged, often willful child. He then bent his neck and jostled Grace's right inner shoulder with his forehead.

When he had stood upright and she smiled, he added: "We'll probably still be here in line when it's afternoon."

"Amos, after going last time you said it'd felt pretty natural."

"I know, Mom. Just, not today. I don't want to go this weekend."

In the end, she met Henry at the sale and, leaving the choice to buy or not to him, as she didn't care about makes or models, she finally got on the road at one p.m., after a quick stop back at home that took an hour. A mile from her street, she remembered having gone home partly to eat. But then she thought how, unless there was bad bridge traffic, she would be at her new favorite pizzeria in forty-five minutes.

She would get a special pizza to take to the hospital. If she felt kindly, she would get another for her boys. Given the winter temperatures, it would be okay to leave this latter in the car for several hours.

She thought with satisfaction how it had slipped her son's mind and her husband's to ask her to bring a fig and Gorgonzola pizza back.

They had found this pizzeria on a night when the main chance was that whatever mystery restaurant they stopped at would make them sick. It had been a Sunday in October, soon after Alicia's ongoing fever was diagnosed. Grace, in her own view, had made a mistake by forcing them to come. It had been a bad scene, as it had three days before, when she had come alone. But now Henry's bluster and the muteness of Amos kept her from giving care to those most in need of it. She had also been unable to keep a calming metaphorical hand on her own heart.

They had left the hospital in darkness, sometime after a rainstorm had stopped and as the temperature was falling fast. Before they were in their car, Henry and Amos had begun to squabble.

"But I need to eat," the boy said, as if making a moral judgment.

"We're going home," said his father. "I've got things I have to do."

The hospital was forty miles southwest of the bridge, in a suburban area they didn't know. Henry made a wrong choice on his second turn out of the lot and their first few miles, the portion of the trip on local roads, took half an hour. Grace saw that Henry was starting to blow, a condition caused to a lesser degree, she felt, by his own empty stomach.

Amos was quiet, but Henry went on defending his point in the argument. "It's usually a mistake to pick a place out of a hat," he said as they saw the first sign for the highway. He looked at Amos in the mirror. "Let's stop back at the food court in the mega mall."

"No!" said Grace, in a rare use, for her, of the imperative. "I need food now. Turn off somewhere before the entrance ramp."

Henry after a second gave a mock salute, but began, taking his eyes somewhat off his driving, to look across the oncoming traffic at the storefronts. "Eyes left, son," he said, seeking a helper. Grace, turned to her right, put her forehead and then a palm to the window glass.

"We may want to use the heater after dinner," she said. She then thought how she had just been too warm for hours in her surgical mask.

"Pizza at ten o'clock, Dad. I see the sign."

They were in an area unlike their own in being wealthy enough after the costs of housing to support upscale shopping. The pizzeria, at the back of a strip mall behind a wine bar, had wrought-iron stairs and was named, elliptically enough, Wolf. Henry, Grace guessed, was won over by the sense that this might be a find. The sharp odor of a grating cheese was prevalent. He looked only briefly at the posted, priced menu.

"Do customers wolf down the food?" he promptly asked their server. Grace and Amos looked up, awaiting a reply. The family chose a Caesar salad to share and, since both toppings were liked and seemed together so adventurous, the large size of the fig and Gorgonzola pie.

"Let's forget the day we've had, for now," Grace had suggested after Amos won agreement for his favorite salad. "Henry, I'll have a beer if you promise to only have one."

He allowed her the needed pint of ale. And then the strong taste of the pie came to be what let them breathe.

When, round and big, it came, its many dollops of jam looked like dark ponds; the Gorgonzola, like frequent snowfields. Henry scraped his fork along an edge and called the crust promising. Amos rotated the pie a jot to grab a slice with three fig ponds; he split one and ate half, like a titan, with a nearby snowfield. Grace, with a first mouthful, felt in a twitching of muscles that her body was finally taking over for her mind. Fruity and sour, cheesy and crisp: wonderfully, the pie was complex.

They ate without gabbing, and Henry upon finishing his beer startled Amos by asking the server for a new round of soft drinks for the table.

"Gracie, once more, you were right," he conceded as they sat full and tired both in spirit and in flesh at the end of the meal.

In December, they had eaten there again, soon after a suddenly scaled back Thanksgiving dinner. Coming once more near the end of a hard day, they had felt unable to risk trying any different menu item. When they were done and feeling a similar release, Henry touched the empty pie tin and said, trying to rally their energies, "The wolf pack strikes again." He then asked Amos, who instantly eyed his mother, about a science project just assigned to him and due in March.

"You know, you'll have to settle on a topic soon."

"Henry," said Grace. "Please. Not right now."

Headed west on this cold afternoon, she found slowed bridge traffic, which made no sense to her given the holidays being over. With a wide view of the sky, she saw that the silky color from the morning had begun to darken. The river, directly below her, was her boundary, on the other side of which was Alicia's sickness. Now, each day, she wanted to cross over. Still, she was very sorry that Amos and even Henry had not seen fit to come along.

Hobbled on the bridge, she thought ephemerally of the great city out of view on her left and the valley purviews on her right. But from when she could flee the congestion and then for her half-hour scramble down the three linked highways, she was consumed by the facts she drove toward. She left the last highway and watched for the turn into the Wolf lot amid feelings of dread. Every rotten thing about this, she thought, moves either too slowly or not slowly enough.

She saw when outside her car that the wind was up and the air more humid—while this air, which had already been darker at the river, was here a pencil-point gray. The parking lot was nearly full and she, passing the wine bar, heard fiddle music. Wolf was busy, too, enough to force a five-minute wait to place a carryout order. She took the time to finally look the larger menu over.

She wasn't in a chance-taking mood, though, as the fig pizza was the one thing in her day she felt sure of. Alicia often ate grilled cheese sandwiches, and had loved the fresh figs bought at that roadside stand in Vermont. The server they had met on their first visit took her order without a sign of recognition; Grace, able to look closer now than when she had been with her men, saw that the woman, in her forties but appearing younger, took good care of her skin and her hair.

"What'll you have for carryout?"

"Two large fig and Gorgonzola pies, please."

"Good choice. This will take about twenty minutes."

Grace, with her purse out, thought how sitting in her station wagon in a strip-mall parking lot on a darkening day would wear her out.

"Maybe I'll have a salad while I'm waiting."

The server scanned the dining room, with its winter squash–colored yellow walls and olive-green oilskin tablecloths. "I can seat you," she said and began to slip out from behind her counter.

"Could I—"

The server, braking, became a statue.

"Could I... could the kitchen cut me off a slice for in here?"

The server's slightly granite smile lit her pretty, pampered face. "Good choice, again."

Grace felt surer. "Before I lose you to another customer, make it three of those pizzas to go, instead of two.... Not too large a slice for in here."

She was given a window table with a view of parked cars and, over a brown wooden fence, the second-story signboard of a musical instrument store. She made the easier of her two calls first, and reached her son.

"How's geography?"

"Oh, Mom.... Okay, here's the truth: the game's geography is a beast. And you don't just learn about places; you create them."

"That'll help a lot when we win a trip to Europe some day, not to mention on your Monday quiz. Is Dad there?"

"No."

"Where is he?" But on a Saturday, he wouldn't know. "Are you alone?"

"Jeremy is coming over. Are you at the hospital?"

"Not yet. Listen: don't eat pizza today. Also, how's the weather?"

"It's winter; anyway, you were just here. Sweet about the pizza, if I've guessed your meaning."

"Yeah, well. Which Jeremy?"

"The latest model."

"Maybe he'd like to stay for dinner… I imagine, around eight."

She held the phone, with her elbow on the table under it, and sought guidance from the décor as to how to proceed. Her tea and salad were delivered by another server and, as her other hand wielded a fork, she sought out the vinegary wallop of the salad dressing. No one picked up when she tried to reach her brother or sister-in-law at home. But, right away, Steve answered his cell phone.

"How's it going, bro? Where are you?" She pushed aside her salad and pulled her tea a saucer's length nearer.

"Oh, Grace. Are you still coming today? It's good you called."

"Why, what's up? Are you and Nan with Alicia?"

"You might want to stay home, because of the weather."

"Steve, I'm already at Wolf, the pizzeria near the highway we come in on. What weather? Are you both at the hospital?"

"Well, isn't it snowing there? It's sure started to here. The girls are in the corridor, taking a walk. I'm in the hospital room."

Outside her window, snow did fall against the shoulder-high fence. It seemed to have begun only in response to her brother's prompting.

"It's only flurrying here. Then Alicia must be feeling stronger. And by the way, who's playing?" She had heard the bark of a sportscaster and—while she and the boys weren't big fans—knew that on a Saturday in January the game was probably college basketball.

"I think one team is N.C. State. But, anyway, the weather's very wintry here. My car's in a garage, but out the window I see ten people scraping their windows. The TV before said some nearby roads might be closing. We may be in a whiteout situation when you get here. And I read online today that two feet of snow could come by daybreak— this after Channel 8 was calling last night for just a few inches."

Grace pitched her eyes above the parking lot fence, but without a reference point besides the signboard angled partly away from her, she couldn't tell what the weather was doing. She found herself for the moment forgetting the call's inner strain and being carried by her legs out the pizzeria door. "Steve, wait," she told him. "I'm going out to check the sky." The wind had stiffened; either that or she now faced it more directly. Holding her phone, coatless, she walked between car rows until she could see the back of the signboard and the fraught western sky pushing against it.

"It's getting snowier here now," she told her brother. But for the associated darkness, the bigger snowflakes would've drawn her smile. As if cued, they began to dance around the signboard. She eyed the storm, felt again the cold air that cheered rather than stung her, and went back into the pizzeria. "But I'll make it," she said into the phone.

"You may be with us for the weekend if you do. Check for your road service card…. Oops, they're back. Nan wants to talk to you, but she's gone into the bathroom."

Grace kept listening, but sensed Steve had put down his phone. She looked out above the fence, signboard, and two nearby trees at the hushed but colicky sky. Hungry, she ate two forkfuls of salad. It was simple and inexpensively made, a mix of two lettuces with the accenting flavors of red cabbage and cured black olives. The cabbage had been chopped along its grain, making for curled slivers; the pitted olives shone and had hills and depressions. She thought with a bedeviled grin of her big, impulsively so, pizza order, some of which would now be spending who-knew-how-long in her car.

"Well, we'll march through it at the hospital," she said aloud, "given enough snowfall and time." The idea of the piquant slice she would soon have made her hungry but torn. Her brother hadn't really said a thing about Alicia.

What happened next was to her the funny part. Listening, eating her salad, and perhaps likewise drawing colic from the air, she heard, after words of argument, the sounds of the phone being delivered to a toilet seat.

"Grace, are you there?"

"Yes, Nan."

"Okay, don't hang up." Grace next heard the symphonic gulping sounds made by the flushing mechanism.

"How is she today?" Dutifully, Grace asked this twice, with more thrust the second time, even as she knew that no one might right then be listening.

"Grace," said Nan, sounding faint, "just… wait for me to get out into the corridor."

"Okay… but did Steve tell you that I'll be there in half an hour?"

This question, too, seemed to go unheard; then the wait was muddled further by the fact of her slice being set down before her. She saw immediately the faithful fig ponds, snowy meadows, and heat-sculpted crust that had won her family over. Past this sight remained the server's midriff. Looking up, Grace saw her, while smiling at the humor in her behavior, make a ring with her arms and aim it at the entrance. Grace's big order was waiting at the cash register. Then the woman pointed out the window at the sky.

The gums near Grace's molars began to soak, but she pushed the pizza out past where her tea first had been. She then put the palm of her other hand against her nose and inhaled stiffly.

"Nan, talk to me."

"Oh, Grace."

"Hold the phone nearer your face. Are you in the corridor?"

"Yes, it's full of wheeled canisters, the lunch dirty dishes even this late in the day. They're the most understaffed on weekends."

Nan, Grace knew, kept her own housekeeping mishaps out of sight.

"Maybe you should walk the hall as we talk—get away from the garbage. Has anything happened today?"

"Well, you know, nurses in and out, a few doctors. She was gone an hour for a test. Your brother has the particulars. I can't keep track anymore."

"Yes, you can."

"You're right, I know. But I feel so worn out, maybe understaffed and overwhelmed, just like everything else here on a Saturday."

"I'll get there soon as a reinforcement. Will you say something to me about how Alicia is doing?"

"She's been okay. Some high school actors, from outside, put on a skit in the game room. It was for younger kids, but they made her a prop—really, they sat her on stage beside the cardboard cutout of a volcano, and at every sound-effect bang had her push her hand up from behind the cutout and wave a red flag. The smaller kids giggled. Alicia groaned, but I think she was enjoying herself."

"She gets that wry look on her face when she is."

"It was there. I wish I could've liked watching."

"Why—oh." These days the back-and-forth wore everyone out. "She'll get better, Nan. She'll start her next treatment this week or soon after, and getting her past it is all we should worry about."

"The resident said it might be Thursday. And I have to say that to a degree she's better today. You know, it's like when I used to hike with you guys. Every new hill I saw made me want to rest." The small hint at humor told Grace that Nan had begun to relax.

"We'll rest all day, as we watch the storm I just learned is coming at us. I'll get there in half an hour. And, listen, I'm bringing one of those fig and Gorgonzola pizzas my gang's gone crazy over—a large."

"Grace, no."

"I thought they'd said to tempt her with calories again."

"We're allergic."

"To what?"

"We both have mold allergies. I do and Alicia does."

"Huh?"

"Gorgonzola cheese is made using a mold."

"I'm an idiot, honey. It is? Well, okay... I remember that you all like barbequed chicken pizza. I'll be bringing one of those."

"Grace, if you bring one, you should probably bring a plain. She still usually does best with the simpler foods."

Hanging up, Grace looked outside and saw that her wait for another pizza might make driving even dicier. Then, at the cash register, she found that the kitchen had been closed. She paid, carried her stacked boxes back to her table, and sat for a moment eating part of her pizza slice and swigging from her tea. Then she hustled on her coat.

At her car, she set the pizzas on her snowy roof and jostled her driver's door until the ice seam broke. She also found ice beneath the snow on her windshield. With surprise, she still sometimes heard fiddle music as she went about her tasks.

She knew it was a time for haste, but inside, with the motor on, she first dug out her phone. Again, Amos answered.

"Not all winter weather is the same, it seems."

"We heard, Mom. Are you okay? Did you make it to the hospital?"

"I'm fine and I'll be there soon, but I may not get home today."

"You mean you might get stuck somewhere."

"No, child. I just won't make the drive unless it's safe. I'll stay with Uncle Steve or at the hospital. Is your father there now?"

"Yes, but—"

"But what? And what are you doing now—still more video games?"

"No, I was just lying on my bed. But listen, I have an idea for next weekend, for visiting Alicia. Can I tell you?"

"Go for it."

"You have to relax, though. You can't just get all negative."

With her car heating up, Grace whiffed the pizzas stacked behind her. "I'm intrigued, if not exactly relaxed," she said. "Tell me."

"It's video games, Mom. Remember how Alicia and I played last summer? I'll borrow Gary's sweet new system and we can use it with the TV in her room. She and I can have a long war. It'll distract her."

"I'm not negative. It's a good idea." Alicia, five months younger, was not nearly the child Amos was, but childhood was still in reach for her, and, taking hold of it, she often seemed better.

"I'm a genius," said her son. "Here's Dad."

"Gracie, we were just getting ready to call you."

"Call off the search party. I'm nearly at the hospital. But, listen, there's something I have to ask you."

"You probably shouldn't try to drive back tonight."

"I won't. Listen: go downstairs. I don't want Amos overhearing."

"Don't get riled up. The same snowstorm is coming to us."

"Do you know what we're facing?"

"What we're facing? Is this that big a deal?"

"Have you gone downstairs?"

"Now. I'm starting to now."

"I don't mean the snowstorm. I mean with Alicia. Do you know what's begun to happen?"

"It began in October, I thought."

"Yes, but it's getting hard again now. And the worst of it is that the way it's getting hard is the best thing we can hope for."

"Grace, can I say something?"

"Two of her last three treatments made her really sick. So I need to ask you something."

"Hold on, will you listen to me?"

"You have to do something for me."

"Just wait a minute. Just wait a minute. Listen, anything you ask of me, I'll do; but there's something I'll say first. It's been on my mind for a while. You won't like hearing it, but you have to."

"It's that," said Grace, "for however long this goes on, it has to be you filling the birdfeeder. If it needs filling every day, or twice a day, or once an hour, it has to be you doing the work. Every damn kind of birdfeeder you can think of. Henry, I don't know if I can get through what I'm afraid is going to happen."

"It's this, Grace, and I won't make myself angry first, thinking I need to repeat the promise I just made. Part of what goes on is about you. This is your third trip there this week—at a time when we hear the treatment's working despite its side effects. That's over four hundred miles of driving! And, don't get me wrong: I see you fight to hold up the world, keep everyone standing, and like everyone, I'm a little in awe. And maybe now's a time for us, Steve's family, when having someone like you is the best thing that can happen. But the fact remains that before this, last May, you went crazy fighting off the campaign against Amos's fifth-grade teacher. And before that came other crusades, not all that seem so important—every ninth grade play you've directed at full tilt over the last ten years, for example.

"My point is that we all see what life hands to us, but we don't all need to be always fighting back."

"As you've brought it up," Grace told her husband, "yesterday, I backed out of co-directing this April's play."

2

The Consolidation Phase

As she drove, seeking her turns through smeared glass, Henry's claim sat with her, though she only partly saw its meaning. Was she then sowing these whirlwinds?

At the hospital parking lot, though, under open sky, she did find rather a diverting whirlwind in the panoramic snowfall. Alicia's fifth-floor room faced east, and when Grace finally looked out its window just after three p.m., eddying snow was all she saw. Ten minutes before, naïve to this effect, she had stood near her car waving her arm.

"Do you see me in the lot?" she had asked Steve, calling his cell phone.

"We can't see much from up here. You should've parked underground."

"It looked full. Listen, I'll be a little while getting there, but when I do you and Nan should go home. The roads are still drivable. Alicia and I will have a sleepover, and you can come back tomorrow once they dig things out."

"No, Grace, we can't do that."

"You can, Steve. I'm sure you both need a breather. Anyway, tell Nan what I said. It's hard to talk on this phone now that I'm moving."

"This is Nan."

"Nan, have Steve tell you what I said. I'll be up in a minute."

She brought no food, but had her teacher's bag, packed with a few promising items, hanging off a shoulder. On leaving her car, she had been inspired to grab her twenty-ounce travel mug. While still outside, she filled it with snow and then, at Alicia's door, removed a mitten and pulled the snow out by handfuls and sprinkled it over her head. Then she got on her protective mask.

Inside the room, she said, "I'm a walking puddle in the making."

An actor gauging her crowd, she looked about to see Alicia, with her sparse hair, laugh, and Nan grin faintly, and her brother be as usual slow to admit liking a joke. The bed nearer the window was made.

"The snow has weight, Steve. It's not so cold out, and the wind is from the northwest and not as bad as it seems from up here. While there's daylight you can easily drive the half hour south to your house."

"Aunt Grace wants Dad and me to go home for the night," said Nan.

"Hang your coat in the shower," said Steve from behind his mask. "You're destroying the floor. We'd begun to talk about what to do.

"Hardly the first floor I've seen her ruin," he told his daughter.

Shorn of her wrappings, Grace moved to the bed, and Alicia used her palms, heels, and buttocks to give her more room by sliding over. She hugged Grace hard, conveying again that she felt better. She still moves like a child, Grace thought, as Alicia's breasts pressed her own. At Alicia's right inner shoulder, the central line was attached.

"We just see wind and snow out these high windows," said Alicia. "It's pretty unusual to have everything else just disappear."

"You know, dear, that it's only an illusion," said Nan.

Alicia looked at her mother before leaning back and smiling into Grace's eyes. "She's been working too much Mom-overtime."

With a wide-faced smile, Steve said, "A snowflake in this wind gets quite the roller-coaster ride." Standing at a window, he put a finger to the glass and swept it in mock wind-driven curlicues.

Grace squeezed Alicia's shoulders harder than might have been best. Alicia touched her forehead to Grace's. Without looking up, she wagged a finger at her mother and said, "Mom."

"Alicia's father," said Nan, "has logged lots of overtime, too."

"But he's a ham," said Grace. "Ham actors run in the Hudson family."

Steve continued his curlicues for a while, but he had blanched and now his sweepings looked forced. Grace felt bad that her heedless talk had exposed her brother's brief performance for what it was.

On the bed, she shared an intimate look with her niece. The girl, with her fever and nausea gone and her count back near where it had to be, said, with her eyes, that she needed diversions and had been waiting for her aunt. And they would have fun, first off, Grace knew, just in being together, for neither knew the other as well as they hoped to. Three years before, Alicia's family had moved from Illinois to a suburb eighty traffic-filled miles from Grace's house. Niece and aunt grew close, but Grace's busy, jumbled life had before the illness kept them from being often alone together. Meanwhile, Alicia, like Amos, had somehow moved up to middle school and gotten busier, too. Then in the treatment's grim induction phase Grace, coming twice a week or more, had been able only to read to her, help her parents as needed, or sit near her bed.

Since the start of the consolidation phase, though, there had been times in which Grace and Alicia had sat talking, playing cards, and even snacking as if at a party. They had been sometimes in her room at home and sometimes in the hospital. But on Grace's last two visits and more worryingly on fully half her visits since the start of the holidays, poor Alicia hadn't felt well enough to join in any kind of play.

"We've had a good couple of days," said Nan, who had plumped up since October and who wore one of her many off-the-rack outfits, this in gold and red, in which blouse, skirt or slacks, and some accessories matched. "I made pecan pancakes, we picked up a milkshake, and she ate it all. We expect she'll come home on Monday."

"Then by next weekend we'll have another treatment in our rearview mirror," said Steve, also addressing Alicia indirectly. Grace saw how her big-hearted but frightened brother's language tripped him up.

Alicia turned to her and, with a hand over her mouth, in a mock whisper, loudly said, "Sleepover." Her hair had thinned more and would now fall out, Grace saw in a glance—weeks after it had seemed this might not happen. And then, like the actress she had half-learned to be, Grace immediately regained her place in the script.

"Once your parents finally leave," she announced, "I'll bring in the cute guys I met at the mall. One is for you and one is for me."

"Your son would find you gross," said Nan. Her sister-in-law could temporarily be distracted from her worries, and had always hated to be left out of any activity.

"All I want is that someone decide," said Steve. At forty-four, her little brother still was very freckled. She thought how his puzzled look here was like the look he'd had back when he saw her act in plays.

Except that here, a puzzled attitude made good sense.

"One way or another," said Alicia, "Dad has to get outdoors soon for his next cigarette."

Nan asked: "Did you bring a change of clothes?"

"Of course not; but I have three big, terrific pizzas in the car that only Steve and I aren't allergic to. I tried to get a plain cheese but they'd closed the kitchen. Steve, you may as well take one home."

"They'll have toiletries here, and fresh sheets if you ask for them, and maybe pajamas. They really try to make families comfortable." Nan smiled at her daughter. "I think it'll be fun. I'm jealous!"

"We *will* have fun, Mom. You should be jealous."

"We'll be back in the morning. But are you sure?"

Grace would go outdoors with them, ostensibly to hand off a pizza. Steve took hold of Alicia's head, kissing her where her hair met her forehead; then he gathered up what Nan had told him to take and went out for his smoke. Nan took Grace to greet the weekend nurses. With her eyes on her route, she spoke of the treatment schedule as they passed a few patient rooms on each side of the hallway. Grace, as had been true for months, had to fight her impulse to tune out what she could. She saw in a blue-eyed, jeans-clad, college-age boy leaving a room the puzzled look she had just seen in her brother.

"Carol," Nan shortly said in a slow, insistent tone to an older woman who sat typing at the nursing station, making her look up, "this is my sister-in-law, Grace, who you must've met. She's offered to wait out the weather in Alicia's room and give Steven and me a breather."

Carol's eyes climbed to the top rim of her glasses and seemed to weigh Nan and then Grace. "The roads will close all night," she said with a cautious look, before starting to smile. "But we'll be fine. Nan, have a bath and a glass or three of wine. Grace, once our princess is asleep feel free to come back here for a late cup of coffee."

Moments later, again in her coat, Grace went down the elevator with Nan, who had quieted. They found Steve against an outer wall of the glass and cement building, shielded from the wind but busy calibrating it.

"The highways will still be drivable," he said. "My bride, the worst case, if we don't get up the hill, will be a night in the hotel. It'd probably do us good, anyway. But I think we'll get home."

Nan had begun to cry. "No, worst case is a two a.m. call and us not able to get back. I'm thinking we should stay, or find a nearby hotel."

"It's not like that now," said Grace. "They say the problems relate to the treatment, not the disease... and that it may grind along in this way for a while. Go take care of yourselves for a few hours."

"If she can't handle the treatments, she could die," said Nan.

"Grace is right," said Steve. "The problems are procedural. You don't really understand."

Grace through wet eyes saw Steve and Nan, and then they all looked at one another. Steve, working down his butt and seeming stymied, was the first to turn away.

"A little boy down the hall is being buried tomorrow, unless the snow holds things up," said Nan.

"We're going home," said Steve. "It's a good idea."

After a moment, Grace asked him, "You'll take one of the pizzas?"

"It's just me eating it, so I'll take a half."

"But there's so much of it. Take one and freeze half."

"Grace, I appreciate your gesture, I really do. But if you want me to have pizza, give me half a pie."

Grace left the windbreak for her car in a nearby row. As she walked, she looked at the seven-story wall of windows. Then she found the pizza in the top box to be cut in discrete slices—lucky, as she would have ripped the pie by hand. Next, the missing slice threw her off. But she had let the snow on her eyebrows and cheeks ease her mood by the time she again greeted Nan and Steve, who had walked out to meet her. With the handoff made, the couple went back inside to ride the elevator down to their car.

Grace feigned a need to get something else from her trunk and stayed outside, keeping imagistic hold of the hospital's south-facing wall and the snow slicing into it. She noted the whites and browns of the ebbing daylight and took off a glove to finger-scoop snow. She allowed herself the distractions because once they ended she would have to go back inside.

At least, she asked her imaginative powers, get me onto the fifth floor, to the ward and room I have to know about. She pictured herself leaving the elevator. But as her flash-forward wore on, she regretted not having taken more time to prepare.

Nearing her niece's room in fact, she had the same regret.

Alicia, sitting up in bed under an over-the-shoulder lamp, seemed to be reading. The room had darkened over twenty minutes and the whirling snow looked farther away. The girl, who had grown curvy the past year, and who was smart and full of enthusiasms, cast shadows of her own.

The shadows said she wanted to confess her real mood.

"How's the bravery business?" asked her aunt.

"I don't know."

"Do you understand what's going on?"

"I'm supposed to think I'm getting better, if that's what you mean."

"That's the main message. Has feeling sick so much worn you down?"

"It's not how much but how long. I'm missing all of seventh grade."

"Two months isn't all year, honey. Isn't that what it's been? You were in school during a lot of November, remember."

"Look at me, Aunt Grace. I won't go back like this—let alone when I start to look even more like some pathetic sad-movie freak."

Grace had dropped her damp coat on a chair near the bathroom door. Now she gathered it up and sat holding it, a few yards from the bed. She saw that Alicia's pale blue hospital gown was the flag around which the IV gear and, in sum, all else in the room rallied. And the body it covered had terrified its owner twice: with an attack on her life but also, in its sexual budding, with an upending of the person she had always felt herself to be.

"I know Nan has shown you scarves, and I have more in my bag, if we want to look at them later. Honey, you'll get used to this again— and to do so absolutely qualifies as bravery."

"You want to know if I'm afraid. Being brave is laughing at fear."

"I don't think that. But this week was hard, and as you said, you've been fighting this now for a long time."

Alicia was still, with her head twisted left and her eyes on a wall whose one adornment was a closet door. The starkness of this view made Grace look around the room: at framed illustrations, one show-ing the Duchess from the croquet game and one Toad; at a photo of zebras on the run; at a lamp to Alicia's right in the shape of a frog. In this regard, the hospital tried, and there were other nods to youthful fancy. She also glanced at her niece, whose pale skin and dewy eyes, extremes already, seemed enhanced by her situation. Her gaze spoke of trying to keep her thoughts inside what felt comfortable.

"Kids' talk isn't supposed to be about dying," Alicia said.

"No, it's not. Does that happen here?"

"Among the older of us, sometimes."

"You're going to stay cancer-free."

"I guess luck is a funny thing."

In her mind, Grace quoted: I guess luck is a funny thing. She had heard in Alicia's voice both the hot tone she sometimes took with Nan or Steve and a new bitterness. No, Grace thought: it's not for eleven-and-a-half-year-olds to know this feeling.

"Hon, I need to ask you something. Do you know what an analogy is?"

"Yes I do, of course, to change the subject."

"I'm not changing the subject; I'm trying to speak to what you see. So, let me lay out my dumb analogy. Have you ever driven a car?"

"Once on my dad's lap, sort of, when I was ten."

"Could you learn to drive now?"

"It doesn't seem that difficult."

"You have a sense of what it would be like to drive."

"Yes."

"Are you ready to be a driver?"

"It's not really what kids do. I'm still too short, for example."

"Okay, now I'll try to say this. Your sense of what driving is like is part of starting to imagine life as an adult. But being young distorts your view—it's again like being too short to reach the pedals. And the more someone stares at a distortion, the more it grows…. You're in the midst of some hard months. You may want to put aside your sympathies for others and do what you need to for yourself."

"Who would ever want to be an adult?"

"You'll be a wonderful adult."

Still with her eyes on the closet door, Alicia smiled, seeming to take the compliment and looking to Grace like a new moon. With a wider smile she asked, "Did you really buy a whole stack of jam and stink cheese pizzas?"

"Well, sort of; they're freezing up on my backseat."

"And they're really called what?"

"Called what?"

Alicia turned to her. "Their actual name?"

"Oh: a fig and Gorgonzola pie. It's the—"

"Did you say pig, or fig?"

Relieved but unsettled, Grace saw that Alicia, with her raven hair falling out, bore a teasing expression. The question seemed silly but for how it brushed her memory. She liked seeing her niece begin to play. Alicia pointed to the Duchess, framed expectantly above a blond, low oak or oak-veneer hospital bureau.

"Ah," said Grace slowly. "Nearly, but not to the scene, so tell me."

Alicia seemed to quote: "'Did you say "pig," or "fig"?' said the Cat."

Grace chortled. "You smart thing. Have you been saving that?"

"Since I heard Mom and Dad grumbling about the stupid pizzas."

"'Please,' said Alice," said Grace, trying to paraphrase, "'can you stop coming and going so suddenly, it, uh… makes me quite giddy.'"

"Can we read some of it aloud? I saw copies in the game room."

In fact they had a dramatic reading after Grace went and—being quick in the game room because to be there made her sad—got two copies in different editions. They decided to begin with "Pig and Pepper." Grace would read Alice, Alicia the Footman, Duchess, and Cat, and they would share the narration. They took a break before starting, though, once Alicia noted that it would be dark out before they had gotten far. Alicia left her bed and, with Grace wheeling the IV stand, came around to the window. Insistently, Grace threw a cotton shawl over Alicia's shoulders and, she felt with more welcome, her left arm over the shawl.

"Here at the window, I see a few lights," said Alicia.

"Tell me everything you see."

"No, you."

"I'm a great listener when a kid's being clever."

"No, you. I'm saving up my energy for the reading."

"Well, okay. First, there are shadows, which show us what it must be like to live with one's head not in the sky but under rocks, sheets of paper, snoring pigs, and all manner of things. Then there's the snow flying up out of gloomy distances. Put your ear to the glass to hear how melting snow sounds."

"You're dumb like Dad again," said Alicia as she bent in and tilted her head and, after listening for a minute, leaned closer to Grace.

"Finally, the lights, looking like red animal eyes from here. Some stay constant, others blink now and then. And some live at street level while others float near us up here like... like a *Cheshire cat*."

A nurse came for a fever check and Alicia, while she didn't have to, got in bed. Then they acted chapter six, using a pillow for the changeling baby and making a crayon drawing, which Grace taped above Alicia to signify the Cat. Reading ornately, liking the word and image trickery, Alicia strode back uphill toward adolescence. After chapter six, they went to chapter one, and had gotten through part when Alicia's dinner was brought in. A minute earlier, sniffing food in the hall, Grace had turned to the flat, dark outside and decided to forego the icy pizza. She saw Alicia walk through a lasagna, green bean, and brownie meal, bashing it as "Monday lunch at school." Then she promised to haul back cafeteria treats when she went for dinner. She made this trip presently, when Alicia, after trying the brownie—Grace, slipping morsels beneath her mask, had liked it and the lasagna—stretched out sleepily.

Grace all day had eaten only an almond pastry and parts of a side salad and pizza slice, so at the buffet she chose lasagna and a Greek salad. Later, she would get popcorn and sundaes high with toppings to bring to the room. There were empty tables and as she made for one she saw the nurse she had recently greeted sitting with a woman, a doctor judging by her white coat, who was just standing up.

"Courage and blessings," said the staff members to one another.

Grace drew near her chosen table. "Alicia's Aunt Grace," said Carol. "Come sit with me if you want."

"I work in a middle school, so I know about needing down time."

"Oh, that's fine. We try to be a big family here. Come sit."

Carol was thin with side-parted gray hair and big glasses. She sat behind an iced tea and a partly eaten tuna-salad plate, whose garnishing pickle spears looked to Grace like blades. Her voice was thin, too, and from its lift at the launch of certain phrases Grace surmised that she often had trouble being heard.

"Well, thanks, as I'd hoped to talk with you, anyway."

"There could be lots of time for talk, though now's okay, too. The snow may not even start to ease before tomorrow night."

"Are you set up with power and food and doctors and whatever?"

"We have two hundred kids. We're set up for everything."

"Yet unexpected events must be always coming up."

"They're factored in; it's all about practicing procedures."

"It feels wonderful here," said Grace, before adding, as she got a first wedge of lasagna onto her fork, "even though it intimidates me."

"We don't want that to be happening."

"I find being here hard to get used to. You come, or I first did, as most people must, full of fear; then I found that everyone I met faces something similar. I find it hard to know how to behave."

Grace ate for a time, but with diminished appetite. The lasagna was barely heated through, as if the snowstorm had affected it.

"I remember you being here a lot when Alicia was," said Carol. "It may be harder to come and go, to be here only sometimes, as she is now; but do you recall the usual commotion? Everyone takes care of the kids, including other kids, and the families take care of one another."

"I might not be enough of a nurturer. Being here is too big a shock. Some kids aren't doing so well."

Grace looked grievingly at the nurse, who seemed to startle in her chair. Grace looked past her to one then another of the bold-colored art posters festooning the cafeteria walls. She was cheered by yet another storybook illustration, and listened for ticks of a crocodile's clock.

"Sorry for my outburst," she said.

"Some in our families," replied Carol, "once their hard times are over, find that it helps them to come back and volunteer."

"I doubt I could ever do that. It's enough thinking back to Alicia's first month of chemo. But you're right in that I see people help each other here. A few times, I've tried to help myself.... And speaking of Alicia, how is she? Should I be worrying again?"

"Your niece is special and also fortunate. Her side effects were to be expected. She's coming along nicely."

"I know that's what my brother has been told."

Without replying, Carol looked back sympathetically. Grace saw her face relax, as if layers of dutifulness and fatigue had given way.

"Do I pry to ask what you and your friend said to each other as she left the table? I thought it was: 'Courage and blessings.'"

"You heard right, and feel free to ask about it. It's not personal, but rather a form some of us use when we greet one another."

"Is it taught, one of the procedures this fortress lives by?"

"No, its just words sometimes said to buck each other up."

"And does it hold some secret meaning?"

"Only what's in the words... "

Back upstairs, she found Alicia awake in a dark room. Grace took two lidded sundaes from a bag—Carol had mentioned having told Nan they could now go unmasked—and was groping for a lamp when the girl called her off.

"Aunt Grace, look out the windows."

"I see it now."

"The wind stopped, which lets us see a bit farther out. There's so much snow, and it's falling in straight lines."

"Oh, shit, oh—I forgot to phone your parents."

"They called; they're back at home and fine."

"I better call my house, too, before it gets late."

"Dad said it might be just you and me here till Monday."

Grace sat on the bed below Alicia's feet and handed over a raspberry sundae. "That's good news. I may have you read lines with me. It's for a play my lazy eighth graders are going to workshop."

"I'm sorry I was sad before. I need to be home, and the storm made me feel trapped here even more... even though, now, the snow is fun!"

"I know being here is hard for you... as I said, you're very brave."

"This dessert is fun, too." For a while they ate and watched the snow and shadows in silence. The processed ice cream was still firm. "And it'll be fun working on your play," Alicia added. "But can I say a last sad thing I've been thinking about? It's more frustrating than sad, actually."

"Get it out."

"I don't want you to be sad."

"Look at the snow out the window as you tell me."

"It's not hard for me; I can even keep eating my sundae as I talk. Okay, well, I know about survival rates, my having like three chances in four to finish high school, which makes me lucky in some comparisons. But this sends my mind down two roads: to the dying I just can't make sense of, and to the way no one talks about survival rates after five years.

"What I mean is, if surviving gets less likely after five years, it makes our treatments less valuable, and someone should tell kids maybe my age and older this, and give us more of a choice."

Gasping, Grace said, "Honey, the chances only get better with time." Alicia then turned to her sundae.

She stayed up for three more hours, until ten o'clock, and when, after spending another subdued half hour in darkness, they lit the room, it was to watch an adventure story on TV. Grace got soft drinks in the corridor and nestled in bed holding the popcorn bag, big as a backpack that she had bought in the cafeteria.

Afterwards, while doubting she could work, she took a script into the corridor and went, first, to the nursing station in search of Carol and then to an area with lamps and hard chairs. Sitting down, she saw the nurse fly into a room. A man who also held a softbound document of some kind sat a few chairs away.

"It's late," she told the stranger, looking at him, "I'm tired and you must be, too, and I've nothing to say, yet listen to me." He was Asian and in his thirties, wore suit pants and a white shirt, and had no coat. He looked at her slowly but not, she felt, reluctantly.

"Is your child here?" he asked.

"A niece. She's in her consolidation phase and sometimes having a bumpy ride."

"She's at a very good place," he said in a consoling tone. "I hope there hasn't been a setback."

"Only in treatment delays; she's cancer-free." Grace liked being able to repeat this. But then she felt sympathy. "Is your child here?"

"A cousin's son; so my situation is a bit like yours."

"How old is the boy? My niece is nearly a teenager."

"Matt is eight; but he's sadly not now cancer-free."

"I'm sorry. Are you filling in for Matt's parents?"

"Well, or helping. Ours has been a two-year ordeal."

"Then my chattering may put further weight on you."

"Not really. Talking can make it seem less unreal."

"I've felt that, in terms of repeating good news."

"Good news is a gift. What is your niece's name?"

"Huh—I find I'm reluctant to say her name out loud."

The man glanced at her and said, "That's all right."

"No, it's horrid. Her name is Alicia Hudson."

"It's okay. A lot of guesswork goes on here."

"Maybe it's the guesswork that scares me. For a month I was here a lot and saw a lot, but it all fled my mind when Alicia started to again be mostly back at home."

"What one sees here is hard to contend with; go easy on yourself. No culture I know of has much to add if the news isn't good."

"Can I ask if you're some kind of a Buddhist?"

"No; only a Minnesotan with a finance degree."

"Making me feel even worse is that I want to hear about Matt."

"He's a scared child who fights hard and sees the guesswork going on around him. And picks up hospital talk: he told me once that when his platelets were down his body had to make more little plates."

"I don't understand the medical terms much better than he does."

"His parents do, now. Sometimes there's a lot you have to know."

"I'm a mother, too, so I have to ask this: How is Matt doing?"

"We'd thought okay before the second relapse; now we aren't sure."

"You know, I think I'm scared here for myself, not others. It hurts too much to hear the stories."

"That it does."

"And just now there must be a hundred adults keeping watch as you and I are. I mean—two hundred kids are here."

"The adult visitors in these corridors tend to all look alike."

"I have to try to help. Unbelievably, I hadn't thought of this. And there's the staff for each ward. Probably almost no one is allergic. And there must be toaster ovens somewhere, at the very least."

"Pardon me?"

"I helped in October a couple of times, then shut it all out. Would you be willing to walk outside with me for five minutes?"

"You mean into the snowfall of the year, this late at night?"

"Just, briefly. I have to get some gourmet pizzas from my car."

Part Two

Grace

3

A Retreat Extended

Waiting at the tent awnings in the parking lot, Grace Hudson first thought that the strangers she found herself among were all friends. But with the nine a.m. gathering more quietly expectant than chatty, she soon felt less alone. Nor did she care if it took her some time to fit in. Hers was a far larger sense of inconsequence, which she hoped would lessen against the patterns of the place. This was why she was here.

Over the winter, Grace had witnessed a niece's struggle with leukemia. Now, with Alicia's treatment in a maintenance phase and her and her parents about to leave for a hospital-run family camp, and with Grace's slightly older son, Amos, at another summer camp, she had carried her self-absence to Seeker. Urged by friends, she took a workshop called "Embracing Sadness"; but at its finish she had merely laughed. Feeling empty and afraid to go home, she had then, with her husband's kind consent and his Saturday, July 4 drop-off of extra gear, extended her stay by joining the support staff for eighteen days. Forlorn, she placed her hope in the academy and its fresh air.

After a day spent—once she had raised her tent—quietly in the sun, and a first night more truly in the woods, she now waited to load luggage. A dozen travel bags of varying sizes lay under an awning. Out of shape, feeling flabby, she tested herself by lifting a big duffle bag to her ribs. A girl half her age yelled encouragement; she wore a white and purple Seeker tee shirt under blue-jeaned overalls, and stood at a table under the other awning. Grace wondered why, amid calm air and a hushed lot, she had not made out the words. She thought: how dazed am I? Then the girl sang "Sophie," ambled over and said, in accented English: "I'm Sophie, from Copenhagen. Do you work with us today? If so you can practice with our barbells." She poked a toe at a pair of duffle bags. "I've learned that, a few weekends each year, someone brings lifting weights, if you can believe it. We drag the sixty kilos in and out of carts. Fridays they go uphill; Sundays, down. It's us staff who get the exercise."

An electric cart hauling luggage pieces pulled up quietly. Two men got out and with Sophie's help began to unload. Grace tried to join in but, hesitating briefly, found that she was already too late. The trio stopped and Grace first registered—indicated by the younger man's shyness—Sophie's physical beauty. She was someone Grace, in her theatricalizing way, would begin to think of as a Venus or Athena of the river valley. An Athena, because Sophie's searching gaze seemed to fly past all that her good looks might easily hand to her.

A dozen workers gathered over the next few minutes. Grace saw that she was the third oldest and that she could be mother to half the team. All seemed to be regulars, except her and a petite young black woman who, in an accent that mixed Scandinavia with Africa, introduced herself as Willa the Wiking. An athletic man a bit older than Grace named Monkfish or Monk (she first doubted what she heard) divided them into three crews, and, with her crew, Grace left the parking lot in a brown van. With Willa and a second girl bracing themselves on the floor in back and Grace in the passenger seat, they began to bounce uphill. Driving was the young guy who seemed stuck on Sophie, silent Trumpeter. Grace decided to wait for someone else to speak.

They rode a gravel path through an area of small cabins, passing the one she had shared with three women the week before. Trumpeter's first words addressed them all: "As Franny knows the routine, she'll stay with the van. You'll both bring luggage from the porches to the path. Be sure that each piece has a room tag."

Thus, Grace's first staff friend was Willa, who had come in June for a two-month stay. They went from porch to porch, encouraging each other and carrying the heaviest bags together. Willa's parents taught in Norway; in September, she would begin graduate school there in sociology—having recently finished a stint in the business world. In Copenhagen, she had lived with Sophie in a group house. They would spend a week together in New York City at the end of their trip.

Willa, in turn, learned that Grace had tried for seven years to be an actress in New York; that she had in time begun to teach English and drama at a lower Hudson Valley middle school; and that she was now—Grace passing over the recent family trial—a more or less typical suburban mom.

The van stopped every hundred feet to gather luggage. Trumpeter exited and they brought bags to Francine, who loaded. This Quebecois girl, small like Willa, was fit enough to toss every bag into the van, singing French pop songs as she worked. She ignored the newcomers mostly but peppered Trumpeter, apparently a friend, with insults and wry remarks. She spoke to Grace and Willa in English—"Ze side door is full. We load now from ze back"—but to Trumpeter in a French he barely followed. Her words ricocheted as she smiled or scowled. Trumpeter at times translated, as in: "Franny here says I carry the lighter luggage; that I don't step up." When he got right the gist of a comment, she grinned and insulted him more in French. When he erred, her tirade was worse. Tight, solemn Trumpeter, Grace saw, seemed to accept the playful lambasting as fun.

During a strenuous two hours, as they three times filled the van and unloaded it in the parking lot, retrieving the belongings of two hundred guests, Grace got Willa's initial take on staff life at Seeker. "It's obsessive here but fascinating," Willa confided. "I've had so much veggie stir-fry that it's in my dreams. At a workshop on choosing careers, the teacher said that if we know what we want the universe will give it to us. What fantasy!... or if not that, proof that one thing people here share is an unwitting privilege."

Grace liked Willa, as well as chatty interactions; but, these days, her emotions wore out quickly. So she was glad when, after a quarter hour, they came to cabins set farther apart and had to work independently. And since workshops ended at noon, they also worked against the clock. The weekend guests must be nervous, Grace felt; the coming and going must force too many changes for that short a time. People near panic and fearing anxiety the most (she put herself in this group) would likely try to leave quickly... and then might spin out if they did not quickly find their bags. Grace knew that her body would ache the next day, as her heart ached from the winter in hell; but she was glad for the struggle. She felt the strain in her biceps and legs above her kneecaps, saw sweat start to pattern her sky-blue polo shirt, longed for heavy hands to massage her neck. Aping Francine, she threw up bags as if they were filled with feathers. Her attention was settled on the task.

By noon, the bags in a third load were laid under the tent and the crew had regrouped. Standing beside Monk, the team leader, Trumpeter—looking bored, with his wry grin gone—sent them to lunch. Walking side by side, Grace, Willa, and Sophie crossed paths with three dozen guests who, skipping lunch, were trudging to their cars. More such departing guests were approaching from the green hill. Grace sensed resignation as the mood of this group: a trip home begun in a hot, dusty parking lot was beyond what she could picture now. Trumpeter and Monk passed in a cart; whether to beat them to lunch or to look for misplaced luggage, she did not know. Once she thought about hunger, she found herself ready to eat.

4

Trying to Meditate

Staff assigned luggage duty on a Friday or Sunday transition day worked split shifts: retrieving bags in the morning, greeting arrivals and ferrying bags in the late afternoon. Guests weren't fed supper on transition days—meals could be purchased in the café, though—so most of the kitchen crew had these afternoons off, as well. After a quick lunch, Grace went with Sophie to a meditation class, offered, she read in the staff mess, beside a class on Hindu Chanting and another titled "Scientific Perspectives on the Supernatural."

During her workshop, Grace had twice climbed to the sanctuary and once gone in. She was stopped the first time by a colony of shoes and sandals in the alcove. To remove *her* shoes, she felt, would suggest beliefs she did not share. She accused the huddled shoes of claiming kinship with her grief. But this was a flash of mood; moments later, she sat on the sanctuary porch, watching lily pads on the cedar-walled pond and hearing the quiet settled on this place of prayer. On a second visit she went in, to find herself alone. She sat on the floor: pressed her feet and palms into the hard-bristle carpet, absorbed the ceiling's volume, felt her emotions begin to surface. After a while, she left.

Hearing this story on their climb, Sophie touched Grace's arm and halted. "Thoughts and feelings often make us spin," she said, amid pattering breaths. "In a quiet place we spin faster: it's as you say. But I think that meditation gets us past this kind of inner disorder. It can help us find ourselves in a deeper sense."

Grace, seeing the sanctuary above and hearing the dining-hall hum below, felt a cloverleaf of confusion. She wanted to dismiss this coded talk, heard all over Seeker, as silly and didactic—more proof that she had been to the end of her experience, from which her goal at the academy was to step back. But she also felt Sophie to be thoughtful and sincere. She seemed believable, like a neighbor passing on a recipe out of simple good will.

In the alcove, they saw dozens of shoes. On entering the sanctuary, Grace's glance met Monk's; oddly, he nodded. It came to her that this peculiar, rangy man was somehow interested in her. She wondered why, thought of romance, and felt herself blush. Then she feared that she would laugh in this solemn setting.

How ridiculous I am in middle age, she thought as she let Sophie lead her to a space on the floor where they could sit.

Calming background music began to play and the meditation teacher prepared to speak. The class members straightened; some sat on black pillows, and Grace, imitating them, felt how to do so raised her buttocks and lifted and lengthened her spine.

"Welcome," began the teacher in an oozy drawl. "I'm Dorothy, a nurse from Texas. Today I start a two-week run as staff meditation teacher. I'll lead meditations before breakfast and supper, and teach meditation instruction to staff. As some here know, I've annoyed you Easterners with my accent for seven years in a row."

It was a heady joke, meant to be relaxing. Grace kept her eyes on this thickset nurse, who had honey-colored hair. She doubted that so enigmatic a person could lead her anywhere. But when, under Dorothy's guidance, the first meditation began and Grace breathed as told to, she felt the air swelling into her lungs assault her over-wound rhythms and discords with—as Dorothy languidly if precisely put it, stressing each syllable—"an inspiriting promise." Grace felt a pressure around her cheeks and eyes, then a tingling near the crown of her head—a place where, she thought wierdly, TV show aliens might hook her from the sky. As if reading Grace's mind, Dorothy told the class to count silently as they breathed, to shake away the images that could climb into their heads.

Moments later, Grace, nearing points of internal breakage, lost her poise and exhaled to a shuddering stop. But Dorothy, catching Grace's glance in a scan of the room, beckoned her to try again, and she did.

It was a struggle to stay, but Grace did for half an hour. Losing track of Sophie, still beside her, she worked on breathing, counting to higher numbers as her lungs expanded. Once she even forgot to count and floated, eyes closed, with nothing in view. Yet the norm this day saw her mind break its count to slide into other channels. Twice she saw Alicia—the second time, wrapped in ungraspable narrative. Then she stopped trying. She stretched her legs, leaned back on her elbows, heard the music, and looked at the skylights: in this way she felt shielded from Dorothy's rapt nursing countenance. The ceiling, two stories high, let her thoughts play more freely for a time. Then, rising discreetly to leave, she saw that fully half of the participants were open-eyed, too.

Bulletin boards stood where the main campus paths crossed. On one Grace saw, beside an events calendar, a notice for a staff concert and poetry recital that night at the café. Two lean-bodied women in their late thirties also read the board—early arrivals, as new guests weren't to arrive before four p.m. One sipped from an opaque plastic bottle; both wore tight, blue, body-length cycling outfits darkened by sweat.

"I saw a staff show last year," said one to her friend and to Grace. "What a hoot. The angry college kids; guys, especially—when you talk to them you get back grunts amid a sense of colliding emotional glaciers. Ten connected words are a lot. But give them a guitar backup and out pops a scowling poet."

"That's how my nearly-adolescent son will turn out," Grace said to them. "And in not many more years, I shudder to add."

"They remind me of some clients," said the other cyclist. "We both," she informed Grace with a laugh, "are psychotherapists."

From three until eight, Grace worked back in the parking lot. With other staffers, she helped arriving guests unload their cars and move to the registration area. Monk led a small crew that took luggage up the hill in carts, while Trumpeter ruled the parking lot. When she returned from her supper break in the early evening, the arriving flow had thinned and, under Trumpeter's direction, she worked the parking lot alone. He spoke only when he had to, and she, tired from the long day, lacked the will to approach him.

Her shift ended quickly, though. At its finish, with the sun behind the western ridge that overlay the camp, she crossed the gravel lot and broke into the woods, heading north. Certain she had taken a wrong path, she instead found that she *did* know the way to her tent. Staff platforms were only a dozen yards apart, she guessed to dampen tendencies among the young for sex under a summer night; but at this twilight hour, with everyone busy, she was alone. The touch of the tent zipper brought a first sob to her chest; or maybe the quiet trees were the carriers, drawing out her feelings as from a tunnel. She waited on her sleeping bag; then through her tent's mesh sides and roof she began to see thousands of leaves, mimicking the oval shapes of eyes. Distracted, as a child can be, she began to look at one leaf and then another. But the day of new labors and acquaintances had done what she had asked it to: so now, preventing for a while another firing of her emotions, she slept.

5

Two Angry Young Poets

She woke forty minutes later, when it was nearly dark, and heard music in the distance. The sound grew richer as she walked toward the café—that of drums and a jazz flute in particular. The path spiraled uphill to the entrance doors; inside, Grace saw the room crowded with about seventy people, drawn from arrived guests and staff. A few musicians played at the far end. She joined the snack line; then a big, gray, pink, mustachioed man of sixty stepped behind her, who with his wife had been in the sadness workshop. "You're our drama teacher," he said. "We found your imitations that one morning to be fun. If you don't remember, my name is Anton Gold."

Grace was surprised to be reacquainted; and their common experience, set against the new faces, made it seem they shared a secret. As the line inched forward Anton learned of Grace's joining the staff for a while; he told her that he and Debs, his wife, came to Seeker a few times each year. "On Friday, we drove to the Berkshires for a concert; now we're back for Nadia Tolliver's 'Past-life Regression' workshop. Then we drive home to our suburb in… to suburban Detroit. But there's more! A week later, we'll fly back for an African drumming workshop Debs insists we do. Our Michigan friends say we are quite the adventurous couple."

Deb Gold, more gestural than Anton, waved from a window table. Grace recalled that she also spoke less calmly than her husband. What they seemed to share was a friendly, persuadable attitude. In the workshop, Anton had called his big body "the support beam for my spiritual beliefs." She hadn't at all known what that meant but had liked how it sounded. Deb stood, smiling, and began to speak before they could hear her. She wore a white blouse embroidered with purple and yellow stitching—likely bought, Grace knew, in a sunny, poor country—and a bevy of bracelets, rings, and necklaces. These ornaments and her dyed chestnut curls played over her trim features and olive skin. All her decorations were on the move.

"Sweetie, you decided to stay!" she said. "I think that's wonderful! Being here is good for you, isn't it? It's healing. Yes, good. What's your job? This is such a healing place." Like Deb's dress, her cadences flowed—as if meant to comfort everyone who heard. Grace knew others who spoke this way, always promising a quick end to some crisis; and Debs was someone she might mimic once she got home. Yet her own style, what she always fell back on, was to give life a chance: a role-the-dice openness that had brought her to Seeker. And so, perhaps aided by her nap and by a soy fudge bar that was surprisingly good, she had the best time of her day sitting with the Golds. Anton, who told stories slowly, recalled the ballet they had seen the night before, while Deb brought up details of audience reactions, dancer costumes, and their own brazen breakfasting on ham and bacon at a bed-and-breakfast.

Trailing in their wake and excitable, too, Grace once laughed so raucously that a prickly, disapproving Trumpeter, looking back from a table near the stage, caught—maybe by accident—her eye.

Willa sat with him; later he went on stage with two others from their table. The Golds and Grace moved up to the empty seats.

"Willa, sweetie, how are you?" exclaimed Deb. Then she addressed the table, waving a tanned arm. "Willa and I met last week. I'd stumbled with my tray toward the picnic tables, and found a seat with people younger than my son. Everyone was smart; and while they were nice to me, I barely followed what was said."

"The conversation was about water," recalled Willa. "And in line with it, you described a Mexican cave lake you once saw that had been a site of human sacrifice." Willa winked at Grace, to show she was irritated by but also sympathetic to the woman's false modesty. Then, pointing to Trumpeter, she told the table: "The Luggage Crew's assistant manager is about to recite one of his poems."

The musicians, playing bongos, bass guitar, and flute, had paused to let their guitarists, Monk and a bald, bearded man in his fifties, set up. Monk slipped a wire harmonica rack over his head; seeing this, some near the stage cheered and called, "Monkfish!" Then, as he broke the lull with a blues harmonica riff, heightened by the strum of his bald guitarist, the chatty rumble of the room switched to a stirred listening.

These blues, Grace knew, had grown from privations that no one there had likely experienced. Still, the listeners from several countries and generations heard notes that brought nearly everyone alive. Young staffers swelled to the music. With closed eyes, Anton swung his arms and tattooed the melody with his fingers. Deb clapped, shouting, "Yeah! Yeah! Ooohh!" Then, joining Willa, Francine, and many others, she began to dance.

After a ten-minute jam, Monk announced a pause but said the band would return to end the evening after two staff members recited poems. Some guests voiced dismay, but the young staff surged forward with excited eyes. Gathered near the stage, they looked to be the children of the guests. Willa moved forward, chuckling self-consciously. Grace, sitting with Anton as Deb went to stand beside a wall, thought of the sweaty therapists she had met earlier. What had they said about the Seeker's poets?

A half hour later, Grace could at least feel that Trumpeter, who ignored but intrigued her, had given the better performance. The band dropped its blue notes to a jazzy background beat and a café worker who had sold Grace her dessert bar began to intone. In line, Grace had seen him joke with friends, but he was as sullen now as he had been when serving her. Holding a script, small, dark-eyed under oily curls, he fumed at his mic: as if to say that his true performance was showing anything other than rage. Each verse let him spit venomous words into the air. Frog nouns, snake verbs, and salamander modifiers leapt at the audience, then hissed collectively when new words of anger entered the room. Monk led the musical accompaniment. The poet's contempt for nearly every imaginable act, relationship, and memory—he seemed to hate memories the most—he countered with visions of "escape." He claimed to find solace in purity: in sex and in women's bodies—he vowed to care only for young women; in fire and earthly destruction; in his sweet knowledge of god.

Grace, listening through her melancholy, sensed that this attitude amounted to no more than a yearning for clarity in the young poet's heart.

Trumpeter, when his turn came, seemed to draw from the same well as his friend. Once he had begun, Grace looked around to find Willa in a grin. But Anton listened, as did Deb near her wall. Trumpeter, tall, puffy, pensive, with brown hair and a matching beard, spoke more of pain, wounds taken in battle, than had the first poet, and he showed less anger. He seemed rather to see the life ahead being made gentle by what he called its "unities."

"Meditation, self-renunciation, kindness, and dutifulness." He twice repeated his list, before adding, "We seekers know ourselves to be living by these practices, anyway, from our collective memory."

As his poem flowed from lament to hopeful vision, flute and bongo made sprightlier sounds, while Monk's intermittent harmonica riffs evoked a mood of ascent. Yet, on ending his poem Trumpeter showed little peace. He dropped his eyes and slipped offstage to stand near a wall; with no reason to be there, he then returned to the table. Anton found a chair, Deb another, and all made room and sat. Monk announced a pause to give everyone a last chance at the dessert line before a blues jam would end the night.

The sullen, first poet was back behind the cash register.

"I felt the power in your words," said Anton. "Listening made me look forward to the coming week. Deep change might be truly possible at the academy."

"Anton cares about deep change," Deb told Grace and Willa, sotto voce and with a hint of irony.

"What, Debs?" her husband asked.

"I said that holistic, mind-body-spirit ideas matter to you." She turned to the table. "Every year, here, Anton buys a stack of books; he reads them during the winter and then he uses his computer to arrange their ideas. Do I have it right, sweetie? You work from November to March in your home office. His printed results look to me like the charts in his dental anatomy books."

"You want to map the holistic movement?" asked Willa with interest.

"To a degree," replied Anton, whose wavy hair was more blond than grey. "For thirty years I've used science in my practice." He inhaled and Deb, making more spousal mischief, did the same. She smiled at the table; he grinned in response. "Still," he went on, "I lack the skills and credentials to scientifically plot New Age ideas—especially now, when there's so much richness and diversity. But the play of patterns interests me, and I hope I can give something back with my provisional mapping."

Grace felt her mind shun even this much abstract thinking; she again wondered if beyond fatigue she was more dazed than she knew. What she had liked in the poetry was its not having to make sense; she was content if an image stuck from each poem—like the first poet's hatred of memory. And it was enough to know he had been angry and the second poet, Trumpeter, what? A dreamer, who wanted life to be sweet.... She knew both positions. And rather than reason, she wanted beer. Seeker forbade such mind-bending agents, yet she sat on a knife-edge. She wanted very much to hear the blues, to dance—what she usually, and always among strangers, feared to do—and to relax.

But not all at the table shared her good, end-of-evening instincts. If time for her had stopped between waking and a need to sleep, or between readiness and a need to relax, others, missing the weak signal of her self-effacing, frozen smile, moved ahead by their own lights. The learned Anton hoped to say more about his patterns; and multicultural Willa, serious yet able to laugh—who Grace felt could be a less-tired version of herself, maybe also wanting beer—mistakenly asked enough of a question to set him off. Deb rolled her eyes, joked, and swung an arm wrapped in pealing bracelet bells over her head. Three others at the table found reasons to turn away or leave their chairs.

Trumpeter, who Anton had just flattered, said: "Every place has its clowns."

The talk and tableside commotion ceased. Deb and Anton, but Deb more so, looked stricken. Her frail confidence and ironic jibes gave way to fear as, frozen physically, her jangling bells grew quiet. Other café sounds fell around them. Stunned, Grace, already watching the stage, saw that, while a guitarist was tuning up, the music was not ready to begin—the bandleader Monk faced away from the crowd. The next handful of seconds passed.

"We aren't sure we know your meaning," replied Willa finally.

It was likely, Grace reflected, that Trumpeter had done no more than turn an idle thought to words; likely too that, a taut fellow, he had spoken without realizing what he said: the insult may have slipped out. Or, for all his poetry, perhaps his sensitivity didn't extend to others, or to everyone. None at the table, which she now thought of as an oasis usually visited by strangers, knew him well enough to be sure.

Trumpeter, alas, for whatever reason, grew vicious. He turned his gaze on Deb, her outline and mass but not her eyes. Then he looked at Anton. "Spiritual seeking is not a hobby," he said. "It's not a pastime for your winter nights. It's about living not in a suburban palace but on the road. People pay to join in this game."

"You're just so stupid," said Willa, with an anger that surprised Grace. "Is your smug attitude different? Does knowing about yoga or Jack Kerouac give you a key to something? I think, anyway, that here everyone is a clown."

The bass guitarist, a balding graybeard with a ponytail, ended this and other discussions by launching the band back into the blues. A wall clock read 10:40, so they could play for only twenty minutes before curfew; but they were free to be fast and loud, and were. Soon fifty people, not just from the younger set, danced near the stage. Willa stood to join Francine, who moved in a sensual yet clumsy way near Monk. Moments later, Trumpeter and the Golds still sat together, perhaps too numbed by their confrontation to get away. Only Monk, watching the room react to his music, was able to catch Grace's eye as—lacking equanimity, and feeling what she knew might even be panic—she rose from the table and slipped out the side door of the café.

6

Breathing and Feeling

By late on the following Thursday, when Grace left the dining-hall after a two-hour duet with an industrial vacuum cleaner, she was thinking she had made a mistake to stay. She was not having a bad time and found it almost pleasant to adjust to the new routines, but she felt no better and asked herself anxiously if she ever would. She was dismayed enough to wonder whether, if she left now, she would remember anything from the experience in another month. Then she saw the alternative, which was to go home, the suction of her front hallway, her uncertainty as to why she even felt so beaten up, and it made her recoil.

This brief stop in the dining-hall had been her fourth job in five days; she knew a cause of her dismay might be that before it she had not worked in thirty hours, and so could only measure time by what relief she attained. After breakfast Monday, she had joined a team that toured the campus in electric carts, bringing materials to workshops. Tuesday after lunch she had joined a crew that vacuumed the carpet and washed the floor in Seeker's largest hall (having vacuumed twice she was an expert); they then put out hundreds of folding chairs and cushions for a major event that night. In her free time—the weekly workload was thirty hours—she began to select from among the copious Seeker menu of things to do. This, for the staff, included chats, swims, walks, and a slew of workshops aimed at rallying one's mind, body, heart, and soul.

She had already met enough people to make remembering names a problem. Once again each, she had worked with Francine and Sophie, but she saw everyone from the luggage crew frequently, though often only briefly as paths would cross. Such serendipity reminded her of life in college and, later, among artist-hopefuls in Brooklyn. Her neighbor in a two-person tent (Grace had her family's rarely used, bigger model) up the slight rise as the path forged deeper into the woods was a red-bearded boy she saw most mornings in the dining-hall, stocking replacement food pans on the buffet line. Wherever else she saw him, he carried a rolled, blue yoga mat. He and Grace began nodding to one another in public settings, but they never stopped to speak.

If there seemed a too large palette of people, she found an equally fearsome abundance of things to do. The first few times she entered the staff mess, she found the row tables crowded with people half her age daunting enough to stop her, as she passed through to the dining-hall, from looking around. Early Tuesday, though, soon after she had seen a skunk just outside her tent, she visited the mess for early coffee. A chill mirrored the pale light, the paths were empty and the mess was too—but for a booted, hairy leg poking out from a curtained-off Internet station. The curtain was buttery yellow and the walls, unlike the wood panels of the dining-hall, were soft green. Morning colors awaiting the sun's animation, she thought. As the coffee warmed her, she began to survey the rectangular room. It was strange to be awake at this hour, or, if awake, to not be home—or, if traveling, to see not her sleepy-eyed family but a stranger's bony knee and before that, a skunk.

She moved first to the broader of two walls hung with postings. Some postings promoted other retreats; in particular, winter retreats in Thailand, Mexico, or the Bahamas. Others announced programs in holistic studies at colleges or special schools. Still others told of festivals based in music, yoga, gender solidarity, spirituality, and other holistic healing themes. A few aggregated, as did Seeker, most such topics. One catching her eye promoted a spiritual retreat in the Yucatan Peninsula with access to coral diving and a ring of lowland Mayan sites. Grace snorted derisively. The pony-tailed guitarist, older than her, grim-faced or only intent, peered out briefly from behind the curtain.

Grace, blushing, sensing she had been reproached, moved to the second wall. Through the screen door, she saw sunlight slant uphill. As her back was stiff, she let fall her daypack. Here columns listed the staff workshops for the coming week. She felt out of her depth but curious. The topics seemed written in a language she did not understand.

Some were familiar: she had learned of them by osmosis, from TV, the Internet, or people she knew. In her suburb, holistic topics had entered conversations that once concerned nuclear bombs, tax shelters, and bundled vacations—much as her parents had seen those topics supplant the gangsters and unions they grew up discussing, and her grandparents had seen gangsters and unions supplant the even older topics of holidays and harvests. We really learn what seems to matter by osmosis, she thought. She scanned for topics she had at least heard of; she read blurbs on yoga, dance, Buddhism, meditation, tarot, tai chi, career guidance, drumming, and what she now summed up as "gender bending."

She could explore those she knew largely as catchwords—as, for instance, she planned to head soon to her first-ever yoga class.

But she lacked energy and confidence, and was worn down enough to know she was at Seeker only to feel. It felt easier to turn to topics she knew nothing of, and even fun to try to decode their titles: "The Sufi Way of Awakening"; "Native Sweat Lodge"; "Thai massage"; "Intuiting Your Health"; "Writing a Vision"; "Remote Seeing"; "Tantric Love." There were many others, but these were enough and she backed up from the wall. The less magnetic distance showed it to have more practical information than she had first thought. Some workshops repeated every week; some, given irregularly, had sign-up sheets that might quickly fill; others were complex enough to require advance reading. Guest workshop leaders led some staff workshops; staff led the rest. Two nights earlier, Monk had led a workshop on male friendship.

She pushed open the door and stepped into a sylvan summer paradise. The rising sun danced with the yielding chill, giving the air a fresh scent. Using a hand as sun visor, she looked downhill and east. At eye level, the treetops across the road seemed to shine with green paint. Farther east, she saw the blue of the pond cut like a belt through the trees. She looked lower and saw the pale yellow undertone that drew a softer green over the lawn. She didn't think to breathe deeply; neither was she calm enough to listen carefully. The fine setting made her feel, if exuberant, also a little scared.

A man emerged from the line of trees and began to walk uphill in her direction. As he left the shaded area, Grace, knowing his shoulders first, saw that it was Monk. He made for the roped-off dining-hall steps, but seeing Grace—midway in his climb, as she was half-hidden next to the building—he angled toward her.

She felt some agitation, worsened by her mind being stuck to the concoction of workshop titles. Trying to shake free, she thought: It's a dumb cliché, but I'm out of the habit of getting to know men.

She was startled by a shirtless youth in a headband, who had come around from the front of the building and wished to go in the door to her left. Mistakenly, she moved toward the boy; after nearly bumping him, she backed so far away that she almost bumped Monk.

"Steady, Grace," Monk said, lightly grasping her right elbow. He backed two steps off and smiled at her.

"Reckless me," she replied, "trying to knock over two pins at once." Further senseless words piled up for release. She closed her mouth.

Monk, waiting but with his teeth visible and a kind look in his eyes, continued to smile.

Quickly but not immediately, Grace surrendered. There's no point in being here if I'm only to hide, she told herself. She floated her left hand back toward the door; then she realized that the mess would be dark looking in from where they stood. More words tumbled out. "I've been reading workshop descriptions. All those strange, or strange to me, journeys they promise. And at the same time, I've been wondering about the poets from the other night: your troops, I gather. Much the same set of journeys seemed to come up in their words."

"They're friends, but I hope not troops," said Monk. "Though you're right about that sort of thing going on here. Both poets do want to be led, actually."

The screen door pushed open and Monk and Grace, making room for a woman who exited, stepped a few yards into the gravel-covered area. On the hill, the sun was now above eye level and the air was warming. A canvas tent Grace had not noticed before had been raised; six folding tables and sixty chairs were set up under it. Monk gestured toward the tent and they, evading questions, found seats at one of two tables that were flooded by sunshine. No one else was near.

"An inch of milk," Grace told Monk as she handed over her cup.

Awaiting him, she thought how in her guess the still-almost-teenage poets hadn't even known what their statements meant.

She also thought how making eye contact again with Monk might give her an important kick in the pants.

Back with their coffees, seated opposite her, wearing hard-toe boots, a red, round-neck tee, and stained, canary-yellow shorts, Monk smiled patiently. Grace felt unsure; she waited. She wondered how much and even *what* might spill out if she really let loose.

"Are they being led?" she asked. "Our grass-green poets, I mean."

Tilting an eyebrow, Monk seemed to accept the implication that they delay speaking personally for another time. Above the brow was a high forehead and white hair; below it, a tightened smile. "I warn you," he told her, "some people here say I'm the biggest bore around."

"You had them clapping in the café. Unless you're saying now that 'Bluesman Monk' is a disguise."

He sipped from a silver thermos cup and met Grace's observation by twinkling his eyes. "I guide them," he said, "when I know before-hand what they think. Their words the other night, basically praising the emotions and saying that to reason is to lie: if this attitude reflects their youth, it's also been the cry of the counterculture, the romantic movement's foothold in society, for three centuries. And the move-ment has always found the same villains: I mean science and business, with numbness and selfishness, that ever-present dark side of human nature, to grease the pot. These were the villains in 1800 and in 1900, and we see from our café romantics that they are still the villains now."

Grace smiled to mask her unease. Monk had blown past her with his second abstract term, "romantic." If she somehow knew his words, she lacked the will to pry their meanings open. Yet at that moment she was seeing a way to perhaps play a part in the conversation.

"Anyway, you lead Trumpeter at *work*," she said. "He seems reli-gious and vicious at once. He sings about peace but then bites the head off the first victim he sees. Are your café romantics always so torn?"

The shirtless boy in the headband emerged from the mess and, with a bosomy, sleepy girl trailing, carried two cups, with teabag strings hanging off their rims, to another table under the tent. Grace searched the girl's face until, disturbing her, their glances crossed.

Turning back to Monk, she found him set to reply. "They are," he said, "and Trumpeter is a good example. He hates his society, which he would say is made up of business, science, and human wickedness—and he hates it enough to think even its internal critics are contaminated. Thus the shelf in his tent of romantic works, by the likes of Nietzsche and Blake, is dwarfed by his many more shelves of Eastern, holistic, and native peoples writings. And the romantics don't really interest him. 'They tried but lost,' he likes to say. 'And now the West sows itself methodically, like its suburbanites sow lawns.' He and his friends from a new generation simply scorn the West. They perhaps can't escape physically; knowing this, they still find nothing in the Western view of life to respect.

"And yes, these views may rip him up enough inside to make him mean."

Grace had listened, but as Monk paused her mind split onto two paths. She wanted to reflect on this sunrise riff by a man she didn't know. And, unexpectedly, she felt drawn back to the nameless-to-her first poet of the other night.

If she had thought him foolish then, she was less sure now.

"This is all a bit deep for me," she said. "I'd say I was agnostic in these matters, but the word may mean more in this setting than I mean it to. Anyway, I found my way to three weeks here largely by chance. Unlike, it appears, a lot of people, I'm no seeker."

Monk relaxed in his chair and let fade the challenge in his eyes. "Here in camp," he said, "a person's story gets around."

The talk had again veered to the personal. She wondered what story he had heard, and about his story; yet she felt resistant. She touched the rim of her cup, and when he raised his thermos cup she raised her plastic one to smell and sip the strongly flavored liquid.

"Why support them?" she asked. "I mean, why a musical backup if you don't like their words? Is it a matter of being kind?"

"But I like their words, or what I think they try to say. And I know taking on society can be lonely work. Posturing often results, which can drive them further to seed—this comes from human awareness being pushed so far down in the imagination. So, I play to help them posture as they are driven to and then say what they can.

"I also hope to show them the merit, as they stumble, of continuing to show up. Because for a while now 'showing up' has been for our kind a way to live in the world."

The falling sound of his final sentence allowed Grace to set aside her fatigue and let his comments register. She smiled in a friendly way and he, rising, and holding his thermos to his cheek, feeling for warmth, smiled back. In a sly ceremony, they shook hands.

"It's reasonably correct that you are a bore," she told him.

Monk vanished toward the hillside behind the dining-hall and Grace thought how her destination now, the yoga studio, was somewhere north of the beach. She found her way by walking some and then flagging down Sophie, who went there, too. The young beauty had an oozy way, which the early hour increased. Waiting for Grace on a gravel path, she squinted as the sun beat at her from its still-intimate angle. She held an end of a rolled, blue yoga mat; its other end brushed the ground. Her thick, rusty-red hair ringed her pale cheeks and brow with a truss of curls. Her squinting grin made a slant along her face.

"So you will join the early-morning yoga class?" Sophie asked.

"Today. I've never seriously tried this before. I don't own a mat."

"There are mats in the studio. I'm no regular, either; usually I'm at the five p.m. class. Now is just too early. But a new teacher began Sunday who people like, and this week I can't go in the afternoons."

Soon they were at the studio. Unlacing her shoes, Grace felt surprise at how high the sun had risen, viewed from the pond's lower elevation. Following Sophie inside, she saw many lithe bodies, which brought her to another sense of fatigue, a holding back. The ceiling was as high as the sanctuary's; the large windows looked on the pond. Sophie helped her find a mat and they laid their things out together. A man in his thirties would be the teacher. He watched from a seated lotus pose, his feet resting on opposite thighs, as forty people gathered, unrolled their mats, and began to stretch.

In minutes, and with more depth by the end of the class, Grace knew why yoga was important to many people. And she felt she would now come every day. She could do only a few positions and only parts of these; she also was happy to be in a corner, where, thinking herself a fat, ugly oaf, she could avoid her reflection in the studio mirror. What mattered was breathing. She remembered how she had liked the breathing exercises at the meditation class and before that in the sadness workshop. How had she lost track of this? Was her confusion only from the past year? How screwed in was it? As she struggled through the poses, feeling blasé unwillingness in her muscles and trying to not be awed by the agility of others, she learned to focus on the teacher's words and, following his direction, on her breathing. The stretching tilted her perceptual axis enough to let her feel her body as she breathed. He would say, "Now deepen your position by breathing into it," and she would slow herself, close her eyes, and feel her body warm as she expanded her lungs an inch wider with each heartbeat.

Lying on her back at the class's close, in what Jorge, the teacher, called a "corpse" pose, she began to see that she could briefly stop it all—could keep quietly within herself—through the simple practice of controlling her breath.

Trumpeter was here, too, and a few others she knew. He wore a tee shirt and shorts, and as he left ahead of her she saw that he took no better care of his body than she did of hers. He was stiff—as if, young and healthy, he would still let his body go to seed.

In this way, too, she thought, as with the anger he and his poet pal had spewed, he resists or misreads or mishandles the harmonious image he tried to conjure in his poem.

Sophie and Grace made plans to meet for breakfast the next day. "It will get us both to early yoga," said Sophie craftily. But then Grace, treading uphill with the others, saw how the calm that had overtaken her in yoga class couldn't survive her way of being in the world. Midmorning, she took a kayak on the pond and cried. At work on a cleaning crew, she said little. A call to Henry she had looked forward to annoyed them both. All evening she wanted distraction. She went to bed too early and rose aimlessly at first light; yet again, two hours later in the yoga studio, she found that she could stretch, listen, and breathe, all more—more! She could feel her frailness.

7

A New Friend's Suggestion

At their Wednesday breakfast, Sophie and Grace soon became friends. They ate alone at a porch table that had been freed up by the wet, cool weather. Near dawn, it had rained suddenly and hard; neither woman had heard thunder, and they shared stories of waking in confusion, zipping tent flaps, and hoping their rain flies would hold. The rain soaked the dining-hall porch and brought chill winds that two hours later still whistled periodically. All but a score of diners thus were cozied together indoors: so nice, hydrated odors of bread, coffee, egg dishes, and cut fruit came out through the window screens. The women used paper napkins to wipe dry two chairs and half of a round table. A glint of sunlight in the east, first pointed to by Sophie as they left the yoga studio, had spread to be a band wide across the sky. So, the storm was at an end.

Grace felt drawn to Sophie. With little hesitation, she dropped the allusions she had taken to using and tried to unpack her mood. "It was hard times and it could be so again," she began. "But now, I hope for ever, Alicia's healthy. The chemo hit her hard and tore us up to witness, and in February she fell back briefly. But the doctors have started talking cure. She's been on a maintenance dose of drugs for six weeks, feels okay, and goes on Sunday with her parents to a hospital-run summer camp. She'll be in school this fall—and not held back a grade."

"She's one of the luckier ones, then."

"Today, most kids with what she has can be cured."

"How are her spirits? Minds can be piercing at that age."

"Time will tell on that. Now, she's intently being twelve."

"I was twelve not so long ago—about when she was born; and at that age, I think, I most liked to complain. So you must tell me what you mean."

"Food, fun, and friends. I hear her friends are being great." Grace smiled, but as the alliterations sounded her smile fell. She looked up past Sophie's red curls at the dripping, snarled oak that overhung the porch railing. Caught raindrops fell in streams; each seemed to ply for her attention. Despondent and sure she looked that way, wanting to have to answer questions, she turned her eyes back to Sophie.

"You seem buried, to use a complicated word," said Sophie.

"Yes, buried, while no one I love was; and isn't that a bright joke! But it's true, joke or not. I wouldn't mind if this tree fell on me."

"Do you mean you doubt that you could feel worse?"

"Yes, damn it—damn me!"

"Is it the fear coming through? You must've had to be brave."

"I don't know; whatever acting classes taught me, I can rarely hide my feelings. The cancer crawled back in February, until they changed the chemo mix; since then, I've felt bad... which is ironic, given her upward slant. But I began to be scared around her and her folks and, later, sometimes, even around my husband and son. That may be why Henry was okay about my coming here, and then hardly complained when I phoned to turn the initial five days into almost three weeks."

Grace looked back over the three-season saga, as if time were space and she looked at an athletic field. Her inner glance jumped from one white-chalked field marker to the next. There had been the struggle in autumn with shock and a lack of understanding; in winter with the force of the treatment regime, lengthened by relapse; in spring with a world that began to push back in. "It feels as if a hand held my heart," she told Sophie. "Took hold of it then and grips it now. I had a look at my own lack of answers."

"Was fear brought up in the sadness workshop?"

"No one breathed for months, I fear, not Alicia and not Nan, Steve, or me," said Grace, seeming to slough off Sophie's question. "It was like a bad play, bad to act in, with us as characters with one thought in our minds. When she relapsed, it was like having to start again at an earlier scene.... Vapid similes! The sadness workshop taught a process of working towards acceptance. But aren't we more the raw materials than the ones who do the processing? Can you imagine how many really sick kids I saw this year? I mean, what's there honestly to accept?"

"Yet you say Alicia may be okay. Are her parents as tired as you?"

"Somehow, no. They're more getting back to themselves. Steve bought a new computer, saying it gave him a better eye on research. Nan's been planning the family week at camp, which I know has got her back inside the malls."

"Which leaves you. Can you help yourself... was trying to do this what brought you here?"

"I'll say 'sort of' to either question. A girlfriend made me come."

Flat toned, thoughtful, Sophie reiterated: "And are you able to help yourself?"

"It seems not. Yet I'm only an aunt. My bruising is fairly minor."

"I feel sad hearing that. It reinforces my sense that you need some help. Grace, you may not get past this using only your will."

It surprised Grace to hear Sophie single out her irrelevant "will."

Sophie, often slow, waited before going on. "Your first workshop may not have helped, but tell me: can you spend a bit more money? If so, I suggest you try Thai massage. Have you heard of it?"

Actually, Grace recalled, she had cackled on first hearing the phrase days before: another exotic flavor off the Seeker menu. More open now, she shook her head, no. At the same time, she wondered silently if her eggs were now too cold to eat. Heavy clouds still stretched above them, even as the sky had brightened in the east.

"I've a friend here," continued Sophie, "an Austrian named Hans. My brother Jonas met him in Guatemala doing relief work. He's led quite a life for being twenty-eight. He taught massage in Thailand; here, he teaches staff. And he massages, charging half the Spa rate. A session lasts ninety minutes and, unlike at your sadness workshop, it's not about words."

Sophie had sidestepped Grace's dour view of sympathy and pledged possible comfort. If, Grace thought, you want to trust a person, hear them out; anyway, I can't feel worse. I suppose Thai massage, whatever it may be, is worth a try.

She agreed. Then, not ready for the conversation to end, she asked Sophie to tell her a little about herself.

After a moment, Sophie, who had taken for breakfast yogurt, coffee, and easily a cup of blueberries, culled from a pan that held melon slices, too, answered. "I must write my brother Joe today, so he's even more in my thoughts than usual. Would you mind if, for now, I instead told you about him?"

Liking indirection, a tool of dramaturgy, Grace smiled.

"Jonas, or Joe, is three years older," began Sophie. "We've a half-sister from mom's remarriage, and, both with straight, brown hair, they look more like one another than like me. Jonas went to high school in New York, where he lived with Dad and Americanized his name. His letters to me for years began—the question comes from a song—'Hey, Joe, wudda you know?' In this way, he conveyed an emerging view of life to an adoring sister.

"At twenty, Joe quit school in Paris to join a relief group. He was in and out of Guatemala for four years, twice going back. Now he's a street artist in Spain. He's full of ideas, but I think confused. It almost seems as if with every new thing he tries he leaves much of the rest of himself behind. The year before last he took qualifying courses to become a lawyer."

"If no psychological bomb is set to go off," Grace observed, "I'd call that typical youthful confusion. Yet who knows what the time in Guatemala adds? Is he in a troupe? What sort of 'street artist'?"

Sophie's worried smile seemed to scar her complexion. "Americans see being confused as normal, even fun," she said. "And from that point of view, Jonas is having lots of 'normal' fun. With others, including an ex-boyfriend of mine, he does street theater; their themes are extremes in sports and the strangeness of middle-class life. The ironic matching seems creative, but I find the skits to be shapeless; and, bluntly, the actors are often stoned. In general, they may waste a lot of time."

Grace, with her own family concerns, and sad to see Sophie garbed in middle-age worries, identified briefly with Jonas and remembered her own youthful irreverence: the effect, for example, a hat or a pair of shoes would have on her senses. Yes, she reflected, I remember the mix of boredom and excitement fondly. A big part had to do with never being tired.

She recalled in particular a green felt hat she had worn in Brooklyn for a year and then again some years later, still before knowing Henry, on a rainy trip to Portugal. She pictured a red band and a peacock feather. Then she imagined her pubescent son seeing her in such a busy hat now. He would read not "fresh irreverence" but her senility.

Sophie's judgments, Grace learned, were shaped by what she called "a need for husbandry." "The time-wasting habits Joe fell into," she told Grace, "fight a conservatism I feel. I see youth as a time for real endeavors. This for some means learning to weed and plant; for others, to take risks. But to toy with life, as my brother does now: this I find hard to understand."

Grace saw that Sophie used a generous, sweet palette even as she painted her brother's disarray. This mix of benevolence and smarts had made Grace listen to her; the delicate word use made Grace feel she could trust her.

8

A Disturbing Conversation

During the nearly two days that had passed since this fine meeting, Grace had felt mostly bad. Again, it was partly the free time: before another session with the vacuum cleaner, she'd had Wednesday after lunch and all of Thursday to fill. She had found things to do but felt detached, and more and more she'd had the arid sense of being a tourist.

Wherever you go, she thought, quoting from a bitter aphorism, there you are.

Her calls home on Thursday had seemed miserably to prove the point.

"Aunt Grace, how's adult summer camp?" Alicia had asked this after answering her father's cell phone.

"Loved one, hi. It's been okay but not yet great. I'm sure you'll all have the better time. How go the trip preparations? And how's your appetite?"

"My appetite—yes, I have to eat less. After all the throwing up, I worry now about getting fat. As for my parents, well, they're strange, in case you didn't know that about them."

"No, the meds cause the puffiness, which *will* go away. Having candy doesn't matter. It's summer now and I order you to eat like a twelve-year-old…. As to certain people being strange: I can't comment."

"It'll be amusing, anyway, to watch them ride horses next week."

"Let's hope your dad doesn't go telling jokes to his poor horse."

"I know. It's sad how people treat animals. Mom's here; do you want to say hi?"

"Good question," said Nan, who now had the phone. "Have you a minute for your weary sister-in-law?"

"Who's shopped till she dropped?"

"Getting everyone ready for a week at camp is no small task."

"I know she's right there, but how's it going? She sounds cheerful."

"Everything's fine. Alicia and your brother have new hiking boots and matching cowboy hats."

"Where's your matching cowboy hat?"

"I have taste. Anyway, my large behind makes me stand out enough."

With others awaiting a pay phone—Seeker was out of cellular range—and a second call to make, Grace soon wished them a fun week and said goodbye. With Alicia doctor-free for a while, Nan's sights seemed set on the carefree life they had once known; she also did not ask about Grace's time away. Henry, saying hello at her next call, breathed unevenly; after a second, Grace guessed that he was out for an evening bike ride.

"It's your wayward wife."

"That's the only wife I have." He breathed in and out. "How's adult summer camp?"

"Alicia just asked that in the same words. They blast off soon to the special family camp. Maybe I should've gone along with Amos."

"Come home and we'll go camping next weekend. I get back on Friday from the Atlanta trade show."

"Well, maybe…. Yet I feel hardly up to even being with strangers. I also want to give this place more of a chance. It's interesting."

"It's nice to hear that life is easier amid strangers. And I still don't know what you're doing there: that fringe stuff doesn't interest you. Maybe you *should* have gone with Amos."

With the phone quiet but for Henry's softening breath, she played over his observations, seeing their root in a disinterest in things not clearly touching his life. She then thought how she had been flung or had half-flung herself at this odd-acting fringe.

"I'm signed up for two more weeks," she reminded him, and felt, in a way she knew to be inaccurate, abandoned.

The next day, even yoga seemed, for the first class in three, to be a waste of time. While the air was already sultry when she shuffled off to the studio just before seven a.m., during the hour-long class neither her body nor her mind warmed. Rather than feeling fluid, she grew critical; and as she didn't want to further berate herself, she picked at the situation. She felt her classmates, lengthening their poses, were ridiculously self-involved. The soothing background music was a lie, the lie of cults or, something similar, elevator music. Jorge seemed not astute, as she had judged him to be, but absorbed in an illusion or practically stoned. Trumpeter, in class after a day away and partly obscuring Grace's line of sight to Jorge, had already shown he could be cruel.

She had to struggle to stay the full hour; yet her tendency to persevere drove her, despite her sniping, to try several times to immerse in the class rhythm. When the class ended and she was outside pulling on her sneakers, she saw Sophie, who had come late. Sophie smiled as she said that what counted most after a bad class was to try again the next day. Then she looked at the pond and said, with a grimace, that she was off to an all-day stint at the Seeker sales office… for what in such fine weather was indoor phone and computer work.

Grace carried her tight feelings to the dining-hall, where hundreds of people intermingled. She dropped her pack on a small table where she might perhaps eat alone. Fearing her piggish mood, she got in a buffet line. At a true mental hospital, she thought, where I probably belong, others would decide what and how much I ate. Here instead was a green light: that and a visual and olfactory banquet of fresh, pungent, colorful foods. And breakfast, many said, was the best meal here. Her belly hunger made her feel less dour, but this confusion of feelings only added to her tension. She feared a crash after eating. Then she decided: When I have my tray, I'll get my pack and find people to sit with. She let the dimensions of the task overtake her. Down the long row were cold and hot cereals, egg and tofu dishes, fried potatoes, yogurt, and grapes, sliced melons, and oranges; along the wall nearest the kitchen, perpendicular to the four buffet lines, were juices, teas, coffees, and milk; along the north- and south-facing walls were breads, muffins, crackers, jam, honey, and peanut and cashew butters. No bacon, ham, or donuts in view—but as had been said on the yoga studio porch: "With fewer distractions it's easier to find the tofu."

In the swing of things, she took her tray (after passing up eggs, which she'd had yesterday, and coffee, which she had filled up on hours before) to where she saw, just sitting also, the Golds. Deb yelled and Anton, pink as rhubarb this morning, introduced her to the others at the table, who were in the past-life workshop. Seeker was often a hive; this was the first time in days that the acquaintances had found a chance to talk.

"Excuse me a moment," said Grace, now wanting conversation. "I think I *will* get a mug of decaf. Can I get one for anyone else?"

On returning, she found a discussion underway about the workshop and its part in the Thursday night show, a weekly event to which all were invited. Each workshop presented for a half hour; a week earlier, Grace had cringed as her teacher and four classmates told preachy stories about the unity of life and death. Yet she had liked that evenings presentation by a percussion class, which got the whole room to make music with instruments, like wooden spoons, taken from daily life.

Tonight, she heard, the past-life workshop would introduce "hypnotic regression." Much of the day would be spent planning and rehearsing.

She saw that Anton had an ear cocked for a pause in the discussion; soon he was asking if she was familiar with past-life ideas.

"Oh, I know little; nothing, really. People recall having lived in other bodies, in other times and places. And from what I've just heard, I guess the memories return through hypnosis. Is that it?"

"Well, yes," said Anton. "Anyway, partly. In fact, we've spent most of the week exploring the two planes of being, physical and spiritual, and seeing what differences if any there are between them.

"I for one see life as physical," he added. "The experiences tied up in other bodies that we remember when we regress really did happen."

"We all think that," said Deb, addressing Grace. "At least we want to. There were only two doubters and one has gone home. The idea

that we can follow a soul through its life in other bodies is very powerful.... But the problem," she added, with a rhetorical smile, "is that
for most of us here it hasn't happened."

"I think Deb means," said Rich, a soft-speaking man in a clipped,
red beard who sat to Anton's right, "that just a few of our hundred-
plus classmates had past-life experiences this week—plus three regressions that we saw our teacher Nadia undergo."

"I want to go back!" Deb cried. Then she grinned widely and said
in a low voice, "But can I bring a giant suitcase? With everything I own
in this life, I'm bound to lack necessities in my other ones."

"Deb has given Nadia headaches all week," said Rich, smiling, "by
pretending to confuse hypnotic regressions with travels in time."

"Her idea of 'karma' is in itself unusual," Anton added.

Grace laughed, feeling breezy as she went at her kiwi slices, yogurt
with jam, banana-nut muffin, and decaf. She then asked if this healing
therapy had spun out of Eastern ideas about reincarnation—a topic,
she added, that she knew next to nothing about.

"In fact," replied Anton, whom she had apparently freed to be
informative, "while the past-life vision ties into reincarnation, it grew
from Western psychotherapy. It began with a few therapists noting
how as they took hypnotized clients back through childhood memories
in search of originating trauma, some seemed to fall through the
memories into past lives. One therapist wrote that it was like finding
hidden rooms in a house. The school of followers that emerged then
said that early trauma, which twists clients up but can be hard to trace,
may in a few or perhaps in a great many cases result from what a person's soul experienced in a previous life."

Grace, wanting to escape or at least be diverted, looked past Anton
into the busy room. She saw a corner of carpet and remembered that
she would vacuum here at eight p.m.; so, she would miss the evening
show.

But Anton had only begun. He gave a layered smile—shaped partly,
she felt, by his love for explanations. "More insights followed," he
said. "One taught that hypnotists could work remotely; this led to a
practice that regressed clients by phone. Another said that past-life
memories could be trapped behind conscious resistance; this led to a

practice whereby a therapist with occult powers visits a client's past lives, like a tomb explorer in a movie, and reports back. Meanwhile the main, academic shoot grown from psychology tilled *its* soil, establishing protocols and conferences and using reincarnation as a way into cross-cultural studies—all to build credibility."

By now, as Anton finished, all were smiling. Grace had also seen the joke. Nearly everyone at Seeker was college-taught and worldly— which today mostly meant being media-smart. So they knew that anything they tried to take on faith—reincarnation was a gaudy example— would confront their habit of doubt. Fortifying this doubt was their sense that of the different calls to faith one heard at Seeker, some were surely nonsense. Yet, they could put such reservations aside and be open to the idea of taking some things to heart on faith.

In fact, Grace saw, a dogged openness shaped the smiles other than her own at the table. The humor lay in how hard the effort was. Eyeing her benevolently, as if sure he gave a gift, Anton carried his tale further. "Grace," he said, "I should say that what I know of these matters springs from my effort, unusual where I live, to open my dentistry practice to new modes of healing. Science and spirit needn't be at odds. Similarly, we in the workshop know to not tie our well-being to reincarnation. And we realize that the many books and workshops on this subject are making some people rich. But we find this sort of synthesis to be stimulating, nevertheless."

Grace quietly smiled back. Then Deb with a knowing look came around the table to kiss Grace's forehead and stroke her hair. Bending, she kept her own dyed-brown tresses from spilling onto Grace's tray.

Leaning over, she spoke both to Grace and the others. "Sweetie, I want to tell everyone about your trial. Grace's niece, Alicia, a sixth-grader she's incredibly close to, struggled with leukemia this year. Alicia's doing better but it's still very sad. And Grace has been totally involved in taking care of her."

Grace said something aloud, but her mind didn't register what. She knew only that it was words meant to not make waves; she had left her instincts to carry on. What she was thinking about were the kids she had seen and sometimes come to know and then about, of course, reincarnation.

Deb returned to her chair and reached across the table to rest her hand on one of Rich's. She turned his hand over and held it. "Rich is a wonderful man with a story he also shared. It's also sad but hopeful, and it tells a lot about why some of us are in this workshop."

"Before Rich begins," interrupted Anton, half standing, "I want to make a last point about the past-life model. Because while it relates to Eastern reincarnation, some people also tie it into our Western idea of the imagination. It's not important, they say, that past-life memories be proven or even claimed as factual. Instead, we can group them with dreams and stories: they let us hear what the heart wants to say. Memory becomes a kind of metaphor, a fiction."

Deb quieted; Grace guessed that she would be used to such interruptions. Then she grinned, not at Anton, Rich, or Grace, but at the two others at the table. They were a couple, Grace felt— notwithstanding that since her own arrival neither had truly spoken up.

Deb continued; her eyes danced. Grace sensed that she alone had not yet heard the story. "Rich's smile betrays his kindness," said Deb. "He works for a big corporation, but he says that he's often chosen a balanced life over his career. He tutors inner-city kids in math and sings in a choir. But as we look at his kind face, we find sadness, too; he has his own story of loss. Rich's wife died in a car crash five years ago, soon after she'd become pregnant with their first child."

Grace felt herself drop more fiercely into dismay. She had sought a diverting yet casual chat. Now she was being led to this unmasking of a stranger. She felt connected only in the sense of being drawn in by a horror movie, wrapped in its fear. She watched as with an encouraging nod Deb turned the tale telling over to Rich.

"Five years later," Rich said, "I can talk about it, largely because I've seen how in time we all know tragedy. The lesson was hard but I've made peace with my sadness, and doing so has brought me closer to other people. I've become a better listener.

"While I haven't found the right relationship, I began dating three years ago, and it was about then that I felt myself coming to terms—I said that once—with what happened. Time the healer... a new apartment; a new hobby, squash; tutoring in Harlem. Twice-a-week yoga and a summer yoga workshop up here—my introduction to Seeker.

"Then, near the third anniversary of my becoming... a widower, I twice dreamt I was a black man. In each dream I was split: an invisible first me watching with no apparent feeling a black second me. A month later, I saw a field at the north end of Central Park and felt that I'd known it as a child. But in my vision, I was a black boy of seven. And since then, I have the vision whenever I'm near the field—if not a clear vision, I have impressions. And while I haven't seen my wife at any time, I have a strong sense that her spirit is there, too."

"How," Anton asked attentively, "do impressions and visions differ?"

Rich, seated beside Anton, turned his chair so they could see each other. "Impressions are psychic pulls," he replied. "I see the wooded hillside above the field and feel a sense of home. The visions let me see someone I know to be me, beside people who seem familiar and with objects I recognize in this familiar setting. I see a drinking fountain at the field both as it looks now and as it was sixty years ago, with people from back then actually standing around it."

The conversation went on a bit longer. Deb reminded everyone of a point Nadia Tolliver had made. The man whose name Grace did not know then spoke up, to describe a book in which a fifth-grader in St. Louis recalled details of a Ukrainian village, ruined in World War II, that only someone there in the 1930s could have known. Nadia had reviewed the book glowingly on its front cover, he added. Deb then said that while she had not regressed that week, she had always felt that she had once been a dragonfly. This caused Anton to point out that instead of soul migrations the more scientific explanation of molecular memory might be involved.

"We all gain and lose molecules each day," he said. "Maybe molecules once in a dragonfly merged with Debs and took root in the area of her biochemical makeup that affects her memory."

9

One Man's Avocation

The crash Grace feared happened while she was still at the table, trying not to listen. By two p.m. that day, she found herself back at her tent, with (ironically, as she thought back to breakfast) little memory of what she had done in the intervening hours. As usual, her tent area was empty in the afternoon. She had cluttered the tent interior, and if she didn't yet have a wash to do—Henry had taken home her first days' laundry—she lacked the will even to tidy up the dirty and clean clothes, water bottles, flashlights, books, clock, and Seeker pamphlets scattered near her sleeping bag. Four hours would bring supper; two more, some work. Her family, from whom she felt a welcome if strange sense of distance, would get real derisive pleasure if they could see this tent now. The gabbing about past lives had made the whole Seeker program seem foreboding; as for nature, the fact of it deadened, not lifted, her spirits. She found the idea of having once been a dragonfly inviting. What must truly be horrid was the opposite: a poor dragonfly burdened by human feelings and moods.

Putting aside these thoughts, she read her Chekhov biography, a gift that had sat waiting near her bed since Christmas. She next wrote a letter to Amos; then, rather than go swimming or sit under one of the shade trees that backed up the beach, she showered. Returned, she changed course and got into a bathing suit; but, ready to walk to the beach, changed her mind again and took photos of her messy tent. Thus, she lay alone on the raft napping when the supper horn sounded. The sun—Phoebus Apollo to her eighth-graders reading

Oedipus—had fallen behind the close western hills, so she had a cool, shadowy swim back to the shore.

Now the big vacuum cleaner was back in its closet, Grace had built a sweat, the carpet looked combed, and it was ten p.m. This job, which she must again do Saturday, had deepened her solitude. For two hours she had only heard a companion motor. Leaving the dining-hall through the staff mess, she felt too dirty, seven hours after her shower, to stop by the café for a snack and maybe company. On this moonless night, she reached into her damp daypack and found—it just fit with everything—that she had forgotten her flashlight in her tent.

Still, the way back to bed passed Seeker's café, and she knew the walk through the night air might be invigorating enough to change her mind about stopping in. The herb garden was dark and quiet; she could hear and sketchily see the café porch tables that overlooked the path. As she drew nearer, Sophie called down from a table.

"Here is Hans," she said, once Grace had climbed upstairs. "He's been in Brooklyn for a few days, but is back now. I told him you might be a customer. He'll pay me a fat finder's fee if you sign up."

Hans was a somewhat slight, blond man of thirty with a quiet smile. A green rucksack worn smooth in patches leaned near his chair, as did, rare for Seeker, a tennis racket. He seemed to like Sophie's kidding. He looked at Grace and, before Sophie could, invited her to sit.

"I think you've been working," said Sophie.

"Only for two hours, vacuuming the dining-hall. But I've had a long day."

"I saw you there," said Hans, "but didn't know who you were. I came from the train too late for the buffet, but got food in the kitchen. I was the guy eating in a corner, the one person left in the dining-hall as you worked. You seemed dedicated."

"Over-focused, maybe, and broken in spirit. I'm glad I didn't suck you into my machine by mistake."

"I've told Hans what you went through this year," said Sophie.

"Not so much, really; anyway, he's done relief work in Guatemala," countered Grace.

"Perhaps that experience helps me help others," replied Hans. "I do have skills it might be good for you to learn. Would you like to try

Thai massage?"

"I don't really know what it is. And by 'learn,' do you mean you'd *teach* me this? I thought it was something you did *to* me."

"To me it's an experience that we go through together—though I do the active work and receive the pay."

Grace looked at Sophie and broke into a soft smile. "It's strange to me and at least unusual," she said. "But I find Sophie to be insightful and sincere. As she suggested this, I guess I'll give it a try."

Sophie grinned. Yet for the first time Grace saw concern beneath her cheery attitude. Could it pertain to her, a new, casual friend? Grace felt this was unlikely.

She then asked Hans to tell her what the experience would be like.

"Thai massage builds on yoga stretches," he replied. "It's physical, but we work together to see neither of us is hurt. We both wear loose clothes. And any talking grows out of what our bodies have to say."

Grace's dismay returned at this allusion to what Seeker folk called "bodily knowledge," and she wondered if she was foolish to go on. Well, she thought, Thai massage either will be silly or not; but as long as my back doesn't break, the results probably won't matter. She and Hans agreed to meet the next morning at ten.

The unlit, chilly walk back to her tent felt delicious but scary. How brave and natural she was, crossing the parking lot under a million uncivilized light pricks of the cloudless sky, then exposing herself to an even darker wood. For a time she leaned against a car, to let her fear find its larger parallel. She felt not small but unsteadily large when juxtaposed to this encircling indifference. The forest by contrast felt supportively domestic. A dozen steps into it, she stopped again. Her eyes acclimated to the darkness and she picked out bushes, the path at her foot, a tent corner, the trunk of a tree. She listened for sounds from the café but heard only nearby, barely audible creaks and whooshes. Moments later, she was zipping up in the sleeping bag—which she hardly saw, having found and briefly flicked on her flashlight, ruining her night vision—with a feeling of accomplishment.

10

Breaking Through

The first session with Hans—she would have three over five days—left her with a sadness in her chest that made her feel as if breathing was itself a new pain she would have to accept. He drew the feelings up and out of her with his actions. The labor was hard, and as she equaled him in weight, they often seemed like wrestlers. He would stretch her into one of the yoga poses she had been learning; then, using their combined mass for leverage, frame against frame, he massaged her intensely along the line of the pose. "You must tell me if your body begins to hurt," he sometimes said, repeating these words exactly. He used as excavation tools his elbows, knees, heels, fingertips, and thumbs. He usually progressed only by an inch or two.

Beneath everything was sadness, she knew, and his achievement was to break through it with his style and force. She first doubted there was much to say, and understanding it now she liked this other language of the body—a reenactment by pantomime. During all the time she had felt toppled by Alicia's struggle she had in fact been an oak, perhaps the strongest one there. Her layered boughs beckoned above all, beyond her brother, sister-in-law, and others in her family, to her niece. Often she was a wreck, swimming instinctively upstream to her duties like a battered salmon. She rarely led; instead, she did odd jobs: buying food for Nan, or getting relatives at an airport. She even mangled such simple tasks. Once she came a day late to a meeting with the doctors. Yet Alicia had laughed at Grace's haplessness and been consoled by her presence. "My aunt is so real," she once had boasted to a nurse as Grace stood nearby. "I think a lot of people are drawn to her."

Hans worked for ninety minutes; when he finished, they talked in the small cabin he had found to use. Grace now saw her lungs as a cistern for sad feelings. Attuned to the heat and stillness, she decided to skip the commotion of lunch. With surprise, she heard Hans say that beneath his vocation he was a common Westerner, bred to compete with his mind and his flesh, a philosophy M.A. who had been on a European pro tennis circuit as recently as two years ago—this after a first, eighteen-month trip to Thailand and then Central America. When Grace, grateful and relaxed but still sorrowful, asked if he was sure about this change in his direction, he merely smiled and shrugged.

She saw how her question had been obscure, for her and probably him. She wondered: sure about what?

"Must it to be one way or another?" she asked. "I mean, our common, everyday life, or something apart from it?"

He looked at her, and she felt trapped in her suburban mom persona. The many habits she lived by seemed to stop at the door of her mind.

"I try to live differently," said Hans. "But the life I was raised into may come at me more as time goes by."

"Many people here try to live differently. There's so much passion—but maybe also lots of pretending. Nor am I sure that the two-car garage everyone is running from is the real problem."

The brief exchange separated them. Hans looked pensive but said no more. Grace realized how glibly she, who had been staggered in part by the suffering of strangers, could voice opinions about problems that might be common to them all.

At one p.m., as scheduled, still sad-hearted, she found the crew she was assigned to and for three hours readied rooms for the incoming weekend guests. The work was harder than she had expected: the mandated hospital bed corners and precisely placed pillows, etc., exceeded her standards at home; and the crew worked to a deadline. She chatted some with the others but more often listened as they talked about workshops, teachers, and campus mishaps. It struck her that the people she met here, joined mostly by common interests, might not know each other well. Without regular ties of family, job, or proximity—she saw little meaning left in the word "neighborhood"—without this resonance, there seemed to be less risk. I wonder, she asked herself: Is Seeker a good place to try things out? Or is it merely a fake?

She had a second massage the next day, on Saturday afternoon. On Friday night, she had cried as much as ever for her niece: who just then might have been with friends at a teen romance movie, or been home getting ready for her special camp. This sadness returned with the first touch, knee against calf, from Hans. He tried to wait out her sobbing, but she rolled away and held a hand out to warn him off.

"Can I tell you?" But rather than say more she laid an arm over her belly and hunched her shoulders and began to wet her swollen face. "For six months"—she stopped, without enough air in her lungs to go on—"for all those months"—she stopped again to steady her breathing—"for all that time we were in and out of the hospital. All the kids and families trying to scratch out a minute of normalcy: it's a place brave, sharp, and dreadful. Everyone wants most to be elsewhere. And the staff tries so hard. But there's a hitch in their response when things aren't going well. We're guessing maybe Monday, a nurse might say. It's impossible to envy them the things they know."

"Lay with an ear and cheek against the grass matt."

Grace did this, and felt less inflamed. She was on her right side, with her right arm pointed past her head. Hans put a wispy blanket over her, and a hand on it at her left shoulder.

"Take your time," he told her. "Talk only if you want to."

Back in January, over the three days a snowstorm had kept her in the hospital, she saw the workings of the ward and met its people. She especially got to know Matt, the eight-year-old second cousin of the man she met on her first snowbound night. Matt, who would die in June, as she worked hard but informally on her middle-school play, saw pizza with jam baked into it as a great food idea. The stink cheese daunted him but Alicia, the next morning, liked seeing her aunt cut away the Gorgonzola humps on two slices. "We may have enough to waste a little," she said, sanctioning Grace's effort.

Matt was shy, like his grown cousin Philip, and maybe depressed. His room, where Alicia and Grace brought the pizza-jam wedges first warmed at the nursing station, was hung with a flag honoring last year's World Series victor—Game 1 having been played, Grace re-

membered, on the day Alicia was diagnosed. Philip coaxed his little
cousin to try the pizza, and then to talk about his favorite sport.

"Crunchy and chewy and sweet all at once," said Philip.

"It's pretty good," said Matt. "I never thought of this."

"Is pizza what you eat at baseball games?" asked Grace.

Matt put down his wedge and waited watchfully.

"Remember the stadium," said Philip. "It's where they put every
slice in its own box."

"My dad said it's so they can charge you more," said Matt.

"If you want to, later," offered Alicia, "we can play the baseball
board game in the playroom."

They did play this later, with Grace and Philip joining in. Then the
kids began playing cards with a little girl. Grace walked the corridor for
a time, marveling at Alicia's generosity; then she sat with Philip outside
the playroom. Phones hadn't worked in a day and the word was they
were marooned until the morning. The snow had ended a hundred
miles west. The bare-boned weekend staff was tired. Grace had
watched TV storm reports earlier, but Alicia was uninterested and this
made her feel self-conscious. So much was going on where she was.

"I'm having trouble knowing how to act here," Grace told Philip.
"I mean, except with regard to my niece."

"It's hard to fit in… though we see other visitors helping out."

"I wonder where they get the courage."

"The staff works hard to get us involved."

"Would you… I hope I'm not being inappropriate, but would you
tell me about Matt?"

Philip looked at her. After working on Saturday, he had worn his
suit to the hospital, and his bosom flashed a crumpled white fabric.
When he replied to her, she heard some guiding principle in his voice.

"Would it help you understand what others go through here?"

"That would be my hope."

Grace, in the massage studio, stopped remembering and rolled over
to look at Hans. Tears welled up, making her wait. Philip remained in
her imagination, ruffled but having decided to help as he could.

"I once was snowed in at the hospital," she told Hans. "It was impossible to miss what went on, miss seeing the frail, beaten-looking kids tied to machines—no, they had been beaten. But people can teach themselves to overlook a lot, and I first left Alicia's room wearing a big, phony sympathetic smile. Such a smile even lasts as you help out in a game room. But then I spent time with a child named Matt, and learned from his grown cousin that Matt had been in a war for three years—for what should have been his first years of school. He'd had twenty hospital stays, been cancer-free four times, and endured a transplant. I met him six months ago, four before he died. And was he brave, someone strange to him like me wouldn't know it, because I only saw questions in his eyes. When I went to his room with Alicia, she got him talking but he and I just were watching one another. I did better with other kids on the ward and their families, found ways to get closer in, but I never really did with Matt."

"Did you ever go back to the ward after the snowstorm?"

"To visit Alicia; then five or six times as a volunteer when she was at home."

She signaled a readiness to resume the massage, and again cried at his touch, when he stretched her in the pose they had broken off and put his knee on her calf. She knew that for a time she had given up on Matt, a little boy who wanted her attention. Hearing about him before she was ready, she had begun falsely, and then given up to begin to try to help others. All that weekend and on her next visit she watched for him, and felt fear when they saw one another. She had betrayed his cousin Philip. It wasn't until early in February that, walking with her amigo Betsy, she had been able to face this. At her request, they went back to the car and drove to a trail they less often took across a cemetery. "Why," Betsy asked, "wouldn't you think this would be hard?" Hearing the question let her start again. Every story in that hospital was hard to hear. The following Saturday, on a roundabout trip to Alicia's house, she stopped at the ward. She filled out the form to be a volunteer and spent two hours in the playroom with Matt and his dad.

Near the end of the massage, she put aside her modesty and let Hans work around her breasts. The young Austrian, now a friend, bent with restrained force to wring out the pain gathered along each rib and around her chest muscles and bones. Once she had lain a second time curled up crying beneath a blanket and his steadying hand, she felt lighter. Yet the session saddened him: he spoke of the uncertainties associated with his choices.

Grace searched for questions she might ask, but then kept quiet.

Nonetheless, as, once they had hugged and separated, she followed the ridge that showed a nice, downhill view of the Seeker garden, she found herself thinking that, despite being mute then, so much of this—what Hans had achieved but also gorgeous, careful Sophie, prickly Trumpeter, and whoever else—she would roll much of this into stories for girlfriends and even, maybe by next summer, for her maturing niece and son. Out would come impersonations, quotations, and scenes. Nor would the stories soon fade: rather, they would bloom, aided by exaggerations, listener riffs, and, sometimes, beer. Because whether or not she truly watched over the people she went through life with, she knew it somehow fell her way—this truth had lain buried all winter long—to be their bard.

Part Three

The Seeker Gathering

11

Misunderstanding on the Raft

The weekend passed, sending Alicia's family to camp and Henry to a trade show, and now on Monday afternoon Hans and Grace were on the raft tethered thirty yards offshore. Grace was being chatty and Hans, smiling to find her so, wondered aloud (causing her to grin) if she was winding him into one of her tales. Willa, whose sometime-prickliness puzzled Grace, was on the raft, too, with a few others. At this hot, humid hour, a quarter of the staff was in or near water: in the swimming area, on the pond in kayaks or canoes, under the cluster of shade trees behind the beach. Inland, Seeker hummed, as hundreds of guests joined teachers at activities. All at the pond heard, as would beachgoers hear that whole week, drumbeats, for a drumming work-shop was under way in a nearby studio. The drums rang in rapid bursts amid longer silences: it was a first, awkward day of practicing. But an-other workshop must use drums, too; for on the raft was heard, from somewhere on the wooded hillside, a fainter, repeating drum song—the beat of music both accomplished and wild.

Those on the raft also heard the yelps of children, the Seeker day-care crowd gathered by the beach. With a counselor near, three tod-dlers sat at the water's edge. Some yards away a second, lean-as-a-plank counselor with a lush, black ponytail and beard splashed up foot-high waves, taunting his preschool-age charges to come after him.

Around the raft, life moved slowly, curbed by the play of senses.

Water gurgles, warm planks under wet flesh, a searing sun... the smell of wet wood. Three people floated on air mattresses, one on his belly with his arms in the pond; a second, on her back, shielding her eyes with an upturned hand as she talked with someone on the raft.

Chatting lazily with Willa and Hans, Grace found that this where-land-meets-water play of the senses forged a mix of reactions. In her, it stirred memories; in Willa, ideas. Hans seemed drawn most to how the responses would vary.

"On beaches from Thailand to Mexico," he had reflected, "it's the same: middle-class travelers at play under a simplifying sun, amid a calming lap of waves. You sometimes, but rarely, see the local people join in."

"Beach sports like that only recently got big," said Willa. "My dad says that on his first trip to Greece, as a student from London, when the island towns were still mainly fishing villages, the locals found the tourists strange. They could understand the flight from cold weather, but they felt it should lead to relaxing at cafés or on boats. The swimmers and joggers—even more so the windsurfers and hang-gliders who came next with their sophisticated gear—made them smile.

"Now this scene is further south, down Africa's coasts. It's even odder for a black African to picture sunscreen tubes down there."

Taking a different slant, Grace said that the relaxing thing for her just then was the lack of kids under her care. "To me a beach means noise," she explained, "so much so that I can remember sounds from past beach days now—sounds especially of my son Amos with his body board and fun and games. At ten, he had one of his last childhood meltdowns at a Hudson River beach near our house. It was my fault: I'd left him in the water too long and he about had sunstroke."

Seated, leaned back on outstretched arms that bent behind them like tent poles, they gazed at the beach and swimming areas and at a cove thick with lily pads to the sunlit south. Grace's reminiscence drew their eyes to the shallow water, where a few children played. She smiled inwardly and, about to say more, turned to find Hans looking at her.

"I was about to add," she said, pointing to the beached boats laid in a row where the cove and swimming area met, "that it was during all those days that Amos advanced from body boards to sails and came to love boats. Now he's at a camp whose crowning experience is a three-day sail on Long Island Sound! It's his second summer; he was too young for the sailing trip last year, and he's looked forward to it since."

She smiled; then her mood dimmed. "Last winter he built two model sailboats," she added in a less watertight voice. Momentarily, she had forgotten what else the winter had brought.

Still faced forward, Willa said, "Grace, you seem not to care about the larger forces that shape our lives."

Grace didn't at all know what the surprising statement meant. She wondered how the scourge of cancer could possibly mean more than itself.

Time dawdled; then Hans saw and pointed out the misunderstanding.

"Grace," he said, facing her, "Willa and I had begun to wonder what water means in different cultures."

Grace felt confounded. Willa seemed impassioned and her voice had been pitched high.

"It's only," said Willa, "that, intending to or not, you changed the subject. We'd begun to ask why some cultures are devoted to sports. But you perhaps assume that all cultures are. The assumption then becomes a kind of larger context for your son's adventures.

"Yet it's a fact that some cultures view bodies of water like this lake as essentially sacred locations... not as sites for games."

Grace felt chagrined and a bit scalded. She knew to let go the scalded sensation, as she didn't want Willa to see the shadow creeping up that opposed her niece's luck to her son's. As to the rest of it, she had seemingly trampled a desire Willa had to bring order to life.

But how can life be orderly, she wondered philosophically?

"I may've mistaken one conversation for another," said Grace.

Hans asked, "But what do you think of what Willa just said?"

"I think I long ago stopped seeking life's larger meanings."

"Yet you like to chat about the life that files past you."

"Yes, I do. I guess a lot that I see draws my interest."

Grace thought how the distinction they had made was interesting. She told herself: At least it helped to drive the death shadow away.

"You're a vital person, Grace," said Willa. "People see that—even if you've been quiet a lot since we met."

Grace smiled. "Lately, the scripts get read internally."

"And your actress years touched you; still, you seem glued to life's day-to-day events. But to question our culture or just wonder at being alive"—Willa waved a hand from side to side and then pointed it skyward—"is a part of life, too."

This was a big, murky comment. But Grace, who had felt since October that she lacked a stable idea of herself, knew that Seeker—where Willa had been for some weeks—pointed more at the philosophical in life than at the day-to-day.

She looked inquisitively at Hans. He had gotten into a half-lotus pose, with a straight back, ankles locked under opposite thighs, and wrists on his knees. He seemed to be listen, thinking, or both. His hands looked small for the degree of force she had felt flow from them.

"It's our everyday routines versus whatever else," said Willa.

"Not quite; that doesn't quite get to it," said Hans. "Because that 'whatever else' is what gives shape to our days.

"Grace," he said, bending towards her, "Willa's description may not apply to you. But it does to a lot of people, and it's a question whether they make life harder by binding it so tightly to the everyday. To use *your* life as an example, what I think I mean is: this happens, then this, and this; young Amos plays, melts down, and learns to sail; and as events join together the story takes a familiar shape. But does it say enough? Do our private, day-to-day events equal life in the round... or are there elements of inner life and of circumstance that also matter? And if they do matter, are we adding to our confusion by pressing our eyes so tightly upon the everyday?"

"So much surrounds what we experience in a day," Willa added.

Grace replied at once, feeling brave to put what felt familiar into words. "I know, facing a big hurt or problem, that I get evasive or quiet. I lack the skill to ask the larger questions."

"It may be more not having the will than the skill," said Hans.

Yet, Grace wondered, what richer story can soak up such sadness? She thought of Hans in his role as a masseur, and of her responses.

Talking of this, he seemed again to search for the ledges where pain hid.

Turning to him and to Willa, she shook her head in an affirming way, indicating more understanding than she felt. Then they all quieted.

Grace hoped to dodge Willa's challenge, at least for now. Her method now became to study her challenger, who had flipped onto her stomach. She had seen her seem, with a dull stare, to envy Sophie's beauty, for instance, and to be, at twenty-two, awkward with men. Yet men, or the careful ones here, must find appealing this girl with pretty, brown skin and an incongruous Nordic lilt in her voice. Her social involvement must only add to this appeal. Willa was, after all, drawn both to improving the life around her and to enjoying herself—even if in regard to the former she could be a scold, chiding herself and everyone else.

"I want to make a better world." She had once said this in Grace's hearing. "This fall I begin graduate work in international development; here, and in the U.S. overall, I hope to deepen my understanding." For the summer, anyway, she had taken to calling herself "Willa the Wiking."

Grace wondered how long Willa's Nordic resolve would endure.

Yet a sign that it might endure had been her spirited dancing on the night when Monk had played the blues and Grace had sat frozen in her chair.

Willa lay with a hand in the pond and her face turned sideways on the raft, near its edge, where water sounds surrounded her. Flipping over again, she rose up on her elbows. "I like," she told Grace, "how you share a name with a great American river and live near it, to. But is 'Hudson' your husband's family name?"

"No, I'm the Hudson. My husband's name is Ross and my story is typically American. I'm from Iowa, half Anglo-Belgian, and I'd hardly heard of the Hudson River before moving east. Our family saga is of my mother's Latvian dairy-farmer ancestors, in a land I've never seen. And swimming meant mostly backyard pools, diving boards, and flip-flops. Then at a street fair in Brooklyn I meet this Henry Ross. A year later, visiting *his* suburban parents, he has to escape… so we head up the river valley. Raised a half-hour drive from the ocean and as near the great river, he, too, is a product of backyard pools. And so, misfits both of us, once we find the Hudson, its rooted depth, we make it our anchor. We buy an old canoe, read local lore, get lost on weekend drives, and even join a preservation society: we become part of the river's mongrel following.

"Then my brother's company moves him to New Jersey, not that far across the Hudson from where we live, and the fates settle in."

"American swimming pools," said Willa, smiling vengefully. "That's what I mean. Oh, there's Francine… "

On shore, Francine, thin but sensuous in a red bikini and a straw hat, was climbing the lifeguard tower to talk with a friend. The friend raised a hand in warning and Francine remained on the tower's ladder, hanging by her left hand and foot from its upper rungs.

"In my Oslo high school, we read about American pools," Willa said, "and about manufacturers' efforts to sell them in Europe. But back then our bourgeois families weren't used to such extravagant possessions; and the house lots were too small. Yet, now, with a wealthier populace and enough advertising, we start to have big houses and the swimming pools, too. Another new consumer need is established! It's a sickness."

"What's sadder," said Hans, "is how we even more than our parents fly south on weekends to share the beaches with Americans. And how we begin to agree when they call the Mediterranean 'dirty' compared to hotel pools. That worse than its garbage, because less correctable, are its rocks and aquatic life and sand.

"Of course," he added, "swimming pools, like steam baths and saunas, may be a European invention, one more upper-class luxury. Though, even then, didn't they mainly provide hygiene and relief from hot weather?"

"They signify a lot more," said Willa. "They're ostentatious and they waste resources. I see them as a sickness of capitalism."

I've not heard *that* phrase in ages, Grace thought: "the evils of capitalism." Caustically, she pictured Willa visiting on her way to New York. She foresaw a dour day, cloudy gray heat, and Willa with a liking for good white wine. She would bring her to Betsy's patio and pool.

Grace, on her back, warm and languid, scolded herself. Where did she aim her malice, in this exchange that had almost randomly—quite a few Seeker exchanges seemed almost random—gotten onto swimming pools? And of course, she hoped Willa *would* visit. "Have you seen the impressive Hudson?" she asked her friends. "It runs just west of here. There's a park somewhere nearby where one can walk alongside it for a mile."

"I've seen it and the mountains only from a bridge," said Hans.

Willa, who shook her head no, seemed to be listening to the drums, raised again on the western ridge. There were two, and they had been at it for a while. The beat continued and Grace, following Willa's shoreward gaze, saw Francine dancing to the music, twirling at the water's edge near where the toddlers played. One, a girl, stood and began to dance, too, in tune less with the drum rhythms than with Francine. The best she could manage was to intermittently stomp her right foot. But even this was more than her balance would bear, and she quickly fell down.

12

A Stranger's Tears

The talk on the raft gave way to an appreciation of the moment, its warmth and repose, as soon they would each rejoin the Seeker schedule. Willa had an eight-hour kitchen shift ahead, while Hans would teach a class. Grace, who had worked late the day before, again on the luggage crew, again with the fussy, laconic Trumpeter, hoped to sit and listen near the drumming workshop for a while. Then she would join Willa for a four-hour stint in the kitchen.

Grace, especially, was sorry to leave the raft; for as they were about to dive in the pond Monk glided up in a kayak. Ten yards away a sharp-eyed woman Grace's age, with brown hair in pigtails, feathered her paddle to keep her kayak in place. Monk and Willa smiled at each other as he slid up to the rear of the raft. "Ahoy, raft dwellers," he said; then: "Yes, Willa, it will be tomorrow, a special dawn performance."

"And I'll be cleaning pots until almost midnight tonight," she said with mock distress. "Ah, I know; at the gazebo."

"For the Buddha," he replied, smiling; then he looked at Grace. "I hope we can talk again soon." Grace nodded. He grinned at Hans. "Hands," he said, raising a splayed-finger hand. Then he pushed forward along the raft. As his kayak, slim and green, cleared it he turned with a broad, arcing stroke to rejoin his companion, who had impressed Grace, too. They paddled off together.

By the time the swimmers were back on land, Francine had tripped off and the day-care contingent, toddlers and rapid runners alike, was under a shade tree, snacking through bent straws on packaged juice. "A lot of wrapping for a dozen sips of liquid," noted Willa. Under another tree, a man and a woman lay in adjoining hammocks. The hammocks had intricate patterns and were made from an oatmeal-colored fiber that looked like hemp. Hans left the path that led across the tree-rimmed lawn to the road; then he called his companions over and continued on to a shack with an open door that stocked life jackets and paddles. He pointed to printed letters, each a hand's-length high and faded black against the cloudy gray values of the wall.

"It's Hebrew," he said.

"I know the story," said Willa. "European immigrants built this camp as a retreat from the city. Monk says they were socialists, who in time sold the place to a Jewish cultural society. This second group would have put up the shack. The word means 'women,' so we can guess this was a changing room. The camp ran for seventy years; but I think it'd long been closed down when Seeker came along."

Hans looked pleased. "I like knowing that people I would probably have respected cut these paths."

"Monk says that a few Seeker regulars went as children to the cultural camp," added Willa. "I think he may be one of them."

At the top of the lawn, Grace waved goodbye and took the path veering right. As the Hebrew word had surprised her by bringing up time, the forest surprised her by erasing all but the present. One need only stop, an experience that seemed fresh and repeatable, to find an intact natural world, a play of color, light, and movement that always was unique. Now the air felt dry. The sun, no longer directly overhead, bore down heavily. So, the day was a bit overripe.

If, as Grace knew, a unique event had taught her a language of fear, fear wasn't, she believed, the measure she used for life when things went well; and she *was* better. Here in the forest, she thought less about what had happened than about the moment: nature itself, and the people she had begun to know. While it was odd, she could enjoy this respite from her life at home. What *was* it like, she wondered, to *be* or *need to be* in an exotic place like Thailand for half of each year… to again be idealistic, like Willa, or brave like Sophie… this completely funny place? What was Monk about—or Trumpeter?

The path took her over a creek on a handsome footbridge and then turned her back toward the pond, a quarter mile north of the beach. Through foliage, she glimpsed the studio she headed for, and then became aware that the drum sounds had quieted. She stopped to listen for the more distant music, but it had stopped, too. Another turn in the path brought her to an open area with a clear view of the studio. Ten people flitted near the porch; a bald man walked toward her on the path. The workshop was on a break.

Wondering if the break would soon end and too shy to ask if she might listen on the porch once it did, Grace detoured into a women's toilet that occupied half of a small building near the studio. Inside, the overhead lights were switched on despite the midday hour; and once through the door she saw a woman of about her age standing in tears at a sink. A guitar case seeming not to suit the drumming workshop leaned against the wall.

Grace had entered the toilet without really needing its services, and she was briefly stymied. Most often, she knew, when something like this arose the right behavior, barring a view of blood, was to mind one's business. Over time she had been more bullied than anything, even by Amos, into acting this way. She herself tended to be curious and kind. But she knew it was one thing in the city, another in her suburb. And it was one thing if the hurt person dressed, spoke, and smelled like her, another if the person did not. This attitude bothered her, but it also was true that people sometimes guessed badly. And beyond one's own area, it was indeed about guessing, not judgment. But if nothing else, she could note the human ugliness. Wasn't this what her safe suburb was to some degree about?

Still, this was neither city nor suburb, but a retreat, a place to study and recuperate that offered a break from one's situation. It was situation—however arbitrary the fact seemed from here—that bred habits. People in this abstract sense were uncomplicated and sad. The woman was thin and had straight, mostly black hair streaked with gray that ran down to her shoulders. A few gray strands stood out. She wore jeans and a black, shiny blouse; leaning against a sink, she folded her arms across her midriff. Each arm, pearl white and thin, lacking tone, holding tension, was bare below the bicep. She shook her head and laughed, now with someone else present, in a way that seemed both self-calming and self-diminishing. At the same time, she continued, a stray tear here and there, to cry.

"Can I help?" asked Grace.

"No," the woman replied, in an overseas English accent. "I'm only being stupid. I just have to admit that I made a mistake."

Again, Grace felt stymied, as she still had no reason to be in the enclosure. Should I, she wondered, pretend to use a toilet or a sink? She thought of what to say next.

"Are they still on the porch?" asked the woman, whom Grace now saw had long, lean fingers and did not wear a wedding ring.

"Do you mean the drumming workshop? Yes. Are you part of that?"

"No. I was on the path, crying and, I guess, listening. I'd wandered this way following their sound. Then they came outside and I ran in here. I even hid in a stall when two of them followed me in. They surely heard me, though... bloody ridiculous."

"Well, my story isn't so different," said Grace with a sisterly shrug. "I also ran in here feeling undecided and embarrassed. Then I thought about hiding from you. And, until yesterday, I'd cried each night I was here."

"I'll leave this afternoon," said the woman in a more intimate tone. "I only have to calm down and figure out how to get back to the city. I came yesterday on the Seeker bus."

"Are you in a workshop? If you are, but don't like it, maybe you can switch into a different one. It's only Monday. Anyway, will they refund your money?"

The woman turned from the sink and then, in a reverse, back to the sink and small mirror at the elevation of her face. "God, it was only yesterday," she said. "I was so excited. I was sure the week would change my life. And in a day, instead of things changing, I've been sealed in." Now her jaw and cheeks clenched and, lips parted, she began to cry freely again. A few breaths later, they heard the workshop drums sound again, as well.

There was an old bench, which Grace had noticed was missing a seat slat, where the forest met the clearing. Near both the rest room and studio, it must have predated both buildings. Grace asked the woman if she would like to get out of the toilet, with its harsh, redundant light, trapped beetles, and cement floor, and for a time sit and listen to the drumming in the open air. The bench was far enough from the studio, she added, for them to keep talking if they wanted to. She also explained that she was a staff member at the academy, and in a little while would have to head off for work.

The woman's smiling shrug hinted at an accustomed passivity, and she let Grace carry her guitar case and lead her to the bench. A label taped to the case told Grace the stranger's name was Moira Kathleen Marshall and that she lived, despite what her accent suggested, on Staten Island. If she had been crying and hiding all day, Grace asked quietly, had she even gotten lunch?

"I left the workshop at the morning break," said Moira Kathleen. "We'd been writing our songs and I just disappeared. Then I was too embarrassed to go near the dining-hall at lunch. Or maybe I have no real insight into why I do anything. Because when the afternoon session started, I left my hideout behind a tree near the workshop studio and went back in. A few people glanced at me; that was all. Ten minutes later, I ran away again."

As Grace was wary not of getting involved but of making things worse, she made no reply. Here was a complex story, and she hadn't much time. It also was daunting, this leap from her small, new circle to a stranger; the drag on her courage grew as she compared the engaged people she had begun to know with Moira Kathleen. Her fear deepened as the women, sitting on the bench, began to hear the practice session in the nearby drumming workshop. Its pedagogy seemed respectful and frank. The leader used both hands to drum ten or so beats, creating sounds that had a plain precision; then, one after another, the classmates drummed in imitation. Each exercise involved a repetition: leader first, then a student. On occasion, a student who hadn't done well was allowed to try again. At other times, the leader broke a phrase down into smaller ones of a few beats each and had students practice these. Yet, despite this patient framing—a standard Seeker practice, Grace had observed, that showed both good business sense and a belief that learning took time—Moira Kathleen, hopeful at a different yet probably similar workshop, one that welcomed guitars, had frozen up.

"Twenty years ago," she said through tears, "when I played for tips in Dublin clubs and taught piano to children, an American folk singer recorded a song of mine. The next year I earned three thousand dollars in royalties. Then, with an album of new songs in my notebook, I moved to New York. I even intended to ship my piano the following spring."

"I fought to be an actress for eight long years," said Grace. "It brought me to the city, too. So, I fear, I know what you're going to say next."

Moira Kathleen gave her an odd look. She grew more cautious, perhaps knowing, Grace felt, that she both needed help and couldn't handle more disappointment, which to her seemed to really mean abandonment. Then she appeared to choose the hope of comfort over fear. "I haven't truly practiced, let alone written anything real, for sixteen years," she said. "Yet I somehow told myself that during five days at a songwriting workshop, in the Seeker milieu and with a teacher I respect, I could get it back. Well, no, I haven't and I can't. So, its five hundred dollars and my life down the loo.

"I really used to care," she added, in a deeper, less plaintive voice.

Two decades, thought Grace: so much time. No wedding ring and probably no child. Ah, yes, without my comforting habits. She doesn't practice and so hasn't become a music teacher, at least; her graying hair; some other job; a dwelling on Staten Island, near downtown. So, it's likely that she works in financial services.

Grace told Moira Kathleen that she had to go to her kitchen job, and pleaded with her to stay, if only for the night. "You've spent your money, anyway," she argued. "Take a swim, have a good supper, and, if you aren't ready to try your workshop again, go to another evening event. You can always leave in the morning." With an enthusiasm that reflected her unease, she explained how the evening schedule worked. Perhaps the woman would grow acclimated by the next day. If she stayed, they might meet again after eight p.m., when Grace finished work.

Moira Kathleen, already looking lonely, said she would remain on the bench to think her situation through.

13

The Supper Shift

As planned, Grace reached the dining-hall early; nearing the rear door, she saw a parked dairy truck. It was hot in the staff mess, where the sun, before it slipped behind the steep hill at the back of the building, beat in from the southwest. Someone was at the curtained-off Internet terminal; three others, including Sophie, chatted avidly and sipped from paper cups at a table. Grace had learned that, unlike in a city or suburb, friends crossed paths often here and so felt no need to always greet each other. Nor did they feel obliged to include their entire visible circle in what they did. Sophie might easily have nodded to Grace, whom she surely saw; but she stayed intent on her companions. This for Grace was still a bit unusual.

Aside from yoga and massage, Grace had stopped sampling Seeker's mind-body-heart-soul programs the last few days. She liked how yoga made her feel, forced her from bed and even earlier made her wake to see the woods in the early morning. Her habit at home was to waste these summer hours. With her husband down having breakfast or gone and Amos asleep, she would lie amid her bedroom clutter, watch light batter her window shades and give herself up to a talk show. More essentially, she would turn her radio or TV on. When her better nature asked her, as it sometimes did, if she allowed this distraction because it was all she knew to do, or allowed it because she was lazy, she would fade with a wistful, bitten shrug back to an earlier time in her life. Then, the idea of laziness had been a relic of youth and a joke. Now—yes, she liked these shows, liked casting her still-sleepy attention into the pop culture breeze; she enjoyed this joining up. At bottom, it helped her to wake. Was it all she knew to do? No, and in this sense she *was* lazy. But did she need the habit? Of this, she wasn't sure.

As she read the staff activity board, planning her week, Francine and Trumpeter entered from the kitchen to a sound of muffled music. Francine wore a white apron and a blue headscarf and carried a stack of plastic plates, which she set on the counter. She talked; Trumpeter smiled. Trumpeter, whose assigned work was with the luggage crew, split the plate stack and took the top half to the other side of the C-shaped counter, a few yards away. He and Francine then stayed talking in their corner of the room. Grace felt that, like Sophie, Francine had probably noticed her but chosen to not greet her.

Grace reread the descriptions of two workshops she especially wanted to attend. One, the next day, was the Seeker orientation. Among its teachers was a member of the academy's founding collective; a psychologist named Elsa who lived near Boston. Each year this workshop was offered on a few weekends to guests, and a few times as a shortened, half-day staff workshop with a picnic supper. Grace had heard it described as the great if unofficial introduction to Seeker's core practices. A sign-up sheet had one spot left, which she grabbed.

The other workshop beckoning was a Saturday night sampler of gospel singing. It seemed too alluring not to try, if her courage held. The teacher led a gospel-singing troupe in Philadelphia.

Grace would be in the kitchen, her first time at this work, for four hours, and again for four hours starting at ten tomorrow morning. She must be sure to look for Moira Kathleen in the café that night. She had better check in with her husband, too. Afterwards the wellness workshop, with also yoga on Wednesday: so it would be a busy two days.

On entering the kitchen, she thought its gleaming silver surfaces made it look like a big, multifaceted mirror reflecting distorted images. Smells of soap and of foods being cut or cooked in water or oil mixed with the distortions and the sight of a dozen workers in white aprons. With the sounding of the supper horn just two hours away, there was much to do. Grace found a manager and got her assignment: she would begin in the dining-hall and later help with the onslaught of dirty dishes.

The pace was brisk, aided by the loud, lively music playing during prep and clean-up hours, when the dining-hall was closed. Managing the mostly-young crew was Tulip, who had a hard-eyed intensity and was in her sixties. And because what Grace heard was the charged music of Tulip's youth, the blues and R&B brought first to life by an oppressed racial minority, she wondered if Tulip forced the others to her tastes. But passing through the kitchen she saw that many among the staff were singing along, often loudly, to the recorded words.

At first, she was told to stock buffet lines and beverage counters with dishes, cups, and utensils. This work, which most mornings she saw her tent neighbor busy at, he of the rubber yoga mat, placed her near Francine, who prepped the bread-and-condiment tables. Francine greeted other staffers with a hard-edged cheer but said nothing to Grace. Grace felt that a reason for the snub, which she regretted, was the gap in their ages. Loud, social, often caustic, Francine might hit her stride after matrons like Grace went to bed. Yet Grace sensed something else at work, beyond the imaginative failing that made a youth dismiss her elders; so she was not surprised to see the girl's back lift like a cat's when Tulip corrected some detail of her work. Francine might distrust adults and authority figures, and so especially adults who held sway over her.

In fact, questions of authority and duty played out most intensely among the kitchen crew, in what Grace had seen so far. Francine just had transferred into this crew: she would no longer float among the many crews, like Grace and Willa. In fact, many young staff seemed to like the trade the kitchen offered of greater freedom in exchange for more work. Each week the kitchen served ten thousand meals; its crew had to be ardent and organized—while being made up mostly of unpaid workers.

A few days before, as she helped to wash the walls and floor of a dance studio, Grace had heard this problem of keeping young volunteers focused addressed. She herself had raised the issue in an effort to pass time; a half-satiric reply came from her crew chief, a big youth whose face shone humidly from his vitality and thirty extra pounds. Grace recalled his name being "Arnold" or "Arthur." Whatever his name, he had gazed down from the middle rung of a ladder at another man and at her.

"Our managers really need us to work hard," he said. "Yet they can't convince us based on the morals we grew up with, which supposedly taught us to be productive, responsible, and the like, because the feeling here is that our plundering culture and its morality is total shit. So our managers, who have a big, funky place to run with mostly volunteer labor, must refer us instead to the codes taught in Seeker workshops: to monastic traditions of manual labor, for instance—or to an even vaguer notion that seekers should be humble before a shared ideal.

"Which means that the running of this place, with its real dirt and dust, can get"—here, Grace remembered, Arnold or Arthur had held his mop at mid-handle and, with a moist grin, waved the sponge as a banner—"a little philosophical and so a little chancy and a little uneven."

Yet in the end it was a simple matter, she learned as they continued to clean: in support of the Seeker gathering, this work must be done. Standards must be upheld. There were the hospitality norms of tastiness, shine, and aesthetic kick that for good or ill the mainly suburban guests were used to. And, again, there was the Seeker ideal that, however wobbly in fact, was still described nicely by the coequal terms of "dignity" and "service."

What these issues meant for the kitchen crew, Grace, a new member, began to see, was that it even more than the other crews felt pride, and believed that their doing their work made them free. As most were young, this freedom meant largely being irreverent and wild. Signs taped to walls, for example, forbade fighting with food. And, with loud music playing when the dining-hall was closed, there were times when the crew prolonged its shift (hearing this, Grace felt an anticipatory tug of fatigue) by leaving the prep tables and utensils, or, if they washed dishes, the garbage, plates, and sprays, for a dance or game or chase.

As with the wildness, their youth must partly fuel the irreverence— and yet, as Grace's youth had shown her, an irreverent attitude might have other sources, particularly anger. A short ladder, she knew, might bring one to irreverence from deeper feelings of disdain. Among many of these youth raised in material comfort it in fact was a given that the culture they grew into was, to paraphrase Arnold or Arthur, simply shit without a toilet. This was why most of them were here.

This was a glum way of seeing things, surely—but it was one that she could document by quilting together comments she had heard as she worked, ate her meals, and sat in workshops. There were the parents she heard described as strange or lonely or choked by possessions. There were the siblings and friends she heard described as having turned to painkillers—drugs and drink to dull awareness but also the achievement tracks, most prominently professional schools, which, it was said, repeated past mistakes by dispensing roles without understanding. And there were the childhoods she heard described in terms of sad, private castles, abutting each other in suburbs or in tall buildings—and around each castle, like soil around a seed, a thicket of media channels, shopping malls, and, of course, roads.

Grace remembered this category of youthful anger, which seemed to have changed little in two decades. Back then she had known of it indirectly, through the passions of friends. How few of *them* she was in touch with now! She wondered how many had seen their rage burn out. If she could not have made the analogy then, she now knew that their varied reactions might be plotted as a graph, the kind Amos made at school, to draw a sketch of their group with statistics. Some had sat near a trend line of recognized anger, brooding and complaining. She and most others had stayed at the edges, finding their language in the musings of the more vocal. It probably came down to a mix of taste and training, she thought. But the brooders had in fact been the better storytellers, as they struggled with the forces beneath daily life.

As she worked through these thoughts, she filled a dolly with coffee mugs and wheeled it out of the kitchen. And now, stacking cups at a coffee station, she paused, seeing Willa's face in her mind's eye. On the raft, the girl had spoken to these forces of confusion and anger. And now Grace had been reacting to her challenge unawares.

Stopped, with cups in each hand, she became aware that while she was one of her suburb's storytellers, she found her material not in any struggle of forces but rather in (to paraphrase Willa) the crises and passages of the people she knew directly. And by "directly" she meant family, friends, and neighbors—but, ah yes, she must ruefully admit, also some celebrities who would engage her through the media.

Of course, back then the media had been just as persuasive. What technical term did her husband use? Yes, "signal and amplification." The complaints of her idealistic friends and other like-minded people were amplified by the music and images that encircled them. A resistance culture influenced the media. Or was it the reverse: their cries being shaped by stories gotten from the media? Which then was signal and which amplification?

As she pushed her dolly to the other coffee station, watching the crew as if it acted in a skit, she also saw the part played in life by self-selection. It was her zest for experience but serving few goals that back then led her to an artsy crowd. Other groups went about preparing for safer lives. Similarly, these Seeker youth from a dozen countries were here because, for a host of reasons, they weren't at ease in more safely usual settings.

Still, as Willa's questioning spurred her to see, it also was true that self-selection, even to think to choose, was a trait mostly of the well-fed classes. It was no option for the poor. And if Grace rarely talked with these poor, she surely knew of them. Willa was right to remind them that these multitudes were there.

Trumpeter was on an apparent social tour of the kitchen, because at 4:30, when Grace had been at work for half an hour, he was still there. As she swung back into the kitchen to look for clean silver, she saw him talking with Tulip, who stood holding a clipboard and laughing deeply. Trumpeter, the jokester, wore the same sardonic, muffled grin he had worn listening to Francine, earlier in the mess, and during a recent wrangle with the luggage. The look was hot but turned inward, so charged perhaps by embarrassment.

The silverware sat, separated by type, in cylindrical white plastic tubs that were punctured by air holes, one per square inch, almost the size of dimes. Several dozen gleaming forks, knives, or spoons fit in a tub, so when Grace turned to go back into the dining-hall, the six tubs she held, balancing three on each forearm as the silver leaned into her chest, made a heavy load. She divided her squint between the bundles and the swinging door and thus was surprised when, after a few steps, she saw that Tulip had come up beside her. The woman rescued a cylinder from each forearm and was about to go with her into the dining-hall when a cook yelped from behind a silver shelf. Tulip barked Trumpeter's name. A minute later, dour, split by angles, cuter than he likely knew, he was showing Grace where beneath the buffet line this refill stock of utensils should be put.

"Thanks for the help," she said, as she knelt to deposit the last tubs.

"How're you getting on?" he asked, perched awkwardly over her. "I've seen you in morning yoga. Has, well, being here started to help?"

His personal words surprised Grace. She turned and grinned up at him and he uneasily smiled back. She rose, smiling widely. But then he broke eye contact. She wondered if, without his usual scornful manner, he felt exposed. It was fun but also mean to spar with one so cautious. She looked up with a quieter smile. "I'm better this week. The fresh air helps. I was awkward that first day I worked for you. Anyway, the work yesterday was more enjoyable—throwing suitcases felt pretty good."

Her more direct approach worked, for if his new smile was thin, he looked at her and stayed. "Don't worry about it; you've done fine," he said regally. Then he stepped down his mood. "I hear you're doing massage work with Hans... a good choice. Hans is unassuming, but many people here think he has blessed gifts."

"I like him, too. We just were together on the raft." She realized that Trumpeter, if he knew of her work with Hans, might also know about Alicia. And had he really said "blessed"? Seeker contained a surprising mix of reticences, points-of-view, feelings. It was a funny, compressed place, and hard to get a bead on.

"I saw you. Willa was there. Anyway, I shouldn't keep you. Enjoy the shift. Tulip says this is your first day in the kitchen. I told her I was glad you were here, because compared with washing dishes work on the luggage crew is fun. We compete for hard workers at the academy."

During the first, busiest hour of supper she worked not washing dishes but in the dining-hall. At the last minute, she was moved to the task of maintaining a beverage station—likely another rookie's job. Wearing a neat black apron tied at her waist and neck and holding a cotton rag hairy with threads, she kept a thirty-foot counter clean and stocked with drinks, glasses, and cups. It was a fine job, really, as it took little effort and let her view the gathering as an outsider. The slightly abstract tinge brought on by this helper role let her stoke her satiric nature. Watching someone pour a glass of milk led her to glance at the tray of clean glasses and guess when it would have to be refilled. She likewise tried to guess, by a person's dress or posture, which workshop they were in. Who, guessing mostly by these factors, was a teacher, a workshop veteran, a first-time guest? Who, back home, was a meter reader, an artist, or a middle manager? There of course probably were few if any of the first. She weighed the buoyant mood that seemed a mainstay of the academy. Gathered to eat in a hundred groups, amid rich odors and a general din, the Seeker community looked sociable and excited. One might read contentment in its bustle.

Usually this much group classifying sufficed for Grace, and she would turn to finding quirks in individuals; Trumpeter's stiffness, the blond passing in a body-length sari and big green sunglasses... quirks like these. Her cheerful verbal caricatures were made artful by this contrast of type against unique profile, each flawed silhouette setting off the other. It was the caricaturist's method. Now, though, she felt more exposed than usual. Eyeing the room, she realized that, besides her failed workshop, after two weeks she knew little about what went on at the academy. Why, she wondered, beyond the fresh air and good, plentiful food, assuming there *are* other reasons, are the people at the tables here? What do they get from workshops, and at what risk? She thought of Moira Kathleen. She also wondered if some in the crowd, happy as they seemed, really rode off the deep end with pursuits like past-life regression. She decided that for her remaining two weeks she would be more of an explorer.

Then, unexpectedly, with a kick from fortune, she grew from kitchen rookie into minor hero. Two five-gallon steel vats with rims slanting out held a cream-colored substance that looked like paint. They sat with dipping ladles on a table between the beverage counters. What they offered, signs said, was "Cold Fruit Soup," a mix of peaches, spices, and milk. Grace had tried and liked it the previous week. Yet now, rarely did sweet-seekers so much as risk a taste.

She watched and listened as a few people approached skittishly.

"There are soup bowls, but it's sticky for soup," one person said.

"They call it soup, but it's cold," another pointed out.

"Anyway, who eats soup for dessert?" a third wondered.

It was at that moment that Grace, holding her rag and keeping an eye on her assigned work, began to play fruit-soup promoter. She had few takers, at first. Then she found herself thinking to say, as she might to her family, that here was only a smoothie: sweetened fruit and milk, blended and chilled. She shaped a plan. Robbing a juice machine of paper cups and a milk machine of glasses, she stood near a vat, hawking its contents as "cold peach *smoothie*, a delectable dessert *drink*."

"Oh," exclaimed a new group of wonderers, gathered around. "Yes, on this hot afternoon! Thanks!" A line for the new dessert formed.

She was rewarded, though, when cycled back into the kitchen, with a cold eye from Tulip and the least pleasant job at the dishwasher, clearing garbage from plates. "We try not to waste food *or* run out of menu items," a cook said stiffly. "But the peach soup is nearly gone, and the food line will be up for half an hour more!"

Willa, doing prep work at a counter with a bucket of eggs by her side, winked at Grace, enjoying the calamity. Otherwise, Grace was soon ignored. She changed from her crisp black apron to a soft, soiled white one, put on rubber gloves, and, with a quick tutorial from Tulip, took her place on the rubber mats that made passable the soaked tile floor around the dishwashing machine. Francine was the practical leader of the team; she wielded the long-necked water sprayer, holding it by a pistol-shaped nozzle. Grace saw that her right eye was red and half-closed. Still, she was able to pressure-rinse and load rack after rack into the machine. Grace's job, replacing someone on break, was to scrape the solid and liquid waste she found amid unsorted, polluted stacks of pots, plates, bowls, glasses, cups, and cooking and eating tools into tall, brown pails; sort the wiped-off items according to kind; then load it all on racks. A boy who spoke French to Francine emptied the racks that had passed through the dishwasher. Grace saw carts filled with clean plates, etc., sitting on casters at the other end of the dishwasher from where she was marooned. It was plain how the whole system worked.

She dug in quickly, seeing through the drop-off window in the dining-hall how those who lined up to leave trays faced a wall of dirty dishes. But moments later, Francine, sighing dramatically, dropped her nozzle and began to help scrape. Grace was not keeping up. Truly, her movements weren't fluid; her mind lunged past her hands and she found herself, amid similar errors, twice putting coffee cups in with racks of silverware; still, it seemed an impossible pace. Tulip circled near. A man came to work beside Grace. He wore a red bandana and knew the job well. A half hour later, with the rush over and the man sliding off his gloves, Francine complained in English, "Even *here*, bosses do the least work they can manage." His blank look back made her simper with delight. Walter, Grace learned later, thin, curly bearded, quiet, a kitchen manager, in overall charge of the dishwasher, was if anything responsible, even irredeemably so.

With the outside press over and the tempo slower, Francine, like Trumpeter earlier, showed an interest in Grace. The plate scraper even wondered if she had been a subject of their chat. The boy handling clean racks couldn't for hygienic reasons touch dirty things; and the women, likewise, couldn't handle what was clean, so they were largely alone. Francine asked Grace what she had enjoyed thus far at Seeker.

"Yoga and fresh air, especially," said Grace. "Though I guess that, with food, these are the common denominators, anyway. I've had massage. But there's so much I don't know about... so many other things going on.... It's funny," she added, after a pause forced by loud clanking and spray, "but after two weeks, I feel I've been here two months, yet each day goes so quickly. And you... how long have you been here? What do you like?"

"I came for the season. I got here when I could in May and I've asked Tulip to let me help close the kitchen in October."

Grace grinned softly and cogitated, wondering if she should ask about the girl's eye, or college plans, or interests, or wait to hear what she said next. It sounded as if Francine planned to take the coming year off.

"Were you like us when you were our age?" the girl asked suddenly.

"Yes, I think so," said Grace, finding herself, surprisingly, with a lot to say. "My friends and I were uneasy, because we didn't fit in anywhere predictable, which I think is the same.... Whatever 'predictable' might mean. But I see two differences. What happened back then seemed to have a political side; we expected to improve society. And the kind of inner work Seeker aims at was just beginning. I never tried anything like these practices. Instead, perhaps, I tried to be an actress."

"Bending over in high heels and slacks for housewife commercials... ?"

Grace laughed, with enough force and surprise to make her slip and have to regain her balance on the rubber mat. "It came down to that, if you had the luck to be hired. We did voice work or commercials or we worked in restaurants or as temps; then we ran to rehearse avant-garde plays in basement theaters. I never got a voice-over or a commercial. And I think at least some of the plays we put on were pretty dreadful."

Racks ran through the dishwasher on a small conveyor belt and Francine, facing the belt, had usually shown Grace her wounded right profile. However, as most dinner dishes were now clean she began turning in a wider arc, to scan the machine's long shelf for utensils, pans, pots, and other cookware that needed washing. Each time Grace saw anew the girl's infected right eye, she winced at its raw inflammation.

Nor did Francine respond immediately. They labored; Grace felt her usual impatience at a stalled conversation. Yet before long, Francine said: "We did plays where I was in the spring."

"College plays? Did you act or make sets or what?"

"They were more skits than plays, without sets. I suppose I acted."

Francine, with her powder-blue headscarf, red eye, and soaked white apron, was surely enigmatic. The infection was made harder to look at by the sense it was a piling up of illnesses, an unfair burden. Without the infection, the girl's eyes burned with tension and condensed need. Lacking a dramatic entrée to her topic, Grace said what she felt she must: "Your eye must be uncomfortable. Have you seen the Seeker nurse or a doctor?"

"It's nothing," Francine answered with a shrug.

"But when did you get it?"

"Very recently; a week ago... "

Grace was barely able to keep from prefacing her next words with the fact of her being a mother. "You may need an antibiotic to get rid of it. The infection could also be contagious. Has a nurse here seen it?"

Grace, suddenly self-conscious, knew that anyone idly watching their work area would be puzzled, for now Francine moved nervously while she stood largely still. "It's really irrelevant," the girl said, perhaps confusing her English adjectives. "Thank you, though. I wash it with water and use an ointment a friend found at the beach here. And I'm treating it with chanting and other spiritual exercises."

Grace's resolve weakened as she heard these remarks. What ointment? Chanting? Had Grace uncovered or caused the girl's nervousness, which seemed to be on the rise. Still, an eye infection was a practical problem. And if "irrelevant" was not the best word... her problem was surely minor. "Maybe Quebec insurance isn't good here; if so, I can bring you in on my policy," she continued, lying in a minor act of charity. "We'd say you are my cousin, here on a visit. It won't cost any money. And I'd be glad to help you find a local doctor."

Francine finally stopped moving. She shifted her body to point it just past Grace's left shoulder, and turned her head to meet Grace's gaze. The infected eye hollow was now partly obscured. "Thank you, again," she said. "My 'college' dramatics last spring: well, I wasn't really still in school. Doctors saw our skits. They were psychiatrists, bastards who'd seen me enough before. Now I'm done with them and their awful Western drugs. There are other ways to heal."

14

Bowered Oration

Moments later, Francine asked Grace to scout the kitchen for further items to wash before ending her shift. Their exchange, Grace saw, which had almost become personal, was over. She hoped Francine, who plainly craved benign forms of attention, would not see her as someone to fear.

As Grace left the kitchen, she found that the long Seeker evening, divided from the sunset by a ridge, was starting its decline. Even to think ahead was to thrust the shady hour nearer midnight. She walked past the dining-hall, hoping to relax for a time in the kitchen garden. The plants, aided by benches and fine Adirondack chairs, made a meditative area of curls, angles, and scents. She smelled herbs and the fresh evening, antidotes for her damp, soured skin and clothes. The air was cool but still; she could almost wear a pullover. Someone spoke with force in the middle distance; applause followed. Ten people were in the garden, some reading; as she found an empty chair, she heard and glimpsed a crowd under the trees fifty yards further still.

Seeker at this hour was as busy as it could be: some guest workshops ran evening sessions; staff workshops were under way; a crafts studio as well as tennis and basketball courts, hiking paths, the bookstore, the sanctuary, and the café with its patio tables all were open; and there were scheduled and off-the-cuff performances. The garden dwellers were middle-aged or older, and Grace joined them in letting the tickle of senses cleanse her spirit. How funny, she thought, that it's the people aware of aging, life's ticking clock, who find resting happily to be as sweet a thing as they know. And then, doesn't that argue for "mindfulness," the strange word heard repeatedly here?

Two people had entered Grace's imagination. Both Moira Kathleen and Francine were troubled, in ways that she barely understood. She turned to watch a row of basil plants, already producing heartily in early July; and hoped not to get involved. She had limited energy. But was this so: as the saying went, "did she know her own strength?" And would problems brought her way by people in turmoil strengthen or weaken her? Having been tested the past year, she had to ask the question. It might also be true that most people here were deeply screwed-up inside.

She wondered: including me? Then she willed away that question and returned to the one of keeping safe in the face of other people's hardships.

The fresh air helped her to think. And, still feeling Willa's kick in the behind, she found this a good time and place to try to ruminate.

Both rest and action, she knew, could help to fortify her—such rest as being in this garden. But the idea of action was less clear. Seeker's creed said that for an act to fortify it must be mindful. If this meant seeing life's wonder, as she felt it must, then caring for Alicia had been a mindful act; as was raising Amos—getting nutrients down him each morning, for instance; as was letting one's imagination run free.

Yet, she wondered, what of activity that isn't mindful? Do I only distract myself when I play cards, jabber with friends, or watch TV? Is this true also for my work life, when I mostly drift outside myself? Are these regular activities of life, my life, just instances of absence, waste, time gone by without an effort to be present?

This had been a premise in Thoreau, she knew. Once, she had written a paper on it.

Okay then for dreamy Henry David, she thought; but say that half a lifetime and a hellish season later I flip the premise to ask what's wrong with being mindless? With or without a mindful attitude, each day points ahead. And rarely has a deeper awareness played a part in my habits, thoughts, or, maybe the big one, my ties with others. Could a desire to be mindful spring from its being so rarely satisfied? Which makes me wonder if the true distraction is *desire*? I ask from the midlife position of thinking we all deserve the best time we can have.

As, for instance, to distract myself, stop my worrying, I'll turn my gaze to the man in a green cap, sitting in an Adirondack chair near a row of tomato plants. I'll wonder what he thinks about.

I'm guess I'm new to the meditative prospect tried here, yes, and doubtful. But I also see how these thoughts about Moira Kathleen and Francine, a kind of mindfulness, help to build me up.

After a few minutes, the man in the cap rose and walked toward the café. Grace drifted past the garden toward the stage, which stood small and barely elevated in a grove of large-limbed hemlocks and oaks. A man spoke; thirty people sat in folding chairs and fifty stood or sat on the ground nearby. Some who stood—Trumpeter was among them, watching her approach—leaned against trees to avoid blocking the sight lines of others. Catching her eye, Trumpeter pointed at her, then to his wrist and breastbone. He repeated this signal. Grace saw that he wanted her to stay in the grove so they might talk when the presentation ended.

The speaker, in his sixties, had an angular face and white hair combed back from his temples. He wore khaki shorts with flap pockets and a maroon, long-sleeve pullover he had not tucked in. Grace, with her half-rural upbringing and her suburban present, amid which had been stuck a tantalizing decade of big-city life, noted his flair. His shirt hangs loose because the style suits him, she thought. She saw too that he had a regal bearing, as if he felt himself to be on a mission, and to have the crowd in the proverbial palm of his hand. Whatever he meant to say, a lot of practice had prepared him for this stage.

Someone left and Grace took the chair. She wanted a close place to judge what after all was partly a performance. The man's voice rose over a receptive silence; few in the audience would let their eyes leave the stage. But some who, seated on the ground, could easily drop their gazes, did so, as their fingers wove the grass, perhaps mirroring the run of their minds in response to what was said. Settling in, Grace saw passers by watching from adjacent paths—one path passing, a second approaching, the grove. She thought they must have been wondering if they should stop to listen.

It was 8:10 p.m., so the talk was probably just beginning.

"… can be no answers, now," the speaker said, his voice pitched to be enticing. "Rather, it's a time for questions. I may have more comments in the autumn; if so, I'll post them to my website.

"As some of you know, I was a founder here. I taught meditation during our first years, when we met in a drafty old hotel across the Hudson. The hotel was rich in history and fun to be at, even if we saw no charm in its *specific* history—that of helping the managerial classes to essentially rest and re-arm. I'm speaking, not without respect, of the business managers, doctors, and lawyers who brought their families for a week of water sports, card games, and steaks near the romantic river. Such parents raised some of you; some of you are such parents now. I ask that you keep this clichéd image of the business warrior, tanned and eager for steak, in your mind. My talk will turn back upon it soon.

"Back then, we had to teach hotel chefs vegetarian cooking, when we knew only what we'd seen in a few cookbooks. And these brave efforts had forgotten that people *like* to eat. For years, such books could be had for next to nothing, maybe their worth, at yard sales. We reached a crisis in our second year, when an angry chef threw out as trash the vegetarian stew he'd just made. He then fixed us ten dozen cold cheese sandwiches, which we ate happily with bumpy organic tomatoes—knowing only that lunch that day was late. The melee grew sillier as the hotel manager tried to fire his chef, who was refusing to cook for us again. We begged to save his job, but the next year brought our own chef. Three years later, we had our own kitchen.

"I return to these memories because my questions now take me back to our beginnings: to what was sought and left out... because all builders leave things out. Our business-manager fathers—nearly every man I was in school with, a dreary ratio the younger generations here may share—built a landscape of shopping malls and suburbs, but left out knowing much about themselves, their families, and, to be cryptic but quick, life outside TV. Thus our movement began as an escape from a dry culture—well, we saw it in those terms. So, a key to our creation story is its being rooted in dry soil. And, since many people here travel widely, including to deserts, I can add that the vegetation I think we resemble isn't hardy. Touring Arizona or Egypt, we see that many desert roots pull out easily. Life's often superb in these places, just not hardy.

"Thirsty, we moved toward water, which itself stands for spiritual renewal. The journey felt so fine that we ignored what we were leaving, our dry culture but also talk of its reform. Instead, we mined cultures we saw as more spiritual than our own, like India's, for ways to honor the 'souls' we now knew we had. We learned that soul was 'intangible,' and change came 'within.' Yet this new outlook recast our Western history, with its hundred million dead in recent wars, as both an ugly reminder and beside the point. It also recast our current choices, like whether or not to go on eating steak: putting them in a context of what we came to call 'individual spiritual development.'

"Our new outlook also seemed to flip some old maxims, like, 'an apple never falls far from its tree.' This could hardly apply to us—we, who'd been born in darkness but learned to open our eyes to the light.... "

The speaker paused and a quiet punctuated his challenge. Grace saw that she was about to hear an academy insider voice criticism. She felt chagrin, as if she intruded, for after two weeks she knew little about what Seeker tried to do. I take its gifts, she thought, its color and freshness, its milieu that brought Hans here to help me—but I don't join in. She saw nothing in the faces of the crowd to help her. She turned to the speaker and his imperious gaze.

This shows that, when I can, I avoid going deeper, she thought.

The speaker stared pensively.

"In recent years, here," he said, "I often meet the kids of friends, old enough now to be on staff. This reminder of time passing puts me in a retrospective mood and so, as I try to care *for* what I care *about*, on the lookout for assumptions that may do us harm. I'll raise three of them now; yet each fits in a story that must be told all the way through, I think, to make sense. Know that I at least *intend* to be quick.

"I've already sketched the story's first chapters. Chapter one tells how our movement came alive in a desert, chapter two how thirst led us to leave the desert behind. Chapters three and four, which get us to the middle of the story, speak to how, as we learned to look inward, we grew convinced that we could will the world to do the same—and to how, when the world merely shrugged at our suggestions, we felt trapped.

"Chapter five, the first I'll take time with, tells how, ignored, we turned more inward. This gets us back to our maxim that an apple falls near its tree and to a first assumption I'll challenge, that we can live outside society—can escape, I mean, being the fated apple. Those who defend this assumption say that our turn inward shows we can and even did escape—we fell far from the tree, proving the proverb false. Our society's crimes drove us away, they argue, and what matters now is the result: we were blown far from the tree. The clean-break paradigm that this supports is one many people here believe in. Forget the past, it says, and find new ways to live. In fact, I'm called a leader of the clean-break party, because my work explores the inward life—a caring more for meditative awareness than for having more things.

"Still, tonight I mean to test the paradigm, so I'll ask a question I rarely hear. Back home, what has changed? At the community center and mall, yoga, tai chi, and meditation have replaced some less-mindful activities—what I only partly slander by calling our endless competitive sports. But we remain business managers, living lives that business defines. Even those of us with non-business jobs are shaped by what we make and buy: we enact roles the system gives its middle class. If we buy with more care, do we buy less? What choice is there? And does personal choice even matter? Ditto for our roles as producers.

"These questions of course return us to our dry, frantic culture and its history, which we so want to forget."

Grace, sensing a pause, wondered if the people here really did try to hide from everyday reality. I can't see how, she mused. It visits me like an ocean tide.

Wishing she at least knew the speaker's name, she saw him clown with people seated near the stage. He held out a hand and pulled back its digits one at a time, signifying the five covered chapters. He smiled delicately; then, with an expressionless stare, he looked again out at his audience.

"A story told in eight chapters," he went on, "should shift course by chapter six and begin a march to its end. My story does this, too. We've learned already that we were thirsty and went looking for water; that, finding it, we tried to lead the world to it but were ignored; and that some of us ignore the world in return. So far, we've described what we view as a spiritual quest, but now, right on time, comes a shift. In chapter six, our story, exposing a thorny conflict, raises the problem of *justice*.

"In this chapter, we seem less heroic. Because we find that, while we turn our backs on society, we assume a right to its justice. Because while we, quite normally, dislike assault, theft, and fraud, we feel protected enough by the society we seem to scorn to say that its concerns over justice only hinder our spiritual work. We see our own right to it as both a given and beside the point. Yet, here I'll suggest—taking us to chapter seven—that what is called 'spiritual work' changes with time. Think of Moses, cowering on Sinai as he awaited Yahweh's laws, or of the vengeful royals in Mycenae, being persuaded by the goddess Athena to stop killing one another.

"Here, then, is a second worrisome assumption I'll challenge: that pursuing justice isn't part of our spiritual quest. And if we combine the assumptions—that we can ignore our society, but expect its just treatment—they seem even more worrisome. Actually, I'll add a third doubtful assumption, one I'd missed before: that we are like a desert bloom in not being hardy."

Trying to keep up, Grace felt blocked by the earlier phrase, "party of the clean break." Its hard consonants kept repeating in her mind.

Does he call holistic healing types wrong to think they can live outside society? she wondered silently. I lack the context to make sense of this. She considered how she felt now as her better students did when they battled a play like *Macbeth*, which was hard for being clear—because the new light it cast was startling.

Even when one can choose freely, she thought, it's often easier to not let such a disrupting light shine.

"Still," continued the speaker, who Grace saw as receding with the daylight, "even if we doubt our ability to be spiritual in our suburbs, where the scent of grilling meat fills the air on pleasant evenings, it may still be true that most of us here, being of the right class and race, can take justice for granted. And here our clean-breakers speak up, pointing out that, with the world so rotten, we serve everyone's purpose by following our purely spiritual direction.

"And yet, I'll argue, the problem gets more complex as 'justice' is redefined in our time as 'social justice.' We see the poor through the media and inherit even more of them as our technologies closes global distances. Can we also turn away from them?

"Well," the speaker said, his voice rising to a climax, "maybe we can and even must ignore social justice. I'll at least address 'can' by asking, how much of this work Seeker, with its mission to heal, takes on? The question is rhetorical, as I run with the old-timers here, with management, and I know that justice is rarely addressed. My friends voice regret and say it comes down to this not being a problem the community will pay for, since it doesn't face it directly.

"So, we can ignore justice; again, some say we must. And I'll clarify that by 'we' I mean our *community*, not its managers. My friends will get into heaven, as not even the gods punish good managers for mixed results. It is only as community *members* that they may be in the same serious position as the rest of us.

"To close, I'll restate the assumptions that worry me. One says we can ignore society, a second that we can ignore its justice, a third that we aren't hardy—and so would risk a lot to test ourselves in a fight that was somewhat for others.

"Now I mean to listen. I hope I've been provoking; hungry, let's break some proverbial eggs. And to repeat: in the fall, when my book on these questions is finished, I'll add a posting to my website."

There was quiet, and like others nearby, Grace gasped. What was this place, this patch of an already-fabled river valley that rallied such risk taking? And who were these people? It was hard to keep this stuff of opposition in one's head! The speaker was a hero! Too bad Willa was at work: these were her concerns. And Grace had questions for herself. Why didn't she regularly feel this unease? And how had she developed a mostly blind eye over the years to the world's problems?

The crowd's stir implied a general unease; a first comment voiced dismay. "Many of us," said a red-haired woman holding a walking stick, "use what energy we have to get through our days. I'll be honest: unless I'm immersed in a cause, social justice or just finding my way out from under things, I find it hard to know what to do. Life pushes back with a lot of mayhem and confusion."

Someone who, red hair and all, was nearly the woman's twin said from a chair that social justice didn't only concern poverty: they all were victims. Cleaning the polluted world her children would inherit was equally important to her.

Turning back to the speaker, Grace saw, serendipity of red-haired women, Sophie seated pensively on the grass. She wore a thin sweater, loose and brown as mud; she seemed practiced in using stratagems of modesty to damper her sensual glow.

The speaker listened. A man—it was Trumpeter—stepped away from a tree and took some steps toward the stage. He wore a red staff shirt given out some earlier year. "Ken," he said with ardor, "justice gets tied up in politics, which kills the spirit. Our work sits above what politics can understand." His eyes looked raw even in the twilight. He walked further forward. Ken seemed set to reply, but another man rose and began to speak. For the first time since Grace had begun to watch him, Ken showed surprise.

Like others there, the man wore an open-neck shirt. "Excuse me," he said, "but you're not the first person to relate justice to the spirit. And your boasts reflect a larger elitism here—not among attendees, but among those managers and teachers who are your friends."

Kicked further alert, Grace thought: this flows too fast. Elitism, social justice, spirituality... do people talk to or past each other? I can't possibly keep up.

The man went on: "In two days here, I've met lots of people from the social justice trenches: social workers like me but also teachers, nurses and... well, lots of teachers. So I find it odd to hear some guru discuss this as if he'd invented it, when so many of us fight for it every day.

"When I got my first Seeker catalog, I saw that justice was largely ignored. This left me wondering what sort of people I'd meet here. Would they say politics killed the spirit? But, again, many are like me. So maybe it's the Seeker's managers who shut these important issues out."

"No!" sang a woman in back. "Seeker is for us—the socially aware. But I feel we're weaker, more beaten down and tired than we admit. And we are losing ground. What we seek here is the strength to go on."

"The man up front is uninformed," said a man also in the rear, "if he thinks our daily struggles matter much on the spiritual plane."

The crowd quieted before the rough terrain. Trumpeter seemed ready to speak, but then drew in like a turtle. Grace's thoughts swung among opposing views; she felt chagrin at how easily the smooth-talking Ken had impressed her. The last speaker save one now seemed to have it right: those who fight the world's cruelties most need places like the academy. As to the last speaker's notion of a "spiritual plane," she had felt it soar over her head.

Ken, smiling, magisterial and now, to Grace, egotistic, proclaimed the evening ended, in a fine new state of disarray. So, that was it. Grace rose with the others and shook away her stiffness. She wondered: has Trumpeter left? Is his idea really to stay in his reptilian shell? Does he miss the suburban echo? He's a child made raw by his feelings. Grace walked back to Sophie, who stayed on the ground. Trumpeter, back near his tree, talking to someone, twice nodded her way.

Sophie watched her draw near. "It's hard," the young woman said, and repeated: "It's quite complicated and hard." She sat on a green plastic tarp. Joining her, Grace poked a finger inside a metal eyelet near where two edges met. After the patter about soul and society, she wanted to touch something physical; this felt like a genie's ring. Sophie must have had a similar need, as she ran a hand over the slick, shiny material nearest her knees. "What did you think?"

"A lot of things. Mainly, that it's hard to be reminded of all I ignore. I know about the poor, justice, pollution… all of it; yet I forget what I know. Life's a cheat, I guess, in that when the ugliness isn't in our face we find ways to be comfortable. Usually, others have to pay."

"The hard work is to be attentive. I was thinking that, too."

"I came by chance and don't know the speaker. What can you tell me?"

"Oh, a lot!" said Sophie, with a grin. "Even his marketing spiel. After all, my work here is selling workshops. Ken Samuel wrote a book about marriage a few years ago that sold a hundred thousand copies; a new book, about a year spent living 'mindfully' on an Alaskan fishing boat, is also a best seller. He's led workshops in eleven countries and comes here every year. This week here he's 'spiritualist-in-residence'; the workshop he ran ended yesterday."

Their talk began to stray onto simpler topics. Grace learned that Sophie had gone to the city for the weekend to attended a service in a Hasidic synagogue and another in a cathedral. Grace spoke of massage and her kitchen misadventure. They noted how Ken would speak Saturday about his Alaska year. Then the talk grew subdued; its gazes and speech tones fell. Both women seemed reluctant to forget "justice" and fly off on a garrulous breeze—to again, Grace thought, show human nature in its sad, take-the-easy-way-out light.

Trumpeter neared, and they looked up. He kept standing; Grace saw that he was courteous to Sophie. He would court her if he could, and Sophie, who did not know he meant to speak with Grace, may have thought she was being courted now. Grace saw his bit of luck that she and Sophie were friends. Old grandmother, she told herself, give the boy a hand.

"Did you hear about my dining-hall debacle?" she asked him. "Because of me, the kitchen ran out of fruit soup before the food lines closed. I'm not sure Tulip will want me there again."

Trumpeter again was nervous. He stood with a wintry grin and maybe an idea of how the interaction might proceed, but faltered when Grace mentioned the dining-hall. Thus, he didn't respond to her cue or greet either woman. Looking at him, Sophie asked, softly, if he planned to fight a duel with the man who had argued against his point of view, or perhaps with them. This made him pale and step sideways; then he faced Grace. "Your Staten Island friend was being wild at the pond," he told her, in a murky way that made both women wince.

Anxious people, Grace knew, often excel at anticipation, and when given a clue to a problem can turn their minds in wonderful instant circles. She'd had her own sad, recent practice at this kind of behavior but knew she usually was less frantic. So it took her some time to see that Trumpeter was asking that she remember something. She wondered why he had mentioned Staten Island. Then she saw images of buggy light, electric and redundant, in a sticky toilet on a hot day, and of Moira Kathleen, with her dull skin, nerves, and despair. Had the scared woman stayed at the pond and nearby studio area all these hours?

A second puzzle surfaced and she asked how he had known to tell *her;* asking, she re-experienced her sense of the woman's fear. Trumpeter told them—Sophie listened—that Hans was with Moira Kathleen even now.

"I think he met her soon after you did," he said, addressing Grace but often looking away, "when she walked to the beach and he went there for a book he had left. At loose ends, she went to his workshop. When it ended, they talked more and he got food from the dining-hall, which they ate in his workshop studio. I walked by and got involved. Then we took a service road and a path through the woods to reach the pond without being spotted by her classmates. I felt she might break down and brought up seeing the nurse, but Moira Kathleen asked me to find you. She said you were a friend from her generation who would understand."

Trumpeter, grounded by a story he had to tell, was less officious and gentler. Sophie asked to come along, and Grace said she had been kind for only a short time to Moira Kathleen and felt mostly a stranger to her. But sympathy came easily at Seeker; so, not intimate themselves, they walked out of the grove and on to the pond in dusky darkness. On their way, they spoke of the warm night and of being lost. Sophie, perhaps in response to the blights raised by Ken Samuels, found and held a pinecone. Once, she stopped their way forward to slip under a conifer tree's black-green bowers and touch its trunk. Grace, guessing at holistic concepts, thought this might be "mystical behavior," as it sought safety in nature's touch. Trumpeter said little, but when the path made them walk single file he went between them, rather than first or last; he was, Grace sensed, trying to live in this particular moment, without knowing he was safe.

He at least knows to try, she thought. I fear that among the men I know even this much openness is usually lost. I lament this in the name of my son.

These last days, she thought, I've begun to come back to myself.

15

On and Around the Teeterboard

They turned onto the forested pond path and saw that, in the deeper darkness, they would have to map the shoreline more by memory than by what eyesight revealed. Sophie stopped and touched Trumpeter's shoulder. "I sometimes fear politics, too," she said. "I felt this the most visiting my brother in Guatemala. As much as their plight, it was my own fear of being used up. It's sad to say, but social activism can wear you out. Yet the poor need political support, not our sympathy. We must almost choose to put their need to be healed ahead of ours."

Trumpeter said nothing and looked unsettled. Grace wondered if he was afraid to reveal himself. Then why had he said much that same thing in a crowd? He might also have a lot to say, or say to Sophie, but be unable to turn on the tap. Sophie herself, adding to her rueful words, had had a hitch in her voice.

Her new friend, Grace noted, seemed also to believe that "justice" meant social justice, and "politics" meant helping the poor.

Hans and Moira Kathleen sat near the water on a child's seesaw. He was in the air and she near the ground, with her fingers in sand and her ankles crossed over the grip handle of the slanted board.

"Good evening," said Hans, in an accent that seemed more harshly pronounced in the night air. "Was Ken Samuel provoking? Sophie. Moira Kathleen, here's Sophie from Copenhagen. She's an avid seeker; but as the sun burns her skin, she seems to only go out at night."

Reaching down, Grace touched the hair of Moira Kathleen, who smiled awkwardly. Hans beckoned Grace over and similarly touched her hair.

"Then I salute Dionysus, god of midnight and wine," said Sophie, masking her native Nordic musicality to sound deadpan and wry.

"I love that," said Moira Kathleen. "It's so creative."

"To me it's thirst-making," said Grace, adding, "swell seesaw."

"Oh," said Sophie. "I'd heard the English word is 'teeterboard.'"

"And I, 'teeter-totter,'" said Hans.

"*Teetering...* that fits *my* life pretty well," said Moira Kathleen.

"We've done massage," said Hans, "and talked about how what we want isn't always what we really need. I told Moira Kathleen what I'd been doing until just a few years ago."

"European tennis star, or wannabe," said his friend Sophie.

"Yes—and how what I thought I should want came to hide my true needs. Family, friends—many people, including me, thought I'd be more successful than I was. Excitement and pride drove me, even as I more and more sensed that I was living the wrong life."

"You won by not qualifying, by losing," affirmed Trumpeter, who seemed to know the story.

"I lost my professional ranking and told my family and then left, the first time, for Thailand."

However, he added, he had left the economic track while still young enough to ignore the financial consequences. "For instance," he told them, "I didn't mind giving up my jazzy car." Moira Kathleen, in their conversation, had educed this aspect of his decision by saying that she had felt similarly secure—until, in her middle thirties, she began to see that the life she had, its habits and relationships, might be all she would ever know. No miracle waited beyond the horizon. She realized then that her neighbors and also the strangers she came upon would view their lives in similar ways. This led her to understand the value of luck.

The unhappy woman began to speak, in her manner that asked hearers to also take care of her. Grace, with insights boiled up from her acting years, saw how this had to do with self-protection. Moira

Kathleen, with her nervous words and movements, seemed to be fending something off.

Everyone there knew the central fact of her being in a crisis, which she faced with self-derision. Her raw laughter about having hidden in the woods made the others want to protect her, but also, in fact, to escape.

Rawness and reluctance illuminate the fear, thought Grace.

"Those hours I spent on the hill above the workshop felt strangely liberating," Moira Kathleen said at one point. "My old lyrics moved me and my imagination came back. I even sang from the heart as I think I did long ago. But when I'd look down at the studio or hear chords coming out its windows, I'd start to sneer at myself again."

Grace began to see how Moira Kathleen would tend to lean back on her crutches. One crutch was a lost dream of being a songwriter—the other, a set of beliefs that seemed to tell her not how to fit into life, but that fitting in was possible.

For years, she told them, she had taken classes at the New Meanings Institute, in Tribeca. "It's a feeder organization for Seeker, where its founder teaches every summer," she said. "But the work it does relates only to spiritual worldviews. It doesn't get into the kinds of experiential things that go on here."

In an irked tone that startled Grace, Hans said that he found Seeker *too* caught up in spiritual worldviews, adding, "I mean, in philosophies of life based on beliefs in higher powers. In fact, we almost seem to teach them all. That we do became clear to me last week, as I again browsed the 110-page catalog. I saw that workshops were offered on Islamic Sufism, Jewish Cabala, Christian mysticism and African voodoo. And there were others, too—on Native American religions, on astrology, on Buddhism and other Asian creeds."

After browsing the catalog once, feeling curious, he had, he said, begun again—looking now for workshops that drew lessons from these beliefs. "New Age teachers," he told them, "like to uncover lost teachings in different traditions—or, more oddly, from within their own imaginations. They then draw on these teachings, to create 'wisdom' books and workshops around practical subjects such as aging, beauty, romance, and self-discovery.

"What's more," he continued with rising irritation, "some teachings further intellectualize the search by taking as their concern the soul, the human organ most prone to mental fancy. They project a realm of being they call 'spirit world,' which most of us can only imagine. Then they tie our well-being in this world to the journeys our souls take in the spirit world—journeys that can range across past, present, and future.

"Finally, they tell *us*—whatever, in fact, *we* are, perhaps the flesh that these souls wrap themselves in—that we have the power to go on these journeys in our minds."

"Laid out that way, it's funny," said Grace. "It suggests we all want to leap out of our heads. And, Moira Kathleen, if you feel boxed in hearing this, all I can say is: welcome to the party!"

The sliver moon and some stars were out; they could almost read each other's faces. Grace felt Trumpeter's scowl. You may be right, she mused. Hours before, she had witnessed Moira Kathleen's fear. Now she was joking in her presence about these daunting, even menacing subjects.

"I miss your meaning," said Moira Kathleen. "Spiritual worldviews put us in touch with our higher powers. This brings out the true selves that our materialist culture tries to kill."

"I agree," said Trumpeter. "They get us past the Western vanity that poisons spirit and matter alike. The West makes medicine from tree bark, a practice it stole from shamans, and then has the nerve to think it alone has all the answers."

"These worldviews show us life in mystical, holistic terms," Moira Kathleen affirmed.

Unsure what these words meant, Grace was again lost; she also saw an incongruity. Yes, she'd been glib, but the philosophical salad Hans spoke of and the ache it announced *were* funny. If I laugh, she wondered, is it from being so caught up in my little life—my bigger-than-I-can-handle life, too—that I don't remember what I've lost?

When I repeat all this back home, won't Betsy fall over laughing?

Hans, on the teeterboard with his feet in the sand, stirred things up again. "In a crucial way, these spiritual worldviews seem both like each other and like their shared enemy, materialism," he said. Grace was surprised by his willingness to argue—and surprised again by Sophie's subsequent interruption of him in mid-thought.

"With a good talk at hand," said Sophie, "we might adopt the old trick of using a stick or some other token to let people speak uninterrupted. The token can pass among us in any order we choose." She added, "I sometimes feel that conversations here tend to fall apart, with so much being talked about and so little that is sure."

Her suggestion led to a silence. In a way, Grace saw, Sophie only sought to emulate the helper role a teacher played in a classroom. On the rare day a class of hers was drawn into a discussion, Grace would quiet down and listen. Yet discussions between adults usually flowed more freely—even if in practice this meant that the many motives and points of view that people had made them talk *at* rather than *to* one another, making speech an element of force.

Yet, being adults, those at the pond took this metamorphosis for granted. Thus Sophie's against-the-grain suggestion seemed odd.

Still, no one contested it. They poked around in the inky air for a stick. Hans found one first and leaned it against the seesaw; sensing it would slip to the ground, he took hold of it again.

Grace, Sophie, and then Trumpeter, drew nearer the teeterboard.

"You'd been saying that all worldviews were alike," said Sophie.

With a low laugh, Hans regained his point. "I'd begun to say that they share something big, a role each one takes as explainer. Now, it's true that I bring a bias—that I root my life in feeling, especially touch, which was my bridge from tennis to massage. Still, browsing the workshops I saw how they all give explanations. 'Reading the Sacred Octagon,' 'The Heart's Precepts,' 'Four Ways up the Mountain': dozens of such workshops are in the catalog."

"Spiritual wisdom opens us to higher powers," said Moira Kathleen, somewhat repeating herself. "It provides mental and physical as well as emotional tools, which all must be explained."

Too late, she looked across the board at Hans, who held the token.

In the darkness they saw Hans shift position, to show that he now found the teeterboard an awkward roost—given the grown-up themes, that he and Moira Kathleen should probably stop their children's game. She stood slowly, with the board under her lean bottom; then, he in shorts and she in her jeans from the morning, both stepped away. Hans stayed near. Moira Kathleen drifted a few yards away.

Sophie retrieved the stick. "Moira Kathleen," she said, in a gently rhetorical tone, "I also have a spiritual ache, which I'm just learning to talk about. So, I'll ask what you mean by 'mysticism' and by 'higher powers.' Or not just you: I wonder what these terms mean to others."

They waited for her to go on. Moira Kathleen was quiet. Sophie pivoted the stick, keeping an end in the sand. "I may've been wrong about our token," she said. "I'd meant it to stand for a sense of community. But we may not yet know enough about each other or what we actually want to talk about for that."

Her having said this might help us to know ourselves, Grace thought.

"Maybe I can contribute by saying why I'm here," added Sophie.

Waving a hand, Grace said, "Sophie." With a grin Grace could see in the darkness, Sophie, interrupted, handed over the stick.

"I know I'm beyond my depth here," said Grace. "I can't in any real way define 'mysticism' or 'worldview'; the words don't evoke things I often think about. But I'm starting to care—if more about the speakers than what the say. Or maybe it's that people must have meaning for me first. With help from Hans, I recently swam up out of a personal numbness. Since then, I've often felt startled by what I see and hear."

"Startled good or startled bad?" asked Trumpeter.

"Well, both. Yet, in either case I don't know why. But I'm drawn to the sincerity, which leads me to a request that came to mind when Sophie brought up 'community.' As we pass the stick and I guess philosophize, I'd also like to hear what brought people here."

"I come," said Trumpeter, "to escape our brainwashed society and to connect more with the universe."

"We must all come mostly for those reasons," said Hans. "This isn't a soccer camp."

Grace reminded Hans that she had come for different reasons.

"But your friends felt the academy's practices could help you. And these practices all reflect the seeking after deeper connections."

"Grace, I think I get your point," said Moira Kathleen. "Once you know what people care about, the things they say seem more real."

"That perspective makes too much of the self," said Trumpeter.

"But it's a fair place to start from," said Sophie. "So I'll take up that challenge as I go first." She got back the token from Grace.

"In Denmark," Sophie continued, "I've finished a year of Ph.D. work in public policy. I may quit, but I'd stay if I felt the work mattered. At twenty-four, I want to believe that the world I live in can become better. I don't want to think that constant flux is all there is.

"I was here last July and returned for this summer. I'm learning if I have the knack to be a healer. And so for weeks I've pushed past my doubts that a spiritual presence even exists. This has led to wonderful experiences, various meditations, and I'll be here six weeks more. But a new question has come up, nearly the opposite of those that brought me here. I sense something ominous behind our search for spiritual connections. And the only way I see to even find out what I mean is to begin to doubt again and try to think the question through."

Grace had kept an eye on Moira Kathleen, fearing the wispy woman had been left behind. Slow to react, Grace now saw why Trumpeter had scowled at her. Moira Kathleen's bred-in-the-bone problems, a likely barren life and fears that happiness had passed her by, might be lost in this philosophical debate. It's another case, Grace thought, of how words lose focus, obscure levels, slide from the mark. Shoreline shadows kept her from seeing the face of this woman, who might not but also might like what was being said. I may be wrong, Grace mused. She's spoken up, and may want this ruminating to continue.

Moira Kathleen did, in fact, then make what Grace took to be a late reply to Sophie. "I think wisdom, the explaining we need, comes finally through intuition, which only comes if we let go," she said. "When we fall, the gift of intuition rises up to meet us. But we rarely let go, as we get tangled up in things." She grew louder as she echoed what Grace felt must be a precept of the Tribeca institute.

"Cars, computers, and the like," said Moira Kathleen, "distract us from inner meaning. By doing spiritual exercises, we get in touch with what really matters."

Grace snuck a glance at Trumpeter. She wanted to speak but had nothing to say. Where did she stand in this parley, with its pleading sense and its mood that seemed anxious for exposure and yet hard put to defend itself? Here again were the themes of exposure and protection. They hadn't in ages mattered to her; then Alicia got sick. Trumpeter and the others made Grace think of not herself but of her niece and her son. Alicia could plead now; and the sensitive Amos, as he matured in the next few years, might come to ask what truly mattered in life.

Hans had backed away enough to face them all. "I too find intuition a gift, one our culture hides from us," he told Moira Kathleen. "But I see it as a feeling, first, and it's in regard to my capacity to feel that I distrust philosophies. Buddhism, Hinduism, materialism: they all work to program the mind."

"You have it wrong," said Trumpeter.

"I may, T," replied Hans. "Massage therapists can be quiet types, and I'm often quieted by uncertainty. Yet, here, around the teeterboard, is a chance to see how far words can take me—to try to say what led this massage therapist to where he is now in his life.

"I'd first say that I was more pushed than led. And it wasn't my failure on the tennis court; that only took me from one set of habits to another. Remember, I studied philosophy. Like massage, philosophy and tennis are disciplines. I know that I'll always look for guidance.

"So, I'm prone to have what some call a compulsive character; but it's just this, together with a lesson I once learned, that makes me wary of explanations. I'll get to the lesson after I first say a bit about my uncertainty."

He builds his phrases like his yoga poses, thought Grace. She listened in an attentive if not surely comprehending way.

"Practicing touch," Hans went on, "teaches me to feel for the core, and a core personal truth is that I only really trust myself to work on practicalities. I can read an anatomy chart, I mean; facing a mirror, though, I often don't know where as a person I begin. I lack the words but fear also that beneath words it's all a muddle. And so, with regard to my self-confidence, I compare badly with the frogs we hear croaking nearby.

"I know this is a problem of the mind, of lacking good explanations, because when I involve my body I get guidance from my senses. Then I often find my way to intuitions—I mean, to finding relationships in life that I don't have to try to have explained.

"I sweat a lot out, and try to limit and grasp what comes in."

He grew silent, but Grace knew he would soon begin again.

"Much of this is obscure," Hans said. "As I find obscure much of what I hear others say. Which returns me to the lesson about materialism I was a long time learning. It's a lesson that others may have learned.

"To begin what is finally a fable, I see myself as a child, being passed, like something made in a factory, from spelling and counting on to science. It was just what the old knew to teach when I was young, I know that now, but no one ever said to me: 'Hans, before your mind fills up, gather some perspective. Learn that you have choices that lead elsewhere than to money and to things. Get the story's sense and when you have it, write a response, adding one word each day when you wake up.'

"But this context was never laid out; and now, as I practice yoga and massage in this careful way, I feel my old lessons stripping off of me like varnish. Explanations, about what moves us, feeds us, and holds us in place, drift down for later sweeping up. And as I'm the one being stripped, it hurts a lot.

"Still, such pain can be instructive, and it's my sense of being misled by teachers, carried by a mule that had lost its way, that makes me wary of holistic worldviews. I prefer my lessons to be small ones, gained, whenever possible, as I've said, with my hands."

"With respect, you miss the meaning," said Moira Kathleen in a low voice. "What you call 'holistic explanations' grow from our faith that we're included in a mystical union. Besides, doesn't your healing touch point to that union, too?"

Like Trumpeter, thought Grace, Moira Kathleen doesn't like to be challenged. Both seem to first look for signs of danger… I sort of follow this. Though I couldn't repeat what's been said or pass a vocabulary test. Who here could? And I don't know if what I'm hearing is truly intelligent or insightful.

How many similar discussions are going on right now at the academy?

"Moira Kathleen, I only voice my concern," replied Hans. "Which is that people poor in perspective and therefore simple are being varnished by theories. And yes, I think we are simple! In fact, that's a key. If we know there's not much we understand, well, we bear a heavy load, we may be trapped in many ways, but at heart we are simple."

"By 'simple,' I trust you don't mean *stupid*?" asked Trumpeter.

Hans grew quiet. In the darkness, Grace saw his loose frame, surely a benefit of yoga, and guessed that he didn't see people around him as stupid. She also knew him to be kind. "I think," she said, "that by saying 'simple' Hans is rather throwing us all a compliment."

"As do I," said Sophie. "He's saying we feel our confusion and lack of confidence. And that we're no longer comfortable in our class: the middle class that centuries of artists have beaten over the head."

"Oh, right!" said Trumpeter scornfully. "My affluent parents have lots more money than their parents did. Having more, *they do more damage*. And my time in business showed me that my generation, once it takes over, will make it all even worse."

Yes, he's in his mid-twenties, reflected Grace, and so must have done something beyond college by now. But he seems so insistently a non-participant.

Eyeing Moira Kathleen, she saw that, while quiet, the woman stayed taut. She might also be cold in her thin blouse. Grace wondered again if this plunge into ideas further estranged or interested her. Did she like the game?

As if raising sail under cover of darkness, Trumpeter now spoke of himself. Grace, pleasantly surprised, felt this might be his shy way to get to Sophie. "I've also scraped off my schooling like dead skin," he began. He then told a story more eventful than what Grace had guessed. He had gone to two prep schools, a public high school, a state university, and a Jesuit college. Twice he had been expelled after arrests for selling hallucinogens and marijuana. "I guess I sucked at it," he added in a sheepish tone. His third arrest, in the Jesuit student center, led a judge to offer a deal. Since, while loathing success, he was good with technology, he could for three years either work or go to jail. "I made two courtroom pledges. One was to take a job—the other, to myself, was to take drugs every Sunday for three years." He kept both promises. "I left Michigan for California and work with an ambitious company. After a promotion I often traveled. Life was unreal but on Sundays, even in hotel rooms, I was myself. I had partners at first, but the last year I hallucinated alone."

On doing his time, Trumpeter, at a celebratory dinner with his boss, once the wine was uncorked, turned down a third promotion and quit without notice. He began to follow a spiritual path centered in mind-bending drugs, and had been on it, living off savings, for four years. "I read Eastern and aboriginal writings and take workshops from profoundly spiritual people. I know beyond the report of my senses that I sometimes see God when I trip."

His way to live in Hans's deluded world, he added, was to turn away from it, as Ken Samuels had mistakenly warned against. He worked the Seeker schedule and wintered at retreats in warm places.

"You must stop listening to the noise," he told them. "When you do, you find the sweetness. Materialism threatens us by denying the spiritual presence, not by being seductive. But the spirit laughs back. Soon a shift will come to the Aquarian Age. The materialist West will war against itself and maybe destroy itself."

"Do you believe this?" asked Grace, referring especially but not only to his final point.

"I almost could," said Moira Kathleen.

"Hans generalizes too much," said Trumpeter. "What we were taught in childhood was evil, as he says. But that doesn't make all explanations evil. Some come directly from the godhead."

Still, for Trumpeter evil remained powerful and near. It even corrupted the academy. "In the end, I respect your choice," he said to Hans. "Answers *must* be private and small. Received wisdom only takes us part way. And institutions rot; think of the rot here. Money pours in and the talk turns illusory, to personal health and happiness and even to politics. I don't see myself coming back to Seeker next year."

"Where *can* you see yourself being?" asked Sophie.

"In his car!" exclaimed Grace, unwisely. She had felt a sudden fear on his behalf. "Oh! Pardon me! I was as much thinking about myself."

Grace felt too mortified to gauge how the others, even Trumpeter, were reacting to her gaffe. Oddly, she felt the tap of a ruler on her wrist. She looked down at the token, which Sophie wanted her to take.

This appeal was gentle but prompt. "Now is a fine time for you to answer your own question," she said. "Why are *you* here?"

Grace felt caught; everyone there knew parts of her story, and she didn't want to include in her defense Alicia's illness, or the fear and grief of other families she had been led to see. So, doing her best, she was honest yet brief. No one spoke when she was done.

"I guess I came for a workshop on managing sadness," she added in due course, "and stayed hoping its remedies would work. Which begs a further question of why, now, I wouldn't at all want to leave."

Her thoughts whirled and wouldn't settle. A startling breeze pitched across the pond from the east, where she faced. She sought a summing-up she could use.

"I'd thought just before," she said, "that what goes on here seems so earnest but also brittle… the speaker in the hemlock grove touched on the brittleness earlier tonight. I'd also wondered if my pimple-faced son might find his way here in a few more years… I'm away from my usual duties, yet being here somehow knocks back at the door of my maternal feelings."

"There are a hundred other things I'd almost like to say."

She heard her words echo, and waited. Having embarrassed Trumpeter, she owed him this chance. Then with a nervous hail she gave the token back to Sophie.

Hans observed softly: "We're all of us kept here by those hundred things we're not yet ready to say."

"It's wild here, like a kitchen at a cooking school," agreed Sophie. She upped the gently ironic tone in her voice. "Most dishes, we aren't near being ready to cook; among those we try, we regularly mess up. It's enough just to get a sense of the ingredients… I think that, not knowing each other well, that's all we've been given tonight: brief glimpses of some interesting ingredients."

"What big problem do you sense?" asked Trumpeter with some defiance.

Grace felt Sophie move into a state of quiet fermentation. It was hard to know the nature of Trumpeter's challenge.

"Winding down as we seem to be," declared Sophie, "that's kind of a big dish to get in the oven. But I'll say something—I'll at least hint at what the dish's flavor might be.

"A common theme tonight has been our culture's destructiveness. Hans takes the extreme of fearing his thoughts because society plays so large a role in shaping them. I don't go that far; nor am I drawn to Trumpeter's promise of apocalypse—even if it comes, it is fantasy now. I'm more tentative; I also lack the route into the spiritual realm he says he has with drugs. I can only try to go deeper.

"And again, as I explore non-rational healing methods—better, possibly, to call them nonscientific methods—I sometimes fall back on my habits of reasoned reflection. I do that now, as I consider the many uncertainties that make us afraid.

"Forgive my awkwardness. Responsibility is a hard theme." Sophie went quiet again. "Well, you know," she said in time, "I now, like Grace, feel silenced by a lot that I'm unready to say."

Moira Kathleen had something to add. "When you know Western music," she blurted out, "our destructiveness hurts even more."

On this down note, the conversation ended. Sophie inhaled sadly. "In no way would a beer be destructive," said a tired Grace. Sophie patted her knee. Trumpeter stood, and Moira Kathleen backed a few barefoot yards into the pond. The air was dark, with the sliver-moon not yet up. They had now, Grace thought, to act as a group—which might make demands other than those made by their wild conversation.

Buccaneering Sophie; heedful Hans; hidden Trumpeter; mysterious Monk; embattled Moira Kathleen; wild Francine; Willa the Wiking; a recovering Grace Hudson, whom the river alone couldn't cure... and loopy Deb Gold, soon to return.... There was, Grace thought, a fine passion among the people here.

"Moira Kathleen," said Trumpeter, "you helped to begin this. We take on the big questions here." Then his scornful mood changed as he saw the fact and humor in what he had said. Grace saw his body relax and his expression, just barely readable, fall back into a grin.

"We try to help," added Hans. "We'd meant to be a sounding

board."

Moira Kathleen, backed up further, was posted in the pond, with her arms crossed and her pant legs pulled above her calves. Hans added: "We aren't teachers. At best we can say, as Grace did earlier, that like you we are trying to figure it all out."

"Despite my flip-out, I think I like it here," said Moira Kathleen.

Grace echoed her words. "Tonight gave me a better sense of what goes on," she said. "I'm glad for that. It's true that the debate is above me, the catalog confuses me, and some workshop titles scare me. I don't understand much and, well, I'm probably a typical person outside the academy. Still, it's fascinating and, like Moira Kathleen said, I like being here."

It was time to go and as the others got ready, Moira Kathleen left the pond, dried her feet on the spiny beach grass, and slipped on her sandals. "Grace is not as typical as she believes," said Hans as he began to walk up the path.

16

Evening Frivolity

They trooped silently and Grace, given up to sensation and thought, felt she had understated her high spirits to the group—or from another perspective, had gotten a look at her usual wasting of words. At home she would be glad if it didn't rain, or if the pizza crust came crisply baked, or if she got back from shopping in time to watch a favorite show. These happenings spoke of satisfaction and, yes, often, simple ease. Moments managed with little friction. Her gladness now, though, rose from her amazement at the people she walked with. It's not, she thought, that I find them special, or, rather, unique: they seem not unique but *distinct*. Each person here can fully fill my senses, surely touch and smell but also wonder at all I can't know. Though let's be clear that I don't think them superior. It's that the talk and themes and ungroomed lovely night and sense of pilgrimage let me see them with a fullness that when I'm not with Amos or, more recently, with Alicia, I'm rarely allowed.

What I've understated is my present awareness; is it this or a sense of what my life usually is like that has me ready to cry? Which set of paths should *I* be on?

Those I go with now must be asking themselves similar questions.

When the trail ended at the road, they turned right. Sophie said she was thirsty, and they drifted toward the café. Grace, less intent than she had become at the pond, looked up and saw that the night was clear, if dark under the sickle moon. She tallied a dozen stars in the thin band of sky splitting the forest canopy. The dining-hall, a dominating presence here in daylight, was a shadow; the one light they saw was from the café, itself a vague reflection as its windows faced the other way. Someone walked ahead of them. Hans looked left, as if at a night sound. Then before he or the others could turn, Willa and Francine besieged them; the girls, coming downhill from the dining-hall, had seen them and run furtively their way. Hans on the left and Grace lost gazing at the sky were the most startled as the girls burst on them with a rustle of air and an immediate, loud yell.

"Quebecois! Wikings! Take no prisoners!" chortled Willa, gaily free of the kitchen and its odors after eight hours. Pleased by the strike, she even jumped in the air. Francine leapt onto Trumpeter's back.

Laughingly, Willa and Sophie joked together in their Scandinavian patois.

Moira Kathleen was introduced and seemed, a gain from before, glad to make more friends and even giddy to be with people so young. Still, as the group spread apart she moved ahead to walk with Hans and Grace, others who were near or over thirty. Hans noted her better mood and asked if she now knew what she would do in the morning.

"I can't leave. I've lived through so much in the last twenty-four hours. I was ready to bust with sadness when I got here. But I may've cried myself out, and I actually feel good. I'm not so ashamed. And I needn't go back to what the TV world would call my 'so-called life' until Friday."

"I'm sure your workshop will let you join back in," said Grace.

"Well," said Moira Kathleen, "or I'll rest, swim, and go to yoga class, read and eat and chat up strangers. I could take a day browsing in the bookstore. I'd also like to meditate again, for the first time in years, and hire Hans to give me one of his famous massages."

Hans smiled amiably but also, Grace believed, somewhat hesitantly.

Willa and Francine, two wild students, were bent on heading into town to get, as Francine proclaimed in her Quebecois accent, "a leetle hammered." That is if they could find someone to drive and remain fairly sober. "Now, Trumpeter has a car and is responsible and easy to manipulate"—she said this while riding his back and thumping her heels into his side. Thus their glee when, a minute's walk past the kitchen door, after leaving late because Tulip had been on a burn, they had spotted his gait as they themselves walked down the hill.

"Nothing by accident," said Willa, inflecting the Seeker truism with irony. She reached up to pat Trumpeter's shoulder. Francine, about to jump clear, said with a final, rough kick that perhaps Sophie and the others would come along, too.

"My dream comes true," said Grace, who suddenly felt trapped without her car.

As they passed the building housing the café—on the second floor, it still faced away from them—Trumpeter asked them to wait briefly. Grace and, less so, Sophie would not let Hans or Moira Kathleen beg off, as each tried separately to. Soon Trumpeter returned—his poet friend must have let him jump the line—with a plastic quart bottle of strawberry juice. The group crossed the road and walked to the rear of the parking lot, where Trumpeter's worn station wagon was backed in neatly against a thicket where the forest resumed. They waited as he poked inside; they could see a legion of vehicles, a few people walking, and, mostly, no lights that seemed to be nearer than the stars.

Grace loved the stars and drink, and wanted sentimentally to hug her friends.

Trumpeter produced a cyclist's water bottle and a bottle of tequila. Francine poured half the juice in the water bottle and tequila in both bottles. She gave Grace the water bottle, saying: "Your dream, then, comes true." She drank at her toast, before giving the juice bottle to Trumpeter. He drank and, as Grace drank and gave her bottle to Willa, then to Sophie, he drank a second time.

"That's all for me tonight," he said as he gave his bottle to Hans.

There came now a discordant half hour, moments of whimsy punctuated by the shared belief that with this ceremonial drinking it was a time to try to be gay. The night was deep in darkness and the one light not in the sky was the café's weak glow, behind a knoll and sixty yards away. Without the moon's added reflection, the stars lacked presence and were more, thought Grace with a nod to the plays she made her stalky students read, like human whispers than divine echoes. The chill that had rung down at dusk had evened out, and she equated its gentle sensation with that of the water bottle when it came to her again. Trumpeter had gotten chilled juice, and if the plastic bottle had no special feeling, the strong liquid within was slightly cold.

Mood-changing substances, meaning alcohol and drugs, were forbidden at the academy, and they drank with a sense that their loyalty allowed them this misbehavior. The young feel entitled, as do I, Grace mused. Though for me it's less being a soldier in god's army than feeling that a few pulls of tequila do no harm. And yes, we share a sense of safety. Though maybe I, unlike a loyal soldier, see that what we get comes by luck.

Moira Kathleen, knowing bad luck, abstained when a bottle came her way. But seeming to envy the larger comfort, she debated her situation. It appeared someone, if no one there, had refuted her right to join in. "Oh, but I know it'll be okay," she said at last. She smiled, and as Hans put his hand on her shoulder, she took a patently pleasurable swig.

The Scandinavian girls began to lead them. The contest would play with numbers and kinds of words, like a card game but without flickable cards. Willa earnestly spelled out directions; Sophie, imaginative and wry, gave impressions of how the players might fare in this sporting of wits. The bottles sat on Trumpeter's hood, and Grace matched Francine in her number of sips. By the fourth round, they stood together at the car; close, Grace saw that the girl's right eye was now shut with the infection. Francine saw Grace look, but turned and dove into the game. She seemed boosted by the words and play, and as the tequila rose in her she got louder. Trumpeter and then others tried to quiet her—Hans saying, wryly: "Remember, we're trying to be surreptitious." The juice bottle was empty and Sophie had the water bottle pass among them—Francine having one turn, but not four—until it, too, was finished.

Moira Kathleen, as it happened, bore a gift for mental exercise, and was the dark-horse winner in the first two rounds they played. Francine at first was enraged that a person she did not know would defeat her and her friends; then in her harsh, near-predatory way, she laughed and became Moira Kathleen's champion.

"Yes, she's quick," Francine observed, "in spite of having lived for such a long time in this country."

As for Grace, she'd had little alcohol for weeks, and the jubilant mood she had fallen into at the pond began to be expressed. Of the things on which she could focus—game, players, and night—she chose the last two, as she usually chose feeling over wit. As the others played—she did, too, but often went out first—she began to tell New York stories and join Sophie in gently mocking how the other contestants fared. It was a happy, silly group, growing increasingly loud. They saw people wending through the parking lot locate them by following their sound.

Trumpeter hushed them all a second time and Grace, who felt little inhibition but was easily directed, stepped back from the party with childlike chagrin. She was upright but her senses staggered. She eyed the night sky, but it held too many dilemmas; and in her fuzzy state, it seemed a poor cousin to the planetarium sky she had seen with her family in the city. This one, she thought, is indecorously real. She was on the passenger side of Trumpeter's car, and looking up she had a long, unexpected drink of that liquor made not from grain or fruit but from the walk over the horizon that described middle age. She thought of Moira Kathleen, who bore the look of someone who had been trapped for a long time. Many others at Seeker had this expression, including those among the young who, like Francine, might have been schooled in more compressed ways. Gesture and word, this brought one to healing, what Seeker pretended to be about; but what a task it really was!

Brutishly she had pointed out Trumpeter's impasse. So sore and perhaps trapped, where could he be if he couldn't be here? He had let this car become, precariously, his effective home.

Fearing in her new instability to look at the others, Grace, tired by the sky, turned her eyes to the forest. She moved closer to see if what she saw might clarify: a fuzzy mass made obscure in inky night air. The group was now ten yards away. Sophie called her name.

"I'm here," she said without turning. She was happy to follow the unkemptness of the chest-high scrub, which twisted and bent in patterns she couldn't easily make out. In fact, it was foolish to try. Past the scrub, a tree trunk rose as a solid black shadow. The smell inches from the scrub had many threads and brought coolness to her nostrils.

The game, which only concerned cleverness, lost Hans next and after another round petered out. Two threads rose in the conversation. It was ten p.m., so still early enough to go out. Trumpeter again said he would drive and stay sober, and infected Francine was eager to go. A more casual end-of-evening theme rose around summer movies, which Seeker staff rarely saw in season. Willa mentioned hearing of a nearby drive-in theater, a venue particular to America she greatly hoped to visit. Trumpeter said it was more fun and typical to go at dusk and catch two flicks in a row. The group mood relaxed as they began to talk of the blockbuster summer movies that had recently come out. Standing apart, Grace tuned in enough to note that she alone had seen two of the three titles talked about. She had caught both on the weekend of their joint release: amid large, umbrella- or raincoat-dragging crowds in a cold, clammy mall. Yet she heard enough to know that they all knew things about these movies: costs, or the past work of directors and actors, or what things a story demeaned. She guessed they would be as angry to see these films as miss them.

Hans said he must go to bed, and Willa said that having come upon Sophie she would go with her to phone a shared friend in Europe, as they had sworn to; she begged off reluctantly from the trip to the bar. Coyly, she repeated that events happen by design. Trumpeter, perhaps seeing he had lost his chance with Sophie, didn't speak to her. Grace, in touch with her mood, chose to let fatigue defeat her thirst and love for taverns. "I guess," she told her compatriots, "that I'll also make a trip up to my tent."

This left Francine and Trumpeter, who shared an attitude that could as well be called stoicism as fortitude. Abandoned, they would go alone. Then Moira Kathleen, who had never become a full member of the group, spoke up in a way that made Grace think of Cinderella and said she would like a nightcap, too. She should be too tired, she said, but for some reason that wasn't the case.

Part Four

Wellness

17

Word of an Accident

With soft pleasure, Grace's new practice was to rise with the birds. The notes sung solo or in unison and the early light woke her—and today, moving only her eyes, she watched as a skunk foraged in a clearing. She had woken days before to see one, inches from her tent mesh, close enough to make her fear to stretch or move in her sleeping bag; the animals might not know how unusual it was for her to spend nights in rugged areas. But this skunk nosed—she guessed the verb fit the circumstance—near a tree, leaving her free to adjust her position. Yet she lay still, for on balance it was nicer to rest her body while her mind explored. She could look at leaves, guess the day's weather, think ahead to events, or recall past ones. A little drunk last night, she had made tracing bushes and trees a somber fetish. Yet now all was darkly fresh and delicately wrought and rich with promise. She liked to be guided in this way by the clear hand of nature.

She thought of Willa and her idealism. Perhaps she liked her so because Alicia was coming to be similar: her niece, for instance, who had been so empathetic in the hospital, had also grown angry as she learned about some of history's outrages. "How could we," she had asked on hearing certain stories, "have done that to them? And how could god have hardened Pharaoh's heart?" Alicia was also like Willa in the way she wouldn't be placated by irony. Willa didn't at all think that life was ridiculous, and she was ready to fight.

I'm sorry, Grace thought: I can't think about Alicia and the oncology ward now. "Instead"—this last word alone she spoke, loudly

enough to startle birds—I'll do what I must before I shower. The birds
quieted. Grace saw that she still hugged herself as she had in sleep,
with her arms crossed and her hands tucked in opposite armpits. It
struck her, as she freed her hands and shrugged her shoulders in an
initial stretch, that Willa was, however, unlike Sophie, her university
friend. On the raft yesterday, Willa had been opinionated and critical—
even gently so of Grace; but a quickness warned that she might not
know herself enough to deeply root the things she said. Sophie, differently, seemed to keep her gaze on the middle distance. It was as if she
could see where life would take her but was unsure the trip was
worthwhile. And yet, to live that way could not be fully comfortable.
As time went by, Grace thought, Sophie might often have to look for
what was good in life anew.

Having to pee, and hoping the skunk would let her pass, she un-
zipped her tent flap. As direct sunlight wouldn't touch this wooded
patch for half an hour, the arboreal colors and the skunk's white mark-
ings both were muted. Wearing yesterday's clothes, she put clean underwear in her bag with a plastic soap bottle and a towel and headed
through the tent area to the bathroom. Where the trail ended at the
road, she climbed the steps to a unisex toilet and shower. Its screen
door creaked badly, and at six a.m., the creak offended. The trail had
been quiet, so this stock theatrical noise ruined a fine spell—one that
had made her just another natural presence in the forest.

The bathroom shared thin walls with staff dorm rooms, so night
users had to be quiet. Then why, Grace wondered, can't a janitorial
team oil the damn screen door? She put her towel and soap in a cub-
byhole and slipped into a toilet stall. Relieving herself, she heard a car
door shut. An engine fired and the car rolled briefly; its door shut
again near the bathroom. Someone bounded up the stairs and opened
the creaking door. Grace heard Willa whisper her name and then rap
softly on the stall door just to the right of where she sat.

"I'm in here," answered Grace in a low, curious, welcoming voice.

"Come downstairs as soon as you finish. We'll wait."

When Grace opened the screen door, she saw a van idling in the
shadows. Willa sat in the passenger seat, looking tired or grim, with her
night-dark arm crooked and hanging out the window. Nearing the van,
Grace identified Monk as the driver.

"We saw you go in," said Willa, quietly. "Francine and the others were in a car crash last night. Trumpeter and Moira Kathleen, the woman you met yesterday, are mostly all right. Francine may be hurt badly."

Monk, bending his head, caught Grace's eye through Willa's window. "We're off to the hospital," he said. "We thought you might want to come."

"Monk was there earlier," added Willa. "He came back for the van."

The van's removable rear benches were in place; Monk and Willa had gotten them from the service shed across from the rest room. Grace hesitated, and then climbed in behind her friend. As they rode through camp, a menu of personal needs rose before her, keeping fiercer thoughts away. She wanted coffee, and felt some hunger. She touched her bag, picturing both her clean underwear within and the layers of dirty clothes she still wore.

"Where are we going?" she asked.

"Paramedics took them across the river," said Monk, "to a better-equipped hospital than the one nearer here... a half hour in light traffic."

"At least you will get to see the Hudson River," Grace told Willa.

Leaving camp on the gravel road, they saw, resting in a hollow, two deer and a fawn. The van, with its lights off, had almost passed them before they showed a first urge to bolt. The road swung right and then steeply uphill, to end at a stop sign beside a paved road. Waiting to turn, they saw through their tilted windshield the northeast sky. Hills blocked the sun, but three striated cloud layers lit from the east promised a morning that would be humid and perhaps wet.

They passed through the village of Ephesus, only a traffic light and a general store catering both to locals and to people who slipped out of Seeker for snacks—visiting once, Grace had seen one-dollar and four-dollar bottles of beer. Willa, who had been quiet, noted that the store's outside bulletin board told her a lot about rural America, with its church suppers, patriotic signs, and power boats for sale. "And," she added with a small change of subject, "while I'd hoped to visit places with aboriginal names, like Wenatchee, Algonquin, or Saskatoon, in this European-settled part of America I come instead to Ephesus, Rhinebeck, and Rome.

"It seems redundant," she concluded, with a flatness that was not meant to cheer.

Grace saw Monk glance twice at Willa. She guessed he would represent Seeker at the hospital, and she wondered what other Seeker mechanisms came into play when such a bad thing occurred. Had Francine's family been called? She waited to hear more about the long night; but, not eager to be in another hospital, and having learned in the last year that curiosity carried risk, she lacked the will to ask. They entered the sleeping town, a mile off their route, for coffee. It felt more boutique than did the towns in her lower valley, with their richer mixes of ethnicity and class. Down the long main street, each building seemed to blend with its neighbors. The café with its big bay window was in one such building; looking up, Grace saw, above ten yards of red brick, an identical window with a dozen glossy bicycles ready for sale. Monk parked the van as Willa went in for coffees. He eyed Grace through his rearview mirror and then told her that the accident site was nearby. Trumpeter, with two short pulls of vodka in him, as he had told Monk and been persuaded by him to tell the police, had been stopped in a well-lit intersection waiting to turn left when a car flew into them. It struck the passenger door and Francine, with her infected right eye, had not seen it coming. From the backseat, Moira Kathleen had cried out and reached for Francine's left shoulder. Trumpeter had only started to turn at the cry.

On his first trip that night, Monk had passed this way at midnight and again at three a.m., when a crew was starting to clean things up.

Forcing herself, Grace asked about the extent of the injuries.

"Both Trumpeter and Moira Kathleen, the Seeker guest, will ache for a few days, probably starting tomorrow; hopefully, that's all. They all had on their seat belts, at least."

"And Francine?"

"Franny's right shoulder; more seriously, perhaps her back and some internal stuff. She was in surgery when I called half an hour ago."

Trumpeter's mood was raw, he added, while Moira Kathleen was being chatty.

Grace thought: I scorn the Seeker mantra of mind-body-heart-soul. She felt her whole being rebel.

"Willa says she was supposed to have been in the car," Monk said. "She's upset, but I'm unsure how to read her. I often forget what it's like to be so young."

"I do, as well. Maybe it's all her strength boiling up inside…. Did you wake her this morning?"

"Twice a year I put on a performance of sorts for staff. One was to have been starting about now. Willa had a part to play."

Grace saw Monk's forehead in the mirror over the front seat. She felt annoyed at his answer. Was his "performance of sorts" just another Seeker silliness? Why had he wanted her to come along?

"I've logged a lot of hospital time this year," she told him.

"I understand that you have. But I had a feeling we should ask you."

Two men wearing yellow construction helmets left the coffee shop. Monk turned the engine key; soon Willa appeared, and the Seeker van drove away. At the accident site, Monk pulled over. They got out and stood awkwardly sipping coffee. Grace wasn't sure if they had stopped to pay respects, or to investigate or for some other purpose. She wondered if by bringing them here Monk was being solicitous or even moralizing. It was too soon to be pensive, so she didn't know how to behave. Willa also seemed stunned. In any case, here was the town's big intersection, where Main Street crossed a state road. The vehicles had been towed, the debris removed; and the police, to free the streets for morning usage, had ended their work at the scene. There was nothing left to see.

They drove toward the bridge, past a sign pointing to a small college Grace had long heard of, which when it appeared across an ample lawn seemed to be dozing its summer away. Monk recounted a story that Grace found incongruous, given the accident—telling them the school had long defended the principles of humanism. "And an African teaches here now," he added, "whose novels recall her native village and expose the Western forces of its ruin. But while she's honored for her talent and stance—here she is, tenured at an esteemed Western school—she in time came to see that in this country, especially, her village humanism is out of place."

Willa knew the writer's work and seemed mildly surprised to hear that she lived in the U.S. and so near Seeker. Grace, who had begun to reflect morosely on her year—had begun to visualize the hospital's lobby and its bank of elevators— felt surprise to learn in passing that the often-exasperating Monk had graduated, decades before, from this elite school.

Meaning to keep his anecdote alive, Monk added that he had once sought to learn what had driven this writer to his alma mater. "I'd wondered if she might love the river and its lore, like my friends and I do," he told them. "But I found rather that as an exile in Paris she received an offer from the school, which she didn't know of and used a map to find. Then she found it to be a nicely quiet place to work. But in her head and heart, she told me in a note, she always stayed in Africa.... I guess we each live largely in our head and heart."

"Did you get your nickname at the academy?" Grace asked, in a droll tone she felt Willa might respond to. She liked chitchat with her morning coffee, and felt now that, for whatever reason, there would be no immediate talk of the accident unless she herself brought it up.

He was slow to reply, so she looked at the mingled woodland and farm fields that lay north of the college. She had noted before that he often liked to listen before he spoke. "Long ago, in a judge's chambers across the river," he said at last, "I changed my name to 'Monkfish.' I'll only add that I then waited fifteen years for it to kind of ease back down to 'Monk.'"

"Some still call him 'Monkfish,'" said Willa, engaging at last. She turned to face Grace. "Others just call him 'the Seeker Black Sheep.'"

Grace saw Monk smile faintly in the mirror, but he let the subject drop even after seeing that they would still be in the van for a while. They reached the bridge after twenty minutes of driving, with ten more being spent on the coffee run. Thus, Grace assumed that the hospital was close. She had been on the bridge a few times over the years, but didn't know the area. The road climbed through riverside cliffs and then swung with surprising speed onto the bridge. Yet now, with a clear western view, they saw a line of cars stopped in front of them and, further on, big, yellow construction equipment. Grace looked at her watch: 6:40. So the workday had begun and they could be in for a wait.

By now, the sun behind them and their place on the bridge were both high enough to confirm the dimness of the day's weather. Clouds encased the sky, adding white and gray to the blue of the river and the green of the surrounding hills. In the north, greens mixed with browns as the hills climbed into the Catskills. Willa, peering out her side window, pointed to the mountains and then to the river twisting south. Halfway to the center span the van stopped, ten yards behind a red pickup truck. Eastbound traffic was also slowed; bunched-up groups of cars trundled past every few minutes. A bus three slots forward blocked their view of the work site, and they heard no sound of drilling. A pleasant breeze brought the thumping or flapping sound that Grace knew was a sign of high humidity.

In the van, Willa's silence pressed down hardest. Grace sensed that Monk shared her wish to see the girl through this fretful time. Both would sometimes glance in her direction.

"What do you think?" Monk asked Willa, indicating the vista with his right hand. He put the van back in gear to follow the truck further up the bridge. Now they saw both riverbanks.

All but the dark, stabbing blue and the gray sky is green, mused Grace. Can the writer's Africa be lovelier? Didn't touring kings and queens once view this land as a natural holy wonder?

"This view and the accident," Willa began. "It brings up too much for so early in the day."

Grace felt that Willa was in need of conversation and guessed that Monk had a story ready to go. If not, though, she would jump in with an attention-getter of her own.

The thought came that Monk and Willa had likely talked in the early dawn, before they met up with her.

Drilling began, accompanied by a soft jarring. The noise irritated but the drilling soon stopped; despite periodic resumptions, its clamor sank into the background. A dozen more westbound cars came through; Seeker's van arced higher. The view penetrated the riverbanks and, climbing, nearly touched the Catskills. Montreal, Manhattan, the waxen sky—even Lake Erie, a half-day's drive away, seemed near.

Grace's guess concerning Monk, whom she had connected with but hardly knew, had been correct. "Since at least 1800," he began, "people have sought these views. The woods here and even more so to the north hide hundreds of trails. On foot or on horseback, they climbed to views we motor to now, with our hot coffees from a bakery in town. Guidebooks we still use today point to these overlooks, destinations where a swatch of river and hill and distant sky would... would do what?" he asked after a pause, finding a spot where his story could absorb new information and glancing at Willa. He would, Grace saw, try to cajole the saddened young woman into joining in.

Grace couldn't find Willa's eyes in the rearview mirror. "It was the heart taking flight," Willa said unexpectedly, with a rising voice. Grace bent forward, thinking to touch her shoulder in encouragement; then she remembered how Moira Kathleen had tried in this way to warn Francine. Willa, apparently interested but weighted down, tapped two fingers on the windshield and went on: "They must have climbed to get free; though I don't know from what. Were the people here farmers, trappers, or early versions of the tourists we usually see in the village we just left?"

"Or of people living here now in mobile homes and shacks," Grace added. "Who my suburban neighbors like to call the valley's 'rural white trash.'"

Monk reacted at once. "Let's keep clear of what we know is only narrow-mindedness," he said. "I'd like to stick to the escape. What would Europeans settling here have wanted to escape from?"

"Well," replied Grace, trying to go along but hesitant, "they were fleeing poverty and religious war; we know this from history books." She looked at the hills rising into the southern Catskills, seeking a sign of Woodstock, the famed but "just too cute"—more suburban gossip—place for eccentricity and art. But all she saw was forest canopy and a north-south gash that may have been the interstate. Was she trite to bring up this ordinary history, which Amos in seventh grade had studied recently? He would say so. Not only that: she had co-directed a high-school play two years before based on Fennimore Cooper, which laid an egg with a double yoke. The actors had argued that the story's frontier themes, fake muskets, and fur hats suited middle school better. Then, at performances, some parents were condescending. To her, it was not that they belittled frontier risk-taking—after all, their lives were tough enough. It was that they showed so little interest in the struggles of their ancestors.

Monk had led her to this historical reference, with its near-tedious cast. She felt him pointing her elsewhere, too. Well, I get it, she told herself. He's asking me to think.

"I don't see why the farmers or trappers would cut overlook trails," she said. "I mean beyond wanting places from which to survey land. Weren't they Puritans or Victorians, people without interest in beauty? Though in saying this I see how little I know about who they really were."

"We *should* know who they were," Monk said. To her, this sounded preachy and plodding, yet guided by a startling ferocity. His silences also felt fresh. She liked his apparent bravery, a resolve to keep going amid what had to be his doubts.

"The European place names," Willa said, with lingering interest, "make me wonder if the settlers were romantics. This might account for a love of scenery. Back then Europe was full of artists; amateurs, mostly, but also masters like Goethe and Shelley."

"Yes!" Grace said. "Our famous locals, the Hudson River painters, were romantics! Thomas Cole and others, like someone Church, who built a mansion near here… I think they lived during the Civil War. Amos was just learning about them. They thought the valley's fluxes in landscape and climate"—surprised, she heard this idea tumble out—"mirrored its spiritual richness. And they tried to paint with mind, heart, and soul."

"What Seeker doctrine would call 'holistically,'" Monk added.

Grace's mood was pensive. "Yes. River bends, hills and rock ledges, rising mountains… and such changes in cloud shape and light as we see now.

"Like the land itself, their paintings in a museum can make me cry," she added, a little startled by the trembling in her voice.

"Where the heart can take flight," repeated Monk. She watched blond hair curl on his tanned left arm and near his left ear. He's older than me, she thought, yet he reminds me of men I knew twenty years back. His aura of fitness and dislocation and danger is certainly attractive.

"Look behind us and right," Monk said. "The bridge may block our

view, but north of it on the east bank is a park called 'Poets' Walk.' It's
been a haven for two centuries. Grace's romantic artists worked here.
But then this bridge went up, and later a private park became a public
one."

The bridge, Grace saw, did hide the bank where Poets' Walk must
be. She let her gaze drift north along the wooded shore.

"It's pretty country," said Willa, "dramatic from here and probably
charming from below. But charm and drama can be scary; Europeans
understand that big emotions can point to life gone crazy. Think of the
river this one imitates with names like 'Rhinecliff.' In Europe, big emotions led up to the fascists. Something similar has often also been true
in Africa."

Willa's words jogged Grace's memory and she remembered that
history could be dauntingly complex. She again thought of how her
reflective life since college had mostly excluded forces and ideas. But
romanticism tapped dramatic traditions, the history most alive for her.
She recalled Ibsen's stifled, deep-feeling women. Half-randomly, she
thought of Byron, Mary Shelley, and Nietzsche, of Mussolini and Bee-
thoven. It was hard not to first associate these figures with movies
about them; or with her time in college, when their work had lived
more in her mind. In films—she had seen biopix on everyone but
Nietzsche—they were always full of passion.

The passion is what Hollywood wants, she thought. It must be why
films about people of conviction are financed in the first place.

Noting her mental drift, Grace began to fear that she had fallen out of
the conversation. She knew some touchstones of romanticism, in particular
its call to live passionately, which might tie into Seeker's heart-opening exercises. But she then hit a wall of complexity or ignorance that made her leery
to say more. She wasn't sure how fascism or Mussolini related to feeling and
mood, for instance. Yet she felt that much in this history lay at the proverbial tip of her tongue, as stories she knew vaguely. She could be an eager,
thoughtful listener. In fact, her sense of Seeker participants generally was
they at least were eager listeners.

Monk must have felt her withdrawal; trying to keep his lesson alive,
he urged her and Willa to see it as a game and join in.

"Here's a question worth exploring, then," he said. "Among settlers
cutting trail to the lookouts, where did the attention to beauty that

brought them to their work come from?"

But Willa, anyway, seemed weary of talk. She rolled her window up halfway and bent her head to the glass. Grace, looking past her, saw the verdant drop to the river. When, after a delay, Willa again spoke, not in reply to Monk's question and saying only, "Romanticism rejected the idea that human mind ruled the world," her dismayed tone showed that she now found the conversation to be irritating.

Monk turned to the women. "We needn't go on with this and I know there are no answers," he said, again sounding almost tedious. "But I think this stuff matters. And maybe now, as we head to the hospital and what waits there, this stuff matters the most."

Grace was startled and unsure what he meant. Anyway, the exchange had lost force: as his words echoed a silence drew down that would break only for practical comments. She felt that they all wished to escape the treacly scenic beauty and, until they had, to simply look out the window.

18

At the Hospital

Monk's claim still echoed as, minutes later, they got past the bridge-repair work. Only one car was in front of them down the long western side of the bridge—so, not five minutes after Monk could again shift up to second gear, they were beyond the river and in the right lane, slowing to take an exit ramp. They followed its long curve and on entering a flow of traffic found that they were suddenly, as Grace used a stock phrase to affirm, "in strip-mall hell." At this hour, almost every store was closed and the north-south traffic was light, but other telltale signs rolled in through the windows. Grace wondered if the severe change was familiar or strange to Willa. Mustn't Norway and even Kenya be like this now? At a red light, she reached out of her window and verified that the humid, flapping breeze they had felt on the bridge didn't penetrate to the concrete plain. Nor, even muted by clouds, was there generosity to the light as it banged among surfaces. She watched abstract contours clash: poles carrying power and communications conduits, tethered storefronts and surrounding parking lots, fences and intervals of gravel or grass, high mall palaces that blocked the sky. Billboards lined the main sight lines, promoting "Gil's New York Convenience," "Cruickshank Auto Parts," and "Kuala Bear Electronics" amid many other businesses. There at the traffic light, a donut shop, part of a large chain, aimed its V-shaped, orange signage at passers by. The shop's fifty-space lot rallied cars, trucks, and vans which in their solid colors came and went as if they were cherry-red or forest-green, or blue or brown (it tired Grace to feel so mean-spirited) bits of flash that were as passing as the morning's weather.

Monk knew the way; and after he had quipped that they were "like movie heroes now, trying to get by an ambush," they took in the shrill landscape silently. They soon saw that the donut chain, Vinny's, had another branch a half mile up the road; it was in a strip mall anchored by a six-screen cinema. Across a service road, there stood a car dealership and its used-car subsidiary. On passing these businesses, Monk, just as Willa pointed out the relevant sign, turned right into the hospital's grounds. Taking a last look, Grace saw a cluster of buildings, billboards, suburban traffic, and warming pavement that went on for at least a mile.

The hospital was small compared to the pediatric center she had come to know, with new wings cobbled onto an antique building. As an entity, it must have predated the surrounding flow of commerce; likewise, the road it was on would have connected valley villages in earlier days. Monk, ready to park, asked that they stay in the van. He found Grace's eye in the mirror. "I should've asked before about Moira Kathleen," he said. "Our registrar, who I had to wake for information, called her a first-timer. I hear you were with her yesterday. What can you add?"

Grace replied that if Moira Kathleen hadn't been sedated, she would be worn out even if unhurt. "I doubt she's slept much the last few nights, as coming to Seeker meant a lot to her, and she freaked out when she arrived. I suppose that in Seeker lingo we'd say, 'She's just begun her inner journey.'"

Grace watched Monk watch her in the mirror. He asks, she thought, for a simple tip on how he might help someone he doesn't know, and I turn glib. I still deride practices I know little about, when in fact I would love to have some Seeker magic now. I fear going into another hospital. Do Willa, Monk, and, for that matter, Trumpeter really find strength in the things they pursue? Well, I suppose Willa is skeptical, or less prone to this stuff by temperament. Sophie should be here. I also see the irony of Moira Kathleen and Francine being *already* in pain when they left campus last night—almost as representative types, the lost and the sick. Trumpeter, too, I think, in his standoffish, angry-Buddha way.

Monk parked. She thought how with his earnest, receptive manner he reminded her of Sophie. Both were adventurers. Less clear to her, both seemed to want to find and then serve some greater good.

Aloud, she said, trying to be considerate, "I think Moira Kathleen struggles with disappointment. Her life isn't very satisfying. But last night I sensed that Seeker could begin to mean a lot to her."

"She seemed to like it when we played that game," added Willa.

Grace felt glad, surprisingly so, when Monk suggested that they take time to settle themselves before entering the hospital. Willa, afraid or sad, glanced with disdain in the mirror, as if to say that she found a call to contemplation naïve. Then she went along. A girl drove a sporty white car into an adjacent parking space, just as Monk asked them to breathe deeply to clear their minds. How many children from this winter will ever drive? Grace wondered as she took a first draught of air into her lungs. Will Alicia? Then she relaxed and, as she had recently learned to, began using the air to get temporarily free of vexing thoughts. She smiled as with shut eyes she felt what seemed almost to be sea breezes sweep her mind.

"May good fortune again find our stricken friends," Monk said.

This plea, or its idea of asking help from a larger presence, ended her respite and returned her, too soon, she felt, to their situation. Yet, by means of this rest—this checking in with a perceptible stillness—she felt a bit more prepared.

With Monk ready to go, Grace touched his arm. "I hardly know Francine, but at the dishwasher yesterday she told me she'd spent part of the year in a mental hospital."

Monk turned to her. "Franny's heart is pure and she's smart, but a circus plays in her head. We meet this kind of sadness at the academy, among other kinds. Our nurses speak with her Montreal therapist. But she shouldn't have to be facing this now, too."

In the front seat, Willa was staring out through the windshield.

They entered the hospital lobby with Grace determined to keep her thoughts in the moment. With a glance, she saw that the life they found, how they saw it to be organized, would give them all a visceral jolt. The pared-down office sensibility provided a more managed and less pampered atmosphere than at Seeker. Light filled the room uniformly, curbing variation. Low background music and an official hum filled the acoustic plane, masking non-programmed sounds. As Monk led them to the elevator, a strangeness she had always, even before this year, felt as someone healthy in a hospital was amplified by the surreal orderliness. Oh, but her skunk could send a message here! What a long night for their friends. It was past time to help them get away.

She also felt, at every new sight, the shadow of Alicia's hospital. The elderly surprised her, as did the absence of cartoon characters on the walls. Her time at Seeker began to feel like something the wind could blow away. She kept bringing her thoughts back to where she was.

Willa was even more unglued, and after she had bumped into two people in the corridor—one who wore a patient's cloth shift—Monk walked beside her. The thought came to Grace that Willa just might not be ready for this. Later in life she would learn a workaday resolve; but now, wed to her convictions, she might not think about loss, let alone acceptance. Grace recalled how at Willa's age she had sometimes gone looking for trouble, too.

Maybe it always is the same, she thought.

"Wrong way; we go right," said Monk. Willa had gone ahead where a second corridor crossed. She turned back and away, like a wave striking a wall at a diagonal. Monk had to step up his pace to catch her.

Or maybe, thought Grace, she's just scared about Francine; or maybe I have no idea why she's so upset.

Heading to the ER waiting area, they passed stainless-steel food carts and caught breakfast aromas. It struck Grace that since unzipping her tent an hour before she had been increasingly caught in societal rhythms. Nothing new in that, surely, except in contrast with her new tented life. The bridge work and strip malls, but also the van and even coffee that were products of vast business networks. She wondered if more than one skunk visited her. The reversal of fortunes was plain: here it was she nosing past the doors of people rising from sleep. The doors were ajar and under uniform light the patients, en masse—with many showing pain or sorrow and with some unfortunate public nudity—prepared to meet the institutional needs of the hospital: a nutritious breakfast followed by structured efforts to heal. And yes, this, superficially, was how mornings also passed at the academy.

They found Moira Kathleen and Trumpeter sitting at opposite ends of a row of molded plastic chairs. Rising, Moira Kathleen looked at Grace and then Willa, before fixing her eyes on Monk. "The doctors will come by at 7:30 to speak to you," she told him.

"Moira Kathleen—thank you!" Monk said, in a caring tone that pledged to linger with her later. He looked at Trumpeter. "Did the hospital find Franny's parents in Montreal?"

Trumpeter's head turned minutely right and then left. "Her mother is probably living in Japan," he said.

Monk fingered his bare wrist and looked around for a clock. There were forty seats nearby, and at this early hour a third were taken. But the Seeker crew had its corner in the room, and for a moment, they were like actors who hadn't yet been given scripts. Grace found herself thinking of the Seeker catalog, with its remedies for body-mind-heart-soul, and of morning yoga, which must be underway now in the de-lightful bamboo studio. Willa, not Monk, finally drew the group in. She went up to Trumpeter, took two tufts of his shirt in her fists and pulled up, making him rise and, now much shorter than he, wrapped her arms around his waist. Monk gently and wary of bruises encircled his shoulders from behind. Grace feigned a similar closeness with Moira Kathleen; she then felt her act breed true caring, and gave her new friend a hug. I feel it now, she thought—but in thinking this she saw that a part of her didn't connect. The hug back from Moira Kathleen didn't seem desperate and in fact was surprisingly strong.

Both victims had been released by the hospital and were eager to go. Neither had injuries beyond bruising; this news, while bringing relief, enlarged the tragic scope of Francine being injured badly. Her back wasn't broken and she would walk again, but she faced months of rehab. She also wasn't yet "in the clear"—Moira Kathleen, not Trum-peter, reported this—as a blood-related risk factor was tied to her in-fected eye. Moira Kathleen seemed to take no satisfaction in her tale telling; she didn't draw attention to herself, as Grace felt she had on the previous night. Yet Trumpeter watched her with an overt, feral stare.

Grace needed a toilet and Moira Kathleen showed the way. Cross-ing the waiting room, she felt the old discomfort of catching strangers in private moments. This wasn't the unintended viewing of a hospital bed through an open door; rather, it intensified the common experience of seeing people at some public place await the next thing to happen in their lives. This sense of intrusion was, with fear, what had made her avoid strangers at Alicia's hospital. The intrusions weakened everyone, which was the main point to see—even as they happened all the time. Who after all was sick, and who a companion? Just in being here, the people she passed seemed to hold the end-threads of their lives between their fingers. They had no reason to see things differently with her.

As she peed for a second time that morning, after undoing her rank clothes in the ammonia-washed stall, she wondered what Moira Kathleen, awaiting her, would say. She also to her surprise didn't feel haunted by the hospital. Her mind and senses were alive; a start-the-day vigor brought lightness. If only, she thought, that sweet girl is okay—if only, even after painful rehab, Franny walks again. Forget the Seeker talk about finding blessings in sadness. Dodged bullets, she told herself with ire and realism, always are best.

Spurred by the previous night's discussion, she wanted to consider something else before she rose: this point about space and intrusion. At Seeker now, hundreds of people breakfasted in small groups, sitting with others they had not known days or even minutes before. Most had filled their plates with appetizing foodstuffs, cut summer fruit and coarse bread with jam and scrambled eggs and the like, and as they worked down a plate they also dug into themselves in conversations. They talked of illnesses faced and thresholds crossed in therapy and efforts to feel more alive. Listeners then would respond. And it doesn't matter in this context, she told herself, if on reflection a conversation seems weird or softheaded. There's plenty of that, but the point is that people don't hide among each other, as they surely do here. Instead, they are open—many, to the best of their ability. Seeker's milieu allows it. Whatever else I come to think about this imposing place, that's something!

Ah, she thought, I must miss it…. Beyond a visit to the store in Ephesus, this was her first time off the grounds in two weeks.

She sat with Moira Kathleen near the rest room and put her hands on the woman's shoulders. "You're in one piece, at least. Had it been me I'd be collapsing about now, if I'd made it this far."

"I saw the car come at us," Moira Kathleen said with some eager-

ness. "In a flash, I knew to lean away, even as I was belted in. Then I
was just... fine. Trumpeter was dazed, but he also seemed unhurt. I
yelled at him to get out and followed him through his door. I felt in
charge, the one responsible. The car that hit us had bounced back, and
by the time I got to Francine's door, I'd made a plan. I don't know,
maybe the energy and amazing certainty grew from my nerves finally
having an outlet. But I could've believed that, in some way, I was being
guided.

"Trumpeter stood around as I made the driver call for help and put
on his flashing lights, and as I talked to Francine. He wasn't very willing to go near her. And he's hardly spoken to me all night."

"Don't worry about him. He's in shock and maybe feeling responsible and, anyway, from what I've seen, he gets cranky. Monk will take
care of him now."

It took half an hour to get free of the building. Monk greeted the
two doctors who came to meet him with cordiality and pricked care;
he seemed more at ease in the hospital than the others. Trumpeter and
Willa moved off by themselves; they talked quietly, except when Willa
screeched, "It matters even if it had to be!" Grace and Moira Kathleen,
at the other end of the row of bonded seats, watched the room, noting
the phrases freed from Monk's conversation, the paper whiteness of
the doctors' coats, the waiting clock; but they rarely spoke.

Oddly, to this watchful chorus, a nurse passing through the room
actually left it before returning to greet Monk like an old friend. He
lives in the area, thought Grace. He and the nurse, in her forties, may
have dated. Or perhaps she just knows of the academy.

19

Discomfort at a Mall

Francine could not have visitors until afternoon, so in time they began moving to the lobby. With a jittery gait, Trumpeter walked out the main hospital door ahead of the others. It was eight a.m., so the pearly midsummer light—clouds still hid the sun—bore down in earnest. They heard before they saw the rush-hour traffic that overlay the half-rural road, which, Grace felt, might have been bothered enough already by its multitude of stores.

They stood outside the hospital, unhinged by events but also, at this point of returning to the academy, caught between worlds—between Seeker and this more magnetic home. A bit longer spent in this milieu of cars and shopping malls and they would forget there was anything else. Grace sensed that for a moment Moira Kathleen, Trumpeter, and perhaps others would share her lethargic impulse to give up, forget Seeker, and, well, drift into a mall. It must always be a fight to leave home; but these days, with the media such an echo chamber in their lives, the pull of normalcy was especially strong. She felt it was a lot like the habits yoga and exercise tried to instill. They had all seen ads from the chain stores active on this road endless times. And as bodies found what was easy, easy by being familiar, so did minds. There was often a liberating sense when one simply went along.

Monk, whom Grace admired even in his doggedness, thinking him someone she could talk with about her year, had since leaving the ER tried to shepherd together both wounded parties, Moira Kathleen and Trumpeter. But the latter thwarted his purpose by walking ahead. As he made for the van with Willa trailing, the white-haired leader called him back. For a moment, stopping, Trumpeter held his ground; and Willa, planted awkwardly sideways to everyone, looking as if she would remember the moment, perhaps diminished herself, straddled the opposed wills. Then Trumpeter retraced his steps. His silent message palpable to Grace as he rejoined the group was that no one should offer him sympathy.

"How are you doing?" Monk asked him, loudly enough for all to hear.

A car door shut in the parking lot, and in an odd reverberation, an old man intoned that he needed help. The lot quieted. Thirty yards off-road and too far from the river for its complex music to intrude, they were caught in an untidy silence.

Grace saw or thought she saw Trumpeter will himself to partly be invisible. His anger showed only as a kind of wretched smoke. It stung the eyelids and made his governing fire, wretched and charming at once, hard to see. Waiting, he seemed caught under shadows.... Still, Trumpeter was Monk's protégé; and coming to stand beside Moira Kathleen, he tried, while saying nothing, to accede to Monk's call.

As the old man walked past them, using a walker, watching his path, sometimes voicing unease, and being helped by a young woman who resembled him greatly, the group from the academy took a quiet moment in support of Francine. The unfortunate girl—Grace felt an aching in her ears from all that she knew there was to listen to.

Monk asked Moira Kathleen to join him in the front of the van. Willa and Trumpeter took the rear seat, facing backwards. Grace sat behind the driver, alone in her row. The ride's first leg would be short: as they would miss breakfast at Seeker, there was a call, especially from Moira Kathleen, for good coffee. The first idea was to cross the bridge and stop in the picturesque town they all knew—the site of the accident. But that seemed too intense. Their planning was disjointed, with Monk now in a passive mood and the others reluctant or unwilling to participate. Then as they left the parking lot Grace noted that, driving in, they had passed a coffee shop a mile up the road. When no one commented, she added that the bridge, under repair, might be slow for another hour, as the area began its workday.

Trumpeter voiced a desire to get home and out of the "commercial muck" as soon as possible. "It's deadening here. If people need coffee, we can stop at the general store in Ephesus."

Monk, pointing to traffic that already slowed them, said, "I think Grace's idea is best."

Reaching the first stoplight heading north, he flicked his left turn signal, to turn into Vinny's, the orange-colored donut chain store. But Grace said she'd had a different, maybe cozier place in mind. It was on the left, in a mall they could identify by the logo of a discount apparel store chain. Monk saw the place, Hudson River Mall, a moment later. It looked newly renovated and was just beyond Hudson Pastures, a strip mall anchored by an auto parts store and a tire center.

Hudson River Mall was in fact comprised of a single, L-shaped, one-story building. Amid ten tenants, the apparel shop was most prominent; from what Grace saw, only it and one other store belonged to big chains. The small coffee shop had a sugary name: "Café Obsession." The few cars parked near it were, at this hour, alone in the two-acre lot.

"I'd say we are here," said Grace with a chuckle, "but my 'here' stretches the point." She was abashed to have picked this mall. Ten hours before, a little drunk on a dark night, she had sought to charm the vegetation. Now she was showing off her usual habits. Maybe also from habit, Monk parked apart from the other vehicles. Four doors swung open at once—and Grace, moving toward more coffee, could offer a helping hand to Willa, who, hardly bigger than Alicia, had found it hard to climb down out of the van.

Trumpeter, free of the van himself, a few yards away watched this act of courtesy with a surprised look on his face.

They entered a room too cold from air-conditioning and too brightly lit from overhead. Its windows faced south, but at this morning hour, shades blocked the natural light and warmth. Two teenagers, a boy and a girl, ran the counter, with neither apparently knowing the energy cost. This lack of perception extended to service. After the Seeker party had ordered and paid, a time came when Moira Kathleen, squinting from glare and (Grace guessed) upset to be in the same clothes for a day and a night, could say sadly, "At least chain restaurants have training and standards."

Willa pointed to the walls, hung with a dozen pen-and-ink draw-ings, most likely by local artists. "The chain coffee-shops I see don't use living art," she said in an aggrieved tone. "Either it's popular reprints or the faces of famous writers... and always with the tensions blurred away. Anyway, it's about fame or, really, comfort: familiar images make many people feel safe. I'd rather look at local art."

"Local art can be iffy, though," replied Grace. "It doesn't always grab me. The commercial stuff, pretty Monets and the like, which I may resent in my head, still makes my heart beat sometimes.

"Training and standards again, I guess," she added with a grin.

She had said this with muffin crumbs on her lips; she now brushed them away with her wrist. She noted the quiet Trumpeter's seething contempt.

Yes, okay, she told him silently: again, my reflections are sloppy. But you miss the sentimentality in your own point of view.

All ate lightly; it seemed they had stopped less for sustenance than to relax after leaving the hospital. Trumpeter sulked but the others shared fragments of a brighter mood. Comments spilled into areas where numbness had ruled and they began to fold what had happened into a narrative. They spoke of practical details concerning Francine, and took comfort in the guarded medical optimism.

Seeker was at heart a school, Grace knew by now. So, it made sense that even emotional moments like this would drift back on the Seeker curriculum—here, to the misguided faith people today put in what Willa disparagingly called "Western medicine."

"Ah, yes," said Moira Kathleen. "To me it's just the fastest way down into magic."

"Huh!" Monk said with a welcoming smile. "Please say what you mean."

"I'm a hospital accountant," she replied. "And in hospitals you see it all the time: what I call 'medical magic and the common hope.' Last night, with Trumpeter, I experienced it directly."

She explained that, in her view, people coming to a hospital often fell to their knees—driven, so wet with fear that they seemed to risk evaporation, to trust what they didn't understand. "It's coerced trust, surely," she added in a harried voice, "I mean, trusting what you have to obey. And then on the medical side you have cold surfaces, technology that treats people as things, and a priestly caste of doctors."

"A door to this world opened for me," said Grace. "So I see your point. Even when the staff tries to warm a place, the technology makes it cold. You're mostly abandoned, to breathe in germs and face down all the alien surfaces. And if someone who manages the technology smiles at you, you feel more trusting and smile back."

Monk had ordered a glass of grapefruit juice, which, when it finally came, he drank down in two lurid draws. Grace had begun to think him austere, the sort of man who kept hold of what he had. Now she saw that she must take a wider view of his questioning. Listening, he pulled his hands from the table; lanky, he squared up behind his glass. "What grabs me is hearing the tech called cold *and* powerful," he told Moira Kathleen. "This seems to deepen the problem—and suggest why its surface is so resistant to our touch."

"But now the cold technology helps Francine." This was feet-on-the-ground Willa, drawn today to every side of every question. "If she gets well, mustn't we also be grateful for the machines?"

Grace added: "And getting well may be all that finally matters."

"Technologies heal us!" cried a scornful Trumpeter. "Franny doesn't think so. She wouldn't even let a doctor treat her infected eye."

And there it was, Grace thought. We see the beast try to protect her from an infection that, when it seemed harmless, she wouldn't let the beast near. And then, if it can, the beast will mother her for months, easing her pain and recovery with its horrible hands.

Monk complimented Moira Kathleen, noting that she must find hospital work hard given her qualms. The comment seemed risky to Grace, as it invited the woman to magnify parts of her life.

It's what we all do, she reflected. We amuse others with set anecdotes and fool ourselves that they have meaning. I do it more than most. If there's a difference, it's that I need less help than her, as my lucky life has had more satisfactions. And, yes, in this way I see that I am touched by luck.

Confirming Grace's fear, Moira Kathleen showed more of herself than she had the day before. Grace, with her bent for drama, became transfixed. Yet Moira Kathleen grasped only half of what she said. There was her bad luck: a misfired singing career, a marriage ended in a "breaking off of contact," a life of tired habits—all her history she beat into place with a series of half-bitter laughs. But there was also the sense in which bad luck had wounded her character, or even fallen from the wound. In midlife, she knew that people could be sorry for her, but maybe not that they could dislike her.

It was a worrisome turn. Grace saw how Monk's generosity did not always improve a situation. Trumpeter must also be kept in mind. As Moira Kathleen grew more talkative, she might forget why they were here and let her mind slip even regarding Francine. This was a danger with the loyal, strange, and perhaps explosive Trumpeter nearby.

20

A Surfacing of Rage

"It's ugly here," said Willa the Wiking a moment later, breaking cruelly into Moira Kathleen's monologue. Grace, abashed, felt that Willa might have said this as a stand-in for Trumpeter, or from having seen that as a group they couldn't stand the repetitions. And she had probably meant the ugliness in terms of the woman's tone, not words—as Moira Kathleen seemed to always be putting her mental furniture in order, as if a demon always kicked it into disarray. The tone was one that to Grace (who had met the demon before) signified not mental imbalance, but disappointment. Moira Kathleen, with her mind right, could resume her search for a missing key. Once found, it would help her to change her job or friendships or interests or strategies for meeting people—in a way that would bring her to happiness. This rudderless effort seemed to underlie most of her social interactions. For many who spoke with her, it was clear that her utmost need was to simply get along.

Disappointment characterizes her, thought Grace; it's not like I miss the signs. This has loomed large for others I've known; and when I was younger and stronger, it sometimes loomed large for me.

But Seeker's interest, Grace had learned, was in change, not observation. And she had seen how some there took a more martial approach to the many confused people, like Moira Kathleen, who came. The academy, it was said, could be a gate for these people, but they must find it on their own; that was what the workshops, books, and tapes were for, in any case. Yet, not many within the gathering would cross back through the gate to help.

Thus Grace sensed that the young Turks at the table were upset at Moira Kathleen's needing to be heard, with Franny in intensive care and perhaps unconscious. She looked around, waiting for something to happen and feeling currents she could not identify.

The others seemed to be waiting, too—excepting Trumpeter, who looked ready to escape everything he abhorred: the cake crumbs on Grace's cheek, fake breezes on his skin, the step back into the parking lot, and whiny Moira Kathleen. She saw him pick the teabag from his indelicate red cup and fling it inches past a trash bin. Then saying, "That's what I'll use," but without pausing to charge the others with complicities or say what he meant, he rose to leave the café. Given his usual reserve, he acted out of character; Grace saw this fact register in a glance between Willa and Monk, and in his hesitant gait. But as the others watched, he tried to make his own magic. By now a second mall store was open, and workers had arrived at most remaining ones. The parking lot had thus begun to fill. Trumpeter crossed the lane running along the edge of the mall and stepped toward the Seeker van, but after passing a few cars he saw an off-road vehicle and, perhaps liking its geometric lines, he sprang up to sit on its hood.

Watching anxiously with the others, Grace flashed on a movie scene in which men beneath streetlights and rain had sung praises to a shiny new car.

Monk turned his chair to face outside. Beside him, Moira Kathleen hesitated to do the same. She grinned benevolently, but her embarrassment shone through as she looked at Willa and then at Grace. Willa stood and moved forward to stand beside Monk, with a hand on his shoulder.

"What'll he do?" asked Grace, who while captive to Moira Kathleen's need for assurances was also acutely aware of time.

"Let's see what," said Monk. "He's remorseful, but this wasn't his fault and he knows it. Out there, he has the proof he needs. It depends on what use he makes of it."

Trumpeter, on the car's rectangular hood, was examining his left forearm. He looked up squinting at the L-shaped row of stores, as if pretending to see them for the first time. He looked more deeply down the line of stores again. As he slid from the hood—like a chess piece,

Willa left the café at this moment—he began to grin, but in a flushed way that Grace associated with Moira Kathleen. He looked directly at the café's plate-glass window, or perhaps at Willa, who was in front of it, and then turned back in the direction of the van.

"Yes, the van," said Monk.

Grace, with Moira Kathleen following, rose to stand near him.

Trumpeter moved to the van's rear doors. He turned a handle, bent briefly in the cargo space, emerged with a tire iron and slipped off its plastic sleeve. He held the right door open with his right hand and, as if banging in a spike, he cracked the shatterproof window of the left door with the tire iron, held by his left hand. Grace saw him close and turn the lock latch of the right cargo door. He then twice drove his hammer hard into that window's glass.

"Stay with the van," said Monk, apparently to Trumpeter.

Willa was almost in reach of him, but he hip-faked her to skip a few yards away. He pointed the tire iron in front of him, as if warning her off. She still came toward him and he backed further off, and before he began to run he smashed in the side window of a small blue pizza delivery car and cracked the car's top, as well. Monk before going after him gave the van keys to Grace.

"Be quick about getting us!"

As Grace made it through the café door, she saw Monk, alongside the delivery car, stepping backwards through the parking lot. His wallet was out and as he threw cash in the broken car window, he pointed at the Seeker van, sending Willa back to it. He swiveled and ran after Trumpeter, who seemed headed for the storefront at the end of the mall. The nearly speechless Grace swept her charges into the van, saw with relief that it was an automatic, and wondered who else at the mall was watching this go on. She half wanted to laugh at the fun and ab-surdity of the situation, and through the gate of her impishness she glimpsed the emotional currents that had driven the deed to occur. She also wondered whether Trumpeter could be even more destructive. But all of this was meat for a later hour—now, she drove a getaway car.

She aimed for the scene framed by Trumpeter and Monk, who gave his protégé a ten-yard gap. They yelled at each other and fitfully walked sideways and ran. As the van of observers drew near it affected the action—a phenomenon New Age philosophy makes much of in terms of quantum physics, Monk would later add laughingly—with Trumpeter and then Monk turning to sprint for the storefront. It was a carpet store, and the fact of a boy in headphones dragging a rug out its door was what saved Monk from having to try to bring down Trumpeter on the pitiless cement. The boy seemed not to notice as Trumpeter lost his fervor and pulled up short and as Monk, a moment later, took the tire iron away. He did turn to the van, though, as Grace slid up close for her cargo. She saw him watch as she stood momentarily aslant of the painted lines, with her engine idling; and she sensed that he continued to watch as she swung away from the mall and followed the outer edge of the parking lot back to the road.

21

Deciding to Listen

Further confusing Grace, it was Trumpeter who twice tried to step the group down from his minute of turbulence. Maybe the imp had tapped his forehead, too. On the bridge—she drove ten miles per hour but there was no long delay—he told, in flat tones, the story of a Catskill Mountains meditation trip he had taken in early autumn after his first year at the academy. It was an alien tale of unintended smugness, with him as the Martian and with vacationers (from a taut ethnic community he had met in the town he camped beside) as Earthlings. Then, nearing the gravel road into Seeker, he spoke of "Retreat Week." The old mummer Grace allowed him a cautious but much-needed cue by asking what this was. He described it as the one week each year that every workshop had an entirely spiritual theme. Well-known teachers of Buddhism, Hinduism, Sufism, Western mysticism, and shamanism strolled the grounds. Most meals, with seven hundred people present, were taken in silence. This would all begin in five days.

Grace, who could catch but not hold his gaze in her mirror, saw that all her riders—Trumpeter and Willa behind her, Monk nearer the blasted windows in the seat behind them, and Moira Kathleen on her right—had fallen into private reflections. She turned her own mind back to the road and her thoughts. "I'll see some of Retreat Week, then," she said. "I have to go home next Tuesday." She added, with more force than she had intended, "This is all pretty bewildering."

They parked at the maintenance shed near the entrance. Trumpeter, obdurately, and Monk, who had obvious business together, waved their goodbyes as the women headed up the road. Turning in toward the main grounds of the campus at the café, Grace saw that it was the sweet period after breakfast, just before workshops began, when a dozen people lingered insistently in the garden with their coffees. To her relief, Moira Kathleen seemed to still feel the rise in confidence that the midnight crisis had engendered. Grace was glad to see that the ledge she had walked herself onto at the mall had not interfered: the woman seemed able to pick which of her moments she retained. What practice, Grace thought briefly, must lead up to this!

"I'm smelly and tired," said Moira Kathleen with a small laugh, "but I think I'll get my guitar and give the workshop a new try. I guess I have some new things to write about." As she walked off, Willa bent to re-strap her sandals—in fact, she waited for the woman to go far enough down the path for her to follow on her own. Grace above her own dismay recalled that of them all Willa had been the one most turned to rock salt by the accident. Now she had Trumpeter's whipping about to contend with as well. Grace didn't know why the car crash had upset Willa so deeply—why it had seemed to signal not injury and a rehabilitation trial but the end of something.

Willa stood and frowned. "I'll see you later," she said, and began to make her way on the path. Then she turned back. "I know a few of us will visit Francine tonight, unless we go back in a few hours."

"I'm signed up for a staff wellness orientation that goes into the evening," Grace said, speaking fast. "It's time I dug in—I mean, began to really learn about this place. In some ways, I've enjoyed a free ride. Who knows, though, if after all *this* my courage will last into late afternoon?"

Willa rocked her weight onto her back leg but seemed hesitant to move. Grace extended her smile, but felt an underlying agitation.

"Back in the hospital waiting area," said Willa, "he told me twice he'd had about enough of the academy." That again, and more fuel for the fire, thought Grace, but before she could respond—before she could think what to say back—the young woman told her something else.

"He and I share something important," Willa added. "I rarely mention this, but after I took my degree I spent fifteen months working for a media company. I only quit last Christmas. I was shipped around Europe for a year in training programs; then, for what came to be my last eighty-two days, I worked back in Africa."

The question "And?" entered Grace's mind, but before she could speak a staff person she and Willa knew passed, with a little finger-wave hail, in an electric cart. In an afterthought, the woman cut her current and turned to ask after Francine. Grace, splintered by a sense of all she didn't know, suggested with some remorse that the driver ferry Willa to a place nearer her tent. Willa, with a small shrug, seemed to accept this brush-off as minor or circumstantial and got in the cart.

To keep the cart there, Grace put a hand atop its windshield. She smiled at the driver, glanced beyond her, and turned back to Willa, all without knowing what to say.

"Maybe Trumpeter is right," said Willa. "In Africa, I worked on the reselling of old European television shows. What the West brings begins and ends with making money. It's not a culture to live humanly in, let alone sell to others in one's native land."

"I don't know," said Grace. "About all of this, I don't know."

An hour later, Grace reluctantly arrived for her kitchen shift. It hadn't made sense to grab the shower she had missed at dawn, and she instead spent her time in the staff mess rereading lists of workshops and other activities the Seeker staff were offered. It felt like she piled strain upon strain, but she kept at the task. When work began she for the first time acquiesced to the received kitchen wisdom that old-timers like her couldn't handle much. The move backfired, though: she never got into the dining room and instead spent two hours compacting boxes and moving trash and two more at the dishwasher—which seemed ghostly with the absence of Francine. Yet, it may have been the best outcome, as she got through most of her shift in a welcome silence. She saw this as a process—here it truly was a process—where the body just tried to wear itself out, at a time when the mind would not agree to come along.

She took her shower, finally, in mid-afternoon and then loped to her tent. By now, she had seen no one from the morning for six hours. The clouds had cleared finally and it was a beautiful hour for a swim; however, this would have set her on a sure path for missing the wellness orientation, as it began in an hour, and she had to sleep before forcing her mind to a choice. When she started up, seemingly a minute later, it was from a sleep deep enough to ensure that she would feel panic before her deadline and see nothing clearly. Having slid into her warm sleeping bag, she had also begun to cook like malodorous dough. She felt utterly cruddy, knew the feeling would last for a while, and wanted nothing. So, she would have to decide based on form instead of substance.

Correcting herself, she now reasoned: This is something I don't want to miss.

The Ear of the Mind

Seven hours later, as the workshop ended, Grace was in an even more heightened state of overload and fatigue. She walked with the others to the café and, sliding quickly into a lengthening line, bought an iced fruit bar. Taking it onto the porch, she felt how the temperature had actually risen from late afternoon. Passing back through the café, just before it closed, she saw no one familiar to her who would know about Francine; but a staff member at the downstairs guest reception desk had the news that she would completely recover.

For two weeks Grace had been in a regime of early bedtimes, but going to bed now she would either not fall asleep or spring back up at three a.m. She had felt too much that day and, upping the ante, facets within her had been turned toward the light. She walked past the grove in which Ken Samuel had hectored his audience, and climbed a small hill. The path crossed an edge of a manicured field, and peering north she saw heat lightning above what must have been the Catskills. It looked like calligraphic script upon the sky. Although no stars shone there was reflected moonlight, and the covering clouds seemed no thicker than lace. Grace found a bench she remembered seeing, turned it to face north, and lay down. Her muscles arched against the slats; *there* was the tension, as without it she would sag in fatigue. With hints of far-off lyricism, the easy wind gusts teased her skin.

She tried to keep her eyes open as she began to breathe, but gave up, as there was too much stimulation. Listening within herself, she felt the currents that shocked not sky but her blood and bone. Her old deep-breathing trick, while approved at the wellness workshop, seemed toy-like compared to the deeper meditative systems used at the academy. She could bring herself to a slowing of her heart and resulting calm, but had no hint of a presence beyond her senses. It usually took her a few minutes to reach a twelve-second deep-breathing cycle: twelve counted seconds each of inhaling, holding, and letting go. Somewhere near that point she would make a little jump beyond consciousness, often to sleep but always to a moment of self-gathering; she would know of the vault in time by a loss of her count. Her landing *now* was into a form that rested easily on the edge of a magnificent storm. She took an added breath in celebration and on ascending her heart met without trembling a flash in a closer part of the sky.

There were two beckoning topics, Trumpeter's behavior and the wellness workshop. As the workshop, to her surprise, had been full of common sense, she chose to reflect on it first. She felt anyway a strong present need to better understand the academy. It was likely through its lens that she would finally see Trumpeter, as well.

Lying lengthwise on the bench, she put a hand on her breastbone and looked quietly at the heat lightning. The air was damp and she thought it would rain hard where she was in minutes or, likelier, hours. The blanketing wonder was part of what made her feel restful. It settled her as she apprehended her idea of the last few days: that she had stepped off on a journey different from the one she had planned.

The wellness workshop had taken place in an old, screened-in gazebo in a secluded area of campus. There were eleven in the group, with two leaders, and as the gazebo could hold three times their number, they felt huddled together. The dense, enveloping forest was another reason to feel small. To Grace, the tent-like building, with a small stage they didn't use, reflected puzzles that also overlay the workshop. One concerned "spirituality," that guiding idea at the academy whose true meaning she didn't know. A second touched on an idea newly upsetting her: that her prosaic, two-decade family life might grow entangled in a different sort of need.

A sense of what a participant called "spiritual calm"—Grace felt that this included courtesy, besides ideas less clear to her—pervaded the workshop. One leader, Mel, a pensive, thirtyish woman Grace knew from the kitchen, gave a welcoming invocation. Actually, she began by standing, smiling, and remaining quiet.

Grace and the others watched her, eyed each other, and breathed.

"Welcome to The Seeker Academy for Healing Practices," Mel said, finally. "Most of you have been here awhile, even weeks, but we think it's never too late to say 'welcome.' I wonder if we can welcome each other."

"Welcome!" they said collectively. At someone's suggestion, each person turned to welcome whom they sat beside. "Welcome, Mel!" a woman added emphatically.

The other leader, Mike, was tall and cushiony, with gray hair, a melodious voice, and affecting brown eyes. Once Mel had explained how the workshop would operate, Mike had them introduce themselves. The group's accepting ethos came out quickly as a man calling himself "Pythagoras" said he was a shaman from Athens, Ohio. No one smiled at the freighted claim; the man, in his thirties, was matter-of-fact. Yet Grace wondered what shamans—mad whirling dancers as far as she knew them to be—might have to do with the argument-loving gods of ancient Greece?

Mike asked them to more roundly greet someone new to them, whom they would sometimes team with in the workshop. Grace, beginning a mission to better know her surroundings, asked Pythagoras, who wore a black headscarf, to be her partner.

The man, who had a smooth face and a hard stare, looked her over and drew a book from his daypack. He picked out a photo and gave it to her. It was an old picture; at least, it was of a woman dressed in the more formal clothes of a long time back. Aglow like gold neon or an electric filament, a winged, female fairy fluttered diminutively above the human form.

"Here is scientific proof that a spirit world exists," Pythagoras declared.

The workshop really began with what Mel called a "guided meditation," when she asked them each to send "positive energy" to the group. She told them how to sit and act; then she rang a bell and the meditation began. Grace used her breathing trick, but the day's events and a vigor gained from her nap caused a tower of thoughts to rock precipitously over her. On Mel's regular reminders, she tried but usually failed to bring her mind back to her count. She was relieved when a second bell rang and the short meditation ended.

Over six hours, she learned, they would be introduced to disciplines that brought life to the mind, body, and heart. These things Grace now began to pull apart and, to her surprise, apply common-sense judgments to. The final flower in the wellness bouquet, overarching but chimerical, she heard called "soul"—but also "sacredness," "spirit," "religion," and "transcendence." More than the other disciplines, added Mike, which mixed concepts and practices, soul work would be tackled conceptually. This was due to limits of time.

"Mind work, or meditation," he began, "anchors and is the bridge to the other disciplines." The sense Grace had of Mike was of someone reading from prompts: as if a layer separated who he now was from whoever else he had been in a long life. Then she challenged herself to shift attention to his words.

Even if I'm right, which may not be the case at all, she thought. There is laziness in how I usually stop at character.

Mike told them that meditation was ultimately about learning to accept suffering. He said this grimly but added with a smile that such acceptance was the door to being "spiritually present." It let you in on the ultimate reality of god.

To Grace this was a startling yet clear premise, which Mike enlarged on with an explanation of "mindfulness." Another foundation concept at Seeker, it played a part in yoga class, in Seeker marketing, in talks she overheard. "Meditating," said Mike, "we escape our conflicts based in thoughts, feelings, and acts. A mindful state rises, where we wake from the circumstances of life into a larger presence."

Thick black meditation pillows were piled along one wall. Each person who hadn't already done so went to get one, and Grace, musing as she walked, collided with two classmates. I'll put my qualms off for later, she thought. I feel a strong need to pay attention.

Laconically, Mel led the next meditation. She said before starting that while a lot would be discussed in the workshop, they should now merely listen as she took them through the practice. "You already know enough for this," she said. "A key point is that we always already know enough."

Grace clung to her sense of knowing what to expect; as it turned out, this isle of seeming safety was but the first in a chain of distractions during what would be a long quarter hour. Mel and Mike sat facing the group, with their backs straight, legs crossed, and rumps resting on the edges of their pillows. Mel in a second directive told the group to watch their postures. "Meditation is guided by quiet breathing," she said. "Its rhythms are a bridge between body and mind. Quiet breathing is in turn shaped by a balanced posture. Hold your head up, straighten your spine, and think of erectness as a natural sign of dignity.

"Now withdraw from the world to ask for the gift of inwardness. With eyes open or closed, fix your gaze somewhere far on the horizon.

"Then feel how your hand movements represent your moods, and your mouth holds a lot of the worldly stresses that come your way."

Setting up along these guidelines, Grace heard dreamy recorded music that she knew had been playing all along.

The bell rang for the meditation and Grace, with eyes closed, set off in an unfamiliar direction. For now, she had taken it on trust that there was something new to experience. She didn't seek novelty; rather a gathering of attentiveness here at Seeker showed a path she wanted to follow. What she meant by "attentiveness" she could best express with an analogy to her years in theater. There had been periods of reading and seeing great plays and infrequently acting in them—she knew with a wistful sense that she hadn't gone far in her art—when she had glimpsed beyond her everyday life. Her gaze in this direction had been sharply attentive. If in time she had turned back from this soaring experience, it still meant a lot to her.

She saw that a form of this attentiveness grew at Seeker, too. Haphazard Trumpeter sought it, whereas Sophie, Monk, Mel here, and many others clearly possessed it.

Alas, Grace discovered that, unlike theater, which settled an audience by stealing its interest, meditation required a personal discipline she did not possess. So stealth couldn't work. The fluid posture she believed she was settling into turned choppy, and she began to think in an obsessive way of her hands, her mouth, her spine, and her crossed legs. In an almost programmed sequence, these regions tingled as she tried to lose her sense of them and regain her count. "Don't try to stop the thoughts," cautioned Mel, apparently to everyone. "See them rather as the mind's weather, which like most weather we can usually ignore. If you have a thought, note it in passing, as you would a cloud, and return to your count."

Grace thought of her fingers and skin and of how she seemed driven to think these thoughts, and of the idea of destiny, and of her count. She remembered the stormy, May afternoon at the hovering mega-mall near her suburb, with its associations of clammy air, umbrellas, and the crowded movie multiplex. The crowds meant it had probably been a weekend. Such ideas barraged her and sent her back to Mel's guidance, that if we *can* tune out most weather, some we cannot. She gazed out over the strength of her resistance.

When the bell rang again, Grace opened her eyes with a disturbing new sense of her inner turmoil. It flowed not from the past year: Grace knew that, beyond her deflections, she had acted responsibly. Rather, it was turmoil alive beyond the usual reach of drama, yet with true influence. Nor was the disturbance something personal.

She listened to Mike address concerns from others, who had fought their own mental wanderings. "Preparing to meditate," he said, "it helps to go over our resistance. Some may have felt fatigue or self-criticism, attitudes we use to hide from the strangeness of feeling. We all have this resistance, yet the fact is that the real truths of our lives hide behind them. So, we want to keep our resistances from dominating us. This we do by splitting them off from the meditative effort. When you find yourself thinking, turn the thought into an object. Wrap it in a label: call it a 'feeling,' a 'memory,' a 'plan.' Then turn back to your count."

The word "real" is getting a workout here, thought Grace.

Mike then identified stress, flowing from the normal conflicts of life, as the cause of the mind's need for control. "East and West share this view of stress and conflict," he added, "but differ in that the West ties conflict to life choice and luck, the East to karmic laws of cause and effect. Yet, in either view conflict grows in a practical sense from people tripping over each other or themselves. And this struggle only worsens under the Western materialism now spreading globally, where stress is unavoidable. People learn from the get-go to be busy and acquisitive. Few know that a more peaceable life is possible."

Mike and Mel had clearly, Grace saw, run this workshop before and knew what they would say. Mel now took over to claim that in modern society stress was managed with willful diversions. "We escape into movies, sports, and travel. But we don't find peace, because our diversions hide the calming, impersonal energies that flow from spiritual sources. We instead feed on our stress as we drive toward anger, depression, and fear.

"Unlike escapism," she added, "meditation takes pressure *off* the self. It shows us stress objectively, from a viewpoint of not self but freedom and relaxation. It locks the trigger—separating stressful forces from the resulting anxieties felt by the will."

A woman behind Grace contended that this was hard to follow. She didn't know what the idea of "meditative freedom" meant.

"The answer," Mel said, "lies in Mike's idea of getting behind one's thoughts. It's a skill to be discovered more in practice, but we can say that meditation's first goal is to make us present. We learn to separate from our anxious self and join the world. Even if the practice is initially awkward, the goal should seem pragmatic. Think of an experience that awed you enough to let you lose track of yourself. If you can slow enough to hold that feeling in meditation and see yourself objectively, you find a place of letting go and acceptance. You feel more grounded in life, but a little removed from it as well."

Grace knew that while Mel's words didn't quite strike their mark, she aimed at something important: the idea of awe that can quiet the mind. It's funny, she thought. In one sense, I live without awe for months or... as chunks of life slide by; in another, I think I dance with awe every day. I find it by chance; as often, it finds me. Then it slips my mind. Can I meditate to overcome my lack of discipline?

Do I want to lose the serendipity? Do I prefer it to be haphazard?

"Meditation," Mel was adding, "wakes us to a spiritual oneness that holds life's complexity and contradictions. We come to see problems with a detached tenderness, and this feeds our wonder and intuition. It also supports our need to pass through life with real care.

"In this larger reality, conflicts find their own solutions."

Grace was tired. She let her mind run as a recording device as Mike, responding to questions, added that there were ways to bypass resistance; that self-acceptance played a role; and that some practices looked beyond mindfulness. Perking up, Grace heard that these last mentioned sought a mystical connection with god.

When the final meditation began, she worked hard to label the re-sistance she knew must emerge as "the big box," and told herself that she trusted her experience. A time came when her breathing quieted, and she drifted above her conscious filtering in a way that made her feel like the fairy Pythagoras had displayed—she smiled at this second mirage of her self and named it "metaphor." Then she poked at the idea that trouble found its own solution.

The fourth mirage, hardest to dispel, came as a memo from the big box. It showed her the mega-mall, clammy during a June thunder-storm, which ran behind her family's house.

The Ear of the Body

The pressing weight of the big box caused her to join in somberly when, after a break, the workshop turned to bodywork. She felt more at ease in the sense that her introductions to yoga and Thai massage gave her some context. Her body knew both a feel of renewal and some reasons for its heaviness. Her discomfort grew, though, from the same newly gotten markers. Much of the discussion, which surrounded a run-through of basic yoga postures, she could frame as a critique of how she lived in the world. And now her body kept her from dismissing what she heard.

This awakening, when mixed with her latent distrust of society, also showed her the driving force behind the many salves and kinds of bodywork she saw always advertised at home. Yes, she mused. The commercial wheel turns.

"We in the West," said the tall, mushy Mike in a caustic tone, "live in exile from our bodies. And society sells itself so forcefully that it's hard to even see that this is so. Nor is the hatred only for sex: over three millennia, monotheism taught that the flesh exiled us from sacred realms. Then capitalism arose and said that the body, like the earth, was to be exploited. Bodies rot, capitalists were told at Sunday sermons; they saw how the earth was disadvantaged. Both were mere fuel."

Whenever Mike paused for effect, greenwood sounds rose in the distance; a chainsaw worked near Ephesus. Grace met this too-patent illustration of Mike's theme with a sarcasm she aimed at herself.

"Of course," Mike went on, "the masculine, exploitive West most hates the balanced, feminine wisdom inherent in both nature and the body: an Eros that mythologists call the 'glue' between people, creatures, and things! And our reluctance to see life as sacred or the soul as at home in the body is what has brought us to where we are now, choking beside the earth on our human-made mess."

As if meditating, Grace resisted Mike's potent words by returning her attention to him. She fought with herself, as she knew the perhaps-inauthentic man sounded a bell many arduous people had rung for decades or, in changing forms, for centuries. This returned her to Monk's gritty parade of romanticism, and in a forlorn slide to her own lost education. So the claim doesn't die, she reflected, when listeners choose or are made to move on.

With Mike having defined the illness, Mel could show the remedy. Grace liked this pale, round-faced woman for the simple reason that she seemed able to listen to herself and to others, a trait Mike did not seem to share.

"Bodily healing begins," Mel said, "when we submit to nature's restorative powers. A release of control is important, as it frees us to pledge our less willful, spiritual self to help in the body's care. This humbler help takes the forms of listening, learning, and resting."

Mel paused and looked sharply at the group. "As Mike suggests, a big part of the story is political. As we see how cultural interests, including business interests, shape how we see ourselves, we come to look for what our body truly has to say. And what we most often find is stored trauma and self-hurting coping skills. Then comes a time to be responsible: to do the work—if need be, with psychotherapy—to get out from under our defenses."

Mel told the group that, while there were other ideas to cover, she was inclined to do yoga, so their bodies might truly have a turn. But now her listeners were in a boil, with several eager to comment. Grace was quiet; and she felt too fidgety for yoga. I could take a day each mulling over every hour of the last twenty-four, she thought. The Athenian shaman, Pythagoras, then erupted with the claim that the body catapulted its damaged soul parts around the world to protect them from further dangers.

"It's time," said Mel, "with our minds stirred up like this, to do some yoga."

Grace felt overexcited and tired, like a child ready for bed. But a mark of maturity was to endure such a time. She had of course often done so before, but facing plainer objectives: scraping by during a last hour at school, a blow-over fight with her husband, or some such thing. Now, she faced some indefinite change and the risk was higher.

Everyone seemed to enjoy the shift yoga provided. For a half hour the suppertime air flowing in through the screens and the mottled trees and meditative music grew in stature against the quiet directives of Mel, who took the workshop through some core postures. Grace soon broke a sweat and, stretching willfully against her resistance, she was embraced by the practice. But her tottering brain returned when the conversation did.

It was during this quarter hour before the supper break, as the talk swung on a political tether, that Grace gained a context for Seeker's wellness offerings. "Some problems have easy solutions," said Mike. "We can limit stress with relaxation techniques, for instance. Today, much illness grows from people coping badly, via escapism but also the use of biological anachronisms like "fight or flight." We go crazy in situations like traffic jams, when we face little risk. Blood pressure, pulse, and brain-wave activity spikes up; we can even stroke out. A better response is to calm our minds; in the case of a commute, by leaving early to make stress less likely, and, if we get stuck, practicing light meditation or self-massage."

Grace noted how science's hard instrumentation made a kind of tidal reappearance in much of this holistic doctrine.

"But it's wrong," added Mel, "to think only modern stresses keep us from bodily health. Old Asian cultures, whose views of spiritual health include the body, believed all life involved suffering and all healing relied partly on practice. Their patient *listening* led them to find an invisible energy circulating in the body. In China, it is called 'Qi,' in India, 'Prana.' These cultures also saw how stress blocks the flow. This led them to design practices like yoga, acupuncture, and massage, which dispel the blockages and bring the body into balance. They rely on simple breathing, movement, and stimulation.

"Illustrated differently, our state of conflict, of spiritual exile, means we always need practice to reach our animal presence. Therefore, yoga, for instance, creates animal presence rituals through its poses named for animals—like 'rabbit,' 'locust' and 'cobra.' Similar rituals can grow in whatever reminds us that we embody spirit and relate through it to everyone and everything. Mindful stretching and eating—respecting what sustains us—can provide such reminders. As can illness, if we surrender our will to it and remember that while treatment may come from outside the body, wellness arises within."

The Ear of the Heart

The possibilities for where Grace was, other than amidst darkness and flashing light, narrowed only as she lifted her head from the bench and looked down her body at Hans. Most likely, she had woken to his calling her from several yards away, a gap he still held. Her first waking seconds endured dreamily; as lightning lit the sky she recalled the heavy flow of her day. Her body longed for a bed, but her mind in its fragment of sleep had barely caught a breath.

Her heart beat quickly but she felt no agitation.

"Hi," she said, while raising her knees and pulling in her ankles. "Come sit. How did you ever find me?"

"It's been a long twenty-four hours and I'd hoped to run into you. Elsa saw you leave the café a while ago, but that was my one clue and I'd given up, actually. I sometimes sit on this bench at night, myself."

"Elsa?"

"She was a teacher in your wellness workshop." Hans sat, in a motion that coincided with an early sound of thunder.

"Yes, impressive *Elsa*. She came after supper to talk about the heart. Who is she? We saw her on the raft, kayaking with Monk."

"Elsa goes back to when this place began. She's still a director."

Grace looked up at Hans, who turned his gaze on her. She was briefly still; then she began to turn her head from side to side. Her eyes widened as the swinging intensified. Her cheeks crested as a prelude to either laughter or tears.

"I saw Francine tonight," said Hans. "She'll recover physically; but after two months she's in another hospital. It'll be hard for her."

"Yes, another hospital," repeated Grace, with caustic stress. Then, smiling balefully, incredulous, she swung her head sideways again.

"Willa told me about the tire iron, too. Actually, I heard the story repeatedly. I haven't seen Trumpeter, though. Monk says you set up well for a life of crime."

Grace smiled and sat up, lightened by this image of her. She felt a humid, propelling breeze. "Willa seemed undone this morning. How is she?"

"Fitful. Different. She told Sophie she may return to Europe early."

"She kept looking at me all morning. And when we got back to Seeker, she wanted to talk. But I was baffled myself. I think I let her down.

"I feel different, myself," she added. "The day was a magic carpet ride. I may not get back to my old pedestrian self anytime soon."

"You've not had a pedestrian year, either."

"I've been thinking about that, and why I feel differently now. Doing my best for Alicia, I only do what people do when they love. We all do our best; if I help it's due to luck, if only my luck to be strong. But what I flew over recently isn't about strength. Thinking back, some of what I heard last night scares me. And then as Trumpeter flipped out at the mall, I kept waiting to see myself pull up, arrive as another sour observer, with my green Toyota wagon and usual oblivion. In life, you learn to use it for entertainment or pass it by. Then, in the workshop, I began to feel shame."

"Then you missed part of the message. Elsa is surely not into shame."

"I wonder why. What I mean is: I finally paid attention, and what I saw rather knocked me off a ledge. I know they do the wellness retreat all the time here, and people pay to go through it over a weekend and probably leave smiling. I think what happens is they are reminded or begin to learn to be more aware; that at least is how I translate the 'mindfulness' they talk about. My shame is that I've felt this awareness my whole life, but I usually turn away from it. I go off busily in every other possible direction… this while the entire world goes to hell."

She saw Hans smile in the darkness. The storm, mostly quiet and invisible, might be creeping toward them. "Is that because you know I want to talk about the workshop?" She looked at his delicate features.

"I grin because I'm sure you will. And because I think you know that berating yourself is just your way of getting started."

"It's true I need to dump," said Grace, glad for the attention but pensive. "My mind is too full. All the breathless talk about wellness and spirituality—I find it off-and-on silly or based in deep knowing or wrong factually or disturbingly sad. Then, too, I'm caught between my need to trust myself and my great tower of self-contempt."

"Well, there's the outline for a course of study," said Hans wryly.

"The workshop upset me because it spoke to how we live, and I'm not used to that. It was hard, sincere, and thoughtful. Now I'm too tired to sort things out or do anything but try…. Should I begin where the workshop ended, with an overview of spirituality? That seems to be the organizing element here at Seeker."

"I tend to avoid that conversation, as I think I said last night."

"You did; I admit I was probing, as I missed your point then and I'm more curious now. But I accept what you say—and for now, I want to put spirituality aside, too. Well, meditation and yoga more concern doing than talking, at least for novices like me. That leaves what Elsa came to speak of in the gazebo—her break-your-heart idea of somehow healing the heart."

His look back at her was again receptive.

"I think I'd just like to ruminate for a moment," she said.

Grace now evoked for Hans the workshop hour that followed supper. She even backed up to render the break time when, as they ate cold salads—the kitchen had sent canisters and bowls filled with greens, tuna, and bread—they sampled one another's views. Mel and Mike had largely lain back and listened. Yet to Grace this leaderless time had failed, which she saw also as an important lesson. Again, the issue was too little context: as with many other talks not on personal matters she had joined at Seeker, this one lacked the wingspan to keep from falling into self-protection. Pythagoras was not alone in striking a pose of conviction—he showed his photo again and said the earth's soft body was a protector of fairies—because the gathering, whose participants mostly were strangers, was laden with social risk. People made small speeches—some of a few words—in which they gave opinions or made careful points, but as each voice ceased the room filled with a kind of calibrating stillness. Elsa arrived in the midst of this go-round; then on a signal from Mike or Mel she stepped forward to move the workshop along.

Grace thought her manner combined Mike's and Mel's. She spoke clearly, but seemed to only listen carefully at times. Perhaps two decades at a task, Grace thought, makes for a near-saturation, and she only fully wakes when she hears something new. But she did seem to be an effective storyteller, and so, much of the time, a good teacher.

"Our hearts," Elsa had begun, "often resist joy. And often a similar resistance upsets our meditations. Over the years, as we dull the pains inflicted by our conflicts, our resistances harden into armor. This is a human debility—but one the West magnifies by teaching that we are punished by god for our conflicts and bring our conflicts on ourselves with our curiosity and desire."

Reflecting on her Sunday school teaching, Grace thought: What of Jacob clutching the angel, waiting to be blessed? Isn't this desire, and curiosity, too? Then a rich blessing is given. And what of the Virgin Mary? Does Elsa know this basic fare? Does she read it differently?

A lot one hears here, she thought, is opinion. Not yoga posture stuff, but the cultural criticisms. And yet, the historical, Western fever that burns us in everyday life is not to be disputed, either.

"Heart work begins," explained Elsa, who Grace thought looked fit and young for her age, "with a desire to shed the heart's armor and open to life. This means coming to know and forgive oneself—and thus to emotional and perhaps psychological healing. Yet cradling these willful efforts is a sense of deep acceptance.

"The way into heart work," she went on, "is through the magic of stories. Hearing stories, we feel the beating, frightened heart behind the armor. We hear what the heart needs and what it fears. Hearing this quiets our shame and helps us believe in ourselves. Then with fear less effective as a barrier, we can take better care of ourselves.

"The work is hard," she added. "The surrounding darkness is intense: our fears like to lurk behind us. But until we separate from them and feel our boundaries, we don't know ourselves, and so can't put weight on our values and beliefs. To see this absence of self-knowledge and self-confidence manifest, we need only think of the unpleasant behaviors and twisted people we meet in life. The crucial next step, of course, is to grow aware of these traits in our self."

"I was wide-eyed hearing this," Grace told Hans, "since of course it made me think of Moira Kathleen. It's so easy and so much a sign of falsity to write such people off."

"This all involves small, careful work, and I give it my respect," replied Hans.

"You give it your life. You do so far more than I."

In the workshop, Elsa had paused to let her auditors reflect. Then, surprising Grace, she praised them. "Listening—bringing consciousness to life—is a mythic act," she said. "Thus, listeners are heroes. In a way, they are even warrior heroes, of the kind pop culture cheers. But in our 'mindful' retelling of the myth, the villains are named 'Anger,' 'Sadness,' and 'Cynicism.'

"In fact, the quest for mindfulness—authenticity in life—is the mythic core of the hero journey. This is so in every culture: a hero begins stuck, unaware, and mournful, and goes in search of healing magic. The long road winds but it leads to an inner awakening—the hero learns to be attentive, and therein lies part of the magic."

Grace, who's suburban home was full of hero journeys rendered in TV shows, in movies, in games, and in books, kept a lid on her doubts. This idea tying how she lived actually to mythic journeys was appealing. To quiet her misgivings, she glanced about. The others looked happy and at ease.

Elsa nodded to Pythagoras. "As priestly rituals help heroes in other cultures, rituals of therapy help them in ours. And it's in ritual contexts that stories are relived and folded into a larger view of life. They begin as images and evolve into music, dance, visual arts, and literature. The key thing then is to open the pursuit to all: working alone or in groups and with helpers as needed, we can all use our inborn talents to create the ritual stories we need."

"And that," said Grace to Hans, "is about what Elsa had to say, though she went on talking about these things for almost an hour."

"Elsa is brave to marry the hero journey with egalitarianism," Hans observed. "It's a commendable wish, at least."

"That's one idea that has me reeling," said Grace, who was feeling swept away—just as she had after Ken Samuel's talk a day earlier in the nearby grove. Now, as then, she felt that things just said were rising as new belief beams in her mind. It thrilled her to watch the beams go in even as, in a split-off way, she knew they might be temporary.

"What's being created here is important," she added. "I've been backing up from it in my mind, and the farther away I get, the more important it looks."

"I find it important, too. But to you it is urgent and fresh. Remember, also, that I've moved away from the middle-class life. So, I find you, with your green Toyota wagon, to be an exotic as well as a dear. I'll gladly listen if you want to go on."

Grace smiled gratefully and swung her legs back onto the bench. "Two things have me stirred up. One is the welter of ideas here concerned with other ways to live. As I said, I have all kinds of reactions to them, from wonder, to scorn, to a shame at my general ignorance. They're all going off inside me now like rockets. But the bigger fireworks come from my peeling the lid back on how much these changes are needed. I start to ask if my life is built on denial. And in my mind, I keep returning to a rainy spring day at the mega-mall east of my house, headed away from the Hudson. What utter pretension!"

"Why is that pretentious?"

Grace exercised her new mannerism, swinging her head from side to side again. "None of this is new. Inattention, a loathing to even keep track, isn't innocence. Most people I know are locked in the kinds of resistance to feeling the workshop went over.

"Changes!" she added. "Changes? I don't even know what I'm talking about."

It was then, perhaps, Grace thought, as a kindness, or to reflect her fury, that the storm broke over the academy. Two emanations—rain torrents and lightning that unexpectedly hit behind them, toward the kitchen, not the Catskills—struck in tandem. The thunderclap that ended their parley arrived a few heartbeats later. They made a silent dash for the main hall porch, half a minute's jaunt in clear weather.

Now, though, she felt like a soaked sponge before getting halfway. As they ran, a second lightning strike came snapping at their heals. If the air did not cool with the rain, her body slightly did. Turning as they got onto the porch, they looked on a battalion of descending vertical lines that now occupied the field.

"Hans," Grace asked, "do you skip the musings about spirituality to protect what you've learned about wellness?"

She had turned to face him, and saw in his eyes an agility that made her see him as a tennis player. In his dutiful way, he would not speak before thinking. Playing his game, even as a boy, he would—she knew—have kept honorably to his practice schedule.

"Like you," he said, "I see mind, body, and heart as a wilderness. And while claiming not to, I keep an eye on the consensual nightmare, as some people here call middle-class life—I'll at least watch tennis on TV if I can. But I've learned that I'm unfit for the debate and power exercise that comes with talk of god and spirituality. It all usually gets elevated in a way that doesn't appeal to me."

"But your wellness work must be a kind of spiritual work."

Hans didn't respond directly. "I'm a practical person, Grace," he said. "I learned this as I impractically studied philosophy and tried to play tennis for money. It's enough for me to work against the resistances Elsa speaks of with my body. I look forward to a lifetime of study and activity."

It was long past bedtime, Grace was far from her tent, and the rain might pour down for hours. In a tired way, she feared the storm's grandeur, and no less the questions that had entered her heart that day. She lacked the resolution to be logical, so she stored what Hans had told her. Still, her mind took some new little leaps.

"I think Monk shares in your practical outlook," she said.

"Monk? Well, I think, yes and no. *He* goes up on the high trails."

"He shows a kind of obstinacy that seems quite practical."

"Yes, but it's not entirely a sea-level pursuit. His obstinacy may in part come from time concerns."

"Time concerns?"

"Two years ago he was a patient where you were today. The treatment seems to have worked and people say he rebuilt his strength, but one never knows. He's trying to accomplish something here, though. I'm sure of that."

Grace—stunned to hear Monk was ill and feeling the yoke pull again across her shoulders, with her mind tugged back suddenly to the nursing station near Alicia's hospital room—looked out at the falling rain.

Part Five

Spirituality

Just the Right Invitation

The Golds were back! Grace spotted them—she had frankly forgotten they would be returning—crossing a cabin green during the hottest hour of Friday afternoon, as she was herself going with a crew from cabin to cabin making beds. There was time only for a fast greeting, as with a new crowd soon arriving (or, like Anton and Deb, already there), the housekeeping crews were on a tear. Both Golds smiled broadly; they plainly looked on the familiar excitement of the coming days with relish. Grace, with her lower back sore from bending and sweat on her face, a little flustered from her work, made plans to meet them at the café at four p.m., when she was done with her shift.

On her break for lunch an hour earlier, she had found and said goodbye to Moira Kathleen. The airy woman had been hard to spot in the tangled dining-hall: since an early checkout hour preceded the morning's workshops, most departing guests juggled daypacks with their lunch trays. Over three days, Grace had hardly seen or spoken with her. Happily, though, she knew Moira Kathleen had gone back into her songwriting workshop.

She found her at a corner indoor table, talking raptly with two women and a man. The table's two empty chairs fronted food trays and so were taken. A wall beside the table was stacked with daypacks and musical instrument cases.

Grace briefly waited to be seen, and then called, "Moira Kathleen!"

As the tablemates turned to her, a man holding a juice glass slid by and into one of the vacant chairs. Moira Kathleen in a stagy voice said, "Grace, hello!" She then told the others that it was Grace who had convinced her to not give up when, days before, she had hit a wall. Grace smiled, as Moira Kathleen's tablemates grinned appreciatively, with one turned sideways in his chair. Then she moved to the right. Appearing first perplexed then stiffly receptive, Moira Kathleen stood and the women hugged.

"I just today first performed my new six-minute song," Grace heard whispered in her ear.

"What I see in your songwriter friend," Monk had told Grace a day earlier, in their first conversation since the accident, "is how she's like lots of other people here. She's self-occupied, but what is that but a trait shaped by feeling unsafe? Like us all, she seeks a home for the flesh and the spirit. And if she finds one, she may learn to relax. If she doesn't—well, she hasn't yet, so she acts like a child trying to be brave."

Grace had not wanted to ask about his phrase "feeling unsafe."

They had met by chance in the early evening, when he passed a bench on which she sat reading passages in a book Mel had lent to her. He turned when she called, and smiled, as if to show gladness that another chat might now take place. She felt happy, too.

"Can you drive for a burglary next week?" He asked this so loudly that a woman also passing turned their way. "How about going out in a canoe now to hear the plan?"

"Who needs to be a criminal? Life here is interesting enough."

"Well, interesting things do happen. I've been away for a day, so there may be even more that I've missed."

"I looked for you. About now, I'm in the market for a guru."

"I'm not that, but we can talk as one humble teacher to another."

Grace had risen and they were now a few yards apart. "You seemed anything but humble at times back in the van," she said.

"I'd meant humility in regard to the material. But one's acts depend on leaps, I think. Isn't this what your teaching life is like?"

"Sure, maybe for ten scattered minutes every day."

"I'd bet your students tell their mothers you are interesting."

Beginning in this sullen, for her, moment, Monk would be her teacher and friend. Yet, walking to the beach, they were often quiet. Grace felt moved in a way she almost was sure did not confuse her.

"I think I just saw my husband Henry dart behind a tree," she told him. "As they say in the movies, I'm a married woman."

Monk slipped sideways and found his own tree to hide behind. He reappeared. "It's a fair thing to think about, but it may also be a kind of easy self-distraction." They faced each other. "Is it this that has you looking full of zeal?"

"I think not; anyway, I know there are other reasons. I find so much here upsetting." She paused, before adding, "And it's been years since I've thought of sex as just a somewhat easy distraction."

"That kind of thing between us isn't what I want, either."

Grace considered how they had somehow agreed not, absolutely, to *can't*, but to *won't*... and how her thoughts in this direction just might be a type of self-distraction—even if he was good-looking.

Ten minutes later, he was, at her beckoning, starting to reveal how he had read the mood at the mall in the moments before Trumpeter went over the edge. In the bow, paddling, he had glanced over his right shoulder; then he stowed his paddle and swung his body around until he faced her, with his legs again in the boat.

"I've been feeling that when he lost it, I did, too," said Grace.

Monk seemed to consider which of the sentence's threads to address. "I suspect Moira Kathleen's neediness is what set off him and Willa," he then said. "Since, for the young here, being disappointed seems to lack the cachet of being crazy. It's not the kind of thing they want to think will ever last."

"So they meet it with contempt?"

"Well, or the idea of it creeps them out.... But to instead have your mind crack and your emotions head for the hills, to be burdened like Franny—I think they take this to mean bringing all of life within oneself. The outer world can seem to matter less as one battles one's perceptions. The inner world, which they call 'soul,' can instead be the center of attention. And, looking at life in this way, by acting crazily they can show that they are real."

Monk at this moment of attempted sense-making wore a simple green tee shirt. Both knew by now that she had joined his quest, guided by her own concerns, and as he let go his forward motion, looking at her and then at the sky, which had beautifully lost its afternoon shine and glitter, she saw a change in his expression.

Share what you have with me—she expressed these thoughts with an earnest look, which he returned—I can get to work on it as well.

Yet, such sharing was tough to bring about. He had begun to slow down when his phrases called for punctuation.

"Franny's friends see her dancing eyes, and that the world doesn't always count for her. I think they envy this imbalance. And yet, they miss how it may differ only by degree from the imbalance felt by Moira Kathleen. If Franny can just survive to be a little older, she may begin to less dangerously stumble along, as well."

Trumpeter was among those, he added, who read the light in her eyes in terms of *soul*. This idea didn't really scan for Grace, but before she could tell him so, she saw a canoe caught under a tree limb in a shallow area. A rescue ensued; they used a rope in their boat to free two novice canoeists, Seeker guests. Grace, paddling backwards, weighed down, liked the feeling of strain as her back stretched out.

Then, suddenly undutiful, she let Monk guide them back to deeper water by paddling a few times alternately on either side.

"It's a lot to bother about," she said, giving "bother" a neutral reading. In the clear evening light, Monk smiled with his predictably clashing urgency and resignation.

"What our young man gets from Francine," she cued him, finally.

"I suppose that, feeling stuck, he tries to see in her what his own next step can be. And, actually, she may be only one of several gates he relies on to open—any one of them opening will do. What it seems to me they share is verticality. Because Trumpeter, like a Catskill hiker, with sturdy, young legs, is moving up and away from a world that he usually can only face with anger."

"What has him feeling stuck?"

"His fearing that only magic can open any gate."

"The many magical gates of the Seeker Academy."

Both smiled wanly. Then, while Monk's eyes mined the silver interior of the boat, he portrayed some of the gates. Grace felt half lost.

"A magic that could come," he began, "in an insight gained from drugs or through meditation into the silliness—given that life is a dream—of strangling worry. Or in an insight that supernatural forces or the bounce of his soul through a series of lifetimes shapes one's life. Or from some encounter with the supernatural. Or, finally,"—ending his orbit, he met her glance—"from an insight that the crazy beauty that he thinks he sees in Francine, which hints at risk and resolution, is real and might by some practice be made to last."

"What ambitions are these: to want life to be a dream or predetermined, or to be excited at the thought of going crazy?"

"They aren't ambitions to make me glad." He began to paddle again, switching sides as was needed.

Grace watched him work. Soon she said, "At our age, kids are kids... those here and their hypothetical younger brothers and sisters, who I saw tested and injected day after day. Why can't these magic-seekers get it together? Do they know what they have?"

"Is their struggle less than that of people who have physical illnesses?"

Feeling bowled over, Grace thought back to the wellness workshop and, unexpectedly, to her middle-school classroom. "I don't know," she murmured. "You tell me."

Leaning forward, Monk took her hand. "Let me adapt what you said. At our ages, adults are adults. And I do think the struggles here are as real. Also, you should know that I'm healthy now."

"I know next to nothing about your life."

"Maybe we can meet up in the city this October. I think you'd like a friend of mine who's there."

The housekeeping work—to return to Grace's time spent making beds—while often strenuous, was for its conviviality her favorite job. On four afternoons, teamed with several people, she had been assigned to fold and bag clean sheets and towels. With four hundred semiweekly arrivals, the unit's assignment—pull off, send out for washing, fold, and remake—repeating endlessly, done by middle-class workers who earned little or no money, was a managerial challenge.

Laurence, the direct, stoic fellow who ran the unit, was someone everyone liked. Once, passing, she had stopped to chat as he sat smoking
in a tobacco-allowed area near the parking lot.

Laurence promptly showed an interest in her. Single, nearing forty,
with gray creeping into his walnut-brown hair, he asked shy questions
about the household politics that went with having a son Amos's age.
He seemed sad to not be a father. He told her this was his fifth year at
the academy. "Every October I say I won't go back," he said. During
winters, he had sold electronics, furniture, and, on being licensed, real
estate. "Then, each February," he summed up, "one night at around
about four a.m., I get a perspective on my folly."

This hot day, though, Grace rarely saw him as he rode the grounds
like a harried rancher. A ticking watch told him where in its schedule
each crew should be. That was his concern and if he spoke to you at
all, it was about that. Grace, adversely, heard more from her crew
chief, a girl, just graduated from a fine drama school, who would
never, ever, Grace hoped and believed, get her snooty nose in any
door. She can't be talented and she's not pretty enough, Grace thought
spitefully for perhaps the seventh time, as the girl did acting-class
voices while passing among the cabins to check her crews. On laundry-
folding days the girl sang riffs from songs and always steered group
banter to the arts, so she might talk of plays and exhibits she had seen.
Knowing better, Grace garrulously erred in admitting her own strug-
gling years as an actress. After she did so the crew chief—detoured
briefly from suburban comfort and wearing always a belly-baring skirt,
the seductive young woman's fashion that year at Seeker—regularly
put Grace beside people other than herself on the assembly line.

Now, though, Grace was just days past her hospital trip and the
wellness retreat. Here is my method laid bare, she thought, while putting towels and hotel soaps in a bathroom. It is insult and retort, all
tooth-and-claw conflict; and I must like it. I seem to cling to it, anyway. Meanwhile I let so much else in life go by.

Leaving the readied cabin with her crew partner, she considered
how her behavior still only aped what went on around her. This made
her ask if it was her ill-wishing culture—as the wellness workshop had
seemed to argue—or human nature that was at fault.

Laurence drove his twenty-person crew well that day and at 3:30

they were finished. Grace hoped to reach the café in time to refresh herself before meeting the Golds, but when she climbed to the café porch after crossing the still-empty campus, her friends were there. Deb had slipped on a pink-patterned headscarf that Grace remembered her wearing a lot. They had bought a quart of juice and gotten a cup for Grace. Anton quickly went to fill the cup with ice.

Glancing in a café window, Grace saw Willa and Sophie sitting with other staffers.

Smiling but shyly quiet, Deb put a hand on Grace's arm. Then Anton's return broke the dam on her enthusiasm. "Grace, see what we have!" she said. She lifted from the floor a tree stump–sized drum; it was strung with rope, had a skin surface stretched over its top, and was new enough to still have component smells. Anton lifted a second, even larger drum. "Aren't these terrific?" asked Deb rhetorically. "We made a trip to the real Detroit, the African city it now is, to buy them. We hadn't been there, in the true heart of things for those brave people, for twenty years. We drove through a neighborhood my grandparents lived in once."

"We found the rhythm store online," added Anton. "The highways down had a lot of potholes, but even with our detour we made the whole trip, there and back, in an hour and a half."

How funny, Grace thought, as she recalled the Golds' collision with Trumpeter. But then what if their accents had set him off? He too comes from somewhere near Detroit.

"This weekend's drumming workshop is just what we need," Anton added as he tapped a few deep beats on his drum, after wedging it between his knees. "Between our mindfulness work here and our weekly class back in Michigan, we are fairly exhausted. We look forward to letting loose."

Grace then told the Golds of the accident. They of course hadn't met Francine; and while Deb colored at hearing Trumpeter's name, they seemed to hold no grudge and in fact be dismayed. "It's a tough time for youthful idealism," said Anton. They listened as Grace next spoke of the wellness workshop—and of her waking to, or starting *herself* to hallucinate, a kind of vengeful, destructive presence that was now in control of the land.

"But you must see that we have shelters, Grace," admonished

Deb. "Seeker is one and it gets easier to find others. So many good things go on." Like the sun itself, Grace saw, Deb could glance back into darkness.

"I think this whole valley is a shelter," Anton added, "its fine farms and villages and the river, mountains, and hills. It's a wonderful place and something to be grateful for."

"On this notion of wonder," Deb added, looking at Grace, "we are going for an early supper at a wonderful restaurant in town. Sweetie, will you join us?"

Grace quickly said she would, and then had an idea. "Can you," she asked, "also take me by the hospital? I'd only visit for fifteen minutes. Francine may not even want me there, but I have to go. I'm sorry to even ask. At most, the whole side trip will take an hour."

But the Golds were agreeable, and on learning that the hospital sat on a shopping mall-lined road, eager to fill the short wait. The one problem, Deb said, was their need to be back for a 7:30 workshop kickoff. Pooling their knowledge, the trio estimated how long they would need for fifty miles of driving, the hospital detour, and a gentile patio supper. On gaining a figure they dashed—Grace forgot her sweaty clothes and intent to speak with Sophie and Willa—for the Golds' rented car.

Perhaps because her husband was coming for her soon, Grace in recent days had been reluctant to leave Seeker's grounds. So she had hesitated to visit Francine, and now, beyond the ride, she was grateful for the Golds' distraction. The restaurant, she thought, will be lavish with gaiety and color. They plan, in an exchange they see as natural, to buy into its delights with their money. I'll use my wallet craftily, too. Left alone now, I fear, I'd make a more depressing restaurant choice.

A Challenge to Quest On

The visit with Francine was a failure. Grace, beyond her bad temper, felt numb at the hospital, in a way that promised a subliminal storm. Entering the lobby, she recalled in detail her Tuesday visit—almost as if it were rendered in a painting that hung above the information desk. Walking through the hospital, each turn was preceded by a new cluster of memories, from Tuesday but also from the mortifying winter. Francine's mother, due finally that night from Asia, had had her child moved to a private room; the change helped Grace partly snap back to the present. At this new room on a new floor, she knocked twice on the closed door and, hearing only a faint hum, opened it and stepped in.

Inside, she saw Francine, swollen, bandaged, and asleep in bed. The hum Grace had heard was the harmony of four Seeker staffers, none who she knew by name. Two, like Francine, were still nearly teenagers and of the others, both slightly older, one was the chant leader. All sat, with closed eyes, in chairs or on a window ledge. They sang in a low, constrained way, probably due to parleys with a nurse. The style was call-and-repeat, with the leader joining the repetitions. Neither Grace nor—she believed—the singers understood the words. Three or four chants were repeated.

Grace had attended a chanting session at Seeker and knew it was popular, but the activity bewildered her. Her mind jumped to the absurd figure cut by the chanters, here where no one but her looked at the sleeping Francine. Silently she warned them against shutting their eyes to life. Even as *I* less grandly do it all the time, she added. The melodious, pleasant chanting went on, oblivious to her admonition. One singer smiled and all their eyes, the hounded, bruised Francine's included, remained mystifyingly shut.

Walking in the corridor outside Francine's room, with no plan now for the quarter hour, she turned on impulse into a staircase. Dropping down a floor, she found herself at the rest room near where Tuesday she had sat with Moira Kathleen. A follow-on impulse for familiarity drove her to take the seat she had used then. Again, others sat nearby. I'd best try again to clear my head and lose what I can of my pissy attitude, she thought.

She had tried the day before, on the phone with Betsy. She had first thought to tell her husband of her feelings, until she heard the reluctance for surprise in his voice. Well, that was all right: as she told girlfriends, she viewed her marriage as above average; Henry was a technologist, with that sort's taste for order in work and play; he was often a good father; and for periods during Alicia's treatment he had been Grace's knight. What happened to her now, if indeed it was anything lasting, need not yet be about him. So, switching gears, she upon reaching him at his conference had relayed anecdotes from the wellness class, shared incidents from happy (if rare and brief) letters sent by Amos, and made plans for his Tuesday night pickup of her and their drive out for Amos two days later.

Betsy, herself wed to a senior engineer, was a guidance counselor where Grace taught. Colleagues, pupils, and even parents saw her as a woman whose wit hinted at a fine, even fascinating life outside of school. She guided her charges boldly, treating them as ships she was arming for the high seas; so when Grace phoned with her analogy to being like a choral voice in a Greek tragedy, Betsy, who herself kept clear of tedium, the unturned wheel, urged her on.

"Do you know what I mean?" asked Grace. "To open a play, or after a character speaks, they voice their lament. Crops fail, childbirth leads to death, the plague or an enemy strikes. For reasons unknown or unclear, the gods are angry. And that certain gods are angry *now* is a core teaching at the academy. Blockages afflict *us;* what strikes *us* is confusion about our lives, which we only add to with our self-inflicted numbness.

"Is that me talking, Betsy, or the Seeker milieu? I feel as if I've been here forever."

"Grace, you and I may laugh at people thrashing about, but we know that lots of us get involved in Seeker-like activities. The signs are everywhere including among our students, at least as they go on to high school. There, while they do nothing or work in a rage, they drug themselves and talk about transcending consciousness. We don't often find it funny, then. What you are doing now is terrific; stay with it."

"I don't know *what* I'm doing, besides watching habits I live by get torn apart. I almost see a need for this undoing, but it scares me. Then my confidence slips more in the face of the deep searching I see go on. The bookstore with its hundred healing topics is busy from noon to night. Eastern religion, self-help, mysticism... who knows what? I mean, in life we can't work back every action to its causes, can we? Don't we have to take some things for granted? Many people here are trying to back themselves all the way up, though. Even I can't see going in a simple way at the kinds of changes that may be needed."

"Listen and store, Grace," Betsy advised. "Back up, but only a little. We'll have all summer to pore over what you find. Just be sure to remember the funny stuff as well."

Sitting in the hospital, Grace could only long for the stability Betsy's words suggested. Remember, she told herself, Betsy, more directly than I, prepares young people for professional lives. It may also be true that she welcomes life's frenzy more than I. Perhaps I'm more a chameleon, more an actor who fuses with a role; and the role I have now is that of someone who hears and joins in a cry of warning. It's hard to dispute that, at least in the life around me, the mind is distracted, the body stiff with tension, and the heart always seeking a protected corner. Many crops do rot in the field. This Betsy knows, too, in her indirect way. For instance, she'll quickly catch on when I describe the trio from the accident. But the question to ask, at least what a Greek tragic chorus would ask, is what can be done? What bothers the gods and what will return them to our side? Surely, they'd commend the healing practices, the mindfulness, yoga, and heart work taught in the wellness workshop. However, much that goes on here rises above these practices—seeming both to shape larger criticisms and take larger risks.

In the workshop, these larger criticisms and risks had emerged in the discussion of spirituality, a ninety-minute period that found her too tired to listen carefully. But she had still seen a door inch slightly open to a lot that went on at the academy. Whether it was what the angry gods were asking for or not, she didn't know.

Her role, at least what should occupy her last days at Seeker, was to begin to find out. Once, in the hospital, she saw this clearly, she felt less forlorn.... "Listen and store." With some context now in place, she saw that Betsy had been right after all.

27

The Old Story of Fear

The restaurant, in a garden patio off the town's main street, was around a corner from and just out of view of where the accident had occurred. Diners were diverted from the street activity by a grand fish tank, which capped a marine motif that included a large skylight, salmon-colored tiles, and lobsters drawn in kinetic poses on blue interior walls. Style and capital underlay every detail, and the disparities between the restaurant and both Seeker and, from another view, the strip-mall hell startled Grace and even, for a moment, the Golds. Yet Grace's hosts seemed to enjoy the tiny shock. "It's nice to dodge the clamor," said Deb, as Anton eyed the wine list. "Even the academy points you in too many directions. We always try to eat here on the night before a workshop; it lifts us to a nice psychological place. The lobster bisque is just a delirious way to begin."

Grace felt the "lift" but also unease, which she wrote off to her coarse clothes and sense of how dirty she was. Her discomfort lingered, though, and she began to regret having left the academy. Its big-shouldered dining-hall was now a friend. Here it's a bit lush, she mused... and then warned herself, but, okay, relax, and don't aggrandize the people at other tables. The couple by the fish tank could easily be Betsy and Al—or, on a much less frequent schedule, even Henry and you.

The "lift" itself was decidedly theatrical, she saw with uncommon detachment. The hard cue, she thought, if you've not noticed earlier ones, comes when the waiter hands you a menu. Within this simple transaction is a path by which you can be pulled out of yourself. I take the tribute offering, for that is what it is, and step up the ladder to a better view of wealth and its rewards. The aim is to fill my senses. Even in unlit winter, I'd be laid out on a sparkling stage.

Now, though, it was six p.m. in mid-July, and the sun hidden by the building sat a mile west, high above the river's western bank. Grace let herself be seduced, finally, by the crusty bread, which came warm in a basket, as if it had just been baked.

The Golds thought Grace very lucky to be spending several weeks at the academy, and hungered for stories and observations. Deb was also attentive to the low mood that had taken Grace there initially, and its sad cause. Feeling embarrassed, then rueful, Grace told them how the involuntary way in which she had been always thinking of the children's hospital had begun to fade.

"Grace, that's coming to accept god's larger plan," said Anton, as his wife grew slightly tearful.

"I know that to do so leaves a bitter taste," Deb added.

Bitter regret was just what Grace felt, and if her talk with Betsy still resonated, she blamed herself also for having slipped from her blue state into a more active one. Are there links between the two, she wondered? Why all this concern for people I barely know, some who could even dislike me? Is my curiosity—no, my need to explore—a result of sadness or, as I fear, of feeling less sad?

In her searching mood, Grace hoped to lead the conversation to a point where Anton would sketch Seeker's spiritual pursuits. She recalled his map-making claims, and thought both Golds might find it worthwhile and even fun to help her along. But as they ordered their meals, she saw that the explanations would be delayed until the main course or even longer. Deb's eyes remained red, her hand shook slightly when she lifted her wine glass, and she was reluctant to look up.

"We've had a long two weeks, Grace," she said once the waiter, with his order pad satisfied, had finally left. "We're having trouble with Stu, our grown son. You may remember that we were working on our feelings about his unhappy life at the sadness workshop."

Anton gave Grace a lost look she had not seen from him before.

The trouble, Grace did recall, on the surface was less *with* their son than suffered *by* him. He was out of work and, burdened by bad timing, in a custody fight. "I think that the shopping mall we were at set me off," Deb said. "It's a lot like the one near Stuart's condo. In fact that whole road looks like the neighborhood where I take my grandson to the movies."

Stuart, who must have been is his mid-to-late twenties, like Hans and Trumpeter, seemed the sort who fell through the cracks of suburban comfort. He had neither used his opportunities to build his own seat of affluence nor found a clear way to rebel. As Grace heard itemized the result of his failure to root his care anywhere, she thought of talk shows she sometimes caught during school vacations. All our most listless fucking up as entertainment—but such shows wouldn't touch those youth, again like Hans or Trumpeter, maybe, also, Sophie, who just dropped out. If nothing else, being lost to mass culture kept them from being flung onto its fertilizer pile.

Their son had, Anton added, no interest in their healing pursuits. This in no way was his fault, as the cult for such things wasn't large where they lived, and he had never been the sort to be out front. Still, if anyone needed mindful healing, it was he.

"He's out front in his own life, you know," observed Deb. "It's nothing he can help."

Here is one cause of Deb's backward glance, thought Grace.

The lobster bisque was served, in beige pottery bowls that had red circumscribing rings below their rims. "The red crustacean scuttling over the sand," said Anton, as he saw Deb decide with a shrug to step away from their family cares. Like the porous, sour bread and cold wine, the bisque was pungent and crisply delicious. It shocked Grace to be assailed by these tastes after getting used to Seeker's good but less artful food. Perhaps *taste* reflects the spiritual, she thought, in which case I may be less in the dark than I fear. I can understand the word in terms of bounty, our inborn talent to receive. Yet, with other implications, isn't the general talent for taste a major reason for the common greed?

Anton liked Grace's request enough to unfold his cloth napkin and then, at Deb's bidding, head instead for the host table in search of writing paper. Deb looked inquisitively at Grace, before seeming to decide that her step was practical despite the joke. The dentist Anton charted New Age movements—its hive activities—and had useful knowledge. Yet, his was not a door that opened necessarily onto spiritual wisdom. Grace could tell that Deb knew this well—but also that Anton would sometimes forget.

"You've thrilled him," said Deb. "Anton really is funny—though in some ways he's also astute—with his little diagrams and lists."

Grace grinned, the grin of women married to practical men, and confessed her doubt that, on dry land, anyway, lobsters often scuttled.

Over the next half hour, as they awaited and then enjoyed their seafood entrees, Anton began to introduce Grace to Seeker's spiritual explorations. On settling into the task, he got up again, to return with a catalog the Golds had in their car. He looked through its index and contents table, while his wife folded her napkin into a cone and playfully set it on his head. It flopped over instantly and she had to gather it from his shoulder; doing so, she made her point again, with words. "Watch Mr. Wizard," she said.

This was somewhat true, Grace saw. Someone adding thoughtful context to a list, or any crazy set of facts, really did a wizard's work.

Grace described the wellness workshop, with its disciplines used to wake the mind, body, and heart, and its core terms that she understood shakily at best. Though the Golds knew neither person, she spoke of Elsa, with her heroes and heart stories, and of Hans, with his respect for feeling and distrust of active thought. Deb listened with curiosity—Anton, with the calm appreciation of a collector.

When she finished, Anton sat thinking. "Grace," he said shortly, "I see two ways to begin. We can work down the catalog or look at a higher organization I've been teasing out. Should I be more or less pithy?"

"I think be your pithiest."

"Yes, dear, dazzle," added Deb, who seemed to fall back on teasing in the way her husband did his maps.

Whatever his self-awareness, Anton was proud of his critical work. "I think the spiritual practices taught at the academy lead to purity or awakening," he said simply. "Some try to do both."

"Okay, yes, I need more," said Grace. She was too adamant and vexed to feign knowledge of what either term truly meant. "Purity" and "awakening": neither came up often in her life.

Her last thought she had registered aloud. "I mean," she added, "like most families I know, mine gets to church only for weddings and funerals. I myself taught Sunday school for a few years when Amos was the age for that sort of thing. I'd hoped it would prod him to go but he almost never did. I may have only increased the hours each week when I couldn't stop him from playing computer games.... No matter. It made me feel good to be involved.

"'Spiritual awakening' I sometimes think about, if we mean belief in a higher power. The phrase doesn't come up often in conversation.... As to the notion of 'purity,' I can't even imagine it in my life."

Anton had put aside his bisque bowl to look in the catalog. Grace, unsure he had heard her, glanced at Deb, who had. With his left hand, he held the contents table open and pored over its pages; with his right, he jotted on his pad and sipped alternately from his wine or bisque. In the quiet moments this went on, he looked up once, with an absorbed smile that was meant to buy further time.

Yet, he had listened. "The best way in may be through history," he said finally. "But then we begin with purity, not awakening." He showed Grace the table of contents, spilling over several pages. He pointed to workshop titles. "This and these here. Look at Hinduism, shamanism.... You may already know that mainstream Western religions, which the academy largely avoids, understand purity as a miraculous cleansing of sin.

"It's through them that a third idea, 'faith in miracles,' enters."

Grace's besieged look told Anton that he had already gone too fast. He paused to adjust his approach. Deb, with a quiet stirring, let him know that she also was now interested.

The simplified story—with awakening put temporarily aside—Grace now heard was of the ongoing human desire to be free of the fear and suffering life entailed. And only minutes into it, she had realizations that widened her worldview, defined largely by her background in drama, for the first time in decades. A familiar, closed door she had come to disregard opened. She was reminded of old tribal purification rituals she had slid past like a tourist in some college classes. The king or a surrogate would be sacrificed at the darkest time of winter, in the hope that this purifying gift to whatever moved nature would return the sun and allow the land to soften. We regret our errors and our problems seeing them, the penitent people said. In a surer time, people tied symbols of their errors to a goat and drove the lowly beast off. In Asia, though, this wish to be pure had taken a different turn. "Karma" played down the idea that what one did to fix one's mistakes would have much impact on life's ruling forces. It termed human awareness painful and illusory, with cold and darkness as the normal state, and said it was better to not be born. What "right living" did, though, was let your soul, as it was reborn in a new body, pass into a purer strain of life. Over time, many lives, crossing different channels of existence—going low and high—right living let your soul reach a level of purity where it need not be reborn. It instead merged with the undivided whole of being—became a peaceful droplet in the soup.

This graduation motif made Grace think of high school. It also hurt and made you cynical, and you were glad to escape. But then, as life went on, you saw that safety always sat on the horizon. The belief that graduation had really meant something faded, and nostalgia kicked in.

Such philosophizing, she knew, was what Hans disdained. Even if it was clearly a behavior—that fear was ongoing she had now to re-learn—based in trying to survive.

Anton pushed his story farther and she listened with care. Like Deb, she wanted to speak, but Anton asked to instead be left to make another point before the entrees came. As he tied in shamanism, his survey, he said, would start to have legs. Then as they ate, they might talk about spiritual purity in a more fruitful way.

"Modern people like us," he explained, "who are taught to be eager for life, often find in shamanism more hopeful potential outcomes of the fight with fear than karmic religions allow. It is also the case that shamanism, unlike colder beliefs based on giving up hope, touches a trained nerve we have for excitement and hot heroes. In the shamanic tradition, warrior-healers, who take hold of their powers amid inner crises, course through areas unknown to the senses but not, it seems, to the imagination. The aim of these quests into magical space is to find and recover lost parts of human souls, which the hard events in life—note the pervading theme—scatter. People on having their lost soul-parts returned to them then begin to heal.

"What I've said barely touches on these traditions. But do you see how each one—sacrifice, scapegoat, karmic release, and the hero shaman—is a human response to fear? And the fear itself seems to rise from certain sources. One is a fear of the hard things in life, with I guess the hardest being death. A second is a fear that we bring our bad times on ourselves through bad behaviors. A third is a fear that we humans can't ever come to be good enough on our own.

"We often learn, at Seeker, that the way to try to be good is to try to be *pure*."

He had made his last remarks as the waiter delivered their entrees. He put his plate aside and, absorbed, grasped the napkin that lay over the wine carafe to signal his intent to pour its remaining liquor. One hand held the open catalog; raising the other, he indicated support for his explanation. "Two dozen workshops teach karmic separation from the world. That many again teach Celtic, Siberian, and other shamanic traditions. A third group draws on shamanism to promote the kinds of supernatural interventions that as yet can't really be proven."

"By 'supernatural interventions,' do you mean magic?" Grace asked.

"I think this gets us back to faith, as I mean a force beyond what we understand that can and will help us in life. Faith enters if we believe a shaman can use force in our favor. Or if we believe what many call 'superstition': that objects like jewels and crystals have curative powers beyond what science can observe. Or if we are consoled to think that an intervention will eventually free our souls from suffering."

"It sounds as if you oppose these efforts—this purification work."

"On the contrary, I more or less believe in them." He raised and lowered his palms in a counterbalancing way to imitate a weight scale. "Anyway, now I'm only trying to sort out a rich, complex environment."

"But your approach to the supernatural is so rational. It seems contradictory."

"Perhaps, but part of the modern synthesis is understanding that contradiction works. Science teaches this: we can be logical *and* accept the bizarre world we know exists. Think about atoms and genes: do nonscientists know for sure they are real? But they are; and who can say that science, having found fate in genes, won't one day find god? New Age science points this way. It looks for divine footprints, for example by pursuing the cross-cultural belief that energy builds in complex forms like pyramids and crystals."

Doggedly, without knowing why, Grace noted Anton's linking of human fear and religious response with a strong belief in human science.

"I see my amateur anthropology, what this is, as related," Anton added with an air of moral exercise. "I catalog how spiritual movements try to free us from fear. Knowing how this works may help us be more mindful as we go forward."

"We took a workshop on faith and science," added Deb. "We learned that people help make things true by believing in them, and may have to believe some things exist to see them. This is totally in line with the newest science. And we learned—this goes back to Anton's point—of relationships known to wisdom traditions that science is starting to accept: for instance, that invisible energy systems govern our bodies.

"What interests me," Deb went on, with heightened emotion, "is using a spiritualized science to live more in harmony with the universe. Like our finding of phenomena that hide from people who don't believe that the phenomena is real. That kind of knowledge can really make a difference."

As at other Seeker moments, Grace began to fall mentally from a cliff. Is what they say true, she wondered? Whether it is or not, is this the secret language that I'm after? I don't think I could stand to be so closely attentive all the time.

Anton had invoked his weight scale, a tool for measuring. Deb then had smiled to evoke not her old tumbledown reliance on teasing, but new beliefs.

Anton eyed Grace and then, protectively, his wife. "Of course," he said, "this fennel cream sauce reminds me that what I'd like to ignore is less these spiritual phenomenon than my cholesterol count."

28

Sorting What She Then Could

Since leaving the Golds an hour before, Grace, no doubt influenced by Anton's diagram, had been thinking about faces. Were she to say, trying to ease her muddle, that she saw five or maybe six kinds of faces at Seeker, what were her categories? She felt, first, that people like the Golds showed in their faces a hurt at being puzzled, and a pliant and persuadable—see this in others or miss it in yourself, Betsy liked to say—search for answers. A second, morose kind of face belonged to the knowingly wounded, perhaps typified by Moira Kathleen. Such faces were schooled in longing and failure—in, especially, hardships of the latter. They looked inward and askance but rarely *at* others. A third kind—she saw it would round out the first of her two galleries, her gallery of *fear*—was actually an aggressive cousin of the morose face. It showed conviction, gave hints of being out on a limb, and grew defensive if its vision was contested. Some teachers Grace had watched pass through the academy fit unmistakably in this group.

Supper at Le Trout Ordinaire, their Main Street bistro, had been useful and stimulating, though the lesson had not gone past impurity and fear. Grace saw that Anton, like her Henry, was a cask of information who could be tapped or corked. After a while, Deb's bracelet bells began to jangle; Anton took this as a signal to return to his filet. Grace hadn't minded, as she was troubled enough by what she had heard. Yes, she thought, while it's kept under the covers, people see life's not right and are self-blaming. We just learn to find the sun's daily trajectory and put the rest out of mind. It's what a Greek tragic chorus must try for as it waits offstage. More cheerily, Deb had then steered the talk back to Seeker anecdotes, a piquant topic to fit the satiating end of the meal. Some Seeker characters the Golds had met over the years were like the special jellies and pickles that came with certain kinds of feasts.

Back at Seeker, Grace began to plan her final days. Yet, this task was challenged in her mind by the theme of Seeker faces, and all evening she flew between these two things to think about. In the end, though, she knew, they followed a single idea. She must not leave here in four days feeling quite so empty-handed.

It was Friday night, and she knew that hundreds of newly arrived guests, Deb and Anton included, filled the main hall in an orientation session. They would be bursting with hope. Tomorrow, as they spent a day many had looked forward to for months, Grace was free. Sunday she would join the luggage crew in a split shift and finish, happily, her assigned work. Meanwhile, the spiritual retreat week would begin, when Seeker must figuratively brim with jellies and pickles. She could observe the scene Monday if this helped her in her task. Tuesday, though, was the end.

While she had several people to find, she most wanted to spend time with Sophie and with Monk. Vaguely, searchingly, she saw them as emblems of the strength that she sought.

Dusk was at an early stage, one of those moments of heightened outline when the wild, dangling fear Anton had talked of seemed *least* plausible. Each shape was itself but also a part of what was near. The café folded in a knoll looked like a twisting child. This time of day, she thought, is when a hill or a hilly range will first be called "Horse Head" or "The Four Cousins." She climbed the café steps but found the porch empty; from it, she heard collective whoops from the main hall. Monk and Sophie could be anywhere. In the garden, people stood, or sat in slanted Adirondack chairs. She stared at an unfamiliar, goateed man until he looked back up at her.

She headed, in this first fit of departure anxiety, for a favored area, the scalloped, switchback steps that led to the sanctuary. She followed the paved path rising from the café and turned left to cross the back of a southward spur. Lining this path, which led to her hill climb, were five small studios. Sophie sat among others on a white porch just beyond her turn. Seeing her, the younger woman waved—then they approached one another. Sophie again wore blue-jeaned overalls.

"I leave in a few days," said Grace. "Can we find time to talk? I want to hear more about your life, especially your pursuits here, the spiritual healing and all."

She saw care and a pinpoint of concern in her friend's smiling eyes. "I'm free tomorrow," said Sophie. "No office work, I'm glad to say. Can we have a late breakfast?"

Grace found herself replying in an essential way. "I'm just getting more confused. What goes on here as much scares me as inspires me. I expect you heard that Willa and Trumpeter both went a bit crazy after the accident. I hardly know them, yet I'm afraid for them. And then I saw teenagers—kids not much older than my son—chanting with their eyes closed in Francine's hospital room. What do people risk by coming here?"

"Might we carry the risks, rather than find them here?" asked Sophie. Then she smiled softly. "But yes, I'd like a heart-to-heart, about my aims but also yours."

"I may be more aimless than aimed. About Willa: how is she? I haven't even bumped into her in two days."

Sophie, peering out from her fortuitous good looks, with the simple lines, thought Grace, of a red-haired doll, took Grace's hand. "She's unsteady, in a way I'd not seen before. I'll invite her to join us."

They parted, with Grace embarrassed by a self-appraisal that she now thought was misleading.

As two strangers sat near the rock pond where she had thought to stop, she climbed higher. The world here was sweet and softening. I'll begin with Sophie and build a polar opposite to my *fear* gallery, she thought. Rather, I'll try to work it out abstractly. Maybe I see only two kinds of *happy* faces at Seeker. The first is shown publicly: I mean the hundred smiling photo portraits in the catalog. I should think about them, anyway, as they'll be on the quiz I get from Betsy.

Back home, the main link to Seeker was its catalog, which issued each spring. And if she had never really thought to come here, she had skimmed the catalogs for years; her friends did, too. And then what came up first in conversation was its store of blissful faces. Most people pictured looked as if they were smiling not from amusement but from a tap on the brow by a magic wand. Everything is fine, the smiles said; which attracted some people and repulsed others. "If magic is involved," asked the naysayers, "can the heart be, as well? And what could make such blissful eyes frown or cry, let alone laugh at a raucous situation?"

Grace herself wondered if such people, who earned their living from this work, could be believable. Coming from the same half-wealthy class as did she and other participants, could they see further? Where behind a beatific smile would lie crackup, or at least the uncertainties that fell on everyone? Many people pictured taught therapies that, while defying Grace's habits, had won her admiration. Yet, if the therapies led people to not courage but safety, where courage would no longer matter, Grace did not yet see how.

She knew that a weakness in her judgment lay in her having had only brief interactions with Seeker faculty—with the catalog faces. She drew near them at meals: a few times, she had been in tableside groups that included one or two. She also went to some faculty-led talks and shows that were open to or meant for staff. But except during her first week, she had not gotten to know any teachers. This was due to her position as a staff member, not workshop participant; she knew she missed out on a lot. But she had also heard complaints that teacher-student interactions were often distant. The teachers moved busily among workshops, media projects, and what were called their "personal spiritual journeys." It was perhaps natural that they would come to deal with their students in a polished and ventilated way.

So, in her present reflections, she must go by her gut. She would let her intuitions flower into a sense of what the faculty was like. She began to tick off observations. There was the rangy, weathered man who had grasped the hand of a staff person he heard voicing doubts at a nearby table. The man, who taught a workshop on animal spirits, used his thumb to lock the doubter's fingers, before he exhorted him. "Your struggle is *blessed*," the teacher said, smiling widely, "as all is from god." There was also—Grace saw herself wring out disbelief, she hoped as a prelude to something—the blond woman with an Arabic name who taught mystical dance. She was like Pythagoras, the awkward, self-defined shaman at the wellness retreat, in that she saw her reach into magical space as no less real than her capacity, home in her kitchen, to boil water. To doubt this was to leave the circle of wellness and wisdom she maintained smilingly for followers. Grace had observed the dismissive look the dancer was prone to deliver—she had gotten a similar one in the laundry from the budding actress. Maybe as telling, she had seen that same dismissive look on the faces of Amos and his friends, preteens who put up platforms of derision for looking out at the world.

Grace didn't know if people like the rangy man and the mystical dancer were onto something. But she distrusted them and guessed that, beyond the profits, self-delusion, and fakery, they were as unmoored as the Golds. Then again, she warned herself, maybe their spiritual pursuits are real, even as human failings mark their footsteps. And was this so, it would be the skeptical, buttoned-up Grace who missed out the most.

The main hint that she missed something vital lay, again, she thought, with the catalog faces. For if she felt that the blissfully smiling yet morose, aggressive teachers fit in her fear gallery, she saw other teachers differently. Some she found startling and some she wanted instinctively to trust. Those who startled her walked the campus quietly, with receptive smiles. They liked to listen, within themselves or for heavenly messages; it was as if they thought they were radios. Often they slowed food lines. Any item could interest them—the salad bar alone had twenty items, from cherry tomatoes to walnuts. She had first seen this effort to live with a childlike openness as precious and controlling, until she saw it informed by an image of joy. Then she decided that at worst it would prove foolish by making one vulnerable; children, after all, had adults to lead them to practical moments. And yet the effort seemed sincere. Some at Seeker called it "mindfulness in life," and different workshops took it as a theme. Many among the staff and each crop of participants sought to engage in the practice. "In life," they said, smilingly, "the simplest seed leads to and comes from everything." Half of what the bookstore stocked, someone said— Grace had recently thought to seek guidance in the lavish, scented bookstore—expanded on this one idea.

While Grace was drawn to this open, smiling attitude—she now decided that only outsiders thought all catalog smiles were alike—she also saw its quality of social reluctance. If, she wondered, you take life as it comes, find it all interesting, and hold up food lines to look for miracles in a salad bar, don't you lose that part of life associated with context and conflict? And what comes of that loss, especially in a time of such general confusion? She had seen how a skein in Seeker's tapestry led from this love of the moment to a view of society that was squeamish or plainly indifferent. Seeker publications, for instance, called for an idealized politics of peace and nature stewardship. Yet they were silent on grittier issues, like justice—what the Alaskan fishing boat guy had brought up.

Closer to Grace, who listened with more care than she had a few days before, this silence reached its pinnacle around the many collisions in society that were a part of her own uncertainty. She would not pause to list those collisions now, she was unsure she even could, but she knew she would be back home among them soon enough.

The fishing boat guy's name, she recalled, was Ken Samuels. She also recalled that during his talk she had first begun to notice, before seeing why it mattered, a second kind of happy person at Seeker. This sort seemed alive to both conflict and a practice of calming their driving needs. They offered another view, she now saw, of what mindfulness in life could be. At Ken's talk, she had begun to recognize in the words of some staff and guests an effort to both serve society *and* live in the moment. The efforts also shone through in smiles that were modest and brave. Many did the sorts of public or human service work where success was rare. Stories came out at meals, launching the smiles, of weeks filled with excuses, wrong information, vile media reports, pillars of mood or laziness, insights into the fear or bad guidance that framed poor motivation... and so on. The teller at some point would say these were signs of suffering, particularly among those with few economic resources. "The worthy response, if your work is here"—the teller in some way would add—"is to breathe deeply, keep your purpose and sense of humor, and go on. Try to better the life around you. Use the Seeker practices to keep in balance, even as your burdens shift. And, lastly, see and be glad for the goodness in life by which you can be an instrument of good."

Practically, these people she now checked off as "happy" often worked in health care, education, social work, and the arts: areas where they traded some pursuit of wealth for a service ideal. Grace, in this group herself, knew that a tower of ambiguity overlay the ideal. People began or did such work for many reasons, with idealism not always one. And many gave up or moved on. Yet, it was plain why the persevering looked for places like the academy. The work was draining and it was hard to stay well. Grace saw how these people, especially, came to Seeker to relearn—amid a mix of feelings and a modesty that losing fights enforced—that they were happy.

Well, of course, again, she found herself thinking, it's more complicated. In the larger society, its pockets of humanism, anyway—she saw herself use words that usually slept in her mind—happy and forlorn tendencies often tangle up together. Sometimes they lock in opposition, animated by different individuals. More often, the people one knows hold the entanglements within. The slide was uneven and slippery; one went from happy to forlorn after not a lot of trouble. In her school, teachers and students alike arrived daily bearing a host of such stress points and—all right, thought Grace, where am I going with this, isn't this simply life?

Everything at Seeker is meant to help you slide back in the other direction.

I don't see kinds of faces, then, but facial qualities.

What, after all, does it mean to be persuadable?

Grace, weary of reflection, had a final idea to stake. Okay, she mused, even if I'm lost in a muddle, which only shows my laziness over the years, I'll point out one last thing. Some here, who smile in the brave, modest way I seem to trust, pursue an elevated life apart from service. They look past the everyday, which I think they see clearly, to something else. It's not that the life I live escapes them, but the reverse. It gets taken along. Yet, theirs is a trek of intense feeling, defined by them as "spiritual." I can hardly imagine what this word means, except that as I see them on their path I can, through a tunnel the image makes, almost glimpse myself.

Sought-after Guidance

Humid heat returned overnight, but daylight showed that it had not brought clouds. A restless feeling drove her from her tent and kept her once again from going to morning yoga. She walked to the pond and stood for a long while like another shade tree, watching the sun, which just had risen, start its climb. I'm between times in many ways, she mused. A flock of geese, which too often used the beach area for a toilet—a regional problem, but she avoided dwelling on the TV news feature that had reported on it—floated within the ropes of the beginner swimming area with their backsides to the land. Rather than shoo them she left, after a time, when a tai chi class began, to get coffee. At the dining-hall steps, just as a black-aproned Mel raised the rope to let in breakfasters, she noted the many new faces present in this second flock of her day. New workshops had begun. By now, she also knew that some strangers there would be experiencing life as intensely just then as she was.

She chatted briefly near a coffee machine with Tulip, the kitchen manager. Tulip was, it turned out, a chanting devotee, and had sent the group to chant ritually for Francine. Her own practice, she told Grace, had begun years before as she came to grips with the death of her "life partner"; its quieting effect helped pull her through. Her expressions of mood now, Grace saw, seemed touched by an accumulated fatigue. Here is more proof of all I don't know, Grace thought. Looking back on my own hard year, I find few such consoling rituals. However, rather than bring this up with Tulip, who watched over breakfast and whom she knew only casually, she mainly listened.

Outside, the sun above the trees was already a commanding presence. On the porch, clothes having bulk or weight were already hung on the backs of chairs. With an hour to spend before meeting Sophie, Grace went to sit on the fragrant, cool lawn. Scores of people milled about, but an early tranquility endured; however, into it passed, moments later, coming downhill from behind the dining-hall, a color flow that gathered finally into a troupe of staff at a picnic table. Two among the troupe, probably twins—lean, bearded youths six feet tall—stood, possibly naked, together. If Grace wasn't sure, it was because head to toe each was a flux of colors and patterns. One wore a dark blue bikini brief, or paint that was made to look like he did.

"Let's get the trickster in blue to jump around," said Monk, as, with a silver thermos in hand, he surprised Grace by crouching on her right. "It may be the only way to be sure.... Moses!" he yelled familiarly across twenty yards. "Do a dance. Shake it!

"We're lucky Trumpeter didn't dress this way at the mall," he added mischievously as he unscrewed his thermos cup. Moses turned their way and on seeing Monk waved, raised his arm higher, smiled, and did as asked. His penis bobbed comically. Amid free-flowing green, white, and red shapes, amid stars, stripes, circles, and the like that made his body a reckless canvas, his hands were painted the same dark blue color as his loins.

Grace laughed. Nudity was unwelcome here, with a stated firmness that made her think the policy was sometimes challenged. In moments, the swarm of staff that surrounded Moses and his presumably also naked brother headed for the road, going north. A sudden thought made her turn and look up at the eating porch. Some new arrivals were gazing with curiosity at the exhibitionist brothers, too.

"Is it morning for these kids or late night?" she asked Monk. "I've wondered what goes on after old folks like me go to sleep."

"Moses got back this week from a year in India. His brother, called Jesus here, last month finished his first year at some law school. Now they both get a little wild."

"You do seem to cross the generation gap with relative freedom."

"It's partly the guitar, partly my having been here for so long. People hear of me."

"I like to watch them. But I wonder what besides being young creates the wildness, and what forms it will take, and how long it can last.
It makes me think of Francine."

"They are what, my guess is, you see them as: used to middle-class comforts, self-indulgent, bright, and mostly unaware that, for some people, life can
hold choices. Not just Moses, but most of them will drift into the mainstream
as they get older. Others will act recklessly. A few in each category will some-
day find their way to the choices you and I have."

Grace was twice surprised—first, that he seemed to so plainly ele-
vate himself. "I'm just one of the drifters, who's been on her raft for
twenty years," she said. It was rare to hear someone she thought of as
honest and modest speak with such conviction.

"Only we choose, who begin to know who we are," responded
Monk, using his frankly prodding tone. "We trip over this knowledge
or fight to get it; it may not matter which. And I've watched you in this
struggle—two nights back in the canoe, but, before that, at the poetry
slam in the café when I played my guitar."

Grace, feeling warm, recalled the Sunday school story she told each year
of Peter denying Christ. She grinned edgily at Monk. "That's too much optimism for so early. I wonder if seeing life matters, when you're caught up in
it." She heard herself sound resentful, the effect of a colder idea that had risen
as she spoke. Monk must also be a pessimist. Even at a place like Seeker, he
seemed to say, where people come to try out new ways of life, to learn to see
through new prisms, and to act in new ways, and even among the young, the
more robust and malleable, four in five would harden back into the lives they
had been shaped for. This meant that those who did not, even perhaps like
her, were only lucky.

And so Amos, whom she largely let the world shape, and who
might not grow up to have her kind of dopey resilience, which may
only be an inborn trait, would have to make his own luck.

Monk leaned back out of his crouch and sat. He smiled at Grace
and waited for her to wade through her ruminations and continue.

"Moira Kathleen left yesterday, relatively content," she said. "I've
still hardly seen Willa or Trumpeter."

"There is mall melodrama news. Trumpeter plans to leave, on

Monday if his car is ready. And Willa may be going with him."

"Leave? Do you mean *leave,* and *with Willa?* But what she'd started to tell me... but they aren't even a couple!"

"He talks of driving into Canada, and only possibly returning in a month."

"Isn't the academy already the end of the world for him?"

"It was. Now he's smashed those windows; I suppose Canada is next."

Grace's normal curiosity and concern for others was tempered by her new state of doubt. Don't watch them like a tourist, she told herself. Or find them later if you want; now be more basic with Monk. He awaits this. She relaxed and, slightly surprised, spoke of her dinner with the Golds, strangers to him. He smiled as she sketched the philosophical Anton, but was quiet until she asked him in this context—she waved a hand to show that her context was the academy writ large—what it meant to see others as persuadable, susceptible... innocent?

"You know, don't you," she added, "that at best my time here has been for unlearning? I mean I *always* wear blinders! How can I jump on this susceptibility in others?"

"There's an important distinction to be made, Grace, and it goes back to what I just said. You are lucky and can use your luck, and this is all you need know. It only gets you started. Truly susceptible people, or those among them who've been hurt by their bewilderment, need more help than you, and are more at risk here, as a lot of ideas are being sold. What brings them to Seeker? The question is important, but maybe not one for you to ask now. You have to know what matters to you at this moment. Are you here for others or for yourself?"

"You do know I raise a child! Still, I see this must be first about me.... Really, I'm not sure what my reply is. All I can really feel now is that something is wrong."

Behind Monk, people passed, usually bound for the dining-hall steps. She wondered what they would say. "When we talked earlier about Moira Kathleen," she now added, "you said some things about feeling unsafe... "

"There again I think you skip an important question. With your re-treat ending, will you busy yourself with why others feel unsafe or are for that matter bewildered, or with why *you* feel unsafe and bewildered? Where do you want to be looking?"

"Isn't it likely the two conditions, personal and I assume communal, are related?"

"Well, that hits on an important possibility. Yet, relationships vary. And remember: even with your luck, you are just starting. Here at Seeker this question you raise leads in some very different and in some very wild directions."

Grace then told Monk about the wellness workshop, which had filled out the day of the mall uproar for her. Sure he was schooled in these themes, she condensed her report to a few sentences covering mind, body, and heart. She spoke of and complimented Elsa, whom she guessed to be his old friend. Then she told him of her plans to spend that morning with Sophie, in part exploring, with the inspired young woman's help, the academy's forays into "spirituality."

"For me, now," she added, "the word most signifies my own laziness and neglect. So I have no idea what, if anything, spirituality has to do with luck, or susceptibility, or safety."

Monk looked at her, not with the sympathy she expected yet didn't want, but intensely. Then he smiled and stood. "Come to the old gazebo Sunday night," he said. "You'll see one of my performances, rescheduled from the day of the accident. It's fun: I do it twice a year or so and, invariably, at least a few people get terribly upset. You might, as well.

"We try to give newcomers a rounded experience," he added, winking.

"I wanted to hear more about Trumpeter and Willa," said Grace. "Will they at least be *there*?"

Monk, down the path, stopped. "I'm doing my best on that one."

"Also, even though I'm supposed to wait for our day in the city, what about you? You tend to move around here like an actor."

"I am that; so it may be fitting that I begin to tell my story from a stage."

"And what really do you mean when you talk about the crappy 'mainstream'?"

Monk pointed at her; he then more broadly waved, turned, and was gone.

On Perilous Paths

Sitting alone, Grace turned her attention to all the hungry new arrivals and the even fuller flood of words. A while later she began walking to the yoga studio. However, where the path to it left the main road she saw, gathered again, the painted, naked brothers and their friends. The cleared path, running east, set them directly in morning light. The enlarged tribe now included Trumpeter and, as one of three young women dancing indolently around the tribal perimeter, the budding actress from the laundry.

Trumpeter wore tan shorts and sandals, a white shirt, and a careful smile. He thus stood out against the daffodil sun; his multicolored, grinning companions; and, differently, his own dark countenance and beard. Grace did not see Willa but, nearing the crossroad, she spotted Sophie on her way up the path. In a wider arc, enlarging the group's perimeter, Grace moved amid incense scents toward her friend. She felt sympathy for Trumpeter, who, whatever his smile and whatever the group enthusiasm fertilizing it, seemed to be jumpy even here.

She had at first thought to approach him, and again did now. But to do so would embarrass him, especially with Sophie now in the mix.

Sophie carried her blue yoga mat. On getting near enough to see what went on, she paused, as if to reconcile a post–yoga class calm with this spectacle and her tête-à-tête with Grace. She smiled wryly. "They seem sweet in the sun, like young animals," she said. Still in a wry tone, she then expressed an idea that showed she had taken Grace's partial call for guidance to heart.

"Shall we skip the dining-hall," she asked Grace, "and take oranges I have to an empty studio on the hill? It won't quite be fasting… but a light-headed mood might bring us closer to our spiritual hunger."

Sophie had apparently thought her task out even further: on reaching a studio picked, Grace felt, at random, Sophie slipped a disc from her daypack into an audio player on a table. "A workshop begins here in an hour," she said, "I think on how supernatural forces can help us find our romantic partners. When people come we can move to the bookstore."

Grace was eager to start and, with coffee in her, already edgy. She stared back at Sophie and said: "As in, the wee folk and angels do the matchmaking?"

The studio had three large windows, each drawing in a July morning stillness that Grace knew it was wrong to disrupt as she had. The soothing music also seemed to clarify the stillness, in the way a murmuring creek might. Grace told herself: Listen to this. Start in accepting not what you know but what you *don't* seem to know.

Sophie also saw the dilemma. "A lot that seems silly may or may not be, Grace. I'm unsure, too. But I do know that ideas like 'supernatural matchmaking' grow from a change in perception. I think we might spend our first bit of time on this change."

She took from her pack an incense stick and a Buddha figure that fit in her hand. A herbal scent, likely thyme, was in the windows and as the stick was lit, Grace grew annoyed. Aren't summer smells enough, she wondered silently? Can't a "message" be carved out of them?

The few, plain surfaces of the room answered with quiet. The women lay on their backs on the floor and waited, hearing a near-voluminous quiet amid whirs of rare breezes and flies at a screen. Then the music partly gave way to speech. A guided meditation began, similar to one Grace had happened on at an outdoor gathering a week earlier.

First, a man's voice led them to a sense of relaxation Grace now found almost familiar. As she had learned to, she steadied her breath, kept her arms loose at her sides, and locked the thumb and forefinger of each hand. "Be with your fear, fatigue, and doubt," the voice said. "Then imagine these things leading you to flee your habits for a day. You first must escape, and, doing so, note how your empathy for the people left behind only makes you feel worse. Then you arrive in the countryside, where a dirt road leads off to the left. You park your car, begin to walk, and, as you pass a stand of apple trees and see white blossoms, you remember it is spring. The air is warm and at a greater arc endlessly blue. The terrain rises to the horizon. Amid this expanse and silence, you feel subtle energies that seem to flow to and from the nearby rocks, trees, and farm fields, and you, yourself. You feel connected and more cleansed by each breath. You find that even your language has lightened, that the way you explain existence to yourself has become believable, and this makes you feel safe."

The meditation wore on; when, a few minutes later, the tape returned to music, Grace, lying quietly, felt safe still. The trick of sense and memory had reminded her that there were moments when everything lined up, when you saw light as language. Many people had experienced this, and she now saw that anyone could. But was it transient? Even as she began to mull this question over, she felt a wall of disbelief reform. The wall's dangerous mass led her to wonder if, as a fruit of meditation, *it* would have the larger continuing effect.

Studded in the wall were things about Amos, her messy tent, every sick child at the hospital, the shocks that would come in a few days—yes, she mused, flesh and change... a language of not light but difficulties.

And yet, she reflected, it seems that many people here believe in an enduring language of light, whose use can be learned.

She turned onto her right side, planted her elbow and forearm as a post, and laid her head in her open right palm. She looked inquiringly at Sophie, who seemed willing to accept the risk of new experiences.

"I've thought about this," said Sophie. "I wonder about it so much that I wanted to make a believable space for us. And so incense, to represent sacrifice or at least earnestness. So, too, the three sample paths I've decided to show you, in this taste you asked me to provide: three as a mythic number, making this a sort of game, as I'm having to guess. Each path leads—supporters claim—to an inner state that is usually hidden partly or completely by the rush of life. It is known as being 'spiritually awake.'

"I'll add that I've felt awake in this way. And that this feeling is what brought me back to the academy."

"Is meditation one of the three paths?"

"Yes. Has it ever had meaning for you?"

Grace felt a thrill. Yes, Sophie was right to start with what she knew—this was how one built up a child.

With unusual care, Grace began to speak. "I'd only ever *tried* to meditate a few times. But here, especially at the wellness workshop, I've begun to see how it can lead to a kind of stillness, an immediate 'now' that is parallel to everyday life. And I've learned that a lot of people here practice being aware of this stillness, and look for qualities in it that go beyond what I know."

Something else came to mind. "In a way, this stillness reminds me of memory." Sophie eyed her. "I mean, in how I frame memories as if they were photos. In how, as my winter begins to take shape, I grasp it as a series of images. Seeing my brother, Alicia, the other kids, whatever: I relate each story element to a set of images. Maybe contemplation is what the images are for.

"Very differently, everyday life tends to slide by me. I think it might be too much like video, where the past flows through to the future as a kind of a process."

Tangled in metaphor, she felt out of her depth; but with another idea to mine and Sophie still attentive, she went on. "Everyday noise may hide this awareness, but I know it's there. Take what for me is a typical summer beach scene: one where I'll chat or read, watch kids swim, soak up the sun, and in my mind's eye, anyway, brood about something or other. In this way daily life passes through me. But if I see a breeze stir the waves or the sun fall abruptly behind a cloud— either a kind of sign from the mysterious 'now'—my routines lose force. My mind, anyone's, awakens for a time to the larger mystery.... And I agree that such awareness seems to flow—that the visible parts can seem to radiate together.

"I guess that above all it's about attitude. Mustn't wind and water always play in some way, whether I notice or not? It takes a strong, *sudden* change to get my attention.

"But 'mystery' and 'stillness' are tired words. I'm unsure of them."

Sophie seemed to be thinking. Grace sat up and brushed her legs. She took hold of an orange, made a shovel of two fingers and broke through the peel, finding red underneath. She especially liked blood oranges and now she had one to eat.

"Why do you call the words 'tired'? I find them fresh."

After a pause in which they each tasted sections of the orange, Grace said: "I think I see. The suddenness can catch anyone up. It's a sign available to all, not just the devout. Words like 'mystery' and 'stillness' seem tired because we don't often look at their meanings.

"Then again, supernatural mysteries show up in half of the new movies I see. Our need for these signs makes them itches the entertainment business tries to scratch."

"Less so, the stillness, I think," Sophie said. "Business culture misconstrues other signs as causing fear, but less so the stillness. It can't be lied about as easily."

Many at Seeker, Sophie then explained, sought to shape their lives around this spiritual awareness. "Perhaps because we all crave direction, these people expand the rather simple experience we've touched on into a strategy for living." Before she could go on, Grace broke in to say that a dentist here, now at a workshop, had a day earlier given her similar if rawer insights into how spirituality related not to life choices but instead to fear.

"Grace, please," said Sophie, "don't make too much of what I say. My so-called insights fall to pieces when I hear myself talk about them."

"It's true I often turn people I like into heroes," said Grace. "I must think that in a pinch they'll help me to see my own life."

"In a pinch!" replied Sophie, repeating the colloquialism with a tickled grin.

"Fall to pieces!" Grace echoed.

Grace saw that they both had misgivings to announce. And she felt, again after decades, an old crossroads sensation that she associated with being in her early twenties.

An awakened spiritual sensibility, Sophie now added, fueled two related if contending approaches to how one lived. Those who lived in society could be *mindful*. Those who turned away from the cares of others could search for *transcendence*.

"'Mindfulness' came up in the wellness workshop," said Grace.

"I've no idea what 'transcendence' means."

"For another slice or two of orange I'll say what I know. Though I know I miss the deeper meanings."

Grace smiled, complied with Sophie's demand, and ate two slices. But as they left the purer air of spiritual awakening to back down onto the branches of life and life choice, she felt regret.

Sophie may have also felt regret, as she hesitated, with dropped eyes and a thwarted look. Seeing this, Grace noted how she herself was again so occupied by what she faced directly as to forget most other things. This had always been her way and it had helped her learn lines during her actress years. Then as Alicia took ill she had lost sight of friends beyond her suburb and her harder-to-reach students and all but the easiest housekeeping. Now she was again reverting to type, in that her sudden interest in healing—said less emotionally, in the academy as she sensed its importance—was making her lose sight of the people she was with.

For instance, she had caricatured the Golds. She had parodied their words and mannerisms and done likewise with Willa and all three victims of the accident, Trumpeter, Francine, and Moira Kathleen.

Now Sophie was being generous; but while they felt ties of sympathy, friendliness, Grace did not know the younger woman well.

Swiftly, her mind debated. She lived most naturally in the here and now, with the people nearest her. Should she fall back on that manner or go on pursuing what, beneath character and passing incident, their life stories might also be about? Had she the strength to try both together?

Looking up, Sophie found Grace's warm smile. "You're brave to plow through all this stuff," said Grace, "I mean, to do so not for me but for yourself."

Sophie smiled back, but kept her eyes low. "It was always my way to persevere, push the plow forward, so I don't deserve credit. Yet, I'm still a bit surprised to be persisting at *this*."

"Plowing where the major crop is human life?"

"Yes, sure. Just a few years ago, I thought I might become an actual farmer, in Denmark or even in Africa. I worked a summer on a collective farm in the Israeli desert."

"What turned you this way, to being what my third-grade Sunday school pupils like hearing me call a 'fisher of men'? One boy even drew a crayon picture of Jesus beside a fish, both wearing ear-to-ear grins."

Sophie smiled at the image but left the question airborne. She may be thinking she doesn't know me well, Grace mused. She's very smart and I think may come from money and so have gone to the better schools.

"What turned me," Sophie answered, "was seeing the sadness all around. You may recall my lamenting my brother Jonas's sense of drift, especially given his rich imagination. Watching him fall into this gave me, at age fifteen, special glasses that made me think I saw behind all the smiles in the world."

Sophie said this in a direct way, as if unaware of or unbothered by its hopeless sensitivity. Grace saw that her own attentive act had been useful, but she felt confused and also caught in a prior moment's smile. Did Sophie mean to stick by these adolescent insights?

"Isn't that how many teenagers look at life?" she exclaimed.

"Yes, maybe; but as time passed I learned that this sense of being half adult or half child, half many things but wholly nothing, suited the world. My childhood friends, in their mid-twenties now, only care about building their careers. They show little interest in things outside of private life."

Sophie looked down ruminatively. "The people I see more often now call themselves 'activists' or 'artists.' The activists, who I know from school, work on projects that tend to leave them disappointed. And the artists seem self-absorbed, like the mythic Narcissus. They sneer at how most people live, their traditions and habits—at every part of culture. And then, like the activists and my childhood friends, they spend a big part of their day absorbed in new technologies.

"As for the people your age I know, in and out of my family and including my divorced parents, they have their own ways of being half-hearted. They pile up belongings and watch TV and learn to like the entrée listings on every kind of ethnic menu."

Sophie took Grace's hand and smiled, to show a mood lighter and less limiting than her words. "I don't think I exaggerate, but neither am

I as thrown by this as I was at fifteen. I also know it may not be as dismal as I make it sound… or I may just misunderstand. So much new technology, for example, is of course both inevitable and probably mostly beneficial."

Grace, fishing for a response, imagined Sophie as a painting. In word and gesture, she conveyed an ideal. She was a portrait of fresh imagination, resolve, and luck as it began to grapple with the sadness.

I would, mused Grace, paint her watching me, as she sat in a chair wrapped in colors that brought out her red, blowsy hair and pale skin.

"The people I know," Grace said, "rarely talk of being disappointed. Do you mistake a settling in that occurs for sadness?… Or do *we* mistake a sadness that drops on us all for settling in?"

Sophie raised a hand, surprising Grace. It wove the air, pushing words into place. Her unsure grin showed that she was again falling back on her determination.

The Diligent Beauty, Grace thought, now giving a name to what her memory of this hour would be.

"It must be both at once," said Sophie. "There is a settling in, of course—people today often take pleasure in life. There are good times in families, for example. And yet I think our enjoyment outside these good family times is half-hearted. Look at our anxious smirking at the world's strangeness. My brother, who gets his living from this anxiety, tells me stories of couples who marry on TV, of students who teach tricks to machines, and of relief-worker friends who end up working in giant corporations. And you're right that we get used to these harsh sketches—even as their themes often are need and disappointment.

"But some feel the sadness most of all. We hear others and ourselves ask for safety and satisfaction. Our laughs grow more nervous; our likely disappointment is where the craziness comes in."

Grace thought of Trumpeter's mall furor and her own splitting-off to imagine how others were seeing it. His actions had surely been about need and rejection. "Sophie," she asked, "are you talking about politics? Whatever, in our situation, that word even means."

"Maybe, yes, in regard to how problems are solved. But the problems themselves may grow from how the world we make confuses us, how we see ourselves as a species, or other causes. And you know that people hang careers on these questions, as I'm tentatively doing. But to me they seem as soaked in sadness as anything else. What I've found I'd graduate into is a lower rung of status; I'd learn to latch onto powerful people. The falseness of this, the way it ignores my need for commitment, my fear that as I climb the ladder I'll join the half-hearted ones—these factors drove me to the academy."

Grace conveyed an expression of not quite seeing where this led.

"Our view of life may be worn out, Grace, in the way a car engine can be. Above all the specific problems, this may bring on our sadness. The academy, on the other hand, tries to slip past our view of life, or trick it into opening. At times, it even talks to it directly. It draws on many different spiritual traditions in these efforts."

The Gift of Her Footing

They had wandered off course. Grace, feeling forlorn and unable to be quiet, had noted mockingly a parallel between drawing on global spiritual and kitchen traditions. This quieted them, and returned them to the central theme of stillness. But such stillness stayed attached to hopes and dreams. Grace felt tempted to mentally drift off in either of these directions; and the women, who might drift separately, became shy with one another. Grace tried to think about political involvement. With relief, she put this effort aside as Sophie began to speak again.

"The ideas of 'mindfulness' and of 'transcendence' anchor a lot of what goes on here," Sophie said. "So let's sit with them for a moment. Then we'll move to 'stillness' and another related little teaching aid I brought.

"I'll preface this by saying that 'spirituality' has many meanings here, in part because many ideas are in the air. Some welcome the chaos and say it frees us to take the best from Buddha, Christ, and other teachers. And, actually, many of our beliefs *are* mix-and-match efforts at synthesis, whether believers know this is so or not."

Touching back next on spiritual awareness, the profound sense of the "now," Sophie said it was not about religious authority or personal choice—it undercut both these things. "Feeling the stillness, the vibratory moment, the teachings say, we get past daily life. Not just things like cars but also fantasy—thought and memory alive in the mind.

With deeper vision, we see the constant change around us. Lives begin and end; we bind ourselves to beings and things that don't last. Bound in this way, we suffer as we wait ourselves to cease to be.

"But awake spiritually, the teachings say, we see that daily life is a dream. Beyond conflict, self-interest, and change we find a truer reality that some call 'god's eternal peace.' We stop yearning for our body and its illusions and come into god's acceptance."

As Sophie paused, Grace parroted her: "Flesh is an illusion," she said. "Conflict isn't real."

"Many cultures have believed so. It may be worth your while to hear this teaching out."

Grace smiled, to show a wish to go on. Sophie went back to wrestling with these ideas, bringing her sensibilities to bear on them-after winking to show that the ironies Grace pointed out, she saw, too.

"Mindful living," Sophie said, "comes from seeing that illusions of selfhood make us suffer. They form a wall that keeps us from seeing god in life. But if we quiet these illusions, we feel god's love and, in it, our reality. With detachment, we accept pain and pleasure, impermanence as well as loss of control. Our acceptance shows us the unity of things and leads us to live spiritually in the world."

Grace was disappointed. "I see people living that way here," she said, "always seeming surprised and holding up food lines to gawk at baby carrots. I can just see myself bringing that attitude home on Tuesday."

"Grace, believers think you *should* take it home. They say the mess we are in is due not to practical matters but to the devil of desire... prejudice, greed, and hatred. They say the solution is to learn to live unafraid, with an open heart instead of desire-and to bring this lesson of nonattachment to bear on community problems that we come across."

"Without attachments, why would I or anyone care about community?"

"The ideas of karma and living in god's love come in here. Awake spiritually, the teachings say, we see life's mysterious laws and the compassion they call us to."

Grace saw that something was true, absolutely, in this last idea.

How unsettling, she thought, to scorn the whole argument and then be struck by its conclusion.

"In all this," she asked Sophie, "what could 'transcendence' mean?"

"I feel like the pedantic teacher who is mocked behind her back."

"No, not at all. I want to hear. I need to hear this. I'll be good."

Again, Grace felt drawn to Sophie's need to know where she was.

Sophie gave Grace a layered smile. She picked her sack up by an edge, peeked in, and pulled out a notebook. "I'd best read this to you. Try to sit tight for another minute.

"Never mind for now where I got this… but of transcendence it says"-she read from her notebook-"that it's 'a deepening of attachment without concern for worldly illusions. It bypasses the laws of cause and effect and clings to the experience of awakened spirituality. While any feeling can lead to direct experience, including the compassion a cause-and-effect world creates, if you strip away the feelings, the attachments that lead to the experiences, you see you aren't alone. This lets you give up life more fully. You see how all experience, including suffering, feeling pain, say, from cancer or injustice, fits in a spiritual script that unfolds perfectly. It is even joyful to watch. To wake into transcendence is to see that one's suffering ultimately isn't real.'"

"To me," responded Grace, fiercely, "this is all about fear. It's about bailing psychological water with a sad little bucket while your very real lifeboat is beginning to sink…. I'm also shocked at how much these ideas repel me."

"Yet they've been taught through the ages. In one way or another, many religions preach god's perfection and charity and the pain-causing illusions of human selfhood and perception."

"Where exactly does 'charity' come in?"

"In our ability to be spiritually awake… some call this 'an act of god's forgiveness.'"

"We are to be forgiven for becoming what god created us to be?"

Sophie, having announced her own misgivings, was quiet.

"Though I see how scared people will want forgiveness," said Grace.

"There's too much fear and suffering," Sophie said. This idea hung in the air as the women again became aware of the room and the summer vines outside its windows. Grace heard two men talk, and wondered if they had been near for long. She looked at Sophie, wanting more without knowing what.

"It is hard to keep this simple," Sophie said after gathering her thoughts. "Yet maybe spiritual awareness isn't the same thing as its consequences. Maybe the latter is what people choose to argue over.... A clue here is how we've turned from the heart to the head."

"I felt that shift," said Grace.

Sophie pulled from her sack a big book. Two sets of folded, stapled papers fell free as she opened it. She handed a set to Grace.

"How are you feeling, now?" Sophie asked.

"Stymied and confused... "

"Me, too. I'll replay some of the tape. Let's get back to the stillness. We'll look at what is written on these sheets in a little while."

Over the recorded music, Sophie asked that they both empty their minds. Grace, never sure if she truly meditated, tried to push away the troubling talk. But she felt fitful. Life throws up enough problems, she thought, without my having to be confused about this bedrock stuff. Her strong reaction against Sophie's teaching was proof enough that she saw life differently, but what was her perspective? She didn't know, and the fact that she didn't made her temples ache.

Start with what you do know. These words returned and caused her to note her situation and again try to empty her mind. Now she was more successful. She slipped to an edge of restfulness, where breath and count filled awareness. That she stayed at a slippery edge became apparent when Sophie, a bit later, while asking her to remain quiet, stopped the tape and began to speak. Grace, with closed eyes, sensed that Sophie read poetry, likely off the sheets fallen out of the book. She felt attentive to the words. They were curious, and at Sophie's finishing a first short poem, Grace asked that she more slowly read it again.

"I'd only read a stanza or two," Sophie replied, "but I'll start over. The poem's title is 'Say Yes Quickly' and it begins:

Forget your life. Say, God is great. Get up.
You think you know what time it is. It's time to pray.

You've carved so many little figurines, too many.

Don't knock on any random door like a beggar.

Reach your long hand out to another door, beyond where

you go on the street, the street where everyone says, 'How are you?'

and no one says, How aren't you?"

Within Grace, something trembled. The commands in the poem, telling her what and what not to do, struck around her heart like the heat lightning had while she talked on the bench with Hans. *Say. Forget. Get up. Don't. Reach.* As on that night, her act beforehand of self-quieting allowed her to greet the external force with welcome rather than her instinctive defensiveness. She didn't cringe to think of forgetting her life, or of it being time to pray, or of admitting her lack of dignity. She who easily had six clocks back home—but didn't, it here was plain enough, know the time. She asked Sophie, who had begun another stanza, to read slowly. What momentous door had flown open to allow in this image of being asked how one was *not?* Could she ask this of herself? Could she handle the possible floodtide of her response?

"The poet, named Rumi," Sophie told her, "wrote a thousand years ago." She added that she read from translations, if apparently moving ones. Grace, who felt she must concentrate on the door that had issued and opened, let the words of explanation pass. The important part of concentrating was to breathe. She would let all the rest filter in from the sides.

Sophie read, over fifteen minutes, several poems, all by Rumi. Grace quickly forgot the titles and divisions between poems; what she heard primarily were the eruptions caused by phrases and thoughts striking within her. She found the violence suitable in the way violence suited the happy breakthroughs of spring. "'Stop the words now,'" Sophie read. "'Open the window in the center of your chest, and let the spirits fly in and out.'" Hearing this, Grace felt a release in the sense that her listening, remembering, and thinking began to break free of their confinements—of how she often kept them separate. As Sophie spoke, the phrases Grace heard began to mix with prior ones and her thoughts to make new meanings. "'And if one of our instruments breaks,'" Grace heard, "'it doesn't matter. We have fallen into the place where everything is music.'" Then, "'Inside you there's an artist you don't know about. He's not interested in how things look different in moonlight.'"

If everything is music, thought Grace, perhaps breakage doesn't matter. So, yes, stop the words now. And work less hard to catch life in its most flattering light. Yet, do I really do this? I know I hunt for heroes and the kind of sad or sad-funny stories that heroes are apt to ride around in. Dread waits in this.

"'Last night,'" she heard, "'that moon came along, drunk, dropping clothes in the street.'" The line landed on her heart and made her laugh. "'There are hundreds of ways to kneel and kiss the ground.'" This teaching made her feel grateful. Then a new stanza fortified her will. "'Don't think all ecstasies are the same! Jesus was lost in his love for God. His donkey was drunk with barley. Drink from the presence of saints, not from those other jars.'" Welcomingly, as it gave more guidance, she heard a new clarification: "'Until the juice ferments a while in the cask, it isn't wine. If you wish your heart to be bright, you must do a little work.'"

"This is ecstatic poetry," Sophie had said, adding, as if Grace did not see this, that it was another path to spiritual awakening. These poems, Grace saw, pushed everything else aside, reminding one's mind and body that the soul is the governing organ. Yet, how long, given her involvements, might soulfulness last? Soon, though, a new poem further steadied and affected her. "'This being human is a guest house. Every morning a new arrival. A joy, a depression, a meanness, some momentary awareness comes as an unexpected visitor.'" And half a dozen lines later: "'Meet them at the door laughing and invite them in. Be grateful for whatever comes, because each has been sent as a guide from beyond.'"

As Sophie's voice quieted, the studio's screen door opened. Grace opened her eyes to see two men in the doorway, apparently ready for their workshop on romantic relationships.

"'Is what I say true?'" Grace heard, distinctly, amid silences. "'Say *yes* quickly, if you know, if you've known it from before the beginning of the universe.'"

Grace raised one foot. "I have a toehold," she said, aloud but softly, to everyone.

Giving Time to One's Pursuits

It was nearing midnight when Grace's day finally ended and she returned to her tent. The temperature had begun to cool in late afternoon, during a second, longer stop at the bookstore. When, after
breaking her impromptu, daylong fast at supper, she went at seven
p.m. to join a chanting session in the sanctuary, but then decided to sit
at the meditation pond before moving on, she regretted not having
carried a sweater. Not so resistant, she heard the bountiful melodies
that infused the chanting and gave her heart rest. This third path
Sophie had prepared into spiritual awareness Grace chose to delay
journeying on, perhaps for a future visit, another year. I've gone as far
as I should for now, she thought. Instead, wanting above all, including
above all her surviving bewilderment, to channel her deep emotions,
she joined a gospel singing session that had first caught her eye earlier
that week. She considered how gospel singing and Hindu chanting
might not be too different, but, this evening, she wanted to know what
the words she sang meant. She greatly enjoyed the comedy of being
grouped with fifteen other awkward altos amid groups of tenors and
sopranos; she loved how after an hour they could sing of god in a way
that wouldn't bother the Almighty's ears, and how after two hours the
newly formed community could nearly bust out the windows on the
place. They all left after ten p.m. with sweat on their necks. Outside,
under heady stars, the air felt almost icy.

She'd had an idea to skip lunch as she walked from the studio to the bookstore with Sophie. She was grateful to her, but wanted suddenly to be on her own. Foregoing food seemed one way to keep temporarily intact; another was to lighten things up. Sophie, with her watchful eyes, seemed at first to understand and go along. When Grace turned to gossip, the world outside herself, the particular, funky tale of Willa and Trumpeter, Sophie eased her own mood of concentration.

"I suppose they may end up among the igloos!" Sophie said with gentle amusement.

"Do you feel worried?"

"Worried about what... and for whom?"

Grace responded with a laugh that, like the question, held mischief and foreboding. "I guess I fear that 'bad' can really mean bad," she said. "Trumpeter is wound so tightly. And as for Willa, overnight she seemed to stop being who I'd thought she was. She once seemed confident; the day I met you both, she introduced herself as 'Willa the Wiking.'... Unless, of course, it's Trumpeter she wants to conquer."

"No. More goes on with her, though I think that for a while at least they may end up in a relationship."

"You know, I was sure he wanted you... all that insolent stomping around when you were nearby."

"I did feel that and even, I admit, enjoy it. But I've kept the summer for my pursuits, which include getting to know many people here. I may also still have a boyfriend back in Europe."

Grace wanted to learn more about Sophie's personal life, but felt it might be the wrong topic for the day. "I'd hoped Trumpeter would interest you. I fear for him."

"In a way he's brave. He seems to know he's blind and stupid now, yet sometimes he still tries."

"Is Willa also stupid?"

"I wonder if it's even harder for her, because her confusion is new. You're right in that at school she often was confident. Now this begins to be in doubt. And possibly also rising up are insecurities that grow out of being a black from Africa."

"Do you mean she feels exposed among all the white faces here?"

"I'm not sure. But she told me that it scares her when mainstream white friends look so lost. I think she sometimes uses us as models." Sophie mused briefly. "In a basic way, I do watch over her. I'll try to see that we fly home together in six weeks. And she and Trumpeter will endure their arctic journey: I suppose I mean that, yes, life will go on. Also, Willa has practice living in the North. I think we don't have to worry."

Grace was cheered by this appraisal, as it further freed her to be detached and self-occupied during her final days at Seeker. She knew that in the months to come she would think a lot about people she had met here; but she wanted no such responsibilities now. Hours are the measure of my remaining freedom, she thought.

As Sophie did, she would give time to her pursuits.

Her mind, though, soon swerved onto paired images, seeing Willa's forehead bleakly bent to the car window the morning after the accident, then ghostly Trumpeter, standing by the naked, painted brothers. I've tried hard these last few days, she thought. But while concern for this oddly paired duo has driven me, I've not tried to get to know *them*. Not better, but at all. And now they might be gone from here before me.

Wending downhill, she and Sophie looked out on the mowed field from which she had watched heat lightning build after the wellness workshop. Far beyond it, she saw the structure that housed the café. She tugged Sophie's arm to lead her off the path in the direction of her favorite bench. Thirty members of a workshop filled the field; in a meditative exercise, they took independent directions and walked their impossibly slow half steps in silence.

Sophie once looked at Grace as they detoured, but said nothing.

They sat in the middle of the bench with their upper arms touching. "I wish I could take your advice to not worry," said Grace. "Maybe it's being older than you, or my knee-jerk concern for my son and my niece, but the thought of being young and so lost in life scares me."

"We all eat well enough and seem to be fairly resilient, Grace."   ·

"I know that at the age you all are and maybe more so for eighth graders, most everything is endurable. But what I can't help but see is how one goes from being Trumpeter to being Moira Kathleen. The view they share of what I'll call 'Mount Disappointment,' with her in his line of sight, inescapably older than him and beginning to break apart, probably explains why he couldn't stand her.

"When you spoke before about half-heartedness, I didn't see it; your words seemed too much bathed in idealism. They stand out better in the mountain shadows."

"As I said then," Sophie broke in, "I may also just misunderstand. I hardly know Trumpeter beyond his declarations, but about Willa, I know that she thinks her parents embody this uncertainty. Her father is filled with misgivings and never comfortable in Norway or back in Africa. Her mother keeps saying that life will come together—just very rarely in the ways we expect it to."

"I guess I usually go for her mother's generality," said Grace. "That way, every morning you feel safe."

The bench they sat on was sometimes moved, as she had once moved it; but at its customary place under a tree, years of use had scuffed away the grass. Grace tapped the dry dirt with a toe and thought how on that recent night with Hans, under the ferocious rain, the dirt must soon have run to mud.

"I've gotten so involved, here," continued Grace, "but I don't know anyone very well. Not Willa or Trumpeter or Monk and, while you and I connect easily, not you, either. There's not been time… but I may've also forgotten how to act among rebels. My stay-at-home husband, Henry, would be lost in a place like this. But even Amos… sometimes to show friends how well I think I know him, I mimic his moods. But age him some and have him find his way here—give the world a first solid shot at him—and I don't know who he'd become."

Grace peeled free her shoulder, slid away from Sophie, and turned to look at her. Sophie looked back, with a smile into which Grace read interest and patience; but she said nothing. Still, a receptiveness Grace sensed in Sophie helped to calm her down.

"Sophie," she said, "I want to let what I've heard today settle. And for reasons I'm unsure of, I want to go through the bookstore today on my own. Yet, where you have brought me is wonderful."

Sophie picked a dirt speck from Grace's arm. "We'll see each other later, or at Monk's performance on Sunday," she said. "Willa is away, but she promised to try to be at that. Trumpeter's delicate friendship with Monk makes his taking part less clear."

So… Sophie knew of the performance, and that Grace had been invited.

Blowing Off the Chaff

Alone again, Grace drifted. She wanted to keep moving; seeing someone she knew, she would wave in a clipped, busied way. But her pace was leisurely, as she had no destination.

She decided that later that day she would tour the buildings she most liked, to tie her imaginary castles, all she wondered at now, to actual windows and roofs. She thought to do this while making her first climb to the spiritualist-in-residence tent that sat steeply uphill from the sanctuary. She saw a clothesline strung between trees, pinning two pairs of jeans. Oddly, one pair was pinned at the waist, one at the cuff of each leg. She noted, as she trod a sketchy path into the woods, that the tent she had thought was Ken Samuel's appeared empty.

She had first to wonder about herself. As she had told Sophie, she lived so conventionally, yet she could have deep recognitions. And did her bending toward Rumi's freshness signal that her idea of her life was worn out? She knew there was truth in this, but felt also that her essentially dramatic outlook was more than a case of getting lost in the passing moment—or in Rumi's words, "of having carved too many figurines." And yet, was her cold view of transcendence about such idols getting in the way? With more clarity, she recalled Sophie's remark made days earlier: that while she was drawn to spiritual wonder, she wanted also to back up and think.

Down from her hill hike after a while, she wasn't sure until she neared the dining-hall, finning toward it with a hundred other people, that she *would* keep her fast. The smell of hot food wafting over the porch steps turned her back in the direction of the bookstore, where she arrived at noon, just as it opened for the day. She entered with a hopeful feeling, brought about by what waited inside and its appealing presentation. Like the dining-hall, she saw, the bookstore was meant to feel bounteous and safe. Its nutrients were made not of protein, fat, and carbohydrate, but rather shelf upon shelf of books, tapes, and mind-body-spirit paraphernalia—things like incense and yoga mats. The shelves were labeled as crisply and with as much reasoned strength as the buffet stations, where posh cursives listed the ingredients for every entrée at a meal. As scores of interactions could blossom in the dining-hall, here there were enough recesses for thirty people to lose themselves in thought. Snaking among the shelves, Grace saw a bookstore staff person light incense in one location and then another.

She used her hands frequently, to pull out and peruse a book or less often a video, but also to simply touch the materials, in the sense that they were things. She had left the lunch crowd in part from feeling oppressed by its plainspoken hunger. She had wanted not to escape but to touch these others. In the bookstore she could enact this fantasy, having words and ideas stand in for the people who sought them. She remembered Sophie, in a heightened state, groping the bark of a willow tree. The world is there for touching, Grace thought. Ideas are part of that world.

This first visit lasted ninety minutes. She sought a lay of the land; she wanted to shape her experiences, insights, and questions of the past few weeks into a hardened material she could hold. "Gather and store," Betsy had said, and this was part of that effort. She made a great advance in coming to see, in the broadest sense, that a third of the collection was occupied with wellness and a third with spiritual awakening. Was it too simple to think that the remaining third would be concerned with fear?

Start with what you know, she thought again. In the maze, she found the wellness shelves and browsed there for half an hour. I find this all so practical, but in a hard-to-get-at way, she mused. She recalled Mel's comment that the practices had spun out of old traditions. As they can vault across centuries, Grace thought, they must be rooted in parts of life that all people share. She saw, with some perplexity, more than a dozen yoga styles being celebrated in an inescapably competitive way. The teachers of the styles, anyway, if one went by their smiling book-jacket photos, were pleased with the choices they had made. Grace knew little about yoga beyond the way it stretched and put one at ease, and the common claim that these medicinal benefits were the gift of a deeper commitment. As she moved among the bookstore topics, going from bodywork to meditation to therapies apt for wounded hearts and minds, her method was to grasp a book's spine and skim its back-cover blurbs—she wanted hope to take home with her, not information. She wanted to believe that some of these authors had earned the right to teach.

She had brought a small notebook, and wrote down some titles. She looked for authors whose names she knew from the Seeker catalog. She saw how some books used such celebrity credentials as having been on a talk show to build an author's stature... and how a smaller group of authors seemed to have sound scientific credentials. So wellness, she thought, which sees the soul, an imaginary organ that science can't study, as the source of healing, must have champions and even pioneers in certain scientific fields.

She wondered if scientific stature, which she knew little about, was similar to celebrity stature. It was a side consideration and one that might branch in many directions. Why it matters, even if I must let it drop, she told herself, relates to trusting what you hear. This is important because an inability to trust—here was age-old theatrical fodder—imprints itself as fear.

In this half-sensory, half-ruminating way, Grace went on exploring the Seeker bookstore. Her questions were unformulated and she likewise felt too edgy to read carefully. When she segued from wellness themes to those of spiritual awareness, passing on her short physical journey Lawrence, who ran the laundry, and an older man who leaned on his cane as he read, she sensed that her touch must even be lighter. She must trust her responses and guess what she was after. On coming to a dozen titles by and about Rumi, she registered how she took every line as a challenge. She pulled out and fingered several books. The commands she had heard earlier rang within her: *Say! Forget! Rise up! Don't! Reach!* Using a last reserve of clarity, she rose up enough to be attentive as, going from feeling to thinking, she read the section topics. Hinduism, Sufism, Buddhism, Western mysticism, a few others.... The premise of each tradition must be, she reasoned, that an enduring stillness is in reach. Perhaps this is what they mean this by "peace." But apparently—she meant to question this statement later—this peace sits outside daily life and time.

Grace saw that she knew little about these spiritual traditions, as she was also unschooled in the underlying tenets of practical wellness. I'm no professor or intellectual, she thought; but I may be able to listen now with a more open mind. The question when I get home will be whether I follow up on this. This thought threw her back, dauntingly but briefly, upon the harder questions, raised with Sophie, of what "home" meant for her and what deeper meaning she had for herself.

Feeling good about, meaning trustful of, her glimpses that week into yoga, mindfulness, stories of the heart, and ecstatic spirituality, she bought a collection of Rumi poems and stepped outside. The bookmarks I bring home will carry me forward if I let them, she thought. Over the next two hours, as, with the day's heat peaking, she got her swimsuit and went to the beach, her mind jumped among these themes in just the covetous, tactile way she had handled the books. And she found herself watching people in a strangely analogous manner. She wondered which teachings guided them. As she lay wet and exercised after a long swim into the middle of the pond, down a route safe from algae, she felt the optimism that had carried from the morning wane. I must take home all I find, she thought. I've been here long enough to see that while people reach high, many are also deeply stuck in mud. The notion of fear Anton had first raised came to mind and she thought of the red-haired widower he and Deb had introduced her to, who'd had visions that took him to an era from before he was born. In them, he had been a black child, playing ball near the northern edge of Central Park. He had not met his wife in another body, but her spirit had felt comfortingly present.

With this ideal of comfort in hand, thinking also of the trio from the accident and feeling a little unsteady after twenty hours without food, Grace returned at 3:30 to the bookstore. Her shakiness and stoic resolve—better to bring home everything she saw—together bred a fortitude she rarely felt. This strength is what let me try to help Alicia, she thought. Why is it showing up again now?

As she walked past midsummer foliage, which seemed to grow before her eyes, as the night rain had fed a field before her eyes, or in the
way, turning, she might see wind tease the pond, images of fear rang
down before her. She thought of the knotted fears felt by Trumpeter,
Francine, Willa, Deb, and Moira Kathleen. She thought of her fears for
Amos and Alicia and the perhaps more philosophical fears of Monk
and—yes—Hans. She paged back through several weeks of vignettes
and the many people she had met and found fear often close by.

She saw, as she had not before, a display table near the door that featured
authors who would soon teach at the academy. She had two questions to pursue in the room, where she now felt more at ease. She saw a youth at the register; behind him a woman her age, with the flooded eyes a gardener or a librarian
will sometimes have, battled a computer screen. Grace asked her for a pointer
to books about the spirit world.

"You can look in several sections," the woman said, "Shamanism
and Intuitive Healing, surely. It depends on what you mean. In a minute I can help you."

Grace worked with librarians and knew that the woman's "minute"
could stretch out. Anyway, she had something to pursue first. As she
had swum, she had thought how she could not define the word "spirituality." Was it the awareness beyond daily life Rumi spoke of, or a
sense of god, or of a secret, dynamic reality hidden from the mind and
senses, or what? Did it relate to how one lived? In college, she had
learned that spirit, a Greek word, meant only "breath." Not the body
or anything physical but a breath of life that entered the world. It must
stand for human breath and the breath of creation at once, she
thought. But if this was so, why did Seeker focus on god? Was spirituality really about something outside normal human perceptions? What
of human breath? She had noticed earlier how the bookstore reached
toward mysticism, which she now understood to be the human reaching toward god. This clue guided her as in a scan of the shelves she
saw that something big was missing from the room. There was no
theatre, first off—no Greek tragedy or comedy and no Shakespeare
and no modern drama. Yet, she wondered, isn't this art concerned
with the breath of human life? Neither was there *any* art concerned
with human spirit outside the mystical search for god. The few novels

and the books on music or visual art she found all seemed by their covers to promote mystical leanings.

"A story filled with spiritual messengers," a reviewer of one novel wrote. "A technique that carries your mystical eye into art," said a workbook blurb. Another blurb, on a poetry chapbook, urged readers to "see these poems as sacred, ritualistic word creating."

A chasm opened that she could not now explore. Why, she wondered, is the art I learned to like left out of this collection? Why beside a stress on wellness is there such stress on connecting directly with god? Isn't the conflict-ridden art I know also spiritual? An art filled more with trouble than with mystical messengers and rituals? Excepting that, yes, yes... as with the gods in Greek plays and the seers and faeries in Shakespeare, mystical elements often do fill the center of the dramatic stage.

This was no problem she could clarify easily; pushing it aside, she went back to noting what the bookstore had, not omitted. I'll map our community of souls, she thought. It feels fine to say "community," as it applies to little else in my life. In a gathering mood again, she turned to her second question: what was the "spirit world" that many people here looked to? She thought back to the stern, convinced man in the wellness workshop, Pythagoras, with his fairy photo. She thought of the funny—funny to her—idea that soul was more actual than emotional—that a soul could be wounded in such a way that a human-spirit doctor, a shaman, would have to slip into the spirit world on a healing mission. These aren't ideas first thought of in our loony times, she told herself. But they trouble me. If I hear Rumi but go tone-deaf now, thinking of shamans and transcendence, am I anything more than resistant?

She had actually, she knew, not found the phrase "spirit world" at Seeker, but instead brought it with her. A pop culture catchall, it included the use of crystals or pyramids to gather spiritual force, as in the energy science Anton had talked of. Here also came in tarot readers, psychics, astrologers, and other guides to realities beyond the senses. On TV, it was the joke that drew people only half-jokingly to watch. When she laughed with Betsy, it was this New Age material that set them off.

The spirit world, also, she reminded herself, is home to angels and devils and witches and prophets—all beings of Western religions that people today often have strained yet still emotional relationships with.

In the course of the season there were, it seemed, workshops to address all of these topics. One trend that Grace had only just heard of added the concept of "spiritual coaches," who use their powers to help clients achieve goals related to romance, work, and the like. "We align spiritual energies to get what we want," a coach had written—a bit brazenly, Grace thought—in her workshop blurb.

Cautiously, she browsed books that peered into this world. She found the shelf titled "Intuitive Healing"—subtitled "Spiritual Coaching for Oneself and Others"—and the multiple shelves devoted to Shamanism, the ancient religion that fueled belief in spirit manipulation. As earlier, but with a queasiness growing from her lack of better ideas—her doubt cut both ways—she began to browse book jackets. She saw also that most books had brief forewords, written by New Age colleagues and good for grasping a work's core messages.

She began with the older, shamanic religion, choosing one book in a visually attractive series written by a social scientist. The author, a cover blurb stated, "while studying shaman cultures came to know an alternate reality they call 'spirit' or 'dream world' or 'the sacred.'" And when, after his initiation, he became a shaman, supernatural vitalities concentrated in and energized him. In the spirit world, his awareness merged with the awareness of a shaman ancestor. This gave him "great, possibly world-saving healing powers for our time."

In time, the blurb continued, the scientist-shaman saw that he could teach others to be shaman healers as well. The teaching could be split into levels, and if not all students came to have the spirit world's highest power, an ability to retrieve souls, all who tried got a view of that world. The most gifted soul retrievers, the blurb concluded, as he himself perhaps was, come along only once or twice in a generation.

Staring at his books, Grace saw that one was a manual. Retrieving it, she looked through pages whose paint-by-number format made her think of manuals she owned for learning to sew and to change car engine oil.

Grace was startled, not least by the author's assumed authority. She wondered if someone whose words were untouched by, yes, common humility could have special spiritual resources. *World-saving healing powers?* By humility, she mused, I mean seeing low as well as high—his knowing that he uses his beliefs to make his way in the world, and that he shares with others this need to make one's way.

A big step into spiritual identity must be to see this need as a common human trait.

Say *no* quickly, she said to herself, laughingly, unintentionally, impishly.

"Forgive me, Rumi," she said aloud but softly and with audible laughter.

Feeling derision and parallel self-doubt, Grace moved to the shelf on "Intuitive Healing." I think I know what to expect, she thought, but not what to put in its place. Mattering most, after all, are the questions and terrible longings that put us on these roads.

Any derision I feel must therefore keep *my* uncertainties in view.

She first picked a book by an author who had been famous for a decade and whose work, in bookstores always, sold tens of millions of copies. "We can learn to live in a field of sacred energy," she read on the back cover. "As we find our personal mission, we learn to project energy into this field. Our missions take shape through mysterious coincidences that lead us step by step down our paths. As more of us come to live in the sacred energy field, finding our missions," the précis continued—Grace saw three workbooks on *this* author's shelf— "insecurity and violence will end on the material plane. We all will join the sacred energy as beings of light."

Well, that's reassuring, Personal Mission lady, Grace thought flippantly as she continued to browse.

Rather than offer transcendence, another writer's view of intuition took, as had the scientist-shaman's, a metaphorical middle ground. He preached the shaman's ability to shift among physical forms. A blurb noted that the author, on seeing native shamans fly as birds and run as deer, had realized that humans had a dormant ability to merge with other species. It then struck him that this "shape change" was also the key to progress. It was how we might solve problems like addictions and rotting institutions. "Look," the author counseled, "for the miraculous shape-change possibilities that any life problem presents."

Grace saw that his lesson also began with magic and miracles, before scaling back to use shape change as a metaphor. She saw too that before he had weaseled out—*his* metaphorical shape change—of his promised magic, the writer would have had her son Amos and his crew as fans.

Her rallying glibness and need to lean on Amos signaled the unease awaiting her, but she had a last "intuitive" author to visit. She knew that, as spirit travel was a shamanic teaching, reincarnation was a teaching of the Indian religions. Down through history more people had likely believed in spirit travel and reincarnation than had not. She knew even less about these things than she did about the religions concepts that, in a bleached-out way, she had grown up with. Yet, she saw it as fantasy to think that she could change species or bodies. And it seemed wrong to make this leap into fantasy without knowing the consequences. What made it wrong was that this leap was one many suffering people wanted to make.

She recalled the bewildering past-life discussion she had listened to a week earlier, the man with Central Park memories but also Anton's description of it a social movement. With a name in mind, she found the right shelves. She saw five titles by the author; as she eyed them, the store manager came to stand beside her. "I'm sorry I forgot about you," the woman said.

The manager's gaze was now clear; and Grace, who liked bookish types, rolling the dice with this stranger, expressed both her doubts and her lack of understanding.

The woman—who had a drawn face and a modest crown of gray hair and wore rimless glasses—blinked, as she seemed to be making a decision. "You should know that not all ideas live in harmony at Seeker," she said. "Some people here keep away from supernaturalism and discussions of the spirit world. Yet these things grow from substantial traditions and, as much to the point, they are what a lot of people here want."

"By my estimate they fill a third of the shelves here," Grace said.

"That's about right. The ratio may be far larger in the movement as a whole."

"I find it hard to think I could become a deer now or in another life—that this isn't poetic metaphor. What can I even do with such an idea but be entertained? Is a deer with reading on its mind looking through the window now at all your books?"

With a half smile, the manager gave credence to Grace's words; then she showed with a headshake that she was busy. She may also have not wanted to talk about it more. Seeing the shelf Grace stood at, she led her to another part of the store and picked out a magazine. "You can read this if you don't mind standing. It's an interview with Nadia Tolliver, conducted by another philosopher of the spirit world who teaches here."

She started to go, but stopped. "In the West, before Christianity," she said, "people spoke of mystery religions, not spirit worlds; though in many ways, in especially taking pressure off the self, it amounted to something similar. In Greece, mystery religions thrived before and after the time of Sophocles and Socrates. Scores of them existed as the gospels were written half a millennium later, and Christianity's early history was about defeating this competition. And the Church's final victory, with a few more centuries passed, had a lot to do with its own mysterious stories of a transcendent end to suffering and the unreality of everyday life.

"Life by then had become fearfully hard. It may have been better to decide it wasn't real."

Grace saw her own doubts reflected in the departing manager's words. She wondered if Trumpeter, who seemed, whether in pity or disdain, to see and absorb the hardships of people like Francine, Moira Kathleen, and Anton, would one day try to believe that life was unreal.

What could I persuade him was real in me, she asked herself?

It was thus with a heavy heart that she began to read the magazine article. It was, in fact, an interview, conducted with this leader in joining karmic reincarnation to mental health, Nadia Tolliver. Grace with her teacher's eye saw how the interviewer's gently restless tone suggested that he felt himself more prestigious than his interviewee. He wanted, he told readers, to pursue a link between soul movement and unique planes in the spirit world, seen in terms of energy frequencies—he seemed to mean this scientifically, as with TV or radio waves.

Asked to speak personally, Nadia recounted how she had learned of *her* soul migrations later in life, after decades as a psychotherapist and after, in fact, she began helping patients migrate. In a dream, she saw herself as a princess in a royal family, disgraced and banished for having plotted against her aunt. She had not been killed because of her intuitive powers, which her aunt's priest had been afraid to destroy. In a conscious vision months later she saw herself again, being executed in another era for teaching that souls are reborn. Her rebirth in our time and place more open to intuition was, she added, her karmic reward for having suffered in these past lives.

Grace couldn't help picturing the great trashy movie this story would make.

"Our era is spiritual in response to the destructiveness of the recent past," added Nadia. "Accepting the spirit world and ceasing to fear death are efforts toward species survival." Her labors in this direction had freed her to see wonderful things. "Once we learn we are eternal in god," she said, "we see soul as what matters, which brings us to a new ordering of life. In our society this is unfolding with the help of subatomic science, which is verifying a spiritual belief that the body is not the only vessel to hold being. In my work, the new order helps me learn how the souls of my clients connect—that is, find the next layer of order. Those having great grief in one life, I've learned, are often reborn first. I've also learned that those with strong bonds in one life are often enforcing older bonds—in this way, families move together from one life to the next and lovers find souls they had been in love with during other lives."

Nadia was seeing many more patients recall past lives—something that might signal an evolutionary shift. She excitingly also saw more and more wellness workers, credentialed and not, look for past-life influences as they searched out a patient's source of trauma.

Hans is a wellness worker, Grace mused. He won't even talk about this stuff.

The interviewer, after dutifully asking and hearing Nadia reply to a few questions, raised his belief that souls passing between bodies use "spiritual frequencies," which are planes that hold real (but not visible to the naked eye) positions in space and time. The planes are graded and a soul—hopefully ascending—rests at the level it gained during the life in its previous body while waiting to be born again.

This only began his observations; but Grace, who, while disbelieving the fantasy bred from loss and logic, still feared what this disbelief threw back in her face, decided not to read further.

Say *no* slowly, she told herself, but with firmer emphasis, again.

Part Six

Poets' Walk

An Older Retreat

From where she sat, still a quarter mile from the water, on a bench under yet another gazebo, the river whose name she shared pointed north past the Catskills. On this placid morning, she could see past the Poets' Walk meanders to a fine stretch of blue. Just left, even crowdedly close, the long bridge over the Hudson flowed, high spans, trusses, and all, with romantic majesty. That in its westbound direction it led in less than five minutes to a long strip-mall debacle she would now not forget.

Her two duffle bags and tent bag lay ten minutes back, in grasses near the park entrance. Monk on dropping her off had said her bags would be safe there; he then showed her the park inscription—yes, this *had* been an artists' haunt in romanticist times! Finally, he walked her out to the gazebo before departing.

Now alone, Grace knew that her first layer of surprise rose from the suddenness of her departure from the academy. Her contract ran through Tuesday, but in a call to her no-longer-patient husband Sunday night, just before Monk's performance, he had asked that she leave early and, as it was due him, she agreed. He had taken the next day off, he said. Now it was nine a.m. Monday and in an hour—she had arranged a meeting by the Hudson, where beforehand she might struggle to adjust—he would arrive.

Thinking back tiredly over the last few days, she fixed first on the

hoards arrived yesterday for Retreat Week. Undone by Saturday, inwardly stormy, awaiting Monk's event, and thinking she had days to
regroup, during the first half of Sunday she spent hours on what usually took minutes. Awake at six, she managed to reach the breakfast
buffet only just ahead of its nine a.m. closing. She washed a few
clothes and hung them near her tent. She fell asleep and again almost
missed lunch; then she was hardly aware of the departing hundreds,
people she had cared about and sung with a day earlier. She even forgot the Golds. When, in late afternoon, the transition-time calm broke
before all the new arrivals, out of cars and vans and off buses from the
city, she felt little interest. As a group they seemed readier for Seeker
than had other arrivals—most carried yoga mats and more than usual
wore white head wraps and tunics instead of brimmed baseball caps,
khaki shorts, and the like. She thought, wrongly as it turned out, that
she would have time to observe this exotic gathering the next day.

Only at the lazy staff supper did she start to gather her thoughts.
Beginning at breakfast, meals would be silent that week, but she and
actually some others began the practice then. A man Hans's age, sharing her table for eight, read a "mystical" novel she had seen in the
bookstore, while she eyed the still-spare tableau on the lawn. It struck
her that she now knew something of what Monk's performance would
be about. There were so many awkward layers to get through. There
was her awkwardness realizing that for still-elusive reasons she could
not make the leap, popular at Seeker, to belief in a spirit world. Then
there was the awkwardness trapping Monk when he would try, as he
had tried on the way to the hospital, to bring up history.

No awkward leap was needed, she felt, to see spirit in the world. If
she walked in the city, she could convince anyone she met that this was
so. Awkwardness first arose as one explained why the reverie always
ended; strung together, enough awkward tries at explaining would add
up to illness. Let's not be coy, she told herself, but talk instead of life's
hardships and fears, the opposite of spiritual reverie. Such fears and
hardships must always exist; in addition, there must be times, marked
by events and relationships, historical times, when the burn from them
is worse. Wellness, she now knew, was a practice that lay between the
burn and the reverie. Hans had said Monk tried to get something big
done at the academy. Wellness as it beamed into the world must therefore be his theme.

Watching her tablemate read, Grace saw him look back. She smiled, to show that her gaze had been an empty vessel. *Reverie*, she thought—another word I use carelessly—I know means "dream"; so spiritual reverie must be a dream of creation's breath. How, when I'm home, can I keep this knowledge close to me? How so, when I know I'll slip back into my reckless way of life?

She now, at Poets' Walk, felt for the first time in days, with a sense of sudden saturation, the life she *would* soon return to. Her last thoughts had started this off. She saw her husband's vulnerable, rough face and then, in a sideways slip of memories, the hall closet he had rebuilt when Amos was five, and Amos watching him work, and the boy's end-of-school-year room she had lacked the time and energy to clean the day he went to camp. Once or twice a year Henry picked parts of the house to clean and straighten ruthlessly—but Amos's room would be her job in the time between her return and her son's. When she tried to picture Alicia, Steve, and Nan, home from their hospital-run camp two nights ago, her mental viewfinder stopped at her own front door. Then, returning in her mind to the academy, picturing Hans, she realized that what help she herself gave others usually began with her physical presence. I'll be back there soon enough, she told herself.

With the next days reconnoitered, and finding herself alone but for a few other amblers, she picked up the memory of Monk's performance.

Some Old Masks

Arriving at the screened-in gazebo at dusk, Grace, reading from a plaque she had not before seen, learned that it had been Seeker's first sanctuary. Looking in, she saw Monk, alone by a table on the foot-high stage. A bright candle illuminated him; four others shone around the room. Facing him in a semicircle were two dozen people, including Sophie, Elsa—who had taught here days before—the bookstore manager, and, surprisingly, Hans. She recognized half of those people gathered. She went in, got a black pillow, and took it to sit on beside Sophie.

"Trumpeter and Willa left," said Sophie, touching Grace's arm. "He needed to go. This afternoon Monk took them to visit Francine and then to the home of friends he has in town. Tomorrow they'll get Trumpeter's car out of service and leave directly."

Grace, suddenly regretful, asked: "And they will be fine?"

Sophie shrugged, and tapping Grace's shoulder pointed to Hans, seated at one end of the half circle. He smiled, to say he found value in *some* philosophizing; and Grace, raising a splay-fingered hand as Monk liked to do, then seeing Hans grin back more broadly, felt surrounded by friends.

"Massage Man is a discriminating listener," she said to Sophie.

Grace just before had talked with her husband, and knew she would also leave, too soon, in the morning. As she thought of her departure really for the first time, her daylong tiredness escalated into aching. She recalled the pinched looks of people about to drive home that first day she had worked loading luggage. Driving *her* were logistical issues, taking her tent down and getting to the river and such. Yet far more troubling was a worry that, with all she had found here, something greater, her usual balance, might be lost. Who am I, she thought, to deny the spirit world or whatever other people lean on, or to think I can help Trumpeter and Willa? I don't know anything—except that this desperate need for balance seems sad.

Awaiting Monk, she asked herself what she could expect or at least hope for. Either way, by what was or wasn't said, Monk's talk, performance, or whatever it was to be would climax her stay at Seeker... this, as she was ready to depart. If she left the gazebo wanting, that would be the lesson she could begin again from later.

After what she had seen, and knowing all she would mull over, her hope was that Monk would help her know herself. She meant not her individuality but what lay in support. She had felt enough fear that year and thought of it enough recently to know that who she was individually was not enough. Add enough further pain and she, the known Grace, would just go numb. Whether this meant she would seek a field of energy or a spirit figure, a perfect crystal or a genie to help her along, she didn't know. Though she did feel that to turn, in a like way, to Rumi's kind of pure recognitions would be an insult. His poetic figures seemed to show the wild beauty possible in the human soul and situation, but they weren't really weight-bearing.

It was one thing to look to genies and angels and the like half-humorously; it might be another when life was grave. Was it her known, striving self that she would have to give up?

She now saw in relief the wellness building blocks—the mind, body, heart, and, less clearly, soul work practiced earnestly here. Yet, the fact remained that to conjure wellness required illness. These building blocks had largely the individual as a subject: stretching in yoga, calming the mind... opening the heart. But did illness?

As she turned to bring Sophie her questions, Monk smiled softly at them all. He had the table behind him, with a box under it. There was enough light so all were seen. His shy smile gave no hint of what would follow, here where years of spiritual practice and ceremony had gone on. Didn't he know, she wondered, what this stage had most often been for? If so, why was he pulling an old, grimy rug out of that box?

It was actually a pale yellow animal skin. Monk made it a tablecloth, letting its ragged border drape the table. He then took three racket-shaped items from the box and put two on the table. He raised the one he still held and as he faced his audience Grace saw that what he held was a mask on a wire handle—a sad-face, black-and-white mask made of fabric and wire! She felt stunned.

"Elsa has tragic and comic masks and animal masks," Monk said to everyone. "I ask that you choose one to wear if and when you speak."

With the sad-mask countenance veiling his own, he slowly faced center, left, and right, like an actor, before he went on speaking.

Now I see why we are *here*, Grace thought. Greek theater, which had used sad and happy masks, began on a ceremonial stage. And the rug will of course be a goatskin. I know, though I forget the reason why, that the Greek word "tragedy" meant something like "song of the goat."

Yes, I do remember. The playwright who won each year's festival prize received the honor of sacrificing the ceremonial goat. And what a half-bizarre image, not the blood but the ceremony, that makes today.

"I'm a bit glum," said Monk, beginning, "this since everyone laughs at me and to my face. I started wearing masks for self-protection."

Grace and the others chuckled with varying levels of assurance. Made concrete by the setting, another reframing of their lives—what Seeker did best and what its participants wanted most—was about to take place.

"I'm also glum because this is my third year performing—without extra pay, I'll add—and I still draw small crowds. And I'm glum finally because around here people call this my 'frightened farmer' piece. But I've not spent much time behind a plow." He switched the tragic mask for a comic one he had picked up with his free hand.

More chuckles…. Grace thought, he seems to want to make us groan but not be comfortable.

He faced his three directions and then slowly raised the tragic mask again.

"There is also the matter of my deeper sadness." Saying this, for comic effect he nodded in tragic agreement with himself. "It comes from feeling trapped and afraid. Because what I think traps not just me but us all—please don't laugh—is the power that science and business have over us. Joke at my striking fat targets, my tilting at windmills, but I think these forces control us as much as poverty and nature ever did the farmers who lived before us. For them, tax agents, bad weather, pests, and the like added up to a hungry beast in the yard. But now a more ambiguous beast sees us watch TV, work, walk in malls, and take vacations. It, this beast bred of science and business, may threaten us less but it's just as controlling. It feeds us stories that teach us from childhood how it wants us to see ourselves and behave and even be able to imagine. And as with any beast, it still always promises to eat us if we misbehave.

"Who here can help me describe the hungry beast in our yard?"

Someone took a mask from Elsa's hand and amused the room with a tiger's face, an impressive swiping paw, and a predatory snarl. Everyone turned smilingly to the sound.

Seeing the tiger, Monk had turned to his comic mask. He went back to the tragic one. "I'm sad-hearted again," he continued, "this time for having to wipe away our knowing smiles. Yes, here we grandly seek release from this beast we claim to know well—even as our put-downs of what we call 'capitalism' and 'materialism' show that what we know of the beast is clichéd. But less grand is how this actuality, whatever we call it, may confuse us far more than we know. We could be a long way from our release."

Grace saw that Monk really was, quoting Willa, a Seeker black sheep, for saying this, if for no other reason. While discussions rang out and the staff could be scolded for subpar work, rarely had she heard a healing practice criticized. The Seeker credo was that everyone always found ways intuitively that worked for them. If the range of efforts seemed eclectic, ties at the root showed they all were effective. *It's all good* was even a Seeker maxim. But doubts like those raised by Monk were seen as inappropriate.

His claim is hard to grab hold of, mused Grace. Maybe Monk in his mask fights the TV shows I watch. She looked toward but not as far as Hans, and then turned back to Monk.

Can these everyday forces be *beastly*, she wondered. They surely were pervasive. She remembered having lit on this theme during the dawn car ride with Monk and Willa. And now, again claiming the perspective of her homey tent, she briefly considered the web shaped by science and business that she stepped through in her life. In fact, what *wasn't* a part of it? This objective reality, this stage set then became, yes, much of what the media and also she and others thought about and talked about.

"Young and old," Monk said, "we come here seeking our release. We learn wellness and spiritual practices, hoping they will center us not before the beast but in ourselves. But the confusion I think we share keeps its grip, because we know the beast awaits us when we leave.

"Our young, to start with them, meet the beast as they wonder how they will get by in life. It tells them to settle, walk the common road of school, career, and family—yet they know that most who do wind up making things they are taught to want, and then wanting more things. Still, having grown up with science and business, knowing its touch but not how it works, this fate has not seemed personal—until, taking time here to reflect, they are stunned. Then they linger, as we keep the beast penned. But leaving eventually, they see in the cold way it eyes them that they are trapped.

"This may relate less to walking a common road than to seeing that they will have to one day.

"Will one of our youth play the beast for a moment? It can freely be fierce, as up to this point I suspect we may now agree." A young woman did as asked, yelping fearfully.

Grace wondered if many of her students faced this beast in the years after she taught them. Were they cornered in this way as they looked to the future? And were those who by their nature took a common road—becoming, say, a dentist, like Anton—affected? Did the great, shaping beast frighten everyone?

"We in midlife," Monk continued, "facing smaller decisions, find that our belongings shape our traps. What our young find so suffocating—things like lawn care, diets, and vacation plans, and having it all play back on TV—becomes how we mark time. We know the beast hears each tick and sees us take what it tosses our way. Safe at home, we hardly seem to care, but then—again, among the few who are seekers—when we look out in our yards we see ourselves."

"Do wait!" he added suddenly—Grace, following his gaze, saw that the tiger mask had passed to an older woman. "I'll try to be clearer. I think that what traps us in midlife is, as much as these forces, not knowing if we *are* trapped. Does being shaped by science and business harm us? Like others, I ask this. Should or even can we fight off its control? Is its presence merely irritating? Are we satisfied or even glad? Is our real problem a stale attitude? Science and business cared for our injured Franny this week—we must be honest and see *that did happen.* Is a beast even out there?"

The tiger woman, whom Grace didn't know, stood briefly in the audience. Subdued, she imitated Monk by turning silently and slowly to face the others in three directions.

Grace impulsively got Elsa's tragic mask and did the same. She felt heavy and agitated as she moved, and ached for yoga. Did it matter what forces drove one's daily life? Mustn't there always be underlying structures? Could one even think to break all this apart?

She pictured the gas station she frequented near the mega-mall behind her suburb, and then the strip malls here across the river.

Tiger Woman rose again, crying, "I see the beast!" Grace, still on her feet, holding a sad-face mask, saw in candlelight that the orange tiger mask was rendered nicely. She could almost picture the animal it signified whipping across a delta.

"As do I," said Monk. "I see it leering, plush with power. I see it understanding that if farmers of old saw outward threats, things like drought and exploitation, we whom science and business shape see only ourselves. Some old cultures felt that bad behaviors could wake their beasts. Fear gets to us as we see that our beast has a human face."

Grace was fascinated. Monk's coarse images were themselves a kind of mask. But would the ideas he tried to lead them through adhere?

"This seeing the beast's human face," he went on, "how we bring this on ourselves, moves many of us to self-doubt. At Seeker, while some hate the whole human situation, more turn away from who they now are—seen as people bred to above all buy the products of science and business—and seek other ways to live. What won't reflect the beast, they ask?"

Monk paused—dramatically, Grace thought. This talk to a chorus or whatever they were strained him. Each breath raised his brow over the tragic mask. She saw that the gazebo's window screens behind and to each side of him were now painted in darkness.

"But this turning away also scares me," he went on. "I feel fear as people here exchange their identities for new ones based in other cultures. And as they adopt beliefs that reject physical life, without knowing if they arose among people who were happy, kind, or just. And as they abandon just these hopes to be happy, kind, and just that form another, I think non-beastly part of who we are."

A man at one end of the semicircle stood and moved near the stage. He faced it and the chorus sideways and with both hands held a blue bandanna to his face. It had three holes, perhaps just cut with a penknife. They mimicked two eyes and a mouth to make an eerie geometric mask. The mask's angularity seemed somehow familiar to Grace; so did its wearer.

"We need new identities, as your old ones are dead," the man said. "And nature is no beast—it is good and resourceful. It gives us the strength to make life anew. We only need to build identities that honor it instead of the core *Western* value we call 'greed.'"

Sophie leaned nearer Grace and whispered Trumpeter's name.

The blue-masked man hides in his ideas, Grace thought. In this he *is* like Trumpeter—and like Amos, in the sense that the boy, edging out of his roomful of conceptions, had begun taking potshots at the world he saw.

"But is our way of life so grim?" Monk staunchly asked the blue-masked figure. "Is greed the West's only driving force? What about our humanism—our everyday traditions like liberty and justice for all?"

Grace, empathetic to the man Monk tested, and shielded by a mask, began to speak. As she did, the drama teacher in her saw her step with conviction and a release of frustration into the play. However sad a story, she always liked so to pretend. "I'd say you are the dreamer," she told Monk. She knew this judging of which stance was nearer to her experience had gone on in her mind, not his words, but she felt a need to see it otherwise. "I don't think in your terms, of science and business as a beast. I doubt doing so can help me in my life. But I will say that where I live your humanism is hard to find. What comes up more is endless noise, by which I mean advertising, nonstop images, cartoon politics, being always in cars, seeing people screw up, and so on... with race, class, and using drugs to make life bearable. Many of the kids I teach feel the full weight of this by age fourteen. They might see erasing what matters now, if they somehow could, as a good idea.

"I'd say the noise drowns us out," she added, thinking as she spoke how this idea came from Trumpeter. She gave her mask to Elsa and sat.

Grace felt agitated; her student actors got this way pretending in front of others a first time. It came now from hearing herself speak in this untidy way. Monk was a context. She wanted Sophie to comment—her young friend did, with lowered eyes and a grin that among remoter reflections held appreciation.

My students *do* bring this unease to their behaviors, Grace thought.

When she next looked up she saw the others gazing keenly at Monk, who held up a deer mask. In its curves and hollows and glittering eyes she saw articulated wildness, dread, and speed.

"I've changed masks," he said, "to show that my uncertainty takes me beyond what makes us happy or sad to something wilder. Since, to go on, I think that we are and aren't trapped, do and don't drown in noise... should and shouldn't break free of our identities. Some of you know that the beast I've fought for decades saved my life two summers back. So, this deer mask, which seems always to listen, wait to hear what matters, will frame the next part of my lament.

"Why masks and candles? Why wear wildness and claim to lament? It's that I feel we are more lost than we know. A clue is our frequent use of sarcasm. We react sarcastically if told that we are trapped, or see a beast in the mirror, or can change or even penetrate forces like science and business. But we come here and to similar places to look for ways to feel safe.

"These clues of our sarcasm and our sense of being trapped, and as much our uncertainty that we even are trapped, or, if so, in what ways and how much, puts us, I think, in a tragic situation. We feel disappointed and don't know how to protect ourselves."

Grace thought: My eighth graders learn that stories of strife that end happily are comedies, while stories that begin optimistically but end sadly are tragedies. Of course, they learn this—she had long before made this connection—just when they are losing the butterfly wings of childhood.

We ground them in the premise that they should try to be happy. I also still tell myself something similar.

Where She Was From

Grace had walked down the path to better glimpse the river. She sensed a figure off to her right, whose route, hidden by the land's undulations, might parallel her own. And then where the path forked unexpectedly north and west, she turned her eyes back to the gazebo and saw that someone else, a man grooming a dog, had come up to rest on its rough branch benches. Her gaze returned to the supple, flowing water.

She had realized the first funny thing in all this while tying Monk's claim in with teaching tragedy to her students—she had the background to understand what he was saying! The tragic ideal was a tool in her teacher's bag that helped her to modest achievements every semester. For her, its meaning lay mostly dormant and came alive only as it first did for a student. But long ago, it had engaged her more deeply; and in response to Monk's words, it was again warming in her mind.

She thus had brought a readiness to the next part of his performance. Then each thing said helped her recall more of what "tragedy" meant. Contributing first was his summons to listen wildly for what matters.

And life, if tragic, was funny, too. The other laughable thing about her quest had also surfaced in this middle part of Monk's performance.

Holding up a deer mask, erect as a dramatic figure, and with a tale to unfold, Monk had turned to illustrations from his life. He told them how, like the man in the blue mask, he had once hated who he was. Turning thirty in self-parody, he took a new legal surname, "Monk-fish," happy to demean two honest words. Wanting to escape himself, he came to Seeker in search of magical powers and transcendence. But in time empathy and, he hoped, modesty turned him to practical well-ness. Two more shifts resulted. He came to view the hunt for magic as a sign of not nearness to power but confusion. And he came to tie the hunt and the confusion to being caught in this trap.

"I then," she remembered him saying, "became an oddity here. Still needing a home, and feeling it was here, I returned, but with a new goal. I explored my sense of being trapped. This led me to books about illness, not wellness, which the bookstore didn't carry. I looked again at some traditions I'd abandoned. But as the beast squeezes its critics, it took time to find things that mattered. I had to fight through a disinterest most of us feel. I had to slip past scholarly squabbles to define the past. I had to escape a reluctance to see beyond old tech-nologies and manners to anything vital. But what I found eventually was a saga of battling the beast across centuries or longer that I think the academy needs to consider.

"My friends here, though, felt I'd gone off track. They even met my cries with sarcasm, as the story of science, business, and its critics is one that bored most of us in school. It's taught from sixth grade to graduate school but it rarely interests us. Nor do we even care why; this is true in mainstream culture but also here, where we seek not our roots but what is most unlike us. Our jaded eyes in the mirror come from doubt and from a harder-to-accept cause I'll bring up soon.

"With this general dislike of the subject in mind, and as I always at least *try* to be less alone, I'll wrap the rest of my tale, my dance across history, in misty images. I'll speak from a metaphorical height, as if I stood on a ridge watching two successive storms.

"It's a tale of bumbling, of a sort that wants the comic mask again."

He changed masks, to show the ear-to-ear, stamped grin that Grace now found weird. Then he paused, to her relief. She had been thinking how this all was and wasn't so—it was just the oscillation he described. Not only her students but also she and her friends had to be tricked into looking past their private lives. Some students did well at this, though the connection was usually with achieving, not caring. But was it ever otherwise—was the "tragic" label deserved? She kept her eyes on Monk, sure that the others must also be waiting for him to attack this crux of a difficult presentation.

He now told them that his first metaphorical storm looked back over three hundred years. "It bellows, as big storms do, that our wellness pursuit is just the present adaptation of one side in a war that has split the West that long. The fight has been hard; both sides have been brutal. The Western mind, for its part, has through science and business remade the life we wake to; it gives us a world that won't easily starve us and that we've even begun to play with like a toy.

"And if this coming to toy with the world bothers some of us, a further problem is that humanity itself has begun to be a toy, fit to tinker with and change, of the Western mind.

"Having said this, I can't go further with my skim of a complex story. On one hand, it's far too simplified; on the other, the hall of mirrors it points to is what has brought many of us to the academy."

Elsa rose, holding the tiger mask. She moved to stand beside the man in the blue mask, which now was tied back to his head. At a chance for her to speak, she refrained. Glancing back, Grace noted that the comic and tragic masks were on the black pillow Elsa had sat upon.

"We who seek wellness are divided," Monk said, "by having as parents both sides in this struggle. One parent is the conquering Western mind: few here refuse its food, shelter, medicine, and other riches. This choice puts us in the mainstream, where, as someone said earlier, the riches add up to a lot of distracting noise.

"Our other parent is the opposition to this beast. It has a record of good acts but also acts so evil that humanity still cowers. The crimes done in its name make it hateful: I speak of tyrannies fueled by a hunt for values more fulfilling than the piling up of wealth. Here, later, we can group what we learn in school about subjects like romanticism, socialism, communism, fascism and modernism.

"All this makes us the children of dangerous parents. One is the beast of science and business, which comforts or bribes us but always advances. The other is a moral and emotional opposition to this beast, which still in living memory led to Hitler and Stalin.

"Thus, something our dangerous parents share is a desire for power."

How oddly accepted these themes are, thought Grace. Stripped of Monk's urgency and insights, they're in the books my students read or at least bear around in backpacks when they go on to high school.

"And so at Seeker," Monk said, adding emphasis, "we tend to reject our past and look for guidance elsewhere. We dismiss our exploitive parent out of hand even as we accept most of its gifts. We dismiss our purifying parent as a regrettable failure. Instead, we turn to beliefs as different as possible from what we know, thinking we may find better luck in them. Yet we who've learned to honor traditions, but don't know our own, should and often do see the contradiction."

Grace thought of Mike, who had taught the wellness workshop, and her sense that he had leapt from all he once had been into a new identity. Monk is saying, she told herself, that a clean break couldn't be wholly real or at least lasting.

As Monk paused again, she took his hint and climbed her own ridge. She saw how her life amusements often sniped at this beastly force. Think of your TV stuffed with magic powers, she told herself. Here was another relationship she had missed. Not for decades had she been as attentive to this resistance as she was to it now in the form of Seeker's provoking ideas. Even teaching drama, she forgot that dramatic conflict was meant to lift the human spirit. Romanticism, socialism, fascism—these weren't empty terms. They were if anything the opposite, describing efforts, often turned monstrous, to make life support human nature more than the "beast"—in Monk's terminology, the perplexing actuality of science and business—allowed.

Had she fallen asleep to this struggle? Or did she feel it had lost force—had become the unlucky failure Monk and in a spiteful way Trumpeter talked about, good only as entertainment?

Others may have been thinking along these lines. Tiger-masked Elsa stepped onstage, pointed her free arm, and swung in a slow arc to face Monk. Grace sensed again that Elsa, who had been long at her calling, might often fall back on routinized reactions. As I do in my classroom, she reflected with a smile.

"The greatest scientist of our times," Elsa proclaimed, "taught that problems can't be solved by the consciousness that creates them. Perhaps the Western resistance had no choice but to make monsters."

"I have two responses," said Monk. "The easier is to ask by what rule, if science is part of what bewilders us, we should abandon our painful history of resistance but take on faith what a scientist says?"

Ah, science again, thought Grace. But for relying on it, as I hop among hospitals but also, well, in every way, science is as strange to me as any spiritual concept here. And brought up in this context, it reminds me how far outside my understanding science is.

I'm rooted in this resistance, though. It's the other funny thing in all this. As with being drawn to tragedy, I've let romanticism with its sentimental heroes guide me in life, however lazily and inconsistently. A token of this guidance that I've held onto during even my foggiest years has been the river I live near and share a name with, the Hudson.

Near where Rip Van Winkle also had an unexpectedly long nap.

She again pictured the river's scenery and portraiture, both full of color and conflict. Had the romantics used these traits, as telegraph and rail were coming in, to oppose a lack of appreciation for conflict and color that they were finding the beast of science and business to have?

Reason and Tragedy

Trumpeter was within thirty yards of her by the time she sensed someone's near presence and turned his way. His white travel wear, crisp against the tawny grasses, exposed only his neck and head, cupped hands, and sandaled feet. His expressions again looked more weathered than she had remembered.

"Hi, Grace," he said, once he had halved the remaining distance. She was struck by his swiftness. Then she sensed that his resolve had brought him only to where he could greet her, and he might not quite know what more to say. But the connection she had felt lay between them, never mind how little they had ever yet spoken, had been there in fact.

He could be her older son, grown uncannily to manhood.

"This is a surprise," she said, even if it wasn't so, entirely.

"It seems we are both leaving now."

"And Willa, too, I'm told. Is she here?"

"I'll meet her back in town in a couple of hours."

"Were you in the handmade mask last night? I didn't see Willa."

Trumpeter smiled, shyly; then his expression turned reflective.

"She watched from outside," he said. "I was there with her some of the time. That ongoing role—it results from a promise I made to Monk."

"Do you mean that the things you said were staged?"

"There are always a few actors. It's staged in the sense that he each time has us read things and assigns us points of view and then we improvise."

"Do you rehearse? Is it that contrived?"

"No, it's spontaneous. Monk says it's mostly about listening."

"Theater as meditation—breathing into varied points of view?"

"Well, I guess."

Now, anyway, he seemed to care less about the performance than she did. She was still getting used to having him stand there. "Ask me questions, if you want," she told him.

"Did you get tired of the Seeker food?"

"Only recently… ask real questions, if you want."

"What will you do when you go home?"

She looked in his eyes, then beyond him to the horizon. The river squirreled through the upper left edge of the frame; so, she faced north. The knotted woods behind Trumpeter hid an open view of the Catskills.

With a sudden laugh, she said, "What I'll first do, though you may not like hearing this, is calm down. I'll have to and probably want to." She pointed, to draw his gaze to his right. "In winter, looking downhill from a site on my street, we see both shores of the river."

His eyes had flared at her levity, but he followed her lead. Relaxing, he eyed the Hudson. He doesn't skip past it or counterfeit his effort, thought Grace. That's what Sophie meant when she said he tried. I wonder if I can do the same.

"It's too tightly wound there, you know," she continued. "The goal may be peace but it's a jittery search. Not that I think it can be otherwise—the risk makes it so. What Seeker tries is so much against the grain."

Trumpeter watched the river. "And then what will you do?"

So, he *had* brought a challenge.

"Once I'm calm? I'll need a minute on that question. I'd taken time here to start to ask it of myself. My musings won't yet quite flow; but you can listen along."

In a canoe just days before, Monk had told her that Trumpeter sought an escape hatch. His mood now was otherwise; he seemed accepting—as if he wanted only to face what would come next for him.

"Out in life," she said, "we can't as easily watch the hours go by. We can't hide in the background as people do at the academy."

"So you think that people hide while they are there."

"Not from themselves. But from the way life always knocks us around—oh, yes, they hide from that."

The air felt rich in odors. One thought and then another passed through her mind, but she couldn't touch them; their snub shapes made her think of inchworms. She decided to begin speaking about her family.

"In middle age, I'm made up mostly of roles, being the person others see me as," she said. "So when I'm back settled at home what I'll do is be the mom and wife my son and husband expect. I'll feed one and help the other to relax. These roles and a third as a teacher create endless tasks. I'd say the tasks map my life the way the paths and buildings map the academy.

"Now, anyway," she went on, watching him as he looked away, "you aren't so tied down. I also don't know what the family you grew up in was like."

"It wasn't a happy situation. But I don't hear happiness raised as an issue in what you describe."

"Making my son Amos happy is. It gets less clear after that. I think I can say to you that my marriage, like so many others, leaves something to be desired."

"Meaning that it lacks intimacy?"

"No, meaning the intimacy is tied to terms that exclude some of who I am and maybe of who my husband is. Yet we manage to comfort and often even enjoy one another."

"Do you mean cushion instead of comfort?"

"It may be that, yes, I do."

"Cushioning is what counts in the marriages I've seen." Grace heard dislike and longing mingled in this observation.

"Don't be so sure you understand," said Grace. "I didn't think about my marriage much these last weeks, or other relationships back home. And I don't know that I'll find myself challenging them a month from now. But I think I may *not*—at least due to what I've come across here."

"An open self-examination doesn't appeal to you?"

Grace seemed to hear the stubborn whinny of a horse. "Someone who likes you told me you are stupid and lost," she said.

Trumpeter winced, but didn't rupture. Soon he gave up his grimace for an abashed look. Then he slipped into an embarrassed smile. Such rapid shifts are what lead to his looking older, thought Grace.

But she still felt stubborn. "Examining myself, with whatever 'openness' I can muster, does appeal to me. But I'm not ready to be angry like you. I think I may also feel sympathy more readily— sympathy even for myself. Do you remember when Monk last night brought up *his* learning to be charitable?"

He nodded. Grace saw past the irony to envy his receptiveness. He's so much riper for instruction than I am, she thought. Interrupting her train of thought, she smiled softly. "You're less explosive than usual."

He seemed to swallow the claim whole—she guessed, as he did too much in life. "It's my having chosen to go," he told her. "What's hard usually is deciding. So much of the rest of it, the packing and leaving my choices often come down to, has a numb, robotic feel."

"It masquerades as restfulness?"

"Yes, just in those words."

"Then let me get back to my own thoughts; but be charitable!"

Briefly, I'll echo Monk's struggle on his stage, thought Grace.

"At home," she told Trumpeter, "what may be hardest is to know what to let be. I think this month will stay vivid only if I see how it can affect my life. Unlike some people there, I'm unsuited for sudden, deep change. And actually, unlike twenty years ago, I mostly dislike change now. That reluctance may account for my sense that I'm waking up."

Grace heard false notes as she spoke. She considered how they wouldn't help when, quite soon, she would urge Trumpeter to stop posing. What do I truly mean? she asked herself.

I, too, may look older with every minute gone by.

She saw two hummingbirds but wouldn't let her eyes follow them.

She felt snappishly resistant to the whole Seeker catalog.

"Might everyday life," she began, "sit above this struggle? Might it be that as I work down my daily task list, teaching, fixing meals, being a homework cop, and maybe kicking at my marriage—could it be that I, like others on this daily climb to bedtime, don't have to care about wellness or spirituality? Aren't these things mere philosophy? Don't I already do what I must? Although—ease up, my new young friend; I ask myself, not you, these questions. Then I hate my answers. Why? Because what I think I truly do on my climb is try to sweeten life for the people I care about. So, I live in a private circle—except it's one drawn in chalk on a public floor. And because it is I find I have less control than I'd like, and that getting my private tasks done presents a more complex problem than I believed.

"I mean the world breaks into the circle every way I can imagine."

In a reversal, she was angry and he seemed not to be. She saw him eye her with caring and dismay, but also smugness. I'll go after the latter, she thought, like the feral animal I know myself to be.

"Do you feel superior, hearing me end up agreeing with you?" she asked. "I mean, that ill winds blow through the neighborhood. Do you like having figured it out first?"

"Grace, you misunderstand what I was thinking!"

"I doubt I do. It's always better when it's others losing *their* illusions. But let's see how you like it. Do you remember when, at the pond, before the car crash, you spoke of your three years of weekday work and weekend narcotics? The last year, hallucinating alone every Sunday? It was quite a heroic story. Do you remember it?"

"I remember the experience, and describing it that night." He was a little defensive now, since she pressed so hard; but she felt that they were also drawn tightly together.

"Well, lose the grandiosity. You seem fourteen years old when you slip into it. Talk of that time as if it actually happened to you. Be awake, if you can."

She watched him let pass the challenge of that final sentence. I've guessed right, she thought. He wants most to speak and be heard and hear his works echo. And his best guess is that I know it's hard to really listen.

"The work," said Trumpeter, "being part of a technology business, is in many ways entertaining and therefore easy. It's a game of logic, where the tasks become apparent and you must only find how best to get them done. What creates tension are deadlines and wanting to do well and other players. The first two of these obstacles can even add to the fun.... That teenager you say you see in me—before I got to high school I knew how to get this kind of game-based work done."

"What's wrong with that?"

"It's such a simple, clean model—the work used in that culture is *elegant*. Those who play can start to see all of life as a game."

"Don't such reductions just grease the wheels of life? Am I right? It's okay to take it easy sometimes. Aren't you being too sensitive?"

She saw him look at her without anger.

I pulled a loose thread, she thought. His read on the problem is deeper than mine. For reasons, maybe including personal ones, he sees that a *no* answer to my questions is where lots of journeying begins.

"What I know," he told her, "is that simple, crisp views of life bring out my shame. They always have, whether or not I pretend to go along. If the model is right and life is reducible and cool, so that talk turns to chatter, what do I do with the hot holy mess I feel inside?"

"Being angry and hallucinating better represent your feelings? I mean to ask this plainly as a question."

"It shows anyone who wants to think otherwise that I'm not comfortable."

"And about the hallucinating and general salvation-seeking?"

"Your way of saying that betrays your prejudices."

"I guess it does. Right now, I'd be glad to give a lot of my prejudices a rest."

Hearing her last words hum, glad for them, Grace thought how a need for probing speech that she had painted onto Trumpeter was her need, too.

Trumpeter's tone changed with his next statement, enough to make her again look in his eyes. Speaking as if in the midst of an endeavor, and as if busy with practical actions, he told her that he was leaving the academy to give his own prejudices a rest.

"The experiences can't be described as we stand here, and I'm not done with any of them, probably," he said. "But I'm tired of how I am here and I need a change. The journey can alter course on any day."

"Monk thinks you may be running out of road."

"Monk and I are at odds on that."

"Does Willa make a mistake to go with you?"

"She says she's tired of herself, too. She's a caring girl. We may be good companions for one another."

Grace again rued having evaded Willa's call for companionship on the afternoon after the accident.

"Monk knows how to reach me," she told Trumpeter. "The journey may one day take you a hundred miles south. Will you come to my house in the suburbs and see me?"

He smiled roughly, then wryly. Finally, he looked intimately at her, in the way she looked at him.

To her surprise, he left not on the path to the park entrance, but by backtracking through the tall grass until he melted over a hill. She walked instinctively a little ways toward the river, and sat when she saw it more clearly. He will show up one day, she thought.

Time was passing, and she considered what to do. Well, she thought, one last time on this vacation, hiatus, or whatever it's been, I'll try my deep-breathing trick. I want to clear my head and get back briefly to last night.

The scene could be the one I most often replay with Betsy.

Minutes later, on her side with her lungs open and her pulse quieted to normal, faced away from the distracting river, she was remembering that in the candlelit gazebo, during the flickering moment between Monk's two responses to Elsa, the air had felt full of human strain and capacity. Sophie, not wanting to lose her sense of being enthralled, was avoiding Grace's glance. Grace then had buried an urge to connect with Hans and instead looked back the other way, in the direction of the bookstore manager. But neither the wily woman nor those seated near her—all who seemed to be expressive and absorbed, if solitary—turned in her direction.

Once more, Grace felt grateful for this space—not the gazebo but the academy—that let people have and take time with new experiences.

There were then by her count three bewildering topics in view. First was the claim related by Monk that their everyday world—not any common human predicament but their particular society, spreading globally now—was somehow a trap. Second was the story of an internal resistance to this society, a "romantic movement," if the old name sufficed, that might or might not be a lot of things, including still alive. She grinned at all there was to comprehend. Did the complexity alone make people want supernatural guides? Or was it a despair of small changes? Sophie had neared saying this latter yesterday; now Elsa in her question to Monk seemed to be suggesting it, too.

The third topic Grace counted, though Monk had mentioned it but once, was "tragedy." Of the three, all distant, this seemed farthest. He had said their situation might be tragic. If his performance, which he had twice called a "lament," was winding down, as Grace with her stage sense felt was the case, what he had still to say must concern tragedy. Would he say more about their plight, or talk instead of how in some tragic, against the odds way they might respond to it?

She briefly imagined trying to break all of this down for her students.

Monk had held up an animal mask; she waited with others as his audience and chorus. "My second reply," he now said, facing Elsa, "gets us nicely to my other metaphorical storm. For, if the first storm bore a tale that ran across three centuries, this one covers forty! Because the Western sensibility our problem-solving scientist means to change goes back that far.

"The romantics borrowed from this older tale but then turned against it. Not can it hurt the tale to say that it'll bring us back to our masks."

Grace now heard Monk speak of an approach to human life that, he said, had carried unsteadily across these millennia. He stood behind his deer mask in summer clothes—she only now noticed his bare, muted forearms—and told how Hebrews and Greeks not far apart in eras or geography had arrived separately at human-centered views of the spirit. While still thinking supernatural forces shaped some human experience, they came to believe that the bonds people formed with one another and things and within themselves had deciding roles, too. Even the pious found earthly involvement to be a nicely human way to approach the gods. It developed humility, by showing that one's character helped shape one's fate. The sense of character led to the spiritual need even more than duty to be *answerable*—to express worthy character in action. It was in this way that most people found their way to deeper expressions of spirituality.

"Abraham, Jacob, Antigone, Achilles—Western humanism begins in these stories, which carry the spiritual ideal of human answerability," he added.

The word "greed," part of a truncated phrase, fell softly among the seekers. It had not come from anyone wearing a mask.

Monk waited; his frequent pauses seemed meant to let them look back with care at his words. Grace was struck by how his images of earthly and heavenly spirituality were embodied, perhaps suitably, in the Christian cross.

"And in greed and other human character traits," Monk went on, "and in bad luck. Remember, I address the claim that a problem can't be solved by the consciousness that creates it—that the West can't help to heal itself. My reply is that illness always exists, even as it may *now* be widespread, and that Western self-understanding and answerability can be powerful forces for healing.

"The West's strength comes from its discoveries of reason and tragedy."

As these words spilled, Grace could hardly contain herself.

Making Sense of It

Guessing wrongly, Grace took the trail's north fork for a hundred yards until it entered a forest. She needed clear lines now, she understood at once, so she retreated from the woody ferment, the brush and tree limbs, and turned back to the open meadow. If she climbed the rise before her, bridge and river would quickly come into view. The trail fork that must reach the river, if she still had time to take it, was just up ahead as well.

There was now a refreshing, light breeze, which swept the meadow and tested its winged creatures, its grasshoppers, ladybugs, and rarer but loftier butterflies and hummingbirds. She smelled the grass and wind and, she thought, even the river. This mild scene made her think back to Monk's event, which stayed in her mind, with a sense of less gasping and combustion than sisterly teasing. *Monk* was hardly mild; in fact, he was extreme!

It was time to look at her watch, and doing so she learned that in fifteen minutes she would have to head back to the main entrance. Henry wouldn't look for her in this unfamiliar park even if he saw her bags; after loading them, he would wait near the car or take his own walk. She would be glad and relieved to see him, yet she also knew that, aside from a few expected anecdotes, she would have to put her experiences aside. Normalcy would be on his mind, and he would want to learn quickly that she had recuperated.

Of course, I'll say yes, she thought; though if ever a yes-and-no response were deserved, it's now. The irony and amazed feeling that had carried this reflection gave way, however, to a memory of the wounded children she had seen. She felt a flicker of remorse.

No, she corrected herself: you were and will again be dutiful. So, remember last night if you want. To be dutiful and to be oneself: each extreme act in its time.

And let's find out how close to the river I can get.

Monk's awkward words were no more, she saw, than the result of his extreme points of view. It was as if he had let nature wash over his words until only a hardy few remained, and had then tied these to a pole and walked them back into camp. Science and business, reason and tragedy: what others? Raise your eyes to the words, he had seemed to urge, then say what you think. Perhaps we can layer the complexities anew together.

It was an extreme invitation that even most people at Seeker refused.

And yet, Grace saw, Monk's method was just the one used at the academy. Back there, in fact, the Retreat Week workshops would now be getting underway. Half a dozen halls would be filling. Most gatherings of from twenty to two hundred people would begin with simple prayers, chants, or meditations, all meant to cleanse the mind. Then an idea or two would be introduced and somewhat elaborated—the key point being they were meant to stand grandly in the mind. And this was just the extreme Hans would not go near. Monk, though, more drawn to words than to physical touches, had understood that people assaulted by noise could only really hear what is simple and grand.

Said differently, they can only really hear what is extreme.

Monk sees his situation, she thought. Yet, then, why is he awkward and against the flow? Why do even Seeker folk back off from his extremes?

The only answer she could see concerned complexity. Many people came to Seeker to escape their personal burdens, including words that kept the burdens in mind. They instead sought words that pointed away from them, like "transcendence" and "reincarnation." And Monk's words, while as grand, turned back stubbornly in their direction. One perhaps had to trust Monk or already know his Western story—having meditatively heard it from him or someone else—to see that an easing of human burdens was on his mind, too.

This interpretation seemed sensible; however, near it hovered phantoms that to Grace signified fear and a noisy, crappy mainstream and an ambiguous life maybe better seen as unreal. The phantasms seemed to come out of the ready river now in view. And what the river might be ready for, she thought with a grimace, is to watch me drive south on a parkway it parallels and to watch Trumpeter and Willa head north on the same road. The river's no extreme but it may house them: it may house complicating forces and as well all the simplifying, clarifying forces that seek to rise in their place.

Monk's audacious masks and banner words admit the complex while trying to make life better by making its conditions clearer.

She was twenty minutes from the park entrance, so as near the river as she could go. As the one freestanding bench in view was too far forward, she sat on the grass. The great sky was balmy; still, she chose to think of this spot as one the storm-seeking artists of long ago had favored.

Monk, back at the gazebo and on his metaphorical ridge, surely aware he risked being absurd, had only touched briefly on "reason." Grace recalled two people trailing out the door at this time. Everyone else had seemed, like her, to be receptive in a way that couldn't last. Tension had entered the pavilion, the mood of a chorus wanting not the challenge they were getting but resolution.

Come answerably a little further up the ridge with me, Grace felt that Monk might almost have silently challenged them from behind his mask. Come to know why reason matters. Once you do, I'll have only a final thing to show you.

Sophie, who amid loftier pursuits touched tree trunks and picked lint off her friends, both animal acts, remained self-contained.

"As worked out in Greek and Hebrew stories," said Monk, stepping forward, "reason matters because it unites the mind and the heart. It somehow sees that the mind alone can get lost in thinking and the heart alone in feeling. This getting lost in thinking or feeling, in analysis or instinct, occurs because neither mind nor heart sees life clearly on its own. But joined in reason, they help us contend with those realities of life that might otherwise pull us down.

"Reason first helps us make sense of ourselves. It shows us that we are born to find life mysterious. With the main ways we know, thinking and feeling, so able to surprise and even antagonize one another, could it be otherwise under any circumstance?

"Similarly, reason helps us make sense of our surroundings. Mind and heart together can grasp the way life contains ambition, beauty, and even crime—how people find their way to acts of business, art, and even murder.

"This sense-making, this reasoning out of some of what our world is and who we are, gives us the security to try to be present in life. The feeling of presence we then sometimes come upon is where mindfulness begins.

"Reason grows strong by casting its light on the conflicting urges it sees in the human character. The urges are stopped from festering and the people who have them are led to be more forgiving of themselves and of others.

"And yet despite all that reason—heart and mind together—provides, it's been resisted since it came alive in Western prophecy and art. A clear problem lies in how it has nearly always had to struggle."

Monk had paused, and Grace sought madly to relate his words to her life. This explains something important, she thought. It seems he is saying that the quality of balance I feel stymied to be without must at times be won. There's so much to consider. My drama teacher's ear hears him starting, with a few extreme words, to be elusive; still, if I change from coach to choral member, I can supply all the examples from life that he needs. He wants to rescue "reason," which he says has lost force. Yet the balance of mind and heart it seems to signify I always reach for as I try to be a good mother, wife, teacher, and aunt: all everyday activities and tiring. I see how these activities, in terms of a mindfulness credo, are spiritual. And they usually call my head and heart combined.

Is reason then a gift I've depended on but not understood?

Just asking this made Grace glimpse Seeker's spiritual efforts in a new way, and see why she had refused its offer to leap into the spirit world. I'm sure, she told herself, that I trample the language regularly, but I also sort of trust I'm a reasoning being. I must believe thinking and feeling can protect one another—can each keep its oddball cousin from getting lost. I see, too, how the cousins must be free and accepting of one another for their commingling in reason to work.

So, I don't really believe that supernatural forces pull our strings. No, thinking and feeling make our choices: whether they find a decent balance or not and whether they work through individuals or groups.

Grace lifted her eyes, curious to know if others also struggled with Monk's words. The resolute actor waited behind his mask. Those near Grace showed by their stillness that they were lost in thought and probably, she guessed, in worry. For to choose reason or to see it had always been one's choice was, she realized, to return to circumstances that offer no other easy exit. This made one wonder how durable the united mind and heart might really be.

And we know, she mused, that they aren't durable enough. The maxim summing up this knowledge says, *Life is rarely reasonable*, which explained Monk's point about reason nearly always being resisted.

She sensed that the whole chorus now brought silent misgivings to Monk, grown from his words. If the mind and heart are outmatched by life's mystery and complexity, if we must always settle for unsatisfying glimpses, how do we protect ourselves? Is "answerability" more than an empty pledge if we can't say "to what"?

Why then upset us with passing concerns about science and business?

"Reason suffers from its uncertainty," said Monk, "as I think we all know. It can't see past or pretend to not see the mysteries; and then the heart holds back when the mind is sure, and vice versa. In all times, people who above all want their questions answered find that reason isn't what they need. Here at the academy, these people tend to look up instead of out—to a resolution in the spirit world when they know that none will be forthcoming from the world we inhabit.

"Others, people clinging to reason, again in all eras, face the problem of knowing how to live. They must accept the uncertainty of a spiritual view that begins in daily life even as it may also look up. And what the West says can ease if not resolve this uncertainty is the tragic vision."

Monk had then, Grace remembered, sung the scales of his tragic vision in an especially clear way. I'll bring his song to share with Betsy, she told herself. There again it will be a matter of recovering what we already know. Two things alone I'll remember here, at Poets' Walk, in this moment before I start back. He had said that tragedy defined the effort, always against adversity, to see clearly and behave with as much goodness as one can. And he had said that our always falling short in this and sometimes making life worse by our behaviors was not important.

We cover these ideas in my classroom, Grace thought; but we pay them little real heed and hardly try to gather the heart and the mind.

Monk's mention of goodness had anyway, she recalled, climaxed his performance. He had illustrated the tragic ideal with an anecdote, but he seemed to want to neither tire nor satisfy his chorus more. An exchange like this was only a beginning. His voice lifted for what seemed a final time as he offered his view that in our queer situation— "leaving here, look around and listen," he challenged them—with our daily world so in the control of bewildering social and possibly natural forces, we should center our spiritual effort on how we see ourselves and each other and things.

"But really," he ended, "the lesson of reason and tragedy is that we must base our spiritual efforts at the human level. In effect, both Hebrews and Greeks said that we must suffer to see more clearly, while the Hebrews added that every day we must look for goodness anew. These teachings complement each other and lead us to a spiritual perception... "

However, Elsa would not allow Monk's performance to wind down here. She had stayed masked and at the edge of the stage after quoting her great scientist. Now she turned from facing Monk to the semicircle and bluntly interrupted him. Grace saw that the woman's body had, feigned or not, a steely tension.

The young man beside her, who minimally judged like Trumpeter, held up his coarse, blue mask again. He also turned to the semicircle.

"Our friend is rich in optimism," Elsa said with scorn to the chorus. "He first tells us that we are controlled by bewildering social 'and possibly natural' forces, which he calls 'business' and 'science' as if these labels would lessen our bewilderment. Then he climbs his mountain metaphor to describe history as a set of storms. History and tempest, thinking and feeling—when at last he raises 'reason' directly, we see that it has been his method all along.

"However, as reason often falls short, he must give us a *tragic* way to read our situation when things aren't right. It, really, only asks us to be brave. But it suits his beliefs and gets him back to saying that for all or, at least, most of us, the joined mind and heart show the way to a better life.

"And, yes, this brave stance would be fine—but for the fact that his *social forces* are beyond our means to effect. What really can we do about them when we see them not abstractly but as the everyday noise of screens, shopping malls, and power politics, and just the need we all share to get by? How can using reason make a difference? And if the answer is not at all or not enough, are we brave or unwise to try to root our spiritual lives in reason and tragedy? Wouldn't we be kinder to ourselves to admit that the world is beyond our influence? This is what many religions teach—that spirituality beings in our acceptance.

"Monk perhaps thinks the world can be better than is possible."

Monk's reply was brief, and delivered in quiet tones out of synch with the strong rhetoric of his mask. But he also faced the chorus rather than his fellow actors. "The idea of a beneficial world may be an illusion," he said. "Yet to turn away from the world implies, I think, turning *to* some belief in benevolent gods. And in our shoes, doesn't this seem illusory, too?"

A Veiled Stranger

With such a clear invitation, Grace eyed her low-cut, lead-gray, leather hiking boots, a nice birthday gift from Henry some years back. Looking down her legs, she also saw her matching socks and shorts and her skin that was more toned up and tanned than it had been a month before. In her tent at six a.m., she had seen the day as one when she should look a little nice.

Beyond her shoes was foot-high grass that an east wind pointed at the Hudson, and the river itself that she in her calmed-down mood saw was more subdued than near her home, where it was wider by half a mile and so bent and lengthened itself more regally. Also, whereas here mountain peaks sat above and behind the river like judges, near her home a busier and more compact hill country came up to crowd both of the river's shorelines.

She began to get up but then blinked hard at the panorama, trying to pull her mind back to the moment. It was time to put last night aside, and her respite here, too, and let hearth and home seep back into her awareness. The words she had lived with for weeks— "mindfulness," "transcendence," "fear," and the others—must be left to their woodland home, like the fairy folk one usually sought only in the forest and in one's imagination. She took comfort in thinking of Betsy, who would go in search with her when the time was right.

She pressed a hand down into the silky grass and pushed off from the ground to stand erect. Seeker had left her mind but not been replaced, so she closed her eyes and began to breathe deeply and count. She saw that her senses were still charged by her recent experiences. But with each new counted number, more of these heated images fell away.

The one idea she would try to keep open to as her life swept her up was Monk's equivocal claim that we do and don't live in a self-imposed trap. I can take soundings for this as I go along and then evaluate the data when I have time, she told herself.

Amid a last, ten-second deep-breathing cycle, she let the words about this and about reason and its adversaries fade. She opened her eyes.

What crept back first, as she had known it must, was the pain seen at the children's hospital and, of course, the status of Alicia, whose relative good luck might only be for the short term. She felt as a body blow the fact that she could evidently forget all this when she was otherwise occupied. She hadn't even called Alicia's house the day before. She wondered if she would ever volunteer again at the hospital. When last she had talked to Nan and Steve, after her second massage, she heard in the voices of these people she loved their slightly aggrieved sense that she, in her brief chatter about Seeker, had veered away from the family trauma.

Henry and I will bring over dinner tonight, she thought. They'll like finding me with energy again. I know Alicia will be happy that I detoured here. I did what I had to and now I'll do what I can.

No longer seeing the river amid her inward glances, she turned back toward the gazebo and park entrance and began to make her way. She smiled to think of Henry, now likely minutes away, even as she felt a bit of disappointment. We learn to cook the best we can with our ingredients, she reflected with a grin. Then she laughed to think how in two days they would share in Amos's long-discussed, after-camp junk-food binge.

Yes, it'll likely take place at the mega-mall. And yes, yes, it's just that Amos who I largely let the world shape... as if I had a choice.

She soon was back in sight of the gazebo, where the man still lounged with his dog. Drawing closer, she saw that the dog was small and lean, with a pointy nose. The man occupied the bench she and

Monk had briefly sat on an hour before. They had spoken some of Trumpeter, but, beyond sympathetic laughter, they had left alone Monk's performance and her approaching shift in perspective. They both knew she would be beginning a time of quiet, intermittent pondering, or simple rest.

Weary but striving still, Grace had brought up the romantic art made here and at similar sites. She opined that their stormy skies might have been symbols of a rebellion against industrialization. But Monk had offered a different perspective: that they symbolized a sanctioning, by the settlers' god, of economic progress with its furious conflicts. This brought them back to complexity and got them to chuckling in sympathy with one another.

The man was as thin as his dog and tall, guessing from the way his knees rimmed out like a wall shelf as he sat. Like Monk's musician pal at Seeker, he was a balding graybeard with a ponytail. A walking stick with carvings on its red handle leaned against his bare right leg.

"It's quite the morning to have wings," the man said as Grace crossed under the gazebo's roof. "Have you been out looking at the butterflies?"

"Sitting on the grass, I watched them dance from underneath."

"You could watch a few, perhaps. Here every square yard is another neighborhood."

Grace thought how, while that might be true, she wasn't eager for such distinctions in her last free minutes. She much preferred to feel the wind against her shoulders and to have it dip and turn her point of view as it pleased.

She stopped walking, which drew the dog for a friendly whiff. The man was older than she had thought and perhaps a retiree. To his left, atop a daypack sitting on the bench made of branches, sat a water bottle, a book, and binoculars.

"I've written papers about this meadow," he added. Grace gave a curious look, which led him to touch the book beside him and explain: "Not here, but in scholarly journals. I was a teacher in my earlier career, but then I wasn't able to get tenure.

"Ah, yes," he said again, "it's quite the morning to have wings."

"What did you teach?" Grace asked in a tone that, to her dismay, sounded remote and incurious enough to be rude.

Her tone seemed to not matter, though, as without answering the man bent to a teasing tussle with his pointy-nosed dog.

"I'm about to meet up with my husband at the park entrance, after a three-week separation. I've been at the Seeker Academy, which is near here, if you've heard of it." Grace to her surprise had blurted all this out—and knew she had done so out of wanting to protect herself *and* to respond to the man's shrouded effort to communicate.

With his head near his dog, the man looked up at her and winked in a complicated way. "The holistic healing proprietors seem to be finally settled into that old place," he said with a widening smile.

Grace smiled back, while shifting weight to her forward foot, since she knew it was time to move on. As she raised a hand in farewell, the man went on smiling and rubbing his dog. She turned and crossed through the gazebo. When she was a step or two into open sunlight she heard the man call after her, asking if he might walk with her back to the park entrance.

"I don't talk with people enough, lately," he said. "I'm ready to head back, too, and I'm harmless and I could use the company."

Grace continued to walk, as she thought how her life would change when she spotted Henry, the Seeker world parting from the world of the everyday. She began to anticipate her husband's smell and feel, while Monk stood in her mind as the emblem of experiences that wore against the grain from so much that she knew. And now here was a disruption more immediate even than the academy! The man might be a wreck or a bore or something quite the opposite; he had been in no more rush to show his character than disclose his teaching field, which could still be insect or grass genetics or romantic poetry. And he knew something of Seeker and had a friendly dog and was confessing to being lonely.

Things always came up and it was hard to know which ones to welcome.

This life is a guesthouse, she told herself as, hand on hip, she turned to glimpse the river again and wait for the man and his dog to catch up.